# Earthman Jack

vs.

# The Conclave of Corruption

Book 5 of The Earthman Jack Space Saga

Episode 3 of the Conclave Trilogy

By

Matthew Kadish

Printed in the U.S.A.

First American edition, October 2017

## OTHER BOOKS IN THE EARTHMAN JACK SERIES

Book 1: Earthman Jack vs. the Ghost Planet

Book 2: Earthman Jack vs. the Secret Army

Book 3: Earthman Jack vs. the Intergalactic Manhunt

Book 4: Earthman Jack vs. the Ring of Fire

If you would like to receive updates on the Earthman Jack Space Saga and information on upcoming books in the series, along with special offers and exclusive goodies, please join the official Earthman Jack mailing list. By doing so, you not only get cool stuff, but also help support the series and the author. You can sign up at:

www.EarthmanJack.com

and

www.MatthewKadish.com

To Jude Erin

You Are My Sun & Stars

Thank You For Lighting Up My Life

To Amy,

Keep being Awesome!

Matt J. [illegible]

# AUTHOR'S NOTE

Greetings readers!

By now you know that Earthman Jack's adventures are part of an epic saga spanning many planets, dimensions, and one-liners. This "epicness" is also reflected in the page count, as these books tend to be very long. Well, the third installment in the series ended up being *too* long! My final draft of the story was so large, that it was impossible to publish it in one book.

For this reason, the third installment has been broken up into 3 separate books, which I've dubbed "The Conclave Trilogy." Though the books are physically separate from one another, all three are meant to be read together to get the entire adventure of *The Conclave of Corruption.* The book you are currently reading is the third part of this story, and I would encourage you to read all three books together to get the full experience, as the tale was meant to be read.

The Conclave Trilogy should be read in this order:

- Earthman Jack vs. The Intergalactic Manhunt
- Earthman Jack vs. The Ring of Fire
- Earthman Jack vs. The Conclave of Corruption

My apologies for any confusion regarding this matter. Please remember that these three books make up one installment of the story and all were originally meant to be one book. If there are parts of the book that don't stand on their own or conflicts that seem unresolved by the end of a book, it is because some story threads develop and resolve themselves down the road in other books of the trilogy.

For the best reading experience possible, I'd recommend reading *Earthman Jack vs. The Ghost Planet*, *Earthman Jack vs. The Secret Army*, and then all three books of *The Conclave Trilogy* back-to-back if you can, as the action, tension, and plot twists get more and more exciting as the story goes along.

Thank you for understanding, and enjoy *Earthman Jack vs. The Conclave of Corruption*!

All the best,

Matthew Kadish
Author, *The Earthman Jack Space Saga*

# Episode III:

# Earthman Jack

vs.

# The Conclave of Corruption

# CHAPTER 1

Jack shifted uncomfortably on his feet. The Chamber of the Five Rings may have been a simple room, but the men who populated it - and the circumstances they all found themselves in - served to make him feel out of place. In the past, only the members of the Order of Peers had been present whenever Jack had come to the chamber. Now, senior Paragons from throughout the Conclave were present, and Jack seemed to be the only Initiate in sight.

Masters Highclaw, Hodapp, Savage, and Ravencrow were all present, as were the four members of the Royal Vanguard. Master GorJiro's seat sat conspicuously empty, a reminder of the Paragon's tragic fate. Paragons Blackmane, Krixus, and Desmodus stood in GorJiro's stead, their faces all grim. Mourdock was present, as well, and was the one who had dragged Jack to the meeting. He was standing to the left of Jack while Seqis stood to his right. Paragon Fraiser – who had apparently been part of the Great Seal's research team but was not present during the attack due to an injury – stood before the Order, delivering his report of the events that had transpired.

"We've surveyed the damage the explosion caused to the temple," Paragon Fraiser said. "Structural damage was minimal due to its placement in the Sacred Vault, which contained much of the destruction. Our analysis determined that the overloading of the Weak Nuclear Force Manipulator relic was the cause of the explosion."

"Are you saying someone used an Ancient Relic to set off a nuclear explosion in the heart of the Conclave?" asked Paragon Savage, his face even more dour than usual.

Fraiser nodded. "I fear so, Master Savage," he replied. "Luckily, the ultanium from which the Sacred Vault is made was able to absorb the brunt of the explosion and contain the radiation, otherwise we'd all probably be dead by now."

There was a murmur among the Paragons in the room, all of whom appeared greatly disconcerted by how narrowly they'd escaped being killed in a nuclear explosion.

"And dare I ask about the relics the vault housed?" inquired Highclaw, his sorrowful eyes already appearing to know the answer.

"Gone, I'm afraid," replied Fraiser. "All of them destroyed by the blast."

Paragon Hodapp shook his head. "The greatest collection of Ancient wonders in the galaxy, wiped out in one fell swoop," he muttered. "How was this possible?"

"From what we could piece together, someone accessed the vault after Caretaker Quorquon opened it on behalf of Paragon Pennywise," explained Fraiser. "With Quorquon's subsequent disappearance, we believe he was killed before he had a chance to resecure the vault, and whoever was responsible for his death was also the one who accessed the Weak Nuclear Force Manipulator and set it to overload, giving him time to exit the vault and close it before the explosion occurred."

"Is it possible the intruders who abducted the Princess were the culprits?" asked Highclaw.

Fraiser shook his head. "I don't believe so, Master Highclaw," he responded. "Those who were killed in the Chamber of the Great Seal had injuries consistent with gravity pulse use. From what we've been able to gather about the intruders, they showed no sign of proficiency with Paragon techniques such as that."

"And the one responsible for killing them was also able to defeat Master GorJiro," interjected Blackmane. "I don't care what twisted abilities those intruders displayed. They would not have been able to kill the greatest Paragon Warrior in history in single combat."

Jack frowned. He was indeed disturbed at the loss of Master GorJiro, but the loss of Pennywise stung him worse. After things had calmed down and the adrenaline of the situation had subsided, Pennywise's death had hit him anew, and he'd cried. Pennywise had been a mentor to him, but more so, he'd been a good friend, as well.

"The killer also had to have known how to operate the Ancient relics in the vault, as well as having had knowledge of how to operate the vault itself," said Fraiser.

"So," said Ravencrow. "Our perpetrator is knowledgeable enough to operate Ancient relics, skilled enough to defeat a Master Paragon in combat, and powerful enough to manifest corruption within a Great Seal. It seems to me the list of those capable of such things couldn't be very long."

"Unless the villain has avoided being on the list in the first place," said Savage. "If a Paragon capable of such atrocities has been living among us all this time, then there is a very good possibility that he's developed his skills and knowledge in secret. He could be a Master level Paragon that nobody even knows about, hiding in plain sight."

"I suppose it is possible. With the time constriction and educational philosophy of the Conclave, one could conceivably develop the skills he'd need to perpetrate such crimes without notice," said Highclaw as he stroked the hair beneath his muzzle. "That would require this perpetrator to have been here at the Conclave for a long period of time. Add those who have been here for extended periods to that list of suspects, and let us begin to investigate them, as well. There can no longer be any doubt that a Paragon is behind this sabotage. We must make finding him our top priority."

"That may be your top priority," interjected Seqis, "but the priority for my sworn companions and I is the rescue and safeguarding of Princess Glorianna. And yet I have heard no mention of that aspect of this investigation."

"Forgive me, Master Seqis," replied Fraiser, with a repentant bow. "I did not mean to neglect the kidnapping of the Princess. She is, of course, just as much of a priority to us as finding the culprit behind these recent events."

"I am not interested in apologies, Paragon Fraiser," said Seqis. "I want answers. Who were those intruders? How did they get here? And most importantly, where did they go?"

"Unfortunately, I fear I only have an answer to one of those questions, Lord Commander," responded Fraiser. "From your statements, and those of others who witnessed the abduction, we have concluded that the intruders entered the Conclave through some type of tether."

"A tether?" said Hodapp. "How is that possible? There's only ever been one tether leading to the Conclave."

"A tether which now no longer exists," grumbled Savage.

"We have done an extensive review of the state of the Great Seal after the attack," explained Fraiser. "The corruption that has been afflicting it has taken deeper root. So much so that it has affected the seal's operation."

"What do you mean?" asked Highclaw.

"According to our analysis, the time constriction of the Conclave has lessened," Fraiser said. "The more the corruption spreads, the more time is returning to normal here. Soon, the Conclave universe will be in sync with the prime universe. We believe that the corruption is affecting the Great Seal's ability to create tethers, as well."

"In what way?" asked Hodapp.

"There has only ever been one tether leading here to the Conclave, maintained by the Great Seal," said Fraiser. "However, that is not to say that the seal is not capable of creating other tethers back to the prime universe. We believe Paragon Pennywise's theories were correct. The weakening of the Great Seal from the corruption is breaking down the safeguards the Ancients put into place, allowing the seal to be controlled by those without Royal Blood. We believe that our mysterious saboteur killed Paragon Pennywise's team so he could create a tether which allowed the intruders to gain access to the Conclave and also set it so that when the tether used by the intruders to escape with the Princess closed, the primary tether did so, as well."

"Then, perhaps we could use that to our advantage," Seqis said. "If the Great Seal can be controlled by those without Royal Blood, then one of us could use it to reopen a tether back to the location of the Princess."

"And who here has ever been able to manifest a tether, hmmm?" asked Ravencrow. "It is not exactly a skill we've had a need to develop. The saboteur has apparently had a long time to figure it out. The rest of us wouldn't know where to begin."

"We shall figure it out," declared Highclaw.

"Eventually, no doubt we will," responded Ravencrow. "But by the time we do, it may be too late. This saboteur has an agenda. That much is obvious. Until recently, he's been biding his time, playing the long game. But now things are escalating. With the time constriction of the Conclave disappearing, our learning advantage is disappearing along with it. And if he had wanted us all dead, then he wouldn't have contained the nuclear blast within the Sacred Vault. He'd have let it inflict maximum damage on the temple and all those within it. He's cut us off from the prime universe because he does not want interference from us as to whatever his plans for the Princess are. No… whoever our enemy is wants us contained, at least for now. If we are to get ahead of our adversary, we must find a way to escape the Conclave, and we must do so quickly."

"But there is no other way to leave this pocket universe except through a tether," said Master Hodapp.

"That may not entirely be the case…" said Mourdock.

All eyes turned to him.

"Paragon Skyborn," acknowledged Highclaw. "You know of a way to get us back to the prime universe?"

"Possibly," Mourdock replied before looking over at Jack. "We could use the Earthman's ship."

Jack's eyes widened in surprise at Mourdock's suggestion. Everyone else in the chamber exchanged curious glances.

"The Earthship has an Entanglement Engine, allowing it to teleport anywhere," said Mourdock. "Maybe it could even teleport to the Conclave universe and back?"

"Is that true, Initiate Finnegan?" asked Highclaw. "Could your spaceship allow us transport back to the prime universe?"

"Uh..." said Jack, honestly not knowing how to respond. "Maybe?"

"You do not sound so sure," stated Savage, dourly.

"Well, yeah, what Mourdock said is true. My ship can teleport anywhere as long as we have the coordinates for it," Jack replied. "But I've never tried teleporting it to an entirely different universe before."

"Hmmm..." said Hodapp. "If the Earthman's ship uses a standard three-dimensional stellar cartography coordinate system to choose where to teleport, then perhaps we could figure out a way to modify that so it knows how to access the Conclave's pocket universe in relation to the prime universe."

"Even if we could do that, how would we gain access to the blasted thing?" grumbled Savage. "It was docked in Remnant Station in the prime universe. We can't reach it."

"Jack has a mental link with his ship," replied Mourdock. "He can control it using only his mind."

"Are you able to do such a thing, Jack?" asked Seqis. "Could you command your ship to teleport here on its own?"

"Well, yeah, normally," Jack replied. "I mean... back when the tether was open, I could still sense my ship, you know? Like my connection to it was still there as long as there was an opening back to our universe. But ever since the tether closed, it's like I've been cut off from it."

"Interesting," noted Hodapp. "Tell me, do you require a tether back to the prime universe to access your spaceship? Or will any opening back to it do?"

"I... I don't know," replied Jack. "I guess, as long as there's some way to communicate with it, I could?"

"What are you thinking, Master Hodapp?" inquired Highclaw.

"We may not know how to create new tethers yet, but we do know how to access subspace," the Paragon responded. "We're still able to communicate with the prime universe using our normal means. If we could rig a subspace pocket to open to our universe and the prime universe simultaneously, then perhaps the Earthman could re-establish his connection with his ship and teleport it to us."

"Well, at this point, we don't have much to lose by giving such a thing a shot," muttered Ravencrow.

"Agreed," said Highclaw. "Until such time as we can figure out how to open a tether back to the prime universe, we can attempt to use the Earthman's ship as a lifeboat. Assuming he is willing to help us."

"Yeah, of course I am," Jack said.

"Very well then," Highclaw said. "Master Hodapp, would you be so good as to begin working on the solution to bringing the Earthman's ship to us?"

"Indeed," Hodapp replied. "I'll get the entire Ground Ring on it."

"In the meantime, Paragon Fraiser," continued Highclaw, "proceed with your investigation. Use whatever resources you need to try to find the saboteur amongst us."

"We will assist with Paragon Fraiser's investigation," chimed in Blackmane, gesturing to Krixus and Desmodus. "Whoever killed Master GorJiro has proven to be extremely deadly. Though our master was no match for our mysterious enemy, perhaps his three best students will be."

"Granted," replied Highclaw. "Master Savage, with Paragon Pennywise gone, I leave it to you and the Water Ring to try to find a way to stop the spread of the corruption of the Great Seal."

"It is now our top priority," Savage replied.

"Master Ravencrow, you and I will begin attempting to figure out the means by which we can create new tethers back to the prime universe."

Ravencrow frowned. "Oh, goodie," the Harvshodd[1] muttered.

"Lord Commander," said Highclaw, looking at Seqis. "Until we can find a way back to the prime universe, I fear there is not much we can do short of sending news of what has occurred to Omnicron so that the Empire might begin searching for Her Highness. However, you and your companions are welcome to partake in Paragon Fraiser's investigation, as well, and search the Conclave's

---

[1] Harvshodds are an ugly alien race that are short in stature and resemble trolls.

archives for any information we may have as to the nature of the intruders who abducted the Princess."

Seqis didn't look happy, but he nodded, nonetheless. "The Vanguard shall make ourselves as useful as possible," he replied.

Highclaw nodded in response. "Then this meeting of the Order of Peers is adjourned," he declared. "We all have our tasks. Now let us get to them."

As the chamber began to empty, the other members of the Royal Vanguard clustered around Seqis. "Lugard, Rionknidis," Seqis said. "Go with Fraiser and Blackmane. Despite their bravado, they are not up to the task of battling anyone capable of defeating a warrior such as GorJiro. If there is any trouble, I want you there."

"Good," growled Rionknidis. "I'm worthless at dealing with research. Excellent at handling trouble."

"We'll keep an eye on them, as well," Lugard said. "Frankly, I don't trust any of them."

"Agreed," Seqis replied. "Like it or not, I fear the most likely suspects may very well be the remaining members of the Order. That is why I want you, Dahuud, to keep an eye on them. Put some of that Sisterhood[2] training to use."

Dahuud simply nodded.

"I will go to the Chamber of Knowledge and see if I can find anything about those who abducted the Princess," he said. "Whatever powers they possess, it is clear they are meant to counter those of Paragons. If we are to have any chance of rescuing Her Highness, we will need to find a way to combat them."

"I will come and assist you," Mourdock said. "I want to get Anna back safely as much as you do. If there's any way I can help, I desire to do so."

Seqis bowed slightly. "As you wish, Ascendant," he replied.

"I'll come, too," said Jack.

"No," Seqis said. "Keep yourself available in case Master Hodapp finds a way for you to contact your ship."

"But—"

"Jack, you are the only lifeline we have to rescuing the Princess," said Seqis in a tone which brokered no argument. "Your sole job right now is to find a way

---

[2] Dahuud is a member of the Sisterhood of Whispers, an elite and shadowy group of highly trained female spies and assassins.

to get your ship here. If Master Hodapp should fail, it falls to you to find a way to succeed. Go. Meditate. Try to make a connection without the need for an opening to the prime universe. If you want to help, that is the most important thing you could be doing."

Jack sighed. "Yeah, okay," he relented. "I can do that."

Seqis nodded. He looked at each member of the group, in turn. "The six of us are all united in our devotion to Princess Glorianna," he said. "Time and time again, we have all proven our loyalty to her and Legacy Prime. Going forward, we must trust no one but one another."

Each person nodded before heading out of the chamber. Before going, Jack saw Ravencrow shuffling toward the exit, his twisted legs having required time for him to get out of his chair. "I take it you heard all that?" asked Jack.

"Lord Commander Seqis is many things, but stupid is not one of them," Ravencrow said. "Right now, I'd say he's correct in not trusting anyone but his sworn companions along with you and Skyborn."

"Including you?"

"Oh, believe me, I am the least trustworthy person in this blasted temple," muttered Ravencrow as he walked.

"I don't believe that," said Jack, falling in by Ravencrow's side. "I trust you."

"Well, no one ever accused you of being very smart," Ravencrow replied.

"You once told me that Master GorJiro had been defeated by someone before," said Jack. "Is it possible that person is the one responsible for this attack?"

Ravencrow was quiet for a moment, leaning more heavily on his walking stick than usual as he began making his way down the hall. "I do not believe so," he finally said. "The one who defeated GorJiro all that time ago spared his life. Why would he do that just to come back later and end it? No, the one responsible for this series of unfortunate events is far more malicious and far more bloodthirsty."

"Do you have any thoughts on who it could be?"

"Yes."

Jack looked at Ravencrow expectantly, but when the Harvshodd offered nothing further, Jack frowned. "Care to share them?" he asked, annoyed.

"No," Ravencrow stated, flatly.

Jack sighed. "You think it's a member of the Order of Peers, don't you?"

"Oh, it most certainly is."

Jack frowned. "It's Savage," he said. "It has to be."

"Does it?" Ravencrow muttered.

"Well, I don't think it's you," Jack said. "And I just don't see Master Hodapp or Master Highclaw doing such awful things."

"All the more reason to suspect them," Ravencrow replied. "But that is not something you should concern yourself with now. The Lord Commander is right, you are our only chance of escaping our little self-made prison at the moment. Your sole focus should be on accomplishing that. Whoever our adversary is, they are counting on keeping us contained. We must now trust in The Void to disrupt his plans. That means you and I must do what we are meant to do."

"And what is that?" asked Jack.

Ravencrow smiled. "The unexpected," the Paragon stated.

# Chapter 2

For once, Uleeg Casgor was in a good mood. After what seemed like a long period of time where he'd been dealt nothing but setbacks and political blows, something had actually gone right. Word had come in that the Evenstars had finally agreed to surrender their Legacy to Starkeeper Drucker and the 3rd fleet. Though it had taken a bit of time to negotiate the terms of the surrender, the fact of the matter was that this was a victory for Casgor, no matter how one viewed it. Casgor smirked as he poured himself a glass of brandy and leaned back in his chair to watch the news broadcast in his office.

"This is Danton DeGoosey, coming to you live from the planet of Redwater, where the drama surrounding the dissolution of the Evenstar Legacy is still playing out," the rugged looking Regal reporter said. "The Evenstars sent shockwaves throughout the Empire some time ago when Legacy head Amadeus Evenstar announced that he would be surrendering himself and his Legacy after a long stand-off with Imperial authorities and the 3rd fleet. This effectively marks the end of one of the Empire's oldest and most storied Legacies in one of its most important planetary systems, with the Evenstars being able to trace their lineage all the way back to Emperor Nameer, who is largely considered to be one of the greatest Emperors of all time. Though the Evenstars have enjoyed a great deal of support within their home system, reaction to the news of the surrender has been largely positive, if somewhat bittersweet, for many of Redwater's residents."

The image shifted to "man on the street" interviews as various citizens of the planet of Redwater shared their opinions with the reporter.

"It's sad, y'know," said one Mescalero[3]. "The Evenstars have run things around here for centuries. But at least no one got hurt in this stand-off. I'm just glad it's over."

"First Eudox Evenstar dies, and now his children are going to be banished. It's just awful," said an older Regal woman. "I feel so bad for them. Especially Kimlee. I hope she keeps on making music. My kids love her!"

---

[3] A Mescalero is one of the native races of Redwater, distinguishable by their rust-colored skin, dark hair, and purple eyes.

"Personally, I think it's time for a change," said a young Nakkota[4]. "Eudox Evenstar was great, but his son is too young and his daughter is an embarrassment. As long as Pampam DePamm[5] isn't appointed the new Legacy head, I think anyone will be an improvement!"

The image cut back to DeGoosey, who looked professionally into the camera as he continued his report. "Though news of the Evenstar surrender took many by surprise, even more surprising was the official statement, released this morning, concerning the terms of the surrender. In yet another shocking twist in this ongoing saga, it has been announced that Amadeus Evenstar's sister, the synth-pop singer and reality holonet sensation Kimlee Evenstar, will be the one to officially surrender their Legacy to Starkeeper Mykall Drucker, commander of the 3rd fleet. Some analysts say that this move is meant to ensure the safety of Amadeus Evenstar until the surrender is officially ratified, while others see it as one final insult from the Evenstars to the Empire. Though Kimlee Evenstar isn't widely regarded as a political figure, she is still legally – at least for now – the chief Lady of the Legacy and has the authority to negotiate on its behalf. Many political insiders have stated that the official surrender, which is to be conducted on the 3rd fleet's flagship *The Colossus*, is mostly ceremonial in nature, with the Evenstar Legacy already dragging out the process by negotiating the specific terms by which their Legacy will be dissolved. But one thing is for certain, and it is that Kimlee Evenstar will be the one to officially end her Legacy, very soon. This is Danton DeGoosey, Galactic Imperial News Service, Redwater System."

Casgor smirked as he downed what was left of his drink. He'd laughed when he'd first heard that Kimlee Evenstar demanded to be the one to officiate the surrender. It just seemed so petulant. Yet, if the Evenstars wanted to end their Legacy by embarrassing themselves, he did not wish to stand in their way. In fact, he welcomed the blunder. Though Starkeeper Drucker had initially objected to allowing Kimlee Evenstar to broadcast the surrender over the holonet, Casgor had ordered him to accept the Evenstar's terms.

The Starkeeper may not have been concerned about the optics of the situation, but Casgor was. He could think of nothing better than recorded footage of the last moments of the Evenstar Legacy being handled by a shallow, vapid, fame-obsessed socialite. Not only that, but Kimlee's celebrity would

[4] Nakkotas are Redwater's race of island dwellers, who have lighter colored skin, green eyes, and were typically taller and more robust than other peoples on the planet.

[5] Pampam DePamm is a singer and actress of questionable quality, widely known for being famous simply due to being famous.

guarantee a great many citizens would be watching it, which would only cement Casgor's victory over the Evenstars.

There was no way to chalk this up other than as a win. The Evenstar Uprising had been the first and most visible opposition to his power, and with them not only destroyed but also publicly quelled, it would only cement Casgor in his new position as sole Director of the Empire. Now, if he could only retrieve Princess Glorianna, his ultimate victory would be all but certain. And based on the scheduled appointment he had coming up, he was hoping that issue would soon be resolved, as well.

"Excuse me, Director," came the voice of his assistant over the intercom. "Your next appointment is here."

"Send him in," Casgor replied.

Armonto Virtuoso entered the office, looking like his usual smug yet unemotional self. Virtuoso's demeanor often rubbed Casgor the wrong way, but he was willing to put up with it as long as the man delivered on his assignments. And love him or hate him, Armonto Virtuoso always delivered in the end.

"Uleeg," Armonto said in greeting.

"Have you seen the holonet lately?" Casgor said, still reveling in his victory. "The Evenstars are no more."

"Yes, I heard," Armonto replied, sounding disinterested.

"Well, then, at least try and sound excited," said Casgor as he poured himself another drink. "Not only was I able to vanquish that pesky Legacy without shedding a drop of blood or enduring even more public backlash, but I also was able to do so without contradicting a single order from Verrutus."

"Yes, I'm sure he will be most unannoyed with your actions."

Casgor chuckled. "Droll, as always, Armonto," he said. "So, have you finally come through with the assignment I gave you? Have you figured out a way to retrieve the Princess from the Conclave?"

"In a way. But first, I wish to show you something," Armonto said as he produced a device from his jacket pocket and placed it down on Casgor's desk. The small device was rectangular in shape, with a small arm extended from its top, housing a sensor orb at the end which aimed itself at Casgor and began to scan him with a gridded green light. Casgor eyed the device curiously.

"What is that?" Casgor asked.

"An invention I've been toying with," Armonto said, looking at the small sensor as though it were a misbehaving pet. "Do you recall the reason why we were not able to infect the other Directors with slythru?"

"Of course," Casgor replied. "Our vital signs are all constantly monitored by a nano-sensor network. The minute the trauma of being attacked by a slythru occurred, the Directors would have been teleported to a secure medical facility, and the slythrus would have been discovered before the joining process was completed."

Armonto nodded. "I had been working on this little device to solve that issue," he said. "I designed it to interface with the nano-sensors in the Directors' systems so that false information can be sent back to the network, making it appear as though no trauma is occurring while the slythru infection takes place."

Casgor raised an eyebrow. "If you've had this technology all this time, why didn't we use it?"

"Because, there are some flaws in the design," Armonto replied. "Its range is extremely limited. For maximum effectiveness, it must be within a few feet of the target and must have a clear line of sight with its receptor to get an accurate reading of the nano-sensors. As you know, it is extremely rare for any of the Directory to be alone long enough to get something such as this so close and active without being noticed."

Casgor nodded. "Indeed," he said. "And with me being the sole Director, we no longer have much need for such a device. But, still…" Casgor got to his feet and walked around his desk, eyeing the small machine curiously. "The other Directors are being terrible pains in my side," he continued. "They are still being monitored by the security network. Perhaps we could infect them now simply to keep them from making trouble…"

"Don't worry," Armonto said. "The other Directors will not be troubling you for much longer."

Casgor gave Virtuoso a questioning look. "And why is that?" he asked.

"Because, you'll be too dead to care," Armonto replied.

The sound of the blaster bolt firing had barely registered in Casgor's ears before he felt the searing pain in his belly. He looked down in surprise at the smoking wound in his gut, his hands trembling as he grasped it before collapsing onto the ground.

Wisps of ozone wafted from the muzzle of the blaster in Virtuoso's hand. Virtuoso glanced at the small device on Casgor's desk, looking at it with measured appraisal. "The signal is holding steady. Good," he said. "Nice to know my time spent on this blasted thing wasn't a total waste."

A feeble cry escaped from Casgor as he clutched at his wound. He could feel panic rising within him as the seriousness of what had just occurred settled in on him. "WHAT HAVE YOU DONE???" he cried as Armonto sat down at his desk, calling up Casgor's control console.

"I shot you, obviously," Armonto said as he typed away.

"GUARDS!" Casgor called, coughing up blood as he struggled to speak. "SOMEONE! HELP!"

"No one is going to hear you," Armonto replied. "My assistant is outside with a noise dampener aimed at your door, and I've already disabled all your security protocols, which was ridiculously easy, considering I designed them all."

Armonto's cold and emotionless tone made it sound like he was lecturing in a classroom. Casgor glanced around him, desperate for anything he could use to save himself. "Verrutus wouldn't want me dead!" Casgor said. "He needs me!"

"I'm sure he does," Armonto replied. "I, however, do not."

"So you're not acting under his orders?" Casgor said, grunting as the pain from his wound coursed through him. "Have you gone mad? You are betraying one of the Harbingers? You are betraying the Lords of the Void when we are so close to manifesting their grand design???"

"My confidence in the Lords of the Void and their so-called grand design is not what it used to be, I'm afraid," Virtuoso said as he stopped typing and got back to his feet. He then shot the computer console at Casgor's desk, destroying it.

"What did you just do?" Casgor demanded.

"I have disabled all the security measures for the Omnicron defense grid," Armonto replied as he moved back around the desk to look at Casgor.

Casgor's eyes went wide. "Why would you do such a thing?" he asked.

"To make it easier to destroy this planet and everyone on it, of course."

"But… it's too early for such a thing!" Casgor said. "This… this is not part of the plan!"

"The plan has changed, Uleeg," Armonto said. "And I'm afraid you no longer have a part to play in it."

Armonto Virtuoso fired his blaster pistol one last time, bringing the Casgor administration to an abrupt and unceremonious end. With that nasty little bit of business concluded, Armonto placed his blaster back in his equalarium lined pocket so it would once again fail to trigger the security sensors as he exited the office, and he left his vital sign mimicker behind so as not to raise the alarm too prematurely that Uleeg Casgor was no longer among the living.

Hylda Wahller was dutifully awaiting him in the anteroom leading to Casgor's office. As soon as Virtuoso re-emerged, she shut off the hand-held noise dampener she'd been discreetly aiming at the door and fell in by Armonto's side as they set off for the nearest teleporter.

"It is done," Armonto said as Wahller's eyes went white. "Omnicron is now vulnerable."

"Excellent," Wahller replied. "Now all we must do is wait for Verrutus to make his move."

"And you are certain he will?"

"I have foreseen it," Wahller said.

"It will only be a matter of time before the authorities have discovered what has occurred," Armonto said. "What I've done to the security network can easily be reversed, should they give one of the former Directors access to it. If your master plan is to happen, it must happen soon."

"Patience," Wahller cautioned. "The Princess will break Verrutus's control. And when she does… his wrath will be unbound."

"You are placing an awful lot of faith in our pubescent ruler to defeat your rather formidable peer, Zarrod," Virtuoso said.

Wahller chuckled. "If there is one thing I have learned the hard way, Virtuoso… it is to not underestimate the Earthman. Or his friends."

# Chapter 3

"Scally! Scally! Wake up!"

Scallywag's eyes fluttered open. He hadn't wanted to fall asleep, but after the ordeal he'd been through, he was just too tired to stay conscious, especially while in Glimmer's loving embrace. His entire body was sore from the torture Eisenwolf had put him through. His throat was dry. Worst of all, he had no idea how long he'd been asleep. The last thing a man facing execution wanted to do was sleep.

"What is it?" Scallywag grumbled.

"Someone's coming," Glimmer replied.

Scallywag did not want to leave Glimmer's arms, but he forced himself to sit up, every muscle in his body protesting as he did so. He could hear the door to the brig hiss open and the heavy footsteps of robots hitting the ground. He turned to see Officer Falloran enter, along with two security-bots. Falloran approached the cell containing Scallywag and Glimmer and lowered the shield wall.

"It's time," Falloran said.

Scallywag grimaced. "Ain't even had me last meal yet," he said.

"The Captain ordered you weren't to be given any privileges, Red," Falloran replied as he signaled for the security-bots to take possession of the prisoners with a nod of his head.

The security-bots lumbered into the cell. One immediately clasped Scallywag by his arms as the other grabbed Glimmer.

"Oy! What ya doin'?" Scallywag cried. "Leave her alone!"

"Orders are for the both of you," Falloran stated.

Glimmer's crew in the opposing cell hopped to their feet and began banging on the shield wall. "She's a Blue!" Gage yelled. "She's entitled to a trial, blast it!"

Falloran tapped his datapad and sent a shock to the captives to push them away from the shield barrier. "The Captain is judge, jury, and executioner on this ship," Falloran said. "His word is law, and he has ordered Lady Glimmer to be executed alongside the Red."

Glimmer scowled at Falloran. "And you're okay with this breach of one of our Empire's most time-honored laws?" she asked.

Falloran shrugged. "I'm just following orders, my Lady. Captain's a Blue, just like you. But he has rank, and you don't. Makes it easy for lowly Yellows like myself." Falloran then looked at the two security-bots. "You are to escort the prisoners to Airlock 32," he said. "You are not to stop for any reason. If the prisoners put up resistance, non-lethal methods are authorized to move them along. The Captain wants them both conscious and uninjured upon delivery. Understood?"

"Acknowledged," both security-bots replied.

"Off with you, then," said Falloran as he turned and made his way toward the brig's door.

Scallywag's crew got up and watched as the security-bots led the captives out. Scallywag looked at them, sadly, as each one gave him a final salute, their faces grim. Glimmer's crew also watched stoically as their Captain was escorted away.

Falloran opened the entrance to the brig's anteroom and ushered the robots out to the hallway. "May the Light God have mercy on you, my Lady," he said, before scowling at Scallywag. "And I hope the Dark God flays that dirty skin off you for the rest of eternity, you piece of filth." The Visini spit in Scallywag's face, before closing the door to the brig and resuming his duties.

"I say, that was most rude of Officer Falloran," the security-bot holding Scallywag said. "In my previous position as an attaché android, I believe it is safe to say that spitting in one's face is a most grievous insult in all but three known cultures."

Scallywag raised an eyebrow and glanced behind him at the machine that was currently marching him toward his execution. "Did… did ya just say ya used ta be an attaché android?" he asked.

"Oh!" exclaimed the robot. "Forgive me. This is the first opportunity I have had to reveal myself to you. It is I, Master Scallywag! Dan!"

"Dan?"

"Yes! I do not blame you for not recognizing me, sir. When last we saw one another, I was in my old body."

"And now yer a blasted security-bot on tha *Megavolt*?" asked Scallywag. "How'd that happen?"

"I fear that is a rather long and convoluted story, Master Scallywag – one which I would be happy to regale you about when we have more time. For now, we should consider ourselves fortunate that the many upgrades Master Moriarty insisted I implement allowed me to overwrite this security-bot's programming, effectively transferring my consciousness to this new body."

"Yeah, yeah, very fortunate," Scallywag muttered. "Since yer programmin' is intact, would ya mind explainin' why yer marching me to my own bloody execution instead of helpin' me ta escape?"

"From the moment my consciousness was re-established I have been working on numerous plans to do precisely that, Master Scallywag," replied Dan. "I even have gone so far as to reclaim many of the upgrades from my former body which would allow me to remotely hack this ship's main systems to allow us to get away. However, none of the scenarios I have formulated ends in success, given all the variables of our most precarious situation, save for one."

"I'll take one over none," Scallywag said. "So let's do that…"

"I fear we are currently unable to enact that plan," Dan explained. "It requires that I be able to hack into the ship's main systems, however, Visini military protocol only gives command-level access to its top-ranking officers, and they each have a security code by which the main systems can be accessed. I fear I do not know any of the codes, and the processors of this body are not advanced enough to work them out before you are set to be executed, though I have partitioned a great deal of my computing power to attempt to figure out Captain Eisenwolf's passcode already. If I could discover his passcode, I could indeed save you and your companions quite easily. Unfortunately, there is no way of knowing what the Captain based his code on."

"Then let me and Glimmer go so we can fend fer ourselves!"

"I have considered that, as well, sir. Unfortunately, my counterpart here is of his original programming. He would subdue you and Lady Glimmer almost immediately and then disable me as a malfunctioning unit."

"So yer sayin' there's nothin' ya can do ta help us?"

"I am trying to determine a way to do so, Master Scallywag," Dan responded. "I do, however, fear my efforts may be in vain. I am afraid I am not as good at formulating brilliant plans as Master Moriarty is."

"I'd settle for any blasted plan right about now," grumbled Scallywag. "What are me odds?"

"Of escaping?"

"Of living."

"At this point… zero percent."

Scallywag frowned. "Margin of error?"

"Oh, dear… was I supposed to calculate that, as well?"

Scallywag rolled his eyes. "Don't bother," he muttered. "I'm depressed enough as it is."

"I can certainly understand that sentiment, Master Scallywag," Dan replied. "If it is of any consolation, I shall try my best to increase those odds in any way I can."

Scallywag frowned. "Just promise me one thing, robot," he said, gazing at Glimmer as the other security-bot ushered her along ahead of him. "If ya can't save me, do whatever ya can ta save Glimmer. I don't care if tha odds o' you succeedin' are zero-point-zero. You at least try ta get her out o' here."

"I will see what I can do, Master Scallywag."

It didn't take long before Scallywag and Glimmer turned down a corridor to see Eisenwolf and a small security contingent at one of the ship's airlocks, waiting patiently as the security-bots ushered the prisoners forward to their fate. Once Eisenwolf saw them, he gave a nod and the security guards took possession of the two Visinis.

Eisenwolf glanced at a datapad in his hand and smirked before putting it back in his pocket. "Right on schedule," he said. "I hope the two of you made the most of the opportunity I granted you, for your time is now up."

"Yeah, we had ourselves a right rowdy party," Scallywag said. "We woulda invited ya to join us, but, ta be frank, yer kinda a party-pooper, Wolfie."

"I can assure you, after you are dead, I will be celebrating quite extensively," Eisenwolf replied, looking at the airlock wistfully. "And the fact that you are to be executed on this day, of all days, makes it so much more… *poetic*." Eisenwolf turned back and looked at Scallywag. "You do know what today is, don't you, Red?"

Scallywag sighed. "By all accounts? Me lucky day, apparently."

Eisenwolf scowled. "It is Universal Timedate 10342-163. You mean to say you don't remember?"

"Remember what?"

"On this very date, thirty years ago, you murdered my father and everyone under his command after siding with Harkon the Black," said Eisenwolf, his voice thick with vitriol.

"Really?" Scallywag mused. "Has it been that long? Feels like only yesterday—"

Eisenwolf abruptly struck Scallywag across the face with the back of his hand, sending Scallywag reeling. The Visini grabbed Scallywag by the back of his head and pulled him close, their faces only inches apart.

"Don't dare mock this occasion!" Eisenwolf growled. "This date has been burned into my memory, you vile piece of filth! This was the day everything changed for me! All because of you! And as fate would have it, the stars have aligned so that I may kill my father's murderer on the exact same day as you killed him. If that isn't justice, I don't know what is!"

Eisenwolf released Scallywag and took a moment to smooth out his uniform, composing himself. His gaze then drifted toward Glimmer, who was looking at Eisenwolf with utter disdain.

"I had thought about floating you first, Lady Glimmer," Eisenwolf said. "Force this Red to witness your death so that he may suffer a little more before I end him. But then I remembered that Scallywag the Red cares about no one other than himself, and seeing him die would probably hurt you worse. So, though I am usually a stickler for protocol, in this case, Ladies do not go first…"

Eisenwolf snapped his fingers and the security guards began to wrestle Scallywag toward the airlock.

"Blast it, Eisenwolf! Don't do this!" Glimmer shouted. "Take him back to Visinia! Make him stand trial before the Emperor!"

"And give him that kind of publicity? I think not," Eisenwolf replied. "No, his fate is to be tossed out the airlock into the cold embrace of the void, just like all the other trash."

The security guards shoved Scallywag into the airlock. Scally turned back around as the guards kept their blasters trained on him. He met Glimmer's gaze, her eyes wide and sorrowful.

"I love you!" Glimmer cried.

At that, Scallywag smiled. It wasn't his usual smug, cocky grin. This time, his smile was one of genuine heart and soul.

"I love me, as well," Scallywag replied.

Some of Eisenwolf's men chuckled at his response. But Glimmer recognized the quip for what it was – a heartfelt good-bye, which carried with it a past full of unspoken regrets on behalf of them both.

Glimmer watched helplessly as Eisenwolf hit a button on the console before him, closing the airlock door, which slid in front of her view of Scallywag until locking in place and sealing shut. Through the small porthole in the door, she could see Scallywag's face, his gaze never faltering from hers. And despite her bravado, Glimmer couldn't hold back her tears.

Then, she felt a hand grab her hair and yank her head back, Eisenwolf's hard gaze drilling into her. "You're a traitor to your skin," Eisenwolf sneered. "If you weren't a Blue, you'd be standing in there beside him."

"I'd rather die by his side than stand by yours," Glimmer said through gritted teeth.

"Don't worry, my dear. You'll get your turn to die soon enough," replied Eisenwolf. "Of that, I will make absolutely sure. But until such time, I will be content with his." Eisenwolf released her and turned his attention back to Scallywag. "Any last words, you filthy piece of scum?"

"I think I've said enough," Scallywag responded. "Now do what yer gonna do. I'm eager ta see me brother again."

"I knew your brother," Eisenwolf said, "and I can honestly say, you are not going to the same place as him."

"I'll go anywhere, just so long as you're not there," Scallywag replied. "Now float me, before ya bore me ta death."

"With pleasure," Eisenwolf said as he reached out for the airlock's console.

"No..." Glimmer whimpered as Scallywag prepared himself for the inevitable.

Then, just as Eisenwolf was about to hit the button to open the outer airlock and send Scallywag to his ultimate fate, a flash of light emanated from behind the airlock's hatch, and just like that...

Scallywag had disappeared.

Eisenwolf gazed at the airlock's porthole, at first not comprehending what had just occurred. Then, he rushed forth, putting his face up against the window to look around the airlock, trying to see where his captive may have gone.

"What?" Eisenwolf cried. "Where did he go?"

Eisenwolf turned to his men, as if expecting one of them to have the answer. When his gaze eventually settled back on Glimmer, she looked both surprised and relieved. Eisenwolf scowled.

"You!" he sneered, heading directly for her. "What have you—"

Then, just as Eisenwolf was about to grab Glimmer, she too disappeared in a flash of light.

Eisenwolf looked at the spot where Glimmer had been standing mere moments before, dumbfounded. He glanced around him, confused and angry.

"WHAT THE BLAZES IS HAPPENING???" he yelled, at no one in particular.

"Oh, dear…" said Dan, the robot shuffling up to Eisenwolf's side. "It would appear someone has wirelessly broken your ship's encryption protocol and gained access to its teleportation network just in time to teleport both Master Scallywag and Mistress Glimmer away from your clutches."

Eisenwolf turned toward Dan, looking the security-bot up and down, his eyes wide with bewilderment. "Wha… what?" he stuttered.

"That same someone has also taken the liberty of restricting ship-wide teleportation and communications in an effort to hamper any of your attempts to recover them, I'm afraid," Dan continued. "And I would like to take this moment to apologize to you and your men. I fear you will be too busy fighting for your own lives to put much effort into pursuing us. I am very sorry for what's about to happen, but it was the only scenario I could formulate that would keep you occupied long enough for us to make our daring escape. Oh, and before I forget…"

Dan then hit the button on the airlock's console, opening both its inner and outer doors, before turning back to Eisenwolf.

"Ha. Haha. Ha."

With that, Dan disappeared in a flash of light, just before the vacuum of space began violently sucking all the air from the corridor.

Glimmer appeared on the bridge of *The Reaver* where a bewildered-looking Scallywag was already waiting. The instant they saw one another, they ran into each other's arms and embraced tightly.

"I… I don't believe it!" Glimmer whispered. "What just happened? How did we get away?"

"Turns out I had a guardian angel on me side," Scallywag replied. "Guess I wasn't lyin' when I said it was me lucky day after all."

Scallywag and Glimmer both pulled back, looked one another gratefully in the eyes and then kissed. It was a heartfelt kiss, full of relief and affection. Though the two of them had spent years fighting their feelings for one another, the harrowing circumstances they'd just endured had brought clarity to them both. For in the face of death, they were each forced to finally acknowledge…

They were madly, deeply, in love.

"Oh, dear," came Dan's voice.

Scallywag and Glimmer broke off their kiss to see Dan had suddenly joined them.

"I did not mean to intrude," the robot said, apologetically. "Please, do not let my presence disrupt your oral swapping of fluids for emotional purposes. I shall wait quietly until your romantic exchange has run its course."

"Scally…" Glimmer said, confused. "There's a security-bot staring at us…"

"That ain't just any security-bot, lass," said Scallywag with a smile. "That there is tha new and improved Dan."

"Dan?" Glimmer said. "You mean… your attaché android?"

"Promoted to me guardian angel, as of right now," Scallywag said. "So, ya came through with a rescue after all, eh, robot? Ya sure do know how ta wait until tha last minute. Thought fer certain I was gonna be floated."

"My apologies for the extreme nature of my timing, Master Scallywag," Dan replied. "It was not until I realized how important the date of his father's death was to Captain Eisenwolf that I thought to utilize it to formulate potential passcodes to access the ship's encrypted systems. Once I correctly guessed his passcode, I was finally able to work my way into the ship's network and gain control, successfully saving you and Mistress Glimmer."

Scallywag couldn't help but smile. "Danny-boy, ya brilliant hunk o' scrap! I could kiss ya!"

"Oh!" exclaimed Dan. "Gestures of physical affection are always most welcome, Master—"

"I'm not gonna kiss ya."

"Oh," Dan said, sounding a bit disappointed.

"But I will," said Glimmer as she moved to Dan and gave him a kiss on his robotic cheek.

"Oh!" Dan said, cheerily.

"Thank you, Dan," Glimmer said, genuinely grateful. "You are, without a doubt, the best blazing bot I've ever known."

"Curious," Dan said, tilting his head slightly. "Mistress Glimmer's words have caused an unfamiliar sensation to course throughout my circuitry. It is as though I am experiencing a great deal of anxiety and pride, wrapped up in a copious amount of happiness."

"Believe me, I know tha feelin'," Scallywag said. "Congratulations, robot. Ya just found out what it feels like ta have yer jimmies jerked."

"My jimmies? I was unaware I had anything called 'jimmies', but I must admit, having them jerked feels extremely agreeable," Dan replied, looking at Glimmer once more. "Do it again!"

Glimmer giggled before Scallywag stepped forward and pulled her away. "Right, there'll be time fer that later," he said. "Right now, we still got a lot o' escapin' ta do. Please tell me that beautiful mainframe ya call a brain has a plan ta rescue the rest o' our crew and get us all off this bloody ship."

"As a matter of fact," replied the robot. "It does."

The ear-piercing hiss of the oxygen being violently sucked out through the open airlock assaulted Eisenwolf's ears as he hugged the control console, barely holding on to the bulky piece of equipment as his security team struggled to keep from being sucked toward the breach the robot had opened before teleporting away.

Eisenwolf gritted his teeth and let go of his grip with one of his hands, struggling against the powerful pull of the air until he was able to reach the button that closed the hatch.

Immediately after the inner airlock door slid shut, all the Visinis who'd previously been hanging on for dear life fell to the ground, gasping for breath. An overwhelming feeling of anger rose up within Eisenwolf as he finally had time to come to grips with what had just happened.

"NO!" Eisenwolf cried with rage as he sprang into action, trying desperately to make contact with X.O. Rintin on the bridge. But no matter what he tried, it appeared all communications accessible through his console were locked down. It would seem the boast the robot had levied before it disappeared had not been a bluff.

"On your feet, men!" Eisenwolf barked to his security team. "With me!"

Without waiting for his men to respond, Eisenwolf began rushing down the corridor, looking for any of the emergency network panels that were scattered throughout the ship. *The Megavolt's* emergency network was a closed communication system which used hard-lines and its own battery power so that it would be unaffected in the event of catastrophic power failure or structural damage. If Eisenwolf had any hope of communicating with his staff on the bridge, that would be it.

Finally, he saw a wall panel with the clearly labeled red flame within a circle insignia which denoted an emergency network panel. He ripped it open and picked up the receiver, hitting the button that connected him to the bridge. After a few beeps, Rintin picked up.

"This is Executive Officer Rintin," he said.

"It's the Captain!" Eisenwolf shouted. "Cut all power to the teleportation network! Lock down all the hangar bays! Send a full security detail to the brig and the hangar where we're housing *The Reaver!* Orders are to shoot to kill any of the prisoners they may see!"

"Sir? What's going on?"

"Scallywag the bloody Red is going on, you idiot!" snapped Eisenwolf. "He's trying to escape! And I'll be DAMNED if I'm going to let him!!!"

Officer Falloran sat at his station with his feet kicked up, passing the time by playing a game on his datapad. Suddenly, an alarm sounded and red emergency lights began to flash. Falloran looked around, surprised, before tentatively getting to his feet.

"What the…" he muttered.

Then, the door to the anteroom opened and a security-bot walked in. Falloran looked at it with confusion.

"What's going on?" Falloran asked. "Are they running some kind of drill?"

"Yes, that is correct, sir," the security-bot responded as it closed the distance. "A drill."

As soon as it was within reach, the security-bot shot out its stun prod and incapacitated Falloran, letting him fall to the ground, unconscious. Dan then entered the cell area, where those still locked up were looking around in concern as the alarms blared.

"Oy!" shouted Tarkrane. "Robot! What's going on?"

"It would appear there is a prison break underway," Dan replied as he lowered the shield walls to the cells.

Everyone looked around in shock and confusion until Dan emitted a holographic projection of Scallywag, which made everyone stop and stare.

"Ahoy, mates," Scallywag said.

"Cap'n!!!" exclaimed Tarkrane.

"This here security-bot is on our side," Scallywag said. "He's gonna get the lot o' you outta there. Just do what he says. Glimmer and I are waiting for ya on *The Reaver.* As soon as yer all on board, we're blowin' this squick-heap and not looking back. Savvy?"

"Savvy!" exclaimed Scallywag's crew.

Dan ended the holographic projection and looked to the large group of prisoners before him. "Greetings!" he said. "My name is Dan. Some of you may not recognize me—"

"Oy!" shouted ReeRee. "Less talkin'! More leading us the kitten out o' here!"

"Oh! Yes, my apologies. There shall be plenty of time to get to know one another after we are out of danger. Now, since the brig is shielded from the teleporter network, we shall have to make our way out into the corridor so that I may teleport us all back to Master Scallywag's ship. Please, follow me."

As Dan started leading the group to the exit, Tarkrane sidled up to Gage and gave him a jab with his elbow. "What'd I tell ya, mate?" Tarkrane said with a gleam in his one good eye. "The Cap'n always gets us out!"

Gage was half-tempted to agree with the pirate before Dan opened the door to the corridor to see a full team of armed security personnel racing down the hall, firing their blaster rifles.

"Back! Quickly!" said Dan as he ushered the group back into the brig's anteroom, sealing the door behind him. "Oh, dear," the robot lamented. "My apologies, everyone. I did not anticipate the crew's rapid response to my rescue attempt. In addition to the arrival of an armed security squad, all teleportation within the ship has now been completely disabled."

"What does that mean?" asked Beltran.

"It means that we are trapped at the moment," Dan replied. "And if we do not find an alternative escape route before the security squad breaks through that door, I fear we may all be doomed."

Gage frowned and looked at Tarkrane. "You were saying?" he grumbled.

Tarkrane smirked. "Oy! Robot!" he called out. "Can ya still radio tha Cap'n?"

"Indeed I can."

"Then give him a call!" Tarkrane said. "Tell him ta work his bloody magic!"

Scallywag frowned as he listened to Dan radio in and tell him of the current situation. He looked over at Glimmer. "Tell me ya didn't dismantle tha ship's plasma cannons when ya dressed her up as tha *Bluebell*," he said.

"Give me a little credit, Scally," Glimmer replied. "I'd never declaw such a magnificent beast."

Scallywag smirked. "Thata girl," he said.

As Scallywag hopped over to the weapons console, he saw the bridge's viewscreen display one of the hatches leading into the hangar bay open as security personnel rushed in.

"We got us some company, lass," he said.

"On it," replied Glimmer as she took control of *The Reaver's* forward plasma cannons and began to fire at the incoming soldiers, peppering the area around them and forcing them back into the hatch through which they'd entered. "Whatever you're going to do, do it quickly," Glimmer said. "I can only keep these soldiers at bay for so long."

Scallywag called up Dan's location within the ship on his targeting display. "Not ta worry, love," he said. "This won't take but a moment…"

With that, Scallywag activated the plasma cannons on the topside of *The Reaver*, aiming them upward at the hangar's ceiling. He then opened a communications channel to Dan. "Take cover, lads," Scallywag said. "One escape route, comin' right up."

With that, Scallywag opened fire, blasting away at the levels between decks, opening up breaches until he reached the cell area of the brig, blowing a large hole in its floor. Dan and the other prisoners covered themselves with their arms as the level they were on rattled when *The Reaver's* plasma blasts broke through.

"Deployin' snare winch," came Scallywag's voice over Dan's speakers. "Now!"

A snare winch arm on the top of *The Reaver* extended and fired its cable through the openings the ship's cannon had created. The winch line rocketed forth until its grapple embedded itself in the celling of the brig with a humming *THWANG*.

"Quickly!" urged Dan. "Everyone! Slide down to the ship!"

Kapplan laughed as he rushed to the snare winch cable. "Now this is what I call a jailbreak!" he cheered before grabbing the line and sliding down it.

"Last one there is a smelly crawpatty!" ReeRee cried before following his pirate buddy down the cable.

Gage and Tarkrane ushered the rest of the prisoners to the escape route, making sure everyone got out before they did.

"Ladies first," Tarkrane said, gesturing toward the cable.

"Age before beauty," Gage replied.

"Oh! Is this antagonistic banter used to disguise the fostering of comradery?" asked Dan, excitedly. "What fun! Allow me to participate! Ahem… vulnerable organic sentient life before well-armed robotic being capable of defending itself against large groups of armed assailants!"

Gage and Tarkrane looked at one another before they both acquiesced. "Quick, before we're blasted to bits," Gage grumbled.

"Way ahead o' ya, stoneface," Tarkrane said as he slid down the cable.

No sooner had Gage followed than the Visini security force outside the brig broke through the door. Dan quickly ejected the blaster cannons on his arms and fired at the assailants, giving himself enough cover so he, too, could slide down the snare winch cable.

*Oh my!* he thought as he slid down through the breaches in the decks, looking at various bewildered crewmembers as they watched him speed by. *This is all rather exciting! No wonder Master Jack and the others partake in senselessly dangerous activities so often!*

As Dan entered the hangar bay, he gripped the winch cable tighter, sparking off its metallic threads as he slowed his descent. *The Reaver* was busy firing upon Visini soldiers, trying to keep them from storming the ship. Gage and Tarkrane were topside, at the base of the winch, waiting to catch Dan as he approached.

Dan released himself from the cable and landed soundly on the hull of the ship. Tarkrane wasted no time in ushering Gage and Dan through the ship's hatch, with the one-eyed pirate closing it as soon as he was safely inside. The three then rushed to the bridge of the ship where the other prisoners had gathered.

"Extraction successful, Master Scallywag!" Dan announced. "All prisoners are successfully on board."

"Good job, Danny-boy," Scallywag said as he smiled at his crewmates. "Gents! To yer stations!"

"Aye-aye, Cap'n!" all the pirates responded.

Scallywag looked at Betran and his companions, who gazed at him nervously. Betran frowned. "You were right," the yellow Visini admitted. "We never should have trusted him."

"Hate ta say I told ya so," Scallywag said. "Still wanna ride away from Eionmeer?"

"More than anything."

"Then buckle up. And try not ta get in tha way."

As the Eionmeer survivors did as instructed, Gage approached Glimmer. "Captain," he said.

Glimmer smiled at him. "Gage," she replied. "I'm sure you and I will have a lot to talk about once we're away from here."

"No, we won't," Gage assured her. "I'm with you, Captain. Through thick and thin. I just like to complain sometimes."

"Noted," said Glimmer. "Now make yourself useful. It's time we got out of here."

"Aye-aye, Captain," Gage said.

"I'm not the Captain of this ship anymore, Gage," Glimmer told him. She looked over to Scallywag and smiled. "He is."

Scallywag returned Glimmer's smile and turned to the battered Captain's chair, feeling a sensation of exhilaration washing over him as he took his seat and rightful command of his ship for the first time in a long time.

"Kapplan, retract tha snare winch," Scallywag said. "ReeRee, blow tha hangar's plasma window."

"With pleasure, Cap'n," ReeRee said as he aimed *The Reaver's* port-side plasma cannons at the generators responsible for the plasma window keeping the atmosphere from venting into space. The Visini soldiers barely had enough time to retreat back into the ship before *The Reaver* fired and all the air was sucked out of the hangar.

The hangar's blast doors slowly began to close as *The Reaver* quickly maneuvered out of the bay, just barely scraping by before the doors made the exit impossible to traverse. The crew cheered as they narrowly escaped from *The Megavolt.*

"We did it, Cap'n!" exclaimed Tarkrane. "We escaped!"

"We ain't out o' it yet, One Eye," Scallywag said. "And we won't be until we leave this blasted capital ship in our exhaust trail."

"Yes, about that, Master Scallywag," piped up Dan. "I have successfully locked down *The Megavolt's* plasma cannons, which will prevent them from firing upon us as we make our getaway."

"Excellent work, Danny-boy."

"However…" continued Dan, "I am afraid that once we are far enough away that I am unable to maintain my wireless connection to *The Megavolt's* systems, they will once more have the ability to essentially destroy us."

"And how long until that happens?"

"By my calculations, right about… now."

"Bloody squick," Scallywag muttered. "All power to tha engines! Full thrust! Put some space between us and *The Megavolt!*"

"Aye, Cap'n!" replied Tarkrane.

Scallywag grimaced as he looked at the image of *The Megavolt* on the ship's viewscreen. "Everyone strap in," Scallywag ordered. "This is gonna be a bumpy getaway."

*****

The bridge of *The Megavolt* was in chaos as its crew struggled to regain control over their systems. Officer Rintin stood at the bridge's command center, trying to sort through all the reports coming in. Multiple decks were reporting damage from plasma fire, one of the hangar bays had its plasma window destroyed, and all teleportation was still down.

The doors to the bridge opened as Eisenwolf came marching in, his face a mask of barely controlled anger. Though his skin was blue, his face was turning a shade of purple as rage flushed his cheeks.

"Sir," Rintin said upon seeing the Captain. "The ship has sustained substantial internal damage. Communications are still down. What the blazes happened?"

"The blasted pirate got to his ship and blew a hole in mine, that's what happened!" snapped Eisenwolf. "Tell me sensors are at least still working!"

Rintin called up a holographic display which showed the positions of *The Megavolt* and *The Reaver.* Eisenwolf gazed at it with extreme displeasure.

"It appears they are trying to outrun us, sir," Rintin observed.

"That's because they're cowards," Eisenwolf muttered. "And they know they're no match for the might and fury of this vessel. What is the status of our weapons?"

"They were one of the many systems we were locked out of, sir, but they just came back online moments ago," Rintin informed Eisenwolf.

"Good," Eisenwolf replied. "Bring the ship around and chase that pirate down. Plot firing solutions. Bring every weapon we have to bear on *The Reaver.* I promised myself Scallywag the Red would die today…"

Eisenwolf turned his hard glare toward the bridge's viewscreen, gazing at the image of *The Reaver* like a predator stalking its prey.

"And that is a promise I intend to keep."

# CHAPTER 4

Professor Green and the others had been making their way through the corrupted temple for what felt like ages. The black rock which had covered the structure's surfaces made it hard to navigate, particularly with the slow and cautious pace at which the group travelled. The rock made it feel as though they were walking through an empty void, robbing their surroundings of any distinguishing features they could use to figure out where they were going.

The group's progress was further slowed by the fact that they had no idea what could be waiting for them around every corner. Occasionally, they'd hear the guttural snarls of Deathstalkers in the distance, as though the terrifying creatures were prowling the temple in search of them, causing the group to backtrack or to find an alternate route. Considering Shanks' weakened state, their greatest fear was crossing paths with another Terrormancer. But mostly their biggest challenge was being lost after traveling in circles or running into dead ends.

Green looked down at his Imperius device. Sometimes it would light up, indicating they were on the right track. Other times it would go completely dead, forcing the group to wander aimlessly until getting a signal once more. Green had guessed that their fall to the base of the temple had put them so far out of range of any signal for the portgate that the Imperius device was having a difficult time connecting with it once more (and he could only guess what impact all the black rock was having on the device).

That is why, when the Imperius finally had more than one of its keys light up, Green became extremely excited. "Eureka!" he cried. "I think I've found a signal!"

"About blasted time," grumbled Sawbones. "I'm a doctor, not a tomb raider, daggit."

"Fear not, my grumpy friend!" Green said, cheerily. "I think we might be close to making a connection to the portgate and may finally be able to escape this horrible place! This way!"

Green picked up the pace and began following the signal, growing more and more excited each time his Imperius device had a new key light up. Sawbones and Shanks followed close behind, with Sawbones shining a flashlight to help illuminate the way ahead.

The Professor eventually followed the signal into a circular room with a light blue floor. Though the walls and ceiling were completely covered in black rock, the floor seemed entirely untouched, the metal it was made of apparently having kept the sinister material at bay.

No sooner had they stepped into the room then the Imperius device lit up fully, causing Green to cheer. "This is it!" he cried. "This must be the temple's portgate chamber!"

"Thank King Muskar's mighty mustache," muttered Sawbones. "Does this mean we can finally get out of here?"

"Indeed it does!" replied Green. "Just give me a few moments while I connect to the portgate and have it return us to the surface—"

Shanks suddenly cried out, grabbing onto his head and stumbling to his knees, only just bracing against his staff to keep from collapsing to the floor completely. Sawbones rushed to his side. "Daggit!" she said. "We need to get ya outta here, on the quick, man!"

"No…" Shanks objected as he recovered from his sudden attack. "It is… it is not the soul severance…"

"What else could almost cause ya to keel over?"

"It is the Princess."

Sawbones and Green exchanged a curious look. "The Princess?" asked Green.

"She is here," Shanks declared.

"Yeah? And how do ya know that?" asked Sawbones.

"Because I can sense her."

"You can *sense* the Princess?" asked Green, fascinated.

Shanks nodded. "The last time I made contact with her in my meditations, I imbued a part of my essence into her. It not only allowed me to communicate with her while I was meditating, but it also would make it easier for me to make contact with her in the future. Now, because of that imbuement, I am able to sense her presence, and I sense she is not far away."

"I'm not sure I understand," Green said. "Did you do for her what you did for Jack?"

"No, imbuing one's spiritual essence is different than transplanting a part of one's soul," Sawbones said.

"In what way?"

"The spirit generates energy that can be manipulated and used in many different ways," Sawbones explained. "Ya can use that energy to heal, to discover new knowledge, to make connections to others, and to imbue objects with its power. But that energy can be regenerated. The spirit itself is like its own entity. When part of it is injured or ripped away, it can't be easily healed. It's like the difference between leaving behind a handprint on something and leaving behind your entire hand."

"So… the Princess harbors some of Brother Shanks' spiritual energy, but Jack possesses a part of his actual spirit?"

"Precisely."

"Does that mean you can sense Jack, as well?" Green asked.

"In a way," Shanks replied. "Jack, the Princess, and I… we are all connected at the moment. This is how I know she is here, in the temple."

"But how can that be? We left her at the Conclave. There is no way she could have escaped from there!"

"I also sense a dark presence around her," Shanks said. "Much like the one I felt when we came across the Terrormancer, but much stronger. She is surrounded by many of them. If she were able to flee the Conclave, I would no doubt guess they had something to do with it."

Green frowned. "Oh, dear," he muttered. "If she is indeed here, we need to rescue her!"

"I need to rescue her," Shanks said. "The two of you need to escape this place."

Sawbones grimaced. "Now wait just one daggon minute there," she protested. "If you think we're just gonna leave you behind—"

"There is nothing you can do to help her, my friend," Shanks said. "The last time we crossed paths with a Terrormancer, it took nearly all my strength to guard the three of us from its influence. Now, the Princess is surrounded by them. I will not be able to shield either of you from their powers. I fear you would be nothing but a liability in my efforts to assist her."

"But, Brother Shanks…" Green said. "If you face them alone… you will not survive."

"I am dying anyway, my friend," Shanks replied. "Better to do it in service to my duty. Besides…" Shanks hefted himself back to his feet, gathering what strength he could to stand tall and upright, "when one is surrounded by darkness, only light can save them. I am of the Luminadric, and none shines brighter than we."

Sawbones grimaced, but nodded reluctantly. "And what if your light ain't enough to save her? What then?"

"That is where you two come in. You must escape this place, and you must alert others to the Princess's whereabouts. I shall do what I can to assist her here, but her ultimate fate is in your hands."

"Ya came here to find me so I could heal the Princess," Sawbones objected. "That was supposed to be my role. My purpose is to protect and preserve life. Now, you're asking me to let you walk off on a bloody suicide mission while the Princess is surrounded by Deathlords."

"As you are so fond of pointing out, my friend… you are a doctor," Shanks said, placing his hand on Sawbones' shoulder. "Though you are skilled and powerful in the healing arts, I fear you are ill equipped to deal with Deathlords, let alone the one who is controlling the Princess. Please, do what I ask. Protect the Professor. Find a way to alert the Empire as to what is going on here. If I should fail… then do what you feel you must."

Sawbones frowned, not liking the choice she had to make, but eventually she nodded in agreement. Shanks then looked at Green, who already had tears welling up in his large eyes.

"I never got to say good-bye to my friend Paragon Shepherd," Green said, sniffling. "I've often thought of what I'd say to him if I had. I can't tell you how many speeches I've crafted in my head while imagining I had gotten that chance. And now that a chance like that is here, I… for the life of me… can't think of anything to say…"

Shanks smiled at the Professor, sadly. "I can," he said as he embraced the Trundel. "Thank you for being my friend, Thaddius Rebbabald Green. My life was richer for having known you."

Green returned Shanks' embrace. "And mine for having known you," he replied.

With that, Shanks backed away and looked at his two companions for what would be the last time. "Go," the monk said. "And may the Great Observer watch over you both."

Then, Shanks turned and disappeared into the darkness.

When he had gone, Sawbones and Green both wiped the tears from their eyes and looked at one another. "Enough tearful good-byes, man," Sawbones grumbled. "Get us out of here already."

Green sighed, sadly, before tapping the keys on his Imperius device. The light blue metallic floor beneath them began to glow, and in a flash of light...

They were gone.

Green and Sawbones reappeared on the surface of Eionmeer, back in the park with the decrepit stone fountain, dead trees, and urban waste that used to be the Twin Rivers settlement. The appearance of sunlight after spending so much time in the dark temple caused them both to flinch as their sight slowly adjusted, the empty buildings and stark surroundings around them eventually coming into focus.

"Big Blessed Lightning," muttered Sawbones. "The entire settlement... it looks dead."

The Professor smiled a weak smile. "Well, at least we did not teleport into the midst of zombie hordes or murderous mobs."

"You're a real 'glass half-full' type of guy, aren't you?"

"It never hurts to try to look on the bright side of things!"

"Well, well, well, what do we have here?" came a voice.

Green and Sawbones turned to see Commander Gunner standing not far away, looking at them smugly.

"Master Verrutus told us there were more of you," Gunner said. "You certainly made us wait long enough..."

Slowly, armed members of the Royal Guard appeared from their hiding places, all of them training their weapons on the duo. Sawbones frowned as she watched the Guard surround them. "It certainly never hurts," she grumbled. "But you sure do get disappointed a lot."

"Oh, dear," muttered Green. "I hadn't anticipated that Verrutus might send more of his Secret Army after us. What do we do?"

"Relax," Sawbones said, cracking her knuckles. "I got this."

Sawbones then held out her hands toward all the Royal Guard members surrounding them. However, when they did not react, she looked around suspiciously before settling her gaze on Gunner who chuckled.

"You only get to use that trick on Verrutus once, Paragon," Gunner said. "We were all inoculated against the Bamobuff flu before shipping out, as well as every other known disease in the universe."

Sawbones frowned. "Okay then," she muttered. "Maybe I don't got this."

"Where is the other one?" Gunner asked. "The monk?"

"He… he didn't survive," Green lied. "He died down in the temple."

"Well, if that isn't true, I'm sure it soon will be," Gunner said. "As for the two of you, orders from the Supreme are that you're to join your companion."

With that, all the Royal Guard members closed in and raised their weapons, preparing to fire. Green and Sawbones both braced themselves for the onslaught of blaster bolts, just as they heard a few dull thuds.

Green looked down and saw that three metallic disks the size of donuts had been tossed around them, tiny red lights on their tops flickering rapidly as a high-pitched whine began to escape each of the devices.

"STUN GRENADES!" shouted Gunner, right before the three disks exploded.

A blinding flash of light erupted, accompanied by a sonic squeal that caused everyone to crumple to the ground, each holding his ears in pain. A canister, which began to emit a heavy smoke that quickly obscured the surroundings, landed in the area.

Green couldn't hear anything but a dull ringing as he squirmed on the ground, his eyes unable to focus from the flash of the stun grenade. However, he could feel someone grab him by the arm and heft him up to his feet. Before he knew it, someone had slung Green's arm around his shoulder and was ushering the Professor away from the park.

As Green's hearing began to return, he could hear shouts from the Royal Guard as they also began to recover. The Professor looked over to see a tall, good-looking Regal clad in a tactical suit and backpack, huffing and puffing as he struggled to help Green and Sawbones get away.

"Move your legs!" the Regal ordered. "The smokescreen will only keep us hidden for so long before we're easy targets for the Royal Guard!"

Sawbones shook her head to clear away the haze the stun grenades created and began hurrying beside the man, allowing him to release her from his grip. Green followed suit, and before long, all three were running toward the empty buildings of Little Visinia.

"There they are!" came Gunner's voice.

Green glanced behind him as he saw Gunner and his men emerge from the dissipating cloud of smoke. The Commander pointed toward them, his face flush with anger.

"Kill them!" he ordered.

"Quickly!" the Regal said. "This way!"

The group rushed down an alleyway just as their pursuers opened fire, red blaster bolts streaking by.

Green and Sawbones followed their rescuer as he maneuvered between the buildings, eventually coming to an alley where one of the buildings had basement windows level with the street. The man pulled out a device from his backpack and aimed it at the windows, which slid open.

"Get inside!" he ordered.

Sawbones wasted no time crawling through the opening. Green followed with the Regal not far behind. The instant the three of them were all in the basement, the man aimed his device back at the window and it slid shut once more. He moved Green and Sawbones against the wall and held his finger to his lips, signaling for them to remain silent.

The group could hear the footsteps of the Royal Guard as they tracked their escape route. "Spread out!" came Gunner's voice. "They couldn't have gotten far! FIND THEM!!!"

When their pursuers had moved on, the Regal stood up and peeked out the window to ensure the coast was clear. "Okay, they're gone," he said. "It won't be long before they start searching the buildings, but we've got some time to catch our breaths."

"Who are you?" Green asked, still overwhelmed by their last-minute escape.

The man looked at Green and flashed a cocky grin. "Boone," he said. "Dirk Boone, of the Imperial Intelligence Agency."

"The Imperial Intelligence Agency?" Green replied. "You mean you're a spy?"

"Special Agent," Boone corrected. "Chief Alabaster sent me here to investigate after we discovered a possible Deathlord presence on the planet. When we found out you and your friends were here, Professor, my orders were to assist you, as well."

"I say, that is most fortunate, my good man!" Green said. "Chief Alabaster certainly has a habit of lending us assistance when we need it the most. Tell me, do you know what happened to our companions Scallywag and Glimmer?"

"I fear I wasn't able to help them," Boone replied. "The Royal Guard ambushed them, too. Just as I was about to try and intervene on their behalf, a shuttle from the Visini capital ship appeared. There were just too many hostiles to make a successful extraction. I fear they were taken up to *The Megavolt*. My only other option was to scout the surrounding area and hope to find you and the rest of your companions before Gunner and his men did."

"I take it that's how ya found this little hiding place?" Sawbones asked, looking around the cluttered basement.

"Indeed," Boone replied. "The security system of this building isn't complicated. My remote hacking device easily by-passed their window locks. It was close, abandoned, and fairly secure. The perfect place to lay low until we can find the opportunity to leave and hijack the Royal Guard's shuttle and get off this rock."

"But… that could take hours!" Green lamented.

"If we're lucky," Boone said. "I've been in similar situations which have taken days. Why? You got someplace you need to be?"

"More like we got something we need to do, and fast," Sawbones replied.

"We need to warn the Empire of what's happening on this planet!" said Green. "You were correct that there is Deathlord activity here, Agent Boone, but I fear it goes much further than that. There is an ancient temple the Deathlords have corrupted beneath the settlement."

"An ancient temple?" Boone said, surprised.

"Yeah, and there are some new types of Deathlords, too," chimed in Sawbones. "Ones that can psychically project overwhelming fear. They're called Terrormancers."

Boone raised an eyebrow. "Terrormancers?"

"Oh, and I almost forgot about the Deathstalkers," grumbled Sawbones. "They're like ferocious Deathlord beasts that grow out of the floor."

"They do what, now?" asked Boone, beginning to feel overwhelmed.

"And the Deathlords have taken Princess Glorianna!" said Green. "I do not know what they have planned for her, but we believe the Terrormancers want to use her to harness the power of the temple somehow."

"And whatever that may be for, ya can bet your sweet sweaty patoot it ain't good," said Sawbones.

Boone was quiet for a moment as he processed everything he was hearing. "RNGsus, the Chief wasn't kidding when he said you guys would know what the Deathlords were up to," he muttered. "The Princess being here changes everything. We need to get word to the quarantine ships in orbit. Have them send down every Imperial soldier they have to assist us in rescuing her."

"We need to do more than that, man," Sawbones insisted. "We need to warn the 1st Fleet, the Empire, and everyone within shouting distance in the system!"

"Unfortunately, we are at a severe disadvantage at the moment," Green said. "The quarantine is blocking all long-range ultrawave communications from the planet. And I fear the only subspace communicator available is in the command tower of the settlement, guarded by heavily armed members of the Secret Army. We'd never be able to get to it."

"So you're saying all you need is a subspace communicator?" Boone asked.

"Yes," Green replied. "With one, we could send out a broadcast to all the military vessels in the galaxy alerting them to the impending danger! Without one, I fear we are doomed."

"Well, then," said Boone as he unslung his backpack and pulled out a briefcase-shaped metallic object, opening it up to reveal his subspace communicator. "Allow me to save the day," he said with a smile.

# CHAPTER 5

Anna struggled as Verrutus loomed over her, the tar-like avatar of the Deathlord Supreme having engulfed the form of Anna's dark companion, which worked its claws into her back like a puppeteer controlling a marionette. Sparks flashed in the blackness of her surroundings, giving brief glimpses of what was happening outside her mental construct.

She could see strange hallways covered in black rock. Robed figures with bone-white skin, carrying scythes with ghostly blades. A chaotic tornado of death energy twisted before a platform containing an access orb. And all the while, she was getting closer and closer to it.

*What is this place?* Anna wondered. *What is happening?*

Whatever it was she was witnessing, Anna knew it could not be good. It only strengthened her resolve to fight back against her tormenter, despite the pain of doing so. Anna tried everything she could – calling on every last ounce of strength she had to resist the Deathlord. But no matter how hard she fought, she could not regain control over her own body.

"Resistance is futile," Verrutus said, his voice a dark and hollow rasp as it echoed throughout the void that surrounded them. "You cannot fight the slythru that possesses you now. And you certainly cannot fight me."

"Your slythru has been trying to kill off the last of me for what feels like ages," Anna replied through gritted teeth. "Yet, here I am. Does that sound futile to you?"

"It sounds sad, actually," stated Verrutus. "Just let go, Princess. Drift off quietly into oblivion. It will free you from this pain. This entire ordeal will end, as will your suffering. All you have to do is let go…"

"Never!" cried Anna, defiantly.

"Your choice," Verrutus replied, twisting his claws within Anna and causing her to scream. "Continue to suffer, if you wish. It makes no difference to me. I have full control over your body and mind, and at the moment, that is all I require from you."

"And what is it you plan on doing with my mind and body?"

"You are to be the catalyst for the ultimate victory of the Deathlords," Verrutus said. "With your powers under my control, we will unleash a corruption over this universe that will wash away all remnants of your precious Empire and any who might be powerful enough to oppose us. You may have defeated Zarrod, but my powers combined with those of Mellegogg will be insurmountable. And when it comes time for Ashtoroth to enact his part of the grand plan of our Lords, it shall herald the final nail in the coffin for all life in the universe!"

"You will not win, Deathlord…" Anna sneered.

"Wake up, foolish child," gloated Verrutus. "We already have."

"Zarrod believed the same thing when he had me at his mercy…" replied Anna. "But he did not account for one very important thing…"

"And what would that be?"

"That I am Glorianna of Legacy Prime!" Anna cried out, defiantly. "Heir of Arcturus! Heir of Nameer! Heir of Tarrok! The blood of the Ancients runs through my veins, and that gives me power you cannot hope to stand against!"

"Blood of the Ancients?" scoffed Verrutus. "You think because your ancestors ruled over planets that you have the strength to fight me? Let me show you the domain over which I rule!"

The darkness above Anna ripped open revealing the light of billions of stars. A silver thread appeared, linking her to the galaxy above. A third arm, growing from the tar-like muck that covered her dark companion, clutched the shimmering thread and yanked Anna and Verrutus violently upward.

Disoriented, Anna cried out as Verrutus carried her up along the shimmering psychic thread. She could see the vastness of space around her, and the higher they climbed, the more threads she could see forming, their fine strands leading to every corner of the galaxy like a twisted spider web that was terrifying in its scope.

Finally, they came to a stop where all the threads converged, the tar creature growing six spindly legs upon which to perch at the apex of its dominion. A head formed that extended out so that it could look Anna in the face with its fiery red eyes that burned with hate and malice. Though the dripping black visage of Verrutus was horrifying to gaze upon, Anna forced herself not to flinch from it.

"Look around you!" Verrutus ordered. "This is *my* Empire, Princess! Each of these threads leads to a soul I have enslaved! Billions of souls are bound to my will! And my power not only encompasses your pathetic Empire, but also that of the Visinis, as well as whole civilizations you've yet to discover – all around the galaxy! My conquests dwarf those of your puny ancestors! Look! LOOK!"

Anna could feel the slimy touch of the tar-like substance which made up Verrutus on the back of her head as the Deathlord forced her to look down upon the galaxy. It was almost too overwhelming for her to comprehend. Its spiral arms slowly turned majestically around the supermassive black hole at its center, with billions of silver threads woven throughout it, connected to countless poor souls who had been enslaved by Verrutus.

"My domain is unending," taunted Verrutus. "My soldiers are legion. My power is insurmountable. Tell me again, Princess… how do you plan to stand against me?"

Despite her bravado, Anna was at a loss as to how to answer the Deathlord – particularly in the face of such a display of power. But she would not allow herself to admit defeat. Not while there was still a part of her left to fight back.

"I will find a way," she replied.

"Defiant to the end, I see," Verrutus said, his dark voice thick with mockery. "But it is too late, Princess. Your time has already run out…"

Anna screamed in distress as she began to descend rapidly. Verrutus maintained his hold over her as he slid down the silver thread and back into the mental construct from which they'd come. Anna felt a sickening sensation in her gut from the rapid drop. She'd barely had time to recover before Verrutus once more lifted her head, forcing her to look at an image of what her body was seeing. When the image came into focus, Anna could tell she was standing before an access orb in a large dark temple, which harbored a tempest of death.

"In a few seconds, the Great Death will begin," said Verrutus. "And once it does, *nothing* can stop it!"

★★★★★

"My Queen," said the Terrormancer. "It isssss time."

*Finally!* thought Judyth Skyborn as she took one last look in the mirror. She'd dressed in her finest gown – a strapless, dark blue one which hugged her shapely form, the winged star of Legacy Skyborn embroidered in silver around her bust. Her beautiful blonde hair hung down loose over her exposed shoulders and around a silver necklace with a large gleaming ruby forming its pendant.

Despite the fact there was no one around to appreciate her efforts to look resplendent, she was determined to appear every bit the part of a Queen as she fulfilled her destiny.

Judyth turned and gazed at the Terrormancer with a smile. "Lead the way," she said as she strode forward, anxious to leave the small chamber she'd claimed in the dark temple of Maxima and to enact the one thing she'd waited so long to do.

The Terrormancer bowed and made his way to the temple's central chamber with Judyth in tow. The temple's monolith stood tall in the chamber's center as the two massive double doors leading to the soul vault rumbled open to receive the Queen of Souls.

Judyth stopped at the base of the stairs leading up into the vault, the Terrormancer by her side. She looked up at the twisting tornado of death energy which loomed before her as she would a lover she could not wait to embrace.

"I wonder…" she muttered.

"Wonder what, my Queen?"

"I wonder if Arcturus felt this way before he raised the temple on Regalus Prime and changed the universe forever," Judyth mused, barely able to contain her excitement.

"And what issssss it you are feeling, my Queen?"

Judyth looked over at the hunched Halcyonian servant and smiled.

"Ecstatic!" she proclaimed.

With that, she made her way up the stairs, the train of her elegant gown sliding over the steps as she climbed. Ghostly white illumination bathed her as she approached the deathly tempest, which swirled before her chaotically.

*This is it!* Judyth thought as she entered the vault and made her way up to the platform containing the access orb. *This is the moment I've waited my entire life for! The moment father trained me for! The moment when I embrace my Halcyonian heritage and become the mother to a new universe!*

Many lightyears away, on the other side of the Empire, Anna stood in the soul vault of the dark temple on Eionmeer gazing at an access orb herself as four Terrormancers looked on. Both women approached their respective objects at the same time, as though their actions had been synchronized by some unseen puppet master. They both raised their hands, ready to play their parts in the grand plans of the Deathlords. Right before either made contact, Judyth smiled to herself.

"The time has finally come," she said, "for a new universe… to rise!"

With that, she laid her hands upon the orb.

Judyth gasped as she made contact with the dark temple of the Halcyonians. She could feel every brick that comprised it. She could feel all the souls trapped within it. She could sense the massive amount of soil above it as it was nestled away deep within the planet. The sensation was incredible, like opening one's eyes after a lifetime of blindness. She'd never experienced such a connection before! Though she had trained and prepared for such a thing, all her expectations had been shattered by what it was actually like.

"Rise!" Judyth cried, both as a command and a mantra. "Rise! RISE!!!"

All around her, the temple began to rumble. It was subtle at first, but grew in intensity as she felt the temple move, forcing its way up through the layers of bedrock and topsoil above it.

The ghostly tempest of spiritual energy swirled and groaned as she took control of its power, using it to help dig a path for the temple as it made its arduous journey toward the surface.

"RISE! RISE UP!" she screamed, feeling giddy as the intoxicating sensation of unadulterated power washed over her. "CLAIM THIS WORLD FOR THE GLORY OF HALCYION!!!"

Judyth felt a queer sensation run through her and was aware of the temple changing her as she controlled it. She could feel her Halcyonian genes coming to the forefront, overtaking her Regalus genetics. Her skin grew pale white. Her eyes turned black. Her mouth stretched and her teeth sharpened. But the transformation was not painful. In fact… it was blissful. She was becoming what she was meant to be.

"YES!" she cried as the temple around her shook. "THIS IS MY BIRTHRIGHT! THIS IS MY DESTINY! THIS IS MY KINGDOM! FOR I AM THE QUEEN OF SOULS – NOW AND FOREVER!!!"

On the surface of the planet Maxima, a large, empty stretch of the Hilavan Plateau began to quake, its effects reverberating throughout the land all the way to the bustling city of Highpoint. Zarrod, in the guise of the Paragon Hasatan, smiled to himself upon feeling the tremors as the clueless residents of the city looked around in confusion and concern at the onset of the sudden seismic activity.

*And so it begins…* he thought.

Far away, the surface of the plateau began to crack and splinter as the tip of the dark temple emerged from beneath the ground. The tremors intensified as the temple continued to rise, bursting through the terrain and sending rock and dirt flying as it emerged like a baby from its mother's womb.

The temple continued to rise, its pyramid form unyielding as dirt and debris rolled down its sides, not stopping until the entire temple had fully emerged from the ground, standing tall, dark, and imposing at a height almost equal to some of the mountains that surrounded it.

And when the tremors of the temple's rise finally ceased, there was a brief moment of peace as it stood, revealed for all the world to see, its dark visage soaking in the soft white sunlight. But that moment of peace was fleeting. For once the dust began to settle, black rock started growing from the base of the temple, spreading out across the surface of the plateau.

And with it, Deathstalkers began to emerge.

Safely hidden in a basement in Little Visinia on Eionmeer, Boone and Sawbones watched as Professor Green finished recording his message on the subspace communicator.

"Time is of the essence!" Green implored. "Please, if you are receiving this message, we require immediate assistance! Not only is the Princess's life in danger, but the lives of everyone in the Empire are, as well—"

Suddenly, a tremor struck. Boone and Sawbones looked around in alarm as the building they were in shook. "What the blazes?" exclaimed Sawbones.

"Feels like a terraquake," said Boone.

"Oh, no!" Green said, distracted from his message as he looked around with worry. "Of course! Why did I not see this coming???" Green quickly grabbed the subspace communicator and got to his feet. The building they were in began to shake more violently by the minute. "Hurry!" he cried. "We have to get as far away from the city as possible!"

"Daggit, man! What's going on?" Sawbones demanded as she and Boone followed Green out of the building's basement.

"It's why they needed the Princess here!" Green said, hurriedly. "They're using her to raise the corrupted temple!"

"Raise the temple?" Boone said in disbelief.

"Yes!" cried Green as he rushed out the door. "We're right on top of it! We must make our way to the outskirts of the settlement posthaste!"

"But the Royal Guard is still out there looking for us!" objected Sawbones.

"When that temple comes up, it will bring this entire settlement crashing down around it!" exclaimed Green. "If we stay here, we will perish! Quite horribly, I imagine. Now hurry my friends! We do not have much time!!!"

Neither Boone nor Sawbones voiced further objection as they followed Green, racing through the settlement as the ground began to quake more violently. The group stumbled frequently as the intensity of the tremors grew, sending lampposts and other unsecured structures falling down around them.

Then, the ground beneath them lurched. The group all fell, knocked off balance by the sudden seismic shift. Green hit the ground hard and looked behind him, just in time to see the tall buildings of the settlement begin to topple as the top of the dark temple peeked over the horizon, growing taller and taller as the planet trembled.

Boone sprang back to his feet and pulled Sawbones and the Professor back up. "RUN!" he shouted as the severity of the situation began to settle in on him.

More and more structures started to give way to the violent shaking of the ground, collapsing all around the Professor and his companions as they ran as fast as they could while destruction rained down from above. They heard a mournful groan as the support structure of one of the settlement's tallest buildings gave way, and it began to tilt precariously toward the direction Green and the others were running.

"Great Scott!" Green exclaimed. "That building is going to come down right on top of us!"

"This way! Quickly!" shouted Boone as he directed the others toward an alternate route.

"Daggit, man! I'm a doctor! Not an endurance runner!!!" cried Sawbones as she huffed and puffed, running as fast as her tiny legs could carry her.

The tall building seemed to fall in slow motion, crashing into other buildings on its way down in a domino effect before impacting the ground, sending rolling clouds of dust and debris in all directions.

Green coughed as the dust cloud caught up with the group, stinging his eyes and momentarily blinding him. The ground continued to shake as the dark temple grew taller and taller in the distance. More of the settlement's buildings toppled as the temple rose up from beneath them.

"Don't stop!" Boone called out. "Keep moving!"

Green rubbed his eyes and could see the hazy shapes of Boone and Sawbones in front of him as he tried to keep pace. Debris was crashing down all around while security alarms blared, mixing in with the cacophony of BOOMS from the many structures that were falling to the ground, each one adding to the intensity of the earthquake and almost knocking the Professor off his feet.

Green and his group ran as fast as they could through the destruction, narrowly missing the deadly debris showering down around them. They could see the edge of the settlement where the colony ended and opened up into a dead field of dirt leading up to a rocky mountainous region in the distance. *If we can just make it out of the settlement, we'll be safe!* thought Green frantically as he scurried alongside his companions.

"LOOK OUT!" he heard Boone cry.

Green turned to see a massive building a few blocks away tipping toward them. It was headed right for their current path, forcing them to stop as the building broke in half and tumbled toward the ground.

Boone pushed Sawbones and Green back as the building made impact, knocking them all off their feet as smoke and dust engulfed them. The dust was so thick, Green could not see his surroundings, but he did notice the tremors were beginning to ebb. Finally, the quake that had been ravaging the settlement dissipated, and the ground was still once more.

"Agent Boone! Paragon MacCrusty!" Green cried out. "Are you okay?"

"I just had a daggon city fall on me! I'm pretty far from okay!" grumbled Sawbones as she crawled out from beneath some debris.

"I'm still alive," muttered Boone as he emerged from the cloud, covered in dust and bleeding from various cuts. Boone held his arm, looking at it with a pained expression. "Broke my arm, though," he said.

"Come here, man. I'll fix that for ya," said Sawbones as she waddled over to the special agent while pulling dust and dirt from her beard.

Green looked up and saw the dark temple looming high overhead, nestled among the remains of the settlement. Its surface was completely covered in black rock and seemed to soak up any light that hit it. Green gazed at the imposing structure, his mind racing. *What could they hope to achieve by raising that temple?* he wondered. *How does this fit in with the Deathlords' plans?*

Green then suddenly realized he'd dropped the subspace communicator he was carrying when the final building had fallen. "Oh, no!" he cried, looking around in a panic.

Sawbones looked up from healing Boone's arm. "What? What's wrong?"

"The subspace communicator! I've lost it!" Green said in dismay. "I hadn't sent out the message I'd recorded! We must find it!"

"Relax, Professor," Boone said. "Now that buildings aren't falling on us, we can take a breath and look around for it. It's gotta be here somewhere…"

"Hopefully in one piece," grumbled Sawbones. "But with our luck, I guess I shouldn't be hoping."

The Stonehooligan began kicking over rocks and debris, looking for the communicator. Boone and Green joined in, searching the area for the device. Finally, after a few minutes, Boone called out.

"Over here!"

Green and Sawbones rushed to Boone's location where he'd unearthed the metallic case that contained the communicator. Green breathed a sigh of relief as he looked at the contraption, which still appeared to be in working order.

"Well, I'll be," Green said as he looked at the device. "I forgot to stop it! The communicator has been recording this whole time!"

"Hmmm. Maybe we should edit out the destruction of a whole city thing?" suggested Boone.

"Or leave it in," Sawbones said. "People need to know what the Deathlords are up to down here."

Before Green could make a decision, a queer noise caught his ear. It almost sounded like ice cracking, but in a persistent fashion. Sawbones and Boone heard the noise, too.

"What the blazes is that?" wondered Boone aloud.

Momentarily distracted, Green got to his feet, gazing around for the source of the noise as it grew louder. "I'm… I'm not sure," he said.

"Captain Chester's Chitlins!" cried Sawbones as she pointed toward the direction of the dark temple. "Look!"

The others turned to see black rock growing over some of the buildings in the distance. It moved almost like shadows from a setting sun, spreading out in all directions. Green looked on in morbid curiosity as he noticed a sheet of black rock worming its way under the remains of the buildings in front of them, growing steadily closer to their position.

"What the kitten is that?" asked Boone, not liking what he was seeing.

Before Green could answer, the faint sound of snarls could be heard in the distance. Snarls that sounded all too familiar and sent a chill up the Professor's spine.

"Oh… oh, no…" Green said.

Boone's eyes widened as the lithe and deadly figure of a Deathstalker emerged over the collapsed building before them, looking down upon them and baring its razor-sharp teeth.

"Correction – what the kitten it *that???*" cried Boone.

"Daggit man, please tell me ya got a weapon in that backpack of yours…" said Sawbones.

Boone wasted no time in grabbing a blaster pistol from his pack and firing at the Deathstalker. He hit the creature square-on, causing it to disintegrate in a puff of black dust.

No sooner had that Deathstalker been dispatched than two more appeared, clawing their way over the building.

"And here I thought we could stop running," grumbled Boone as he continued to fire on the creatures. "Let's move!"

The group all began to run before Green stopped. "The communicator!" he cried, having forgotten about it.

Green turned and moved back to grab the device right before a Deathstalker leapt in front of him. Green cried out as the beast slashed at his face with its deadly claws, narrowly missing the Professor as he fell backward.

Boone shot at the beast, dispatching it before it could attack Green further. But more and more Deathstalkers were beginning to appear over the toppled buildings and rubble around the group.

"Get up Professor!" Boone shouted. "We've got to find cover! NOW!"

Green glanced over at the subspace communicator as more Deathstalkers began to close in. The Professor scrambled forward, reaching for the device as Boone continued to fire on the deadly creatures, which were quickly closing in.

Green looked into the camera one last time.

"The attack has begun!" he said. "Please! If you receive this message – come at once! Before it is too late!"

"PROFESSOR!" cried Boone, hurriedly giving Green what little cover he could as more Deathstalkers appeared.

Green ended the recording and hit the transmission button.

He then began running for his life.

# CHAPTER 6

Jack gazed upon the serene face of Pennywise as the Paragon's body lay partially covered with a white sheet, upon a table of the healing chamber. It was one of the larger chambers of the Water Ring, containing what must have been more than a dozen bodies of those killed in the attack. Jack sniffled, his eyes burning from tears. He'd told himself he wasn't going to cry again. That he was simply going one last time to say good-bye. However, upon seeing the lifeless visage of his friend, he couldn't help himself.

*Yet another person I cared about… dead,* Jack thought, bitterly.

Seeing Pennywise made Jack remember when he'd been forced to look at Shepherd as the Paragon's lifeless body lay upon the examination bed of the Earthship's medical bay. The man who'd been his protector and mentor had been taken from him just when Jack had needed him the most. Since the moment Jack had awakened in the Conclave, Pennywise had been there to help him. He had given advice and guidance when Jack had needed both. But most importantly, he'd stood up for Jack and protected him when no one else would.

Jack had lost track of time as he stood beside his friend's body. He wasn't sure how long he'd been there, remembering all the times he'd spent with the man and lamenting over the idea that he'd never get to do so again. At least until a voice snapped him out of his mournful daze.

"What are you doing here?"

Jack turned to see Paragon Savage standing nearby, looking at Jack with his usual glare of disapproval. Jack scowled. "What's it look like?" he replied. "I came to say good-bye to my friend."

"It was my understanding you'd come by earlier when we had the memorial," Savage replied.

Jack wiped the tears from his eyes. "What's it matter? Is there some stupid rule about not being able to visit loved ones after they're dead or something?"

"No, of course there isn't."

"Then back off, dude," snapped Jack. "Just… let me deal with this."

Jack turned his attention back to Pennywise, well aware that Savage had not left. The Paragon came up beside Jack, looking down at Pennywise's body, as well. Savage sighed, deeply.

"I'm sorry for your loss," Savage said. "I realize you and Eldrich had grown close in your time here. What happened to him was a tragedy."

"Just another in a long line," Jack muttered. "It was bad enough losing my mom, my friends, and Shepherd. I'd hoped I wouldn't have to deal with losing people I cared about again. But it's like everywhere I go, death follows me."

Savage frowned. "I know the feeling," he said. "I'm… I'm sorry. I understand this is probably very difficult for you…"

"Just stop, okay?" said Jack.

Savage looked at Jack, curiously. "Stop what?" he asked.

"Stop pretending you give a slap," Jack replied. "You can take your phony sympathy and shove it, *Master*."

Savage grimaced. "You think my sympathy is insincere? I've known Eldrich since he came here as an Initiate. He was one of my brightest pupils. I trained him. Mentored him. Loved him like a son. He was my friend, as well. A good friend. I feel his loss as intensely as you do, only my grief is multiplied by all my other pupils who were so brutally murdered in this most sacred of temples."

"Fine, you feel his loss. But don't act like you care about what I'm going through. You made your feelings about me clear many times over, and none of them involves sympathy."

With that, Jack turned and began to walk away. He'd only made it a few steps when he heard Savage say: "Stop."

The command seemed to echo throughout the quiet chamber. It was said forcefully enough to make Jack obey. He turned toward the Paragon. Savage walked around the table Pennywise was laid upon, a look of sadness on his face as he gazed down at his former pupil. There was even a tear in his eye, which glistened as it rolled down the man's green cheek and into his red beard. Savage had his jaw set, as though he were about to do something he did not want to.

"It's true. I did not want you here," Savage said. "But that desire did not stem from any personal animosity toward you, Earthman. It stemmed from a love of this temple and a desire to protect it."

"Protect it from what?" asked Jack. "Me?"

Savage nodded. "Yes. You, and the danger you brought with you."

"Dude, I'm not dangerous."

"You are," said Savage, forcefully. "You just have no idea how dangerous you are."

Jack crossed his arms. "Okay, then. Enlighten me. How dangerous can a fifteen-year-old idiot like me be to a temple full of the most powerful people in the universe?"

Savage sighed. He looked down at Pennywise again. "Eldrich came to me many times, imploring me to speak with you about this. I refused him each time, because I'd sworn never again to discuss the subject about which he wished me to engage you. My instinct is still not to talk about it… but part of me feels I owe it to Eldrich to do so."

"He asked you to talk to me about Servuchur?" Jack asked, somewhat surprised.

Savage nodded. "It is a subject I am uniquely qualified to discuss. More so than any here at the Conclave."

"Why is that?"

"Because…" Savage replied, reluctantly. "I am the only Paragon here to have mastered its use."

Jack's eyes went wide. "You… you know how to use Servuchur?"

"Which is why I know how dangerous and destructive it is," Savage said sternly. "The action you performed which severed part of your soul is known as a 'soul blast'. It is a technique in which part of one's spirit is projected out like a cannonball. It can be a devastating attack when used properly, and it is an extremely advanced technique, even for those who have trained in Servuchur. And here you were, having done it without any training at all."

"But it almost killed me."

"Frankly, I wish it had," replied Savage. "If you are able to do that without any training, I shudder to think what else you may be capable of."

Jack scowled. "So that's why you've been trying so hard to get me kicked out? Because you were afraid I *might* know how to do stuff?"

"You have no idea the magnitude of what we are discussing here, Earthman," Savage said. "The power you wielded on that shadow port out in the fringes of space is one of the rawest and most terrifying abilities in the known universe. If you somehow learned to control it and unlock even more of its secrets, you could tear this entire temple down on your own, and even the greatest Master Paragon would be powerless to stop you."

Jack gave Savage a curious look. "Is that what happened with the Schism?" he asked.

Savage glared at Jack. "Where did you hear that term?" he demanded.

Jack shrugged. "Since no one would tell me what I wanted to know, I've been doing my own research," he replied. "It came up."

Savage looked unnerved upon hearing the word, his face growing dark. He looked away from Jack, as though he were ashamed, but eventually he recovered his composure. "Yet another thing I swore never to speak of…" he muttered. "But perhaps hearing of it will convince you to finally let this go."

"I'm all ears, dude."

Paragon Savage was quiet for a long moment before speaking. "Back when the Deathlords first appeared… after the destruction of Regalus Prime… there was a large debate here at the Conclave as to the role Paragons were to play in this war we suddenly found ourselves involved in. Many of us, myself included, were eager to join the fight – to avenge the destruction of Regalus Prime and all those who lost their lives on that day. For my part, I may not be a Regal, but I was born on Regalus Prime. It was my home, and everyone I'd ever loved was killed when it was destroyed."

"I'm… I'm sorry," Jack said. "I know the feeling. It sucks."

A sad look came over Savage's face. "As we learned more about the Deathlords, it became clear they were using a technique known only to those of us at the Conclave."

"Servuchur," said Jack.

Savage nodded. "Servuchur was a practice discovered eight thousand years ago and has been marked as one of the few Forbidden Disciplines of our order. It is a dangerous skillset that no Paragon is permitted to perform or train in. A few have studied it over the millennia, but only under strict supervision, and only in theory, never in use."

"When I fought the Deathlords on the Ghost Planet, one of them asked me how I knew it," Jack said. "I didn't know what he was talking about. In lots of ways, I still don't. What is Servuchur, exactly?"

"There are many words I can use to describe it," replied Savage. "But the only one that comes to mind is… evil."

Jack frowned. "That doesn't really tell me much. I have a good friend who likes to brag about how evil he is. And I think he's pretty cool, so…"

"Servuchur is the opposite of everything we as Paragons believe," stated Savage, sternly. "If the true nature of a free mind is the ultimate freedom of the individual… then Servuchur is the enslavement of the individual. It is the technique of exerting one's own will and desire over the spirit of another living thing. It is the purest form of tyranny there is. Does that still sound 'cool' to you, Earthman?"

"No," said Jack, feeling abashed.

Savage sighed, as though simply speaking about this topic were draining him of energy. "When the concept of Servuchur came to light, I lobbied that we here at the Conclave should learn it as a way to use the Deathlords' power against them. The Order of Peers denied my request, believing the techniques to be too dangerous. But that did not stop me. I felt justified that we should learn to harness the power of our enemy, and I was not alone in this. Others felt as I did. Many others."

"It sounds like a legitimate strategy."

"It wasn't. In my anger over the loss of my planet and my haste to seek revenge, I lost sight of the one thing which I should have been aware of."

"What's that?"

"That you cannot fight evil with evil," Savage said, "for when you do, you become just as bad as those you are fighting against."

"Are… are you saying you became evil?"

Savage nodded. "Me, and others like me," he replied. "It started off innocently enough, with the best of intentions. Servuchur, in many ways, is like the teachings of the Wind Ring. Only it gave us so much more control over our own spirits than anything we ever could have believed possible. It allowed us to manipulate our own life force – which is one of the most powerful energies in the universe. We could use it to shield us from harm. We could wield it as a weapon. We could even use it to step outside of our own bodies. It was so powerful a tool, it was intoxicating. But as powerful as it was using it with our own souls… it was even more powerful when we used it on others."

"You mean… like how the Deathlords use it?"

"Yes," answered Savage. "You have no idea of the power you can feel, holding the very essence of what another person is in your hands…"

Savage looked down at his hands, as though he were reliving the sensation he was speaking about.

"It is the ultimate feeling of dominance," he continued. "You see, we were limited in what we were able to accomplish by manipulating our own spirits. In order to truly harness the power of Servuchur, you have to steal the spirit of others to use as your weapon. But when you cross that line… something within you changes. You begin to place less value on the life of others. You see their spirits as nothing more than a way to make yourself more powerful. And the more power you accumulate, the more of yourself you lose. It's as though every soul you steal kills a tiny bit of your own, until there is nothing left of what made you unique in the first place. And at that point, you feel the urge to harness the souls of others… for no other reason than to fill the void where your own spirit used to reside."

"And… and that's what happened to you and your group?"

"It is not something we like to discuss, and it is something few outside the Conclave know about," Savage said. "Those of us who learned Servuchur turned against our brethren. There was a civil war within the Conclave. One which cost many lives. One which… I'm ashamed to admit… I was the cause of."

"The Schism," stated Jack.

Savage nodded. "The greatest internal conflict the Conclave has ever known. A conflict which nearly tore us apart in the very time we needed to be at our strongest. To the universe at large, the war lasted less than a day. However, here at the Conclave, it was a bloody and brutal month-long ordeal."

"A month?"

Savage nodded. "There were not a great number of us who'd turned, but those of us who had were powerful. Many of the Paragons who reside here at the Conclave are not fighters. Artists, engineers, philosophers, academics… they are the ones who make up the bulk of the Paragons who study here. They were entirely ill equipped to deal with those of us who fell under the spell of Servuchur. We harvested many of their souls, adding their strength to ours. The temple was in complete disarray – a constant battlefield. What Fire Ring warriors there still were held the line against us, keeping us isolated in one part of the Conclave, but we were slowly pushing them back. The terror we brought with us over the use of our powers reigned over everyone here."

"But you're a healer," Jack said. "How were you able to stand against Paragon warriors?"

"I was a Warrior Paragon back then, believe it or not," Savage explained. "One of the best. And my mastery of Servuchur made me deadlier than any Paragon ever had a right to be. But I was saved – brought back from the brink of the abyss by a dear, dear friend. A friend who risked everything to save not only my life, but my very soul. And once I realized the error of my ways, I dedicated myself to the healing arts in an effort to make up for all the harm I'd done. But no matter how many wounds I mend or how many lives I save, deep down I know it will never be enough to balance out the pain and suffering I was responsible for."

Savage looked pained as he spoke, as though the memories of his past were physically hurting him.

"Who was he?" Jack asked. "The friend who helped you?"

A small smile grew on Savage's face. "One of the greatest men I've ever known," he said. "You knew him, as well, I believe."

Jack felt his breath catch in his throat. "Shepherd?" he asked.

Savage nodded. "We were Initiates together, Shepherd and I. We'd known one another a long, long time. By all rights, he should have killed me for what I was doing. But he never gave up on me. He kept trying to reach me. Tried to get me to reconnect with the best part of myself."

"How'd he do that?"

"He would seek me out," Savage replied. "We'd fight. But when we did, he'd remind me of our friendship. He'd remind me of everything I had loved and cared for. He'd tell me about the man I used to be, even as I tried to kill him. And then, one day, his words sparked something deep within me. It was as though he was able to rekindle the fire that was my own soul. And when that happened, I was able to fight back and force myself to become the man I thought had disappeared long before. It was through sheer willpower that I was able to recover a shred of who I used to be. With Shepherd's help and support, I healed myself and renounced Servuchur and all it stood for. But despite all that… I could never be the man I once was…"

"Why not?"

"Because that is the curse of Servuchur, Earthman," Savage said. "It fundamentally changes you, and once you've been in its grip, it never truly lets you go. Not a day goes by that I don't struggle with the urge to use it. It's always there, like a little devil sitting on my shoulder, tempting me to give in just one more time. To feel the thrill of that power. To impose my will on others with absolute dominion. It is a constant struggle to keep that desire at bay. I must be ever vigilant in my resolve to never again submit to its temptation. And though I have recovered from my foray into Servuchur, I can never truly heal from it. The wounds it inflicted on me will never go away. I fear they run too deep."

Savage looked at Jack, their eyes meeting.

"That is why I treat you as I do," he said. "All I see when I look at you is the potential for evil. The idea that you, too, possess the power to wield Servuchur makes it so that I can see nothing but the pain, and anguish, and death that I struggle to keep at bay every single day. I do not hate you, Earthman. I *fear* you. I fear what you are capable of. I fear what you may become should you ever tap into the terrible power you seem to possess. But most of all… I fear that should you master this skill you have stumbled upon, I will not have the strength to resist following you down that vile path you'll inevitably walk."

Jack was quiet for a long moment before speaking. "I don't blame you for being scared," he said. "I get scared, too. So many things happen to me, and I don't know what's going on. I don't know how to make sense of it. And this Servuchur stuff is the scariest of them all, because I almost killed myself using it. But if you really understand this stuff… then I need your help more than anyone's. You know the dangers I face. You could help guide me through them…"

Savage shook his head. "No," he stated. "No, I won't."

Jack frowned. "I'm not asking you to teach me how to use it," Jack said. "I'm asking you to teach me how to understand it."

"They are one and the same," Savage argued. "If you truly want my help, then you will heed this advice – forget everything you know of Servuchur. Never use it. Never study it. Never even *think* of it. It is a gateway to evil, Earthman. And once you start down that path, you can never truly escape it."

Jack was about to object when he heard a voice cry out his name behind him.

"Jack! Jack!"

Jack turned and saw Krupp rushing toward him. Both Jack and Savage looked at the large Initiate with concern as Krupp jogged forward, looking harried and winded.

"There you are!" Krupp said, struggling to catch his breath. "The others and I have been looking everywhere for you!"

"What is it? What's wrong?" Jack asked.

"Master Hodapp was setting up the subspace communicator for you to make contact with your ship when we received a message," Krupp replied. "It's from your friends, Jack!"

"My friends?" Jack replied, shocked. It felt like years since he'd last heard from them. "They finally sent a message?"

"They did," Krupp said, gravely. "And they are in *serious* trouble."

# CHAPTER 7

In a section of the outer ring surrounding the Conclave temple, Master Hodapp and a group of his Ground Ring students had cobbled together a contraption made from three of the Conclave's older subspace communication arrays. The bulky pieces of equipment had been jury-rigged together with a repurposed brane accelerator[6] as a central receiver unit, which sported a rather large clear dome at its top. All told, the brane accelerator looked a great deal like a big mechanical ice cream cone.

When Jack, Krupp, and Master Savage arrived, others were already present. Master Highclaw was there, along with Mourdock, Ravencrow, Blackmane, Krixus, and the Royal Vanguard. Jack noticed all of them appeared troubled as he ran up to the group, eager to see the message his friends had sent.

"I'm here!" Jack announced. "What's the message say?"

"Play it again," Highclaw instructed.

Master Hodapp nodded to Scrappy who was among the Initiates helping with the assembly of the subspace device on which the Paragon had been working. Scrappy tapped on a console and the bulky monitor of one of the subspace arrays displayed an image of Professor Green.

"Mayday, Mayday, Mayday!" the message began. "This is Professor Thaddius Rebbibald Green, sending an emergency subspace broadcast to any and all ships in the galaxy! I am sending this message from the Twin Rivers settlement on the planet of Eionmeer, located in the Borro sector of The Great Border. I require immediate assistance from any Regalus, Visini, or civilian vessels in the area. Princess Glorianna of Legacy Prime is here and being held prisoner by the Deathlords. It is my understanding that they plan to use her to control a newly discovered Ancient Temple located on this planet. For what purpose, I do not know, but I'm sure it has something to do with an attack on the Empire. Time is of the essence! Please, if you are receiving this message, we require immediate assistance! Not only is the Princess's life in danger, but the lives of all in the Empire are, as well—"

---

[6] A brane accelerator is a device which creates energy that affects particles known as 'p-branes' which act like a membrane that separates different dimensions from one another. Brane accelerators are necessary to open windows into other dimensions.

Jack continued to watch with a sinking feeling in his stomach as the room the Professor was in began to shake. He witnessed the chaos of Green's run through the collapsing colony, saw the dark temple rise, and the chilling final plea for help before the Professor ended the transmission as strange creatures closed in around him.

"Well, now we know why our saboteur wanted us trapped in the Conclave," Ravencrow said. "The Deathlords are launching an attack in the prime universe using the Princess, and they don't want anyone interfering with their plans."

"At least we have her location," stated Seqis. "We now know exactly where to go to retrieve her."

"That's a rather optimistic way of looking at things," grumbled Master Savage. "If what that message says is true, Princess Glorianna is being held by Deathlords deep inside a corrupted Ancient Temple surrounded by a growing army of whatever those creatures are. Knowing she's there is one thing. Retrieving her is something entirely different."

"The Vanguard is up to the task," replied Rionknidis.

"Are you certain of that?" asked Blackmane. "Not to take away from the abilities of you and your sworn companions, Master Rionknidis, but none of you was a match for the robed figures who abducted the Princess in the first place. And she's most likely still with them."

Rionknidis curled his lip in displeasure at Blackmane's statement.

"The robed figures caught us off-guard in our first encounter," chimed in Lugard. "We will be ready for them this time around."

"We will," Seqis stated, confidently. "The priority now is that we rescue Princess Glorianna before the Deathlords can harm her or use her to complete their plans."

"It is obvious something dire is transpiring in the prime universe," Highclaw stated. "And though I agree we must do whatever we can to assist the Princess and to stop the Deathlords, our first priority must be evacuating the Conclave until we can re-establish a stable tether between this pocket universe and the prime one."

"I am sorry, Master Highclaw, but Legacy Prime must come first," Seqis insisted.

"Master Seqis, I am responsible for all the lives here in this temple," Highclaw argued. "I cannot in good conscience allow our only lifeline to the prime universe to go off into a conflict that it might not come back from before first ensuring the safety of those under my care."

"This whole argument is a moot point if the Earthman can't get his ship here," said Ravencrow, temporarily diffusing the situation. "Hodapp, is this monstrosity you've cobbled together actually going to work?"

"Theoretically," Master Hodapp responded. "As you can see, we've taken the last three remaining subspace communication arrays in the temple and linked them to a central brane accelerator. While the more recently developed compact subspace communication devices can transmit data through the subspace dimension, these early models actually open windows into the subspace dimension before the data can be transmitted. The hard part is going to be opening a window through the subspace pocket and back into the prime universe while simultaneously maintaining an open window from the pocket into the Conclave universe."

Jack didn't really understand what Master Hodapp was talking about, but he knew that the entire situation ultimately depended upon him and his ability to make a connection to his ship. In addition to feeling the pressure from that huge responsibility, Jack was still deeply troubled by the message he'd watched. He hadn't seen any sign of Scallywag, Shanks, Grohm, or Heckubus. There were only two strangers with the Professor, and he had no idea how long Green would be able to survive his current situation without assistance.

"We should get on with this," Jack said. "Time may move slower out in the prime universe, but that doesn't mean we should waste any, especially with what's going on out there."

"Agreed," said Master Hodapp as he approached Jack. "How much do you understand about the concept of stellar coordinates, Initiate Finnegan?"

"Um… not much," Jack replied. "They always just look like a big string of numbers."

"Those numbers are based on a system of mapping three-dimensional space that we adopted from the Ancients," Master Hodapp explained. "The various numbers correspond to a different axis of three-dimensional space. You have front and back, left and right, and up and down. There's also an aspect which takes into account spacetime. So as you can see, there are four different aspects to stellar navigation coordinates. You follow me so far?"

"Yeah," said Jack.

"Since the Conclave is a pocket universe within the prime universe, it can still be mapped using this system of navigation, the only difference being that we add a fifth aspect to the coordinates which signifies that they belong to the pocket universe we are in now. If your ship can recognize this fifth set of coordinates, it should be able to find its way here. Understand?"

"Yes. But… what if my ship can't recognize the fifth set of coordinates?"

"Then it would most likely teleport to an unknown dimension from which it can never escape."

"Oh," Jack said with a frown.

"Don't fret!" said Hodapp, encouragingly. "Though something like this has never actually been tried before, I calculate the odds of success to be in the high sixty percent range!"

"Um… that's it?"

"Better than the fifty percent range!" said Hodapp, cheerily, before handing Jack a datapad with a string of numbers on it. "Here are the coordinates. This should bring your ship right to the docking ring in front of us – you know, if it actually works. Are you ready?"

Jack took a deep breath and readied himself. "I am."

"Then open the windows to subspace!" Hodapp ordered his students. "Good luck, Initiate Finnegan!"

"Thanks," said Jack, looking at the coordinates again and trying to commit them to memory.

The Ground Ring Initiates activated the subspace arrays and watched as the brane accelerator powered up, opening a window into a subspace pocket within the large glass enclosure at its top. The peek into the subspace dimension was an interesting one as it looked like the inside of a large, well-lit tank of milky water.

"Window into the subspace pocket established, Master Hodapp," Scrappy said.

"Excellent! Now, open the window to the prime universe!"

The other two subspace arrays lit up, the creation of a simultaneous opening into the prime universe requiring twice as much power. Within the depths of the visible subspace pocket, another window sparked to life as an area within the dimensional pocket rippled and opened up, revealing deep space beyond.

Instantly, Jack felt a buzzing in the back of his head as his connection with the Earthship was re-established.

*There you are!* Jack thought. *I need your help! I need you to come to the Conclave right away! Here are the coordinates…*

Jack closed his eyes and concentrated, imagining the numbers Master Hodapp had provided him. The back of Jack's head tingled, as though the Earthship were responding with – *I'll be there in a jiffy!*

Light flashed from directly outside the ring Jack and the others were in as the Earthship suddenly appeared. There was a collective cheer from the group as they saw the spaceship, which gently floated toward the docking ring where it connected to the airlock.

"It worked! Good job, Initiate Finnegan," said Master Hodapp.

"Thanks," said Jack, feeling relieved his ship hadn't disappeared into an unknown dimension.

"Now that the ship is here, we still must figure out how we intend to use it," Highclaw stated.

"There should not even be a debate on this subject," said Seqis. "We must go to Eionmeer and the Princess immediately."

"We have still not uncovered the identity of this saboteur," countered Highclaw. "With news of the attack starting on Eionmeer, it could mean he soon plans to strike the Conclave, as well. Everyone who stays in this temple could be in terrible danger. We have children here!"

"If Legacy Prime falls, there will be nowhere that is safe," argued Seqis.

Before Highclaw could reply, Mourdock chimed in. "With all due respect, Masters," he said. "Ultimately, this decision is not up to either of you."

Seqis and Highclaw both looked at Mourdock.

"It's up to him," Mourdock said, gesturing toward Jack. "It's Jack's ship, after all."

All eyes then turned to Jack.

"The Emperor Ascendant is right," Seqis said. "The Earthman is the one who controls our lifeboat. It is his decision as to what to do with it."

Highclaw frowned. "Yes, I had forgotten," he said, turning his golden eyes toward Jack. "What is it to be, Initiate Finnegan? Will you use your ship to aid the Royal Vanguard? Or your fellow Paragons?"

Jack felt awkward having to make such an important decision. He looked at those around him. His friends Krupp and Scrappy – and all the Initiates in the Conclave – would be safer back in the prime universe. But Anna also needed to be rescued and the Deathlords stopped. However, the one image that kept flashing into Jack's mind was the look of fear on Professor Green's face as he'd made his final plea…

*Please!* Green had said. *If you receive this message – come at once! Before it is too late!*

That is when Jack made his decision.

Jack returned Highclaw's gaze, and the Paragon seemed to know what Jack was going to say before he said it.

"I'm sorry, Master Highclaw," Jack said. "I know where you're coming from. The Conclave… it feels like a home to me now. And the people in it are like family. I understand the urge to evacuate them to a safer place. But… my friends need me more, right now. They're in immediate danger and I can't leave them to fend for themselves when I could do something to help them. I wasn't there for Paragon Pennywise when he was attacked, but I can be there for Professor Green. So I'm going to take my ship to Eionmeer. I'm going to rescue my friends."

Highclaw looked disappointed with Jack's decision but nodded in acquiescence. "If that is your wish, I cannot force you to do otherwise," he said. "All I ask is that you do not take any unnecessary risks and return to the Conclave as soon as possible so that we can begin evacuating."

"You have my word," Jack replied.

With a nod of acknowledgement, Highclaw took his leave. Ravencrow gave Jack a nod of approval before he, too, waddled off, his staff clicking on the metallic floor of the outer ring as he did so. Savage frowned but also left without saying a word.

Blackmane approached Seqis. "I will have Krixus, Desmodus, and other members of the Fire Ring accompany you to retrieve the Princess," he said. "You will have all the assistance the Conclave can provide in your endeavor."

"My thanks, Paragon Blackmane. But I must refuse your offer."

Blackmane raised an eyebrow. "I would think you would want all the help you can get in retrieving the Princess."

"As Master Highclaw mentioned, we still do not know the identity of the saboteur hidden within the Conclave." Seqis said. "I cannot risk this mission by bringing along anyone I do not fully trust. And I'm sorry to say, aside from my sworn companions, the Emperor Ascendant, and the Earthman… I do not trust anyone."

Blackmane frowned but nodded. "I understand," he said. "I hope the six of you will be enough to be successful."

"We shall soon find out," Seqis replied.

"Everyone who's coming, get on board," Jack said as he led the way to the Earthship. "As soon as the Entanglement Engine is recharged, we're off to save the day!"

# CHAPTER 8

crappy stood beside Master Hodapp, looking out of the clear enclosure of the outer ring at the Earthship. Though Scrappy had heard Jack talk about his spaceship many times, he'd never actually gotten to see it. Quite frankly, he was fascinated with the vessel.

"Have you ever seen a starship design such as that before, Master?" Scrappy asked.

"No, it is entirely unique," Hodapp responded, also appraising the Earthship with an engineer's curiosity. "There are aspects of it that are familiar, but others that are totally original. Much of it seems inspired by Ancient design, but there are parts that appear entirely uncommon, as though a different design philosophy was involved in its construction."

"What do you think its hull is made of? That metal looks unlike anything I'm familiar with."

"The scans from my exoskeleton have been able to classify it as an unknown alloy," Hodapp said. "There are many aspects of it that are quite intriguing. I would love to be able to study it further, if given the opportunity."

"Maybe once Jack returns, you can ask him if it would be okay to do so," Scrappy suggested. "I'd love to get the chance to study it, as well!"

Hodapp grinned, showing off his many pointed teeth. "Perhaps the request would be better off coming from you, Initiate Celedon," Hodapp said. "You and Initiate Finnegan seem to be quite close, are you not?"

Scrappy smiled. "He's one of my best friends!" the young Trundel[7] replied.

"Then you should definitely be the one to ask," Hodapp stated, encouragingly.

Just then, Jack's image appeared on one of the monitors from the subspace array. "Conclave, this is Earthship Awesome," he said. "Master Hodapp, Scrappy, do you read me?"

"Loud and clear, Initiate Finnegan," replied Hodapp.

---

[7] Trundels are humanoid aliens who resemble turtles, and are known for their good memories and skills at science and engineering.

"The Entanglement Engine has fully recharged. We're getting ready to leave," Jack informed them.

Paragons Blackmane and Krixus came up beside Scrappy and Master Hodapp. "Remember, don't do anything foolish, Initiate Finnegan," Blackmane cautioned. "Everyone here is depending on you to return."

"Don't worry, I'm the most dependable guy there is," bragged Jack, though it was clear Blackmane wasn't buying his bravado. "I'll return as soon as I can. Promise."

Master Hodapp nodded. "Good luck, Initiate," he said. "May the Great Observer watch over you and keep you safe."

"Thanks," said Jack as he held up two fingers in a V-shape. "Peace!"

With that, the transmission ended and the Earthship soon disappeared in a flash of light. Once it was gone, Master Hodapp turned to Scrappy with a curious look. "Peace?" Master Hodapp said. "Does he always bid farewell in such a strange manner?"

"Yeah… Jack says a lot of weird things," Scrappy answered with a shrug. "Nobody gets him."

"Well, now that the Earthman is reunited with his ship, he have no more need of this subspace array we've assembled," said Master Hodapp, looking at the contraption. "Let us begin disassembling it and move it back to the Workshop of Wonders."

"Do we have to?" asked Scrappy as the other Ground Ring students went about dismantling the array. "It was so fascinating seeing a dual brane projection within a subspace pocket! Maybe we could try some experiments based off Paragon Doohan's theory of using subspace to transmit matter instead of just data?"

"Oh, ho!" laughed Hodapp. "I did not know you were so well versed in subspace theory, Initiate Celedon."

"It's a hobby of mine," admitted Scrappy with a shy smile. "I've been trying to learn how to build my own subspace communicator in my spare time. My other passion is matter traversal. I was planning on doing my thesis on teleportation technology. Maybe I could incorporate the two?"

"Teleportation and subspace," said Hodapp with a chuckle. "You sure do have varied interests, Initiate. Tell you what… when we get these devices back to the workshop, I'll have the team reassemble them there and we can look into the possibility of experimenting with this further."

"Really?" said Scrappy, excitedly.

"Of course!" replied Hodapp. "Far be it from me to shut down such an opportunity to enhance our knowledge of subspace after a successful first test. But further experimentation should really be relegated to the Workshop of Wonders. You know, just in case we accidentally erase all of reality."

Scrappy was about to thank Master Hodapp for the opportunity to further indulge in his scientific passions when something strange caught his eye. He looked past his mentor at a rather odd sight that was occurring in the far boundaries of the pocket universe, visible from the outer ring.

"Master!" exclaimed Scrappy. "Look!"

Scrappy pointed upward, through the clear enclosure of the Conclave's outer ring, toward a ripple in the fabric of the pocket universe. An opening was slowly appearing, revealing stars and a planet high above them. Master Hodapp looked at the development with a great deal of curiosity.

"What… what is that?" asked Scrappy.

"Hmmm. It would seem a rather large tether has just opened up," replied Hodapp as the goggle covering his eye transformed into a telescopic lens, zooming in on the anomaly and analyzing it. "If I'm not mistaken, that appears to be the planet of Maxima, from the Rim."

"Maxima?" said Scrappy. "Why would a tether open to there?"

Hodapp increased the magnification of his lens, zooming in on the planet, eventually getting close enough to see a satellite's view of the dark temple and the black rock that was spreading from it, slowly creeping over the surface of the plateau on which it was located. Master Hodapp immediately retracted his telescopic lens, looking alarmed. "One of the Deathlord dark temples is on the planet's surface!" he exclaimed.

"Dark temples?" squeaked Scrappy, suddenly afraid. "You mean like the one we saw on Eionmeer?"

"The appearance of one of those temples on Maxima and a tether to the planet opening into the Conclave universe cannot be coincidence," Master Hodapp stated. "No doubt our saboteur is now making his move…"

Hodapp turned toward his pupils. "Quickly!" he ordered. "Alert Masters Highclaw, Savage, and Ravencrow! The rest of you, come with me to the

Chamber of the Seal! We must put all our effort into gaining control over the Great Seal and closing that tether before the Deathlords can launch an attack—"

Before Master Hodapp could finish assigning the urgent tasks to his Initiates, a red moonfyre blade burst through him, protruding from beneath his mouth and jutting out the clear dome of his exoskeleton's cockpit.

The breath caught in Scrappy's throat as he looked at Master Hodapp's single, dinner plate-sized eye, open wide in shock. Some of the Initiates gasped and stepped back, unable to process what had just happened.

Blackmane stood behind Hodapp, glaring down at the Scollum with disdain before yanking the sword out the exoskeleton's back. Master Hodapp gurgled, still fighting to hang onto life, right before Paragon Krixus manifested his warhammer and brought it crashing down upon the exoskeleton's cockpit.

The group of Ground Ring Initiates all cried out as Hodapp's exoskeleton crumpled like an aluminum can under the weight of the hammer's blow, squishing Master Hodapp soundly in the process with a sickening *CRUNCH*.

Panic gripped Scrappy's chest as he gazed at what remained of his mentor. He looked up to see Blackmane and Krixus, both glaring at the group of Initiates with their deadly weapons in hand.

There were many things Scrappy could have done in that moment. He could have attacked his mentor's killers. He could have manifested a brilliant contraption to protect his classmates. He could have even made a witty quip to taunt the imposing men before him. But instead, all Scrappy could think to do was say one thing, and that thing was:

"RUN!"

The other Ground Ring Initiates didn't need to be told twice. Almost as one, all the students turned and began scrambling down the hallway of the Conclave's outer ring as quickly as their legs could carry them, each and every single one of them in a blind panic as they did so.

Krixus watched them go, a stoic expression on the large Paragon's face. "Should we go after them?" he asked.

"No," Blackmane replied, looking up to the tether and the planet beyond. "They will be of more use alive when the corruption comes."

"They may be able to alert others before it does."

"It makes no matter," said Blackmane with a wistful sigh as he demanifested his moonfyre sword. "By now, Desmodus has destroyed all the remaining communication devices in the temple. There will be no way for them to call for help from the outside."

"And from the inside?" Krixus asked. "The Order of Peers still poses a threat."

"Not for long," said Blackmane with a sly grin. "Now smash that subspace contraption Hodapp cobbled together. Supreme Mellegogg wishes to leave nothing to chance."

Judyth Skyborn stood within the soul vault of the dark temple on Maxima, the temple's access orb still clutched firmly within her grasp. She marveled at the power she wielded through it. The soul tempest before her was at her command. She could feel the life force of each and every being she and her servants had painstakingly added to it over the decades, and each one was her thrall.

*Oh, how I wish you could be here to see this, father!* she thought, drunk on the sensation she was experiencing. *How you dreamed of the day when we would be able to embrace our true heritage! To banish the stain of the Ancients from the galaxy! You raised me to do what you, and all who came before you, could not… and now, the moment of our ascension is finally here!*

Judyth's connection with the temple made her hyper-aware of everything that was happening around it. It was as if she had eyes everywhere touched by the black rock, and that vision was growing the more the rock spread across the land. But her clearest view was of the heavens, as the top of the temple gazed up into the sky.

Her vision extended past the clouds, past the atmosphere, and into space, where the fabric of reality was torn asunder and a large tether to another universe opened up. There, in the center of the portal, was her ultimate target. The crowning achievement of the Ancients. The heritage of Arcturus and all who came after him.

The Conclave.

*Mellegogg has done his part by opening the tether*, Judyth thought. *Now it is time for me to do mine!*

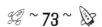

Judyth tightened her grip on the access orb, concentrating as the top of the temple opened up, four quadrants of its tip sliding aside to reveal the soul vault beneath it.

The Queen of Souls focused in on the Conclave temple with her enhanced vision, putting the structure square in her sights as she reached out to the deadly power she had at her fingertips.

She could feel the souls at her command wail and cry out in protest, but they were bound to the temple, and by extension, to her will. She smiled in anticipation as she gathered the death tempest's strength, readying it to ravage the greatest symbol of power the Ancients had left behind.

"Here's to the start of a new universe…" she said.

With that, she unleashed the full fury of the death tempest. Its ghostly beam shot up from the temple, through space, and directly at the Conclave with a terrifying ferocity, which nothing could stop.

As the beam of death energy engulfed the Conclave, a tantalizing sensation of exhilaration and unadulterated power coursed through Judyth Skyborn, making her smile a twisted and evil grin of victory.

"Rejoice, father!" she cried. "Now it is too late for anything to stop us!"

"What do you mean he left?" demanded Morosa.

Krupp frowned. Morosa's growing relationship with Soundwave had mellowed the fiery Femezon a good deal, but when her anger flared, she could still be very difficult to deal with. "He took the Royal Vanguard to go save Princess Glorianna," Krupp explained, again. "It was a very difficult decision, but people needed his help."

"People need his help here," stated Morosa. "There was a nuclear explosion in the temple. We could have all been killed! And the longer we stay here, the more danger we are all in."

Morosa turned and looked at Soundwave, her hard gaze indicating she expected him to agree with her. Soundwave sat back in his chair, relaxed, sipping on a mug of Mellow Mead. There was chipper music playing in The Rec as the group all sat at one of its tables, discussing what had transpired. "I dunno," Soundwave said. "I think it's very noble of Jack to go off to help his friends."

"Are we not his friends?" Morosa demanded. "Why is he not helping us?"

"<Maybe because we are not in immediate danger?>" chimed in Snodgrass.

Before Morosa could reply to that, Scrappy came bursting into the recreation chamber, bumping into numerous students as he frantically rushed by them and toward his friends. "HELP!" Scrappy cried. "HELP! WE'RE ALL IN IMMEDIATE DANGER!!!"

Morosa scowled at Snodgrass. "You were saying?" she grumbled.

Krupp caught Scrappy as he ran up to them, trying to calm his friend. "Scrappy, slow down, breathe," Krupp said. "What's going on?"

"They killed him!" Scrappy cried. "Master Hodapp! He's dead!"

Even Soundwave, despite his usual laid back attitude, sat up in alarm upon hearing Scrappy's report. "Dead?" said Soundwave. "Master Hodapp?"

"<Who?>" asked Snodgrass. "<Who killed him?>"

"It was Paragons Blackmane and Krixus!" Scrappy replied. "They killed him right in front of me!"

The group all sat at their table, stunned. Krupp felt a cold chill travel down his spine. "Blackmane and Krixus…" he muttered. "They're the saboteurs?"

"That makes no sense," Morosa said. "Even if they were, neither of them is powerful enough to defeat Master GorJiro in single combat."

"Maybe not either of them… but both of them might have been," replied Krupp, thinking aloud. "All this time, the Order was looking for the wrong people. Heck – Blackmane was leading the investigation!"

"<But why now?>" asked Snodgrass. "<Why would they reveal themselves now?>"

"Something is happening," said Scrappy. "There was a new tether that opened up…"

"A new tether!" exclaimed Morosa.

"Not in the temple," explained Scrappy. "Out in the space of the pocket universe. It led to the planet Maxima. Master Hodapp was convinced it meant the saboteur was going to start an attack on the Conclave, but before he could do anything about it, Blackmane and Krixus, they… they…"

Scrappy's lips trembled as he recalled the terrible memory, tears welling up in his eyes. Krupp frowned, knowing how much Scrappy had looked up to Hodapp. He placed his hand reassuringly on his friend's shoulder. "It's going to be okay," Krupp said. "We just need to alert the Order. Tell them about what's happened and…"

Before Krupp could finish his sentence, all those in The Rec winced, grabbing their temples as a piercing headache assaulted everyone in the room.

Morosa pushed her chair back, forcing herself up to her feet. "My head!" she cried. "What is happening?"

"Too much caffeine?" suggested Soundwave, half-jokingly, as he accidentally spilled what was left of his drink while grabbing his temples.

"<It's not just us!>" Snodgrass said. "<Look around!>"

Krupp pushed past the pain of his headache to take notice that everyone else in the chamber was struggling with the same issue. "How is that possible?" he asked.

Then, a sound could be heard. It was faint at first, but steadily growing louder. It sounded like screams.

"Does anyone else hear that?" asked Soundwave.

A feeling of dread settled into Krupp's gut. He looked up toward the ceiling of the chamber as the sound grew even louder. Slowly, a ghostly haze seemed to seep through the sandstone bricks of the room, travelling down the walls like a haunted mist.

Krupp's eyes grew wide as he discerned featureless faces with expressions of pain and anguish as they formed within the energy that was slowly encasing the room. He shook his head, forcing himself to focus and ignore his piercing headache.

"GET AWAY FROM THE WALLS!" he yelled. "NOBODY TOUCH THAT STUFF!"

But as the death energy spread across the chamber, everyone could feel an oppressive weight settle in on them, even without touching the ghostly haze. Morosa clenched her fists and gritted her teeth. "What is happening?" she demanded. "I feel… I feel…"

"Wrong…" Soundwave said. "I feel wrong!"

Krupp understood what they were saying. He felt somewhat numb, as though a part of himself was dying while another part was rising up to take over – and that part was dark and angry.

Then, Krupp heard the sound of people crying out. He looked around to see some in The Rec had begun attacking each other. Their skin was turning pale and white with veins within them bulging faint green and purple. People's eyes were turning black, and once that occurred, they violently set upon anyone in their vicinity.

"We have to get out of here…" Krupp said, grabbing Scrappy and gesturing for the others to follow him. "Hurry! Move!"

The group wasted no time in following Krupp as they pushed their way past a growing number of students who were succumbing to the strange transformation the death energy was bringing with it. Though some were giving into the corruption which plagued them, others seemed able to resist it, even as it caused them great discomfort.

Krupp felt sick to his stomach, finding it hard to concentrate, but he refused to give into the sensation that was assaulting him. He eventually made it to The Rec's exit and out into the corridor. When his friends followed, he noticed they all looked pale and weak, but so far, none of them had been fully affected.

However, they had not escaped the death energy which had overtaken The Rec. The ghostly haze was everywhere, seeping from every wall. Cries could be heard from all around as those within the temple struggled with the corruption that was quickly afflicting them.

"What do we do?" asked Soundwave, sounding slightly panicked. "This stuff is everywhere! There's nowhere to hide!"

"We need to call for help," said Krupp.

"<Who can we call?>" asked Snodgrass. "<The only person who can get us out of here is Jack!>"

"Then that's who we need to contact," Krupp said. "Scrappy, where's the nearest subspace communicator?"

"It would be down in the communication chambers in Ground Ring," Scrappy said. "This way!"

The group followed Scrappy as he hurriedly led the way through the Conclave. The temple was in complete chaos as afflicted Paragons attacked those who were struggling against the effects of the death energy. Many times, the group came across grisly instances of violence and carnage, forcing them to change direction and find a safer route. Screams echoed throughout the hallways they traversed – some sounded as though they were from pain, while others sounded as though they were from madness. The temple, which had been a safe place of learning and enlightenment, had turned into a nightmare.

Morosa forced the group to take a detour to the Escrimar arena in the Fire Ring so that they could grab some practice sabers, which she, Krupp, and Snodgrass all used on the corrupted Paragons who attacked them while they made their way to the Ground Ring. Though the practice sabers were not lethal, they did a good enough job of incapacitating the attacking Paragons so the Initiates could continue their journey.

Finally, they'd made their way to the Ground Ring level and found the corridor that housed a series of communication chambers. "This way!" said Scrappy as he led the group to the first one. However, inside they found nothing but destroyed equipment. The same was true of the second chamber, and each one they explored thereafter.

"They've all been smashed," said Soundwave, grimly. "There's no way to call for help."

Krupp frowned. He figured it made sense that if the saboteur had planned this attack, he'd want to ensure there was no way to call for assistance. But just because the equipment had been destroyed, that didn't mean they were doomed. After all, if there were one thing Scofeld Krupp was known for…

It was never giving up.

"Scrappy, do you think you could manifest a subspace communicator?" Krupp asked.

"Manifest one?" replied Scrappy, looking overwhelmed. "I – I don't know. I've studied schematics for subspace communicators, but I don't think I have the skill to actually create one…"

"We didn't have the skills to manifest anything when we first started, remember?" Krupp said. "But we were able to do so when we worked together."

"<What are you suggesting?>" inquired Snodgrass.

"We need to do a group meditation," Krupp said. "Just like back when we were practicing for our Manifestation exams. Scrappy might not be skilled enough to manifest a subspace communicator on his own, but the five of us might be!"

"Well, it's not like we have much to lose at this point," said Soundwave.

"My sweet and attractive man-toy is right," Morosa stated. "If we are to have any chance of surviving this, we must work together."

"Seal the door," Krupp ordered. "Quickly. We may not have much time."

Morosa closed the door to the communication chamber. The group then all sat on the floor and joined hands, trying their best to regain their focus and channel their energies. As death and destruction ran rampant throughout the sacred temple, the inhabitants could not possibly know that their only chance for salvation was a small group of Initiates who had been written off as being the most unlikely of all to succeed.

And now, if they didn't succeed, every living thing in the Conclave would die.

# CHAPTER 9

ilvelm glared at Lord Gebhard Skyborn as he sat on the other side of the desk in the Legacy offices of *The Shieldbearer.* Fred sat at Wil's side as they both listened to Roadblock finish his debriefing. General Wessux and an incarnation of Ambassador Bob were in attendance, as well, standing at Gebhard's side. Though the survivors were now safe and *The Shieldbearer* contingent of the Maxima fleet was making its way back to the system's home planet, the events of Essox were still fresh in Wilvelm's mind. Despite it being considered a victory over the Deathlords, Wilvelm felt anything but victorious.

When Roadblock finished his report of what had occurred on the colony, Gebhard sighed. He met Wilvelm's disapproving glare and frowned. "So… the Rognok was assisting you?" he muttered.

"Frankly, my Lord, he's the only reason any of us are still alive," Wilvelm replied.

"You have to understand where we were coming from when we happened upon you," stated General Wessux. "When your transport did not return, we began searching the area in which you were scheduled to rendezvous for the prisoner transfer. We'd feared the Rognok may have attempted to escape or even destroyed your ship. After receiving your distress call, all we could see was a battle taking place in the colony's hangar. It appeared as though the Rognok had gone berserk and you and your team were fighting for your lives."

"We *were* fighting for our lives."

"How were we to know the circumstances surrounding your battle?" snapped Wessux. "We made the best call we could with the information we had on hand. We acted to protect two Legacy heirs for whose safety Lord Gebhard is responsible."

"I understand why you did what you did, General," Wilvelm replied. "That doesn't mean I have to like it."

Wessux scowled as Fredreek chimed in. "Lord Gebhard," he said. "Setting aside the mix-up concerning your arrival to assist us, the fact remains that somehow Grohm knew there were Deathlords on the Essox colony before we ever even got there."

Gebhard raised an eyebrow at that. "He knew the colony was being raided? How?"

"We never got the chance to ask him," said Wilvelm, bitterly.

Fredreek placed a calming hand on Wil's forearm, signaling for him to ease off. "When Wil and I boarded the mercenary vessel to take possession of him, Grohm asked to see a map of the system. He immediately zeroed in on Essox and demanded to go there. When we asked him why, he told us it was for 'battle'. At the time, we didn't know what to make of it, but once we arrived on Essox, we realized Grohm somehow had known the Deathlords were already there."

Ambassador Bob took a step forward, speaking directly to Gebhard. "Reports from the debriefings of the Earthman and his companions after arriving at Omnicron stated that the Rognok was already on the Deathlord mothership when the Visini pirate and the Princess's security detail were being held captive in what they referred to as 'The Pit'," he said. "There was no indication as to how long the Rognok had been there before they arrived. Could it be possible such prolonged exposure to the Deathlords made him more aware of their tactics, and he was able to guess what their next target would be?"

"More likely it was nothing but coincidence," Wessux said. "The beast simply picked the closest outpost to their location and didn't know what he'd find there. Deathlords or no, Rognok's don't need any particular target to engage in a fight."

"Don't do that," cautioned Wilvelm.

"Do what?" asked Wessux.

"Dismiss Grohm as some mindless animal that seeks only to engage in battle," Wilvelm said. "With all due respect, General, you did not see what we saw out there. Grohm did not defeat the Deathlord battlecruiser sent to kill us by being a mindless brute. His actions were deliberate and strategic. And when he regained consciousness, he understood what Fredreek told him about the situation and acted to come to our aid. He saw the threat the dark monolith presented and he targeted it as a way to end the battle. If he were really just a dumb animal who existed only to fight, he'd have simply engaged the Deathstalkers and not thought about anything else."

Gebhard looked to Roadblock, who was standing quietly at attention. "Is that your take, as well, Sergeant?" he asked.

"My Lord," replied Roadblock. "During my time in Alpha Force, I've seen some crazy things. But I've never seen anything like Grohm. What Lord

Blackfyre says is true. The Rognok isn't some dumb beast. Frankly, after seeing what he was capable of, I wish we had an entire army of Rognoks just like him. I'm convinced they'd make short work of the Deathlords and put an end to this war mighty quick."

"Unfortunately, the Rognoks are all practically extinct," said Ambassador Bob. "There are but a small number still left alive, roaming the galaxy. And that number is even smaller now that this Grohm is deceased."

Ambassador Bob's proclamation sent a mixture of anger and sadness bubbling up within Wil. *Grohm was a hero, blast it!* he thought. *He could have been a huge asset in our war against the Deathlords! And now he's gone because Maxima is run by a group of ignorant morons!*

Wilvelm's clenched fist was trembling with emotion when Gebhard sighed and leaned forward at this desk. "Actually, Ambassador, the question as to the Rognok's current state of mortality is still up in the air."

That statement got everyone's attention – particularly Wil's. "What do you mean by that, Lord Gebhard?" he asked.

"After the incident on Essox, the Rognok's body was taken to *The Shieldbearer's* medical bay for examination. Upon last report from the ship's doctor, though he could find no vital signs whatsoever present within the Rognok, he did mention that its skin appeared to be growing back."

Wil and Fred's eyes widened at that bit of news. They both looked to one another. "After he was caught in the explosion from the Deathlord battlecruiser, he was completely non-responsive while he healed…" thought Wilvelm aloud.

"And that plasma blast from *The Shieldbearer* practically melted his skin off him," Fred said. "If it's growing back, that could mean…"

Fred and Wil smiled at each other, excitedly. "He might not be dead!" they both said.

"The Rognok took a direct hit from a capital ship plasma battery," said Wessux. "Nothing could survive that."

"Nothing Regal, sir," stated Roadblock. "I've seen people melt under blaster fire before. Even bones turn to ash under the intensity of such super-heated plasma. The fact that the Rognok still has a body to speak of is a miracle, considering the hit he took. And frankly, if anything could survive such a hit, it would be Grohm. He's proven to be one of the toughest kittens[8] I've ever seen – pardon my language."

"Whether the Rognok is actually alive or not has yet to be determined at this point," said Gebhard. "We shall need to observe him further to find out if that's the case, which I intend to do back on Maxima. If the creature is by some chance able to recover, then we will need to question him about his 'Deathlord intuition' before handing him over to Imperial authorities."

"Imperial authorities?" said Wilvelm in disbelief. "You can't do that! Grohm's a hero!"

"He is also a wanted fugitive," stated Ambassador Bob.

"You can't be serious," grumbled Fredreek. "Surely he deserves a pardon based on what he did on Essox alone!"

"If it were up to me, I'd agree with you," Gebhard replied. "But unfortunately, the Rognok falls under an Imperial warrant. It's the central government's call as to his legal status. I'm sure his case will be aided by his actions here, along with my support, and the support of your respective Legacies. But ultimately, the Rognok's fate will be decided by Director Casgor and his administration."

"If it hasn't already been decided by blaster fire," Wessux chimed in. "The Rognok's legal status is a moot point if he's actually dead."

"Which is all the more reason to get him back to the planet in short order," said Gebhard. "I'll have the best doctors on Maxima on hand to study him and see if they can do anything to assist in a recovery."

Before Wilvelm had a chance to object further to the treatment of Grohm, Ambassador Bob stepped forward. "Pardon the interruption, my Lords," he said, his translucent pink face looking troubled. "But my incarnations on the ship's bridge have just become aware of a development that requires your immediate attention…."

Practically on cue, a call came in at Gebhard's visual display. He called it up to see the ship's X.O. Commander Neelson on the screen. "Lord Skyborn, General Wessux," he said. "You're needed on the bridge, sirs."

"What is it?" asked Gebhard.

---

[8] The term "kitten" is a well-known curse word in the Regalus Empire.

"It's Maxima, my Lord," Neelson replied. "Something is happening on the planet."

Everyone in the office exchanged a concerned look. "We're on our way," Gebhard said.

The group wasted no time in exiting the office and heading toward the bridge. Out in the hallway, Copperhyde, Lucky, Skeptic, and Missionary were all waiting. As Gebhard led the others to the bridge, the mercenary and Alpha Force all began to follow. "Oy, I thought you wanted us ta tell our sides of what happened on the colony," said Copperhyde as he kept pace with Fred. "Why y'all leavin' in such a hurry?"

"Apparently there's a more pressing matter at the moment," Fredreek replied. "The debriefing will have to wait."

"And what of compensation for my ship and the bounty on the Rognok?" Copperhyde grumbled. "This bloody mess has cost me everything, and I wanna get what's mine and get out of here as soon as possible."

"Don't worry, compatriot," Fredreek said. "You may be a bitter, grumpy, pain in the rear, but you came through for us in the end. You'll have your fortune and glory. I'll see to it you're taken care of once things settle down."

"See that ya do, my Lord," Copperhyde replied. "I ain't no solider. Fightin' Deathlords ain't my thing."

"I fear it's not any of our 'things'."

"Speak for yourself," said Roadblock. "Fighting Deathlords is what Alpha Force is made for."

"Well, if it's any comfort Sergeant, something tells me you may get the chance to do your 'thing' again very soon," said Wilvelm, cynically.

The group entered the bridge to see Commander Neelson standing at a sensor station, alongside two of Bob's incarnations, as they gazed at data on the station's console. The slim and balding Regal looked up from the station as Wessux and Gebhard approached.

"Report," ordered Wessux.

"We were approaching the central oasis of the system's debris field when our sensors picked up an anomaly coming from the planet," Neelson replied. "Calling it up on screen now…"

Neelson nodded to a young, blonde-haired Ensign who called up the image of Maxima on the bridge's viewscreen. There was a strange rippling of space close to the planet and, jutting up from the planet's surface, a beam of chaotic light, which disappeared into the anomaly.

"What the blazes is that?" asked Gebhard, looking deeply concerned.

"It is hard to say, my Lord," replied Neelson. "According to our readings, the anomaly appears to be a type of rip in the fabric of spacetime."

"Uh… that doesn't sound good," said Fredreek.

"Whatever it is, my Lords, our sensors have yet to scan what lies on the other side of it," Neelson continued. "But seeing as how the beam from the planet is not passing through the anomaly, we suspect it may be a portal to another location."

"A portal?" said Wilvelm. "What could possibly open a portal above the planet?"

"And more importantly, what is that being shot through it?" asked Gebhard, looking to Wessux with displeasure.

Wessux frowned. "Magnify the planet," the General ordered. "Focus in on the source of that beam."

"Magnifying," replied an incarnation of Bob as it carried out the order.

On the viewscreen, the planet of Maxima went through a series of magnifications until the dark temple on its surface became visible. A cold feeling gripped Wilvelm's gut as he looked at the structure and the ghostly beam of energy it was emitting.

"What the blazes is that?" Gebhard muttered.

"It's the Deathlords," Wilvelm said, grimly. "Look at the surface…"

The viewscreen was magnified once more to show tiny Deathstalkers – numbering in the thousands – crawling across the black rock as it spread over the plateau. The creatures were headed in every direction, their numbers multiplying by the minute.

"Great Observer!" said Gebhard with a look of growing horror. "The Deathlords have invaded Maxima? How… how is this possible?"

"Open a channel to Planetary Defense Command on the planet's surface," barked Wessux. "Now!"

"We've been trying, General," Neelson replied. "But all comms to and from the planet appear to be down."

"That's impossible!" cried the General.

"Is it?" asked Wilvelm. "The Deathlords have been very good about preventing their victims from calling for help."

"But we have an entire system-wide communications network set up!" argued Wessux. "There are backups and redundancies! Nothing could possibly block all communication, particularly from the planet!"

"What if they're not being blocked?" asked Wil. "What if the Deathlords have found a way to shut the entire network down to prevent anyone from stopping their initial assault?"

"Even if that were the case, they would need access to the network at the highest level," said Wessux. "I just don't see how it is possible, short of them having Legacy-level access to our defense systems. But that level of control is limited to Lord and Lady Skyborn alone."

"For the moment, I don't care how the Deathlords made landfall on Maxima, but rather, what they're doing now that they're there!" snapped Gebhard. "Those creatures are headed directly to our largest population centers! Our cities aren't equipped to handle an invasion of such magnitude!"

"What are your orders, my Lord?" Wessux asked.

"Recall all ships in the system to the oasis zone," Gebhard said. "I want the fleet in orbit, giving our cities cover from those – what did you call them? Deathstalkers? In the meantime, have our ships target that temple. Launch a barrage of Deathscream missiles. I want that monstrosity wiped off the face of my planet, blast it!"

"As you command, my Lord," acknowledged Wessux before turning to Neelson. "Coordinate with our other ships. Target that temple. Plot me firing solutions."

"Understood," replied Neelson as he set about ordering the crew at the ship's various stations to prepare the attack.

Wilvelm looked around as the other ships in the combat group were contacted and the temple was targeted. Half the bridge crew seemed to be incarnations of Bob, while the rest looked like they'd never seen battle in their entire lives.

"What are the Deathlords up to?" asked Fredreek as he quietly thought aloud at Wil's side. "What is it they're firing into that portal? And more importantly, what is it they're hitting?"

"That beam looks similar to their Planetkiller superweapons," Wilvelm commented. "One isn't enough to destroy a world, but that doesn't mean it can't do some real damage. Whatever it is the Deathlords are up to, though, you can rest assured it's not good."

"All ships locked onto the Deathlord temple, General," Neelson informed Wessux. "Awaiting your orders."

"Fire when ready," Wessux said.

*The Shieldbearer*, along with the six other ships in its battle group, initiated a barrage of missiles from their launchers. Twelve Deathscream missiles streaked across the void of space, rocketing toward the planet of Maxima and their intended target. The missiles entered through the atmosphere and impacted the temple, massive explosions erupting all around it.

"Positive contact," Wessux reported as he monitored the strike from his command station. "Direct hit with all twelve missiles, my Lord."

There was a cheer from all those on the bridge, except for Wilvelm and his group. They all continued to gaze at the viewscreen with frowns on their faces.

"If we hit the temple, why is the beam still firing?" asked Fredreek.

As the smoke from the explosions on the surface cleared, a hazy white field could be seen encompassing the temple, as though a part of the ghostly beam it was firing had siphoned off to form a protective barrier around the structure. Though an area around the temple had been affected by the explosions of the missiles, the black rock that had been destroyed there was quickly regrowing from the temple's base.

Soon, all sounds of celebration on the bridge had ceased as it became clear the dark temple was still standing. Gebhard leaned forward in his command chair, his face dark. "General," he said. "Report."

Wessux frowned. "There appears to be some type of protective field around the target, my Lord," he replied. "But… it's not being picked up by our sensors."

"It's like the shield the Terrormancer on Essox created to protect himself," Wilvelm noted. "He used death energy to block our attacks."

"That's right," chimed in Roadblock. "Nothing was able to get past that thing."

"Deathscream missiles were designed to break through shielding," Gebhard argued. "They're meant to take out Planetkillers."

"Planetkillers could survive a planet exploding while they were in its orbit," Wilvelm pointed out. "What if their main weapon beams act like the one from that temple? What if they use its energy to create shields that can't be breached?"

"If the Deathlords have impenetrable shields, how is it we are able to damage their ships?" asked Wessux.

"Maybe because the beams need to be active in order to use them as shielding?" theorized Fredreek.

"Enough of this!" said Gebhard in frustration. "If we cannot destroy the blasted thing, we'll isolate it. Bring our ships in. Create a perimeter around the temple. Bombard it from orbit and let's keep that black rock from spreading until we can figure out how to smash that temple into rubble."

Before anyone could respond to Gebhard's order, sensor alarms beeped repeatedly. Crewmembers at the various bridge stations frantically went to work examining the alerts that were popping up on their consoles. Wilvelm got a sinking feeling in his gut as he glanced around at the worried faces of the crew.

"What is it?" asked Wessux. "What is going on?"

"Sensors are picking up multiple anomalies around the planet, General," said an incarnation of Bob at one of the sensor stations. "More tears in spacetime seem to be appearing."

Wilvelm didn't like that piece of news one bit. He quickly moved to a nearby sensor station to look over the shoulder of the technician who was tending to it. He saw numerous red blips on the sensor display, marking the birth of new anomalies.

"More portals?" asked General Wessux, his face grim. "Where do they lead?"

"Unknown, General," Bob replied. "Sensor readings are jumbled. It is as if the location behind the portals has a completely different set of physics compared to our own."

"Different set of physics? Like from the Conclave pocket universe?"

"Yes, General," Bob confirmed. "But if there is one thing I can tell you, it is that whatever pocket universe these portals lead to… it is not that of the Conclave."

"Multiple contacts!" cried an Ensign from his sensor station. "Sensors are picking up Deathlord vessels emerging from the anomalies!"

"On the screen!" ordered Wessux.

The bridge's viewscreen cut to a wider view, showing ripples in the fabric of spacetime all around Maxima. One by one, large Deathlord vessels began to emerge from the portals, entering the space around the planet in greater and greater numbers.

"Sensors identify Deathlord Dreadnaught-class vessels, General," informed Bob. "Capital level ships previously only seen to accompany small cruiser fleets."

"Great Galaxy!" exclaimed Wessux as he gazed wide-eyed in worry at the viewscreen. "How many are there?"

"Twenty-four and counting, General."

Wil turned to Fred, their look communicating they were both thinking the same thing: *That's not good.*

The entire crew of the bridge watched as more and more Deathlord vessels emerged from the tethers, creating a protective blockade around the planet, practically daring Maxima's smaller fleet to come and meet them, all the while allowing the dark temple to continue firing its beam of death energy into the largest tether above the planet.

Wessux turned toward Gebhard. "What are your orders, my Lord?" he asked.

Gebhard grimaced. "Message the entire fleet," he said. "Tell them to get here as quickly as possible. We must regroup and prepare to face that Deathlord armada that has just appeared around our home. And send out a distress signal across the emergency subspace channels…"

Gebhard sat in his command chair, looking as though the weight of the universe were on his shoulders.

"Let the Empire know a full-scale Deathlord invasion is now at its doorstep," he said.

# Chapter 10

Amadeus was strapped into his chair at the command console of the Redwater vessel *Hightide*, sitting next to General Rustwave as the two gazed at the viewscreen. The ship was running at minimal power levels to mask its energy signature, so the bridge was entirely dark, except for the lights from the instruments needed to operate it.

"We're in position, Lord Evenstar," the pilot responded, his voice coming in through the speaker built into Amadeus's helmet. Everyone on the ship was in full space gear, since all life support systems had to be shut down in order for them to stay invisible to sensor readings.

"Acknowledged," Amadeus said. "What is the status of our fleet?"

"They are in position, as well, my Lord," said Rustwave as he called up the system map on the command console before him, showing the Redwater fleet assembled around Port Longshore.

"Signal the soldiers in the hold to be ready," Amadeus ordered as he tapped on his console, calling up a countdown clock on the viewscreen that was steadily ticking away. "There can be no margin for error here."

Amadeus glanced over at Rustwave, who monitored his console with a frown.

"Nervous, General?" Amadeus asked.

"Extremely," Rustwave grumbled. "This is a very risky strategy, my Lord."

"Risk only exists if one has something to lose."

"You are placing an awful lot of faith in your sister," the General said. "Faith I am not completely sure is justified."

Amadeus nodded. "I understand your concern. But beyond the pop star façade and the reality show trappings, I assure you Kimlee is quite a force to be reckoned with. This plan of hers is a shrewd one and our best shot at victory."

"If it works," Rustwave replied. "If it doesn't, not only will this go down in history as one of the greatest military blunders of all time… but also one of the most expensive."

Amadeus couldn't help but chuckle. "Then let it not be said that the Evenstars fail to do anything big."

With that, the two men sat in their cold and dark spacecraft, watching as the countdown clock ticked away, the imposing image of the 3rd Imperial Fleet filling their viewscreen.

★★★★★

Starkeeper Drucker, along with his Executive Officer Jym Cobbwell and a small security team, stood in the hangar bay of *The Colossus* as the Redwater shuttlecraft passed through the bay's plasma window and came in for a landing.

The shuttle's boarding ramp lowered to reveal Kimlee Evenstar, dressed as though she were going to a formal State function in a long, form-fitting red gown. Her neck was adorned with a golden choker that sported an emerald in the shape of an eight-pointed star, and her hair and make-up were impeccably done. She seemed to glide gracefully down the ramp, followed closely by Sergeant Surior, dressed in a formal militia uniform, and a dozen or so hovercameras which swarmed around her like hungry insects.

Kimlee came to a stop before the welcoming party and smiled sweetly, giving her hosts a tiny curtsey. "Gentlemen," she said.

"Lady Evenstar," replied Starkeeper Drucker. "I fear you make us feel underdressed for this occasion."

"If I am to go out, Starkeeper Drucker, then I fully intend to do so in style," Kimlee replied, sweetly. "I now present myself to you, alone but for a single honor guard, as agreed upon."

Drucker turned his hard gaze toward Surior, who stood stoically by Kimlee's side. His eyes then drifted to the various hovercameras around them. "Those are more cameras than I was expecting," he said.

"Seeing as how this is such an historic event, I couldn't possibly turn down any of the holonet requests to record the end of my storied Legacy."

"No doubt you couldn't. But I can. You may have one camera present at the surrender."

"Only one?" Kimlee asked, looking abashed.

"If I had my way, there wouldn't be any," Drucker replied. "But Director Casgor wants the publicity as much as you do."

"It would seem Casgor and I finally agree upon something," Kimlee joked.

Drucker turned to his security team. "Confiscate all the cameras but one," he ordered. "Search the ship and our guests."

The security team did as commanded, two of them using hand-held scanners to search Kimlee and Surior while the rest boarded the shuttle.

"Are all these precautions really necessary?" Kimlee asked. "As though I could hide anything in this gown."

"Forgive my over abundance of caution, Lady Evenstar," Starkeeper Drucker said. "Frankly, until the accord is signed and your brother surrenders himself, I have every reason to suspect that he may try something in a last-ditch attempt to save your Legacy."

Kimlee giggled. "Oh, Starkeeper Drucker," she chided. "That would be such a foolish thing to do. And I can assure you, my brother is no fool."

"Yes, that is what concerns me."

"Well, if it is a fool you prefer, I am right here," Kimlee said, slyly gesturing to herself. "And frankly, I can't think of anyone more foolish than I."

"Does that mean I should expect trouble from you, Lady Evenstar?"

"Tons!" Kimlee said as she batted her eyelashes. "But only of the vapid, shallow, pop star diva kind. I fully intend to bad-mouth you on my Insta-Rant account once all this is said and done."

Starkeeper Drucker chuckled at that. "Fair enough," he replied. "Seems a far better alternative than having to face your fleet."

"You obviously are unfamiliar with the type of followers I have on Insta-Rant," Kimlee joked. "Trust me when I say a full-scale space battle might be preferable compared to the wrath of social media trolls."

Officer Cobbwell approached Drucker. "The cameras are secure, Starkeeper," he said. "Ship's clean. As are our guests."

"Well, then," said Kimlee, offering her arm to Starkeeper Drucker. "Shall we get on with it?"

Drucker looked at Kimlee's arm, uncomfortably. Kimlee chuckled.

"Come now, Starkeeper. I don't bite."

Drucker sighed and threaded his arm through Kimlee's before escorting her out of the hangar bay.

"My, my, my," Kimlee said, looking around as they traversed the ship. "This starcraft of yours is most impressive, Starkeeper Drucker."

"*The Colossus* is the flagship of the 3rd fleet, my Lady," Drucker replied. "It's the most advanced and powerful capital vessel in this quadrant of space."

"It would appear so. Tell me, in a fight between this ship and the entire Redwater fleet, who would win?"

"We would."

"Are you sure?" Kimlee asked. "We have a lot of ships."

"*The Colossus* was designed to take on Planetkillers, Lady Evenstar," Drucker said. "It's worth twenty of your ships."

"We have more than twenty."

"Indeed, but *The Colossus* has something you do not."

"And what might that be?"

"Me," Drucker replied. "No matter how advanced a starship may be, it's those who command it that determine its capabilities. This ship is worth twenty of your vessels, my Lady. But with me commanding it, it's worth at least fifty."

"Mmmmm. I've always been partial to confident men," Kimlee said, flirtily.

"The same is true of my wife," Drucker replied, coolly.

"No doubt. Though, if what you say is true, it does make one wonder why you needed four other capital ships from the fleet to greet little old me."

"A five-ship combat group is standard formation for operations. With five capital ships, we are able to handle almost any threat to a system."

"Then why did you bring the entire 3rd fleet to Redwater?"

"Because I was ordered to," grumbled Drucker. "I told Director Casgor committing such resources to this blockade was overkill. But now that this is ending, I'll be able to redeploy the fleet where it is most needed once more."

"And five ships are really that powerful?" Kimlee asked.

"Capital class ships are, yes. Your brother seems to realize this. It's why he never tried to engage us. In every single scenario when your fleet clashes with ours, you lose."

"Yes," Kimlee said, whimsically. "Pity we don't have any ships like *The Colossus* on our side. That could have made a difference."

"Indeed it could have," replied Drucker. "But you didn't. And now, here we are…"

Drucker came to a stop before a pair of doors that slid open, revealing a formal conference room. At its center was a long, polished elderwood[9] conference table. The golden orb-within-an-orb crest of Legacy Prime hung on the wall, and a large viewscreen opposite it displayed a panoramic view of space from outside the ship. Drucker gestured for Kimlee, along with her single camera and Sergeant Surior, to enter.

"I'll take it from here, Jym," Drucker said.

"I'll be on the bridge if you need me, sir," Cobbwell replied.

Drucker entered the room, along with three security guards, and stood on the side of the conference table opposite Kimlee as she looked at the view. He placed a datapad down on the table and slid it forward. "Here is the accord of surrender," he said. "Your lawyers have already been through it with a fine-tooth comb. All it requires is your thumbprint and signature as a representative of your Legacy."

Kimlee smiled and looked around the room. "Is there wine?" she asked.

Drucker frowned. "There's water," he said, gesturing toward a pitcher and some empty glasses on a table behind him.

Kimlee gave Drucker an admonishing look. "Starkeeper," she said. "Surely you cannot expect me to sign my family's Legacy away without some wine? And not the bland replicated kind either. The real thing."

Drucker sighed. He turned to one of the guards. "Go to my quarters and fetch a bottle of Nectarplumb for Lady Evenstar, if you would."

"Right away, sir," the guard replied before heading off, now leaving only two guards in the room.

"While we wait for your beverage, would you care to review the agreement?" Drucker asked.

"Legal mumbo-jumbo makes me go cross-eyed," Kimlee said, waving her hand at the datapad like it was emitting a foul stench. "My brother is the one who's the lawyer. Did you know I was to be an Empress?"

Starkeeper Drucker nodded. "Yes, I am well aware of what you were to be, Lady Evenstar."

---

[9] Elderwood is an old, petrified wood that is hard as metal and does not warp, decay, or burn.

“It's funny, you know,” Kimlee said, wistfully. “I was engineered from the ground up to be an Empress. Even when I was in the womb, my mother had Paragon attendants, all working to manifest in me the qualities required of a ruler. But once I lost that purpose when my betrothed was killed, I tried to move on. Become something other than what I was meant to be. But I realize now that was futile. One cannot fight one's destiny. We are what we are, and there is no changing that.”

“Are you telling me you now believe yourself to be an Empress, Lady Evenstar?”

“I'm telling you I've learned to embrace what I am, Starkeeper. And do you know what else I've learned?”

“What might that be?” Drucker asked, sounding as though his patience were beginning to wear thin.

“That Empresses do not surrender...”

Kimlee then looked Starkeeper Drucker in the eyes, her face losing all softness as she dawned the proud visage of a woman embracing her destiny.

“We conquer.”

Suddenly, the camera which had been hovering around sent out two powerful zaps of electricity, hitting the remaining guards and stunning them.

Before Drucker could react, Surior had moved to one of the guards, hitting him across the face and drawing the guard’s weapon, firing a blast into the other guard’s shoulder before moving to disarm him.

Drucker looked at Surior in disbelief as the Sergeant aimed both blaster pistols at him. He turned his gaze back toward Kimlee in abject shock. “What the blazes do you think you’re doing???” Drucker demanded.

“Conquering,” Kimlee said, simply.

“What do you hope to gain by this?” hissed Drucker. “You and your man are in the middle of an Imperial capital ship! You’re surrounded by Imperial soldiers! You have no way to escape!”

“Oh, I’m not going anywhere,” Kimlee said as she checked the clock on the datapad. “In a few minutes, this ship is going to be mine. And as you said before, with *The Colossus* on our side… things will be very different.”

“You are *mad*, woman!” sneered Drucker.

"There is a fine line between madness and brilliance, my dear Starkeeper," Kimlee purred. "You have yet to witness my ability to walk that line. But don't worry…"

Kimlee smiled as she looked at the time.

"You're about to."

Back in the docking bay of *The Colossus*, a countdown timer on the Redwater shuttle in which Kimlee had arrived reached zero. It was then that the doors to a hidden compartment beneath the shuttle opened up, revealing an equalarium-lined cargo bay which lowered down a high frequency electro-magnetic pulse superbomb, already emitting a high-pitched whine as it continued to charge.

Back on *The Hightide*, Amadeus looked at the clock.

"Shut everything down," he ordered. "Prepare for detonation."

In the far distance away from the Imperial fleet, five equalarium-lined Redwater starships all went dark, just as a ferocious electromagnetic explosion erupted from *The Colossus*.

The pulse generated by the superbomb expanded outward, hitting the four other capital ships grouped with the flagship. Instantly, all systems – including gravity and life support – went down on those ships, completely disabling them.

"Now!" Amadeus commanded.

All five Redwater ships immediately powered back up and raced toward the battle group, each one aimed at a different capital vessel. Amadeus looked at *The Colossus* as it grew bigger on *The Hightide's* viewscreen.

"Launch snare winches!" General Rustwave ordered.

*The Hightide* fired its two snare winches, latching onto *The Colossus's* hull and pulling them directly toward a docking ring. With a heavy *THUMP*, the two ships met, and *The Hightide* latched onto the entry hatch.

All those on the bridge unbuckled themselves and stood, grabbing weapons.

"Come along, gentlemen," Amadeus said. "We have a ship to take."

On the bridge of *The Colossus*, the crew members who hadn't been strapped into their stations were floating about, desperately trying to find a way to get the ship back up and running.

"What's going on?" demanded Cobbwell. "Someone! Report!"

"I… I think we got hit by an EMP pulse, sir," replied the Chief Engineer.

"How's that possible?" Cobbwell asked. "Our systems are supposed to be shielded against such a thing!"

"They are, sir!" replied the Engineer. "Our systems should reset any minute. We just need time for the EMP static to dissipate..."

"Someone get me the Starkeeper!" Cobbwell shouted. "Find him now!"

"No need," came the voice of Sergeant Surior as the doors to the bridge opened and Redwater troops marched in with magnetic boots anchoring them to the floor and blaster rifles at the ready.

Cobbwell looked in abject surprise as the soldiers entered the room and quickly subdued the entire bridge crew. Then Kimlee and Surior pushed Starkeeper Drucker inside, closely followed by Amadeus, General Rustwave, and more armed soldiers.

"He's right here," Surior said as he forced Drucker into a chair and strapped him to it.

"I… I don't understand…" Cobbwell said.

"We're being boarded, Jym," Drucker grumbled.

"Not just you, Starkeeper," Kimlee said with a smile. "Right now, the bridges of all the ships in your combat group are being boarded and seized by Redwater soldiers. By the time your systems reboot, they will all be under our control."

"If you think you can commandeer an entire capital ship just by taking its bridge…"

"Our fleet is standing by to approach and unload more of our militia, which will grant us full control over each ship," Amadeus responded. "By taking the bridge, all we have to do is lock down each vessel, open the hangar bays, and then go deck by deck until each ship is entirely ours."

"This isn't possible," objected Cobbwell. "How did you even get here? There's no way you could have snuck up on us!"

"Not unless we had five ships completely lined with equalarium so that your sensors would never even see them," Kimlee said. "It allowed us to get close enough so that when the EMP bomb we detonated knocked out your ships, we had time to board and take control."

"Equalarium?" Cobbwell said. "But the amount needed to line an entire ship, let alone five, would have cost—"

"A fortune?" mused Kimlee. "Considering we just got five Imperial capital ships added to our already considerable fleet in exchange, I'd say we got a bargain."

"You blasted fools!" Drucker said. "Do you really think you can get away with stealing five capital ships?"

"Oh, we're not stopping at five," Amadeus replied. "Once we have full control of this combat group, we're going to approach each of your other groups around the system and take those, as well. If all goes according to plan, we'll have the entire 3rd fleet under our command by the time we're through."

"And once the 3rd fleet has been added to our own ships, we will be a new superpower," Kimlee said. "When word gets out of what we've accomplished, other Legacies will join with us and add their strength to our own. You are all about to bear witness to the birth of the Evenstar Empire, gentlemen!"

"So your agreement to surrender was just a trick, eh?" said Drucker, dourly.

"Make no mistake, Starkeeper. We're still here to negotiate a surrender," Amadeus said. "Only it will be you surrendering to me, now."

Just then, the electronics on the bridge slowly began to return to life. Lights flickered back on and life support was restored. As the artificial gravity came back online, the Redwater soldiers rounded up *The Colossus's* crewmembers and restrained them as Amadeus's men assumed their stations.

"Initiate a ship-wide lockdown," Amadeus ordered. "I want the entire crew boxed in until our ships arrive to take control."

As the men carried out his orders, Amadeus looked at Kimlee and smiled.

"Your plan worked," he said.

"Was there ever any doubt?" Kimlee replied, coyly.

"Tons," Amadeus said. "But you can't argue with results."

Kimlee approached Amadeus and took him by the hands, looking into his eyes excitedly. "This is the beginning, Amadeus!" she said. "The start of our independence! Now, no one will be able to take our power away! Not Casgor, not the World Leaders – no one! We are the masters of our own destiny! Soon, the Regalus Empire will fracture, and we will be the beacon to lead the galaxy into a new era!"

Amadeus frowned. "Yes," he acknowledged. "Though I wish it did not have to be this way."

Kimlee cupped her brother's cheek. "We were not left with any other choice," she assured him. "Despite it all… know that father would be proud of us."

Just then, an alert rang out. Sergeant Surior moved to the communications console where the alert was sounding.

"What is that?" Amadeus asked.

Sergeant Surior tapped at the beeping control panel and checked it. "It's an emergency distress signal, my Lord, blasting across all subspace channels," he replied. "It's the Maxima system. The message says Deathlords have launched a full-scale invasion around the planet. Reports are coming in of dozens of Dreadnaught-class Deathlord cruisers overrunning the system."

Amadeus heard Starkeeper Drucker curse. "Blast you, Evenstar," the man muttered, gazing at Amadeus with a hard stare. "You may have saved your system… but in doing so you just damned another."

"Let the Deathlords have Maxima," Kimlee said. "The Skyborns have never been a friend to us. They are Casgor's strongest ally. Their downfall only strengthens our position."

"Blast your bloody politics!" Drucker snapped. "This has more far reaching effects than a simple rivalry between Legacies! If Maxima should fall to the Deathlords, they will use it as a beachhead for a deeper invasion into Imperial space. The Rim will be cut off from the rest of the Empire, and the Deathlords will be free to systematically wipe it out piece by piece. Billions will die!"

Amadeus frowned, troubled by Drucker's words. He was suddenly acutely aware that all eyes were upon him, awaiting his orders. Kimlee approached him.

"Don't get distracted. This is our moment, little brother," Kimlee whispered to him. "Let the Deathlords have the Rim. What we need to focus on now is shoring up our power so we can mount a true opposition to the Deathlords when they try to invade further. Then, we shall be free to fight them as father always wanted to, without any red tape or interference."

Amadeus weighed Kimlee's words. What she said made sense. The Empire was not a friend to them. And once word got out about the double-cross they had accomplished, Amadeus and Kimlee would both be officially decreed traitors. There was no going back after what they'd just done. The smart move was to listen to his sister and to consolidate his fleet and his system while he still had the chance. And yet, there was a question that nagged at Amadeus. A voice in the back of his head that he could not silence, no matter how hard he tried.

*What would my father do?*

Amadeus stepped forward and signaled to Sergeant Surior. "Open a system-wide broadcast," Amadeus ordered. "I want everyone to hear this."

"What are you going to do?" Drucker asked.

Amadeus returned the Starkeeper's hard stare. "I am going to show the galaxy, once and for all, what the Evenstars are capable of."

Kimlee smiled at her brother's declaration. Drucker hung his head in defeat. Amadeus turned to the holographic transmitter in front of the bridge's viewscreen as Sergeant Surior began the broadcast. Amadeus's image was sent to every ship, visual display, computer, and datapad in the system.

And what he then said would change the course of history forever.

# CHAPTER 11

Green cried out as he tripped and stumbled, landing hard on the skewed surface of the collapsed building he'd been running up. Tiny pieces of rubble caused him to lose his footing and slide backward before Sawbones grabbed onto his wrist to keep him from tumbling down the slope. The *click-clack* of sharp claws on metal and stone was incessant as the Deathstalkers that were pursuing them closed in.

"Daggit, man, back on your feet!" barked Sawbones.

A few Deathstalkers pounced, soaring through the air and landing not far from Green's position before they were dispatched by some well-placed blaster shots from Boone, sending them off in puffs of black dust.

"Keep moving!" Boone ordered. "Hurry!"

Green scrambled back to his feet and began following his companions once more. He'd lost all track of time since they'd started their hasty getaway from the ever-growing army of feral Deathlord creatures. The Twin Rivers settlement had become a virtual maze after its collapse when the dark temple rose. In their mad dash to get away from their pursuers, the group had become hopelessly lost. Everywhere they turned, they were met with either Deathstalkers or dead ends. To make things worse, the longer they searched for a way out, the more the black rock spread, and the more Deathstalkers sprang from it.

Their current predicament had occurred when they'd run into an area where their path was blocked off by rubble and Deathstalkers had boxed them in from every direction. Their only option had been to climb up onto a collapsed building and to run across its face, hoping it would lead somewhere safe.

But as the three reached the apex of the collapsed structure, they skidded to a stop. The vantage point from the top of the fallen building allowed them to finally see how truly dire their situation was. Deathstalkers were everywhere, prowling throughout the remains of the city before them like a horde of swarming insects.

In that moment, it became terrifyingly obvious that there was nowhere left to escape to.

"Blast it," muttered Boone, desperately looking around for some way out of their dilemma.

Green glanced behind them and saw a group of Deathstalkers scurrying up the building, bearing down on them. "Oh dear, oh dear, oh dear," he said. "What do we do now?"

Sawbones frowned. "I'm afraid there ain't nothing to do," she said, dourly. "There's nowhere left to run."

"Don't give up hope!" insisted Green. "There must be some way out of this!"

"Daggit, man, I'm a doctor. Not an optimist."

"My apologies, compatriots," Boone said. "My mission was to rescue you. I'm sorry to say this is one mission it looks like I'm going to fail."

"Apparently, Agent Boone isn't an optimist either," muttered Sawbones, sadly.

Green frowned, turning to see the Deathstalkers scurrying closer. "It's okay, Agent Boone," he said. "You helped us warn the Empire. If we're to die… at least we die knowing we did our part to help protect it."

Boone checked the plasma clip of his blaster. "I don't have many bolts left," he said. "I'm wondering if I should save them for ourselves."

"Slag that," muttered Sawbones, defiantly. "If I'm going down, I'm gonna go down fighting! COME AND GET ME, YOU BLASTED DEATHLORD DROOG-DOGS!"

Sawbones stepped forward and put up her fists, as though she were preparing to engage in fisticuffs with the encroaching Deathstalkers. Boone stepped forward, too, bolstered by the bravery of the Stonehooligan and raised his blaster. "Going out in a blaze of glory, eh?" he said. "I think you got the right idea, little guy."

"Guy?" muttered Sawbones. "I'll have you know, I'm a woman, daggit! And a mighty fetching one at that!"

Boone raised an eyebrow. "You're a female?"

"Of course, I am! Can't ya tell by the size of my beard?"

"Oh… right… I see it now," lied Boone.

With that, Agent Boone began to fire, hitting the multitude of Deathstalkers which were closing in around them. The creatures began to emerge on all sides of the collapsed building, hissing as they clawed their way forward toward their prey.

As the group made their last stand, Green heard a sound. It was faint, but it sounded an awful lot like that of an engine. The Professor turned toward the noise, his eyes growing wide as a broad smile grew on his face.

It was the Earthship, swooping down from the sky as it raced toward their location. Just as the Deathstalkers were about to descend upon Green and the others for the kill, the Earthship screamed by overhead, teleporting them away just in the nick of time.

Green, Boone, and Sawbones all appeared on the bridge of the Earthship, suddenly safe and sound. The Paragon and the Secret Agent looked around in relieved surprise at their new surroundings.

"Well, deforest me and call me Kelley," muttered Sawbones. "We're alive!"

"Looks like HQ won't be marking this mission down as a failure after all," mused Boone.

"See, my friends?" said Green, cheerily. "Never underestimate the power of positive thinking!"

"Professor!" said Jack, hopping out of the ship's command chair and smiling as he approached. "So glad you're okay!"

"Jack! My boy!" said Green happily as he embraced Jack. "Your timing, as always, is impeccable!"

"Sorry for the last-minute rescue. I'd have come sooner but, you know, I was in an entirely different universe. Jeez, that's something I never thought I'd say..."

Green saw the Royal Vanguard standing nearby, watching the exchange. The Professor's elated expression was replaced with one of worry. "Oh, dear," he said. "Are... are we in trouble?"

"Huh?" asked Jack, glancing at the Vanguard before realizing how much the Professor had missed out on. "Oh, no. Don't worry. The Vanguard are here to help save Anna. They're not mad at us for kicking their butts anymore."

"That's not what happened," stated Lugard.

"Not even a little," growled Rionknidis.

"They are still kinda sore about it, though," whispered Jack, before turning his attention to Boone and Sawbones. "Who are your friends?"

"Boone. Dirk Boone. Of the Imperial Intelligence Agency," Boone said as he shook Jack's hand. "Thanks for the save, Earthman. Thought we were goners, there."

"And this is Paragon MacCrusty," said Green, gesturing toward Sawbones. "One of the best healers in the galaxy."

"Glad to have you all on board," Jack said, nodding toward Sawbones in acknowledgement. "I know after all you've just been through, you probably just want to get the heck out of here, but we can't leave just yet. We have to save Anna first."

"Yes! Of course!" Green replied. "The Princess is in the corrupted temple."

"You're sure of this?" asked Seqis.

"Brother Shanks was," Green replied. "He stayed behind to try to rescue her while we called for help. He told us he could sense her presence. And seeing as how one of Royal Blood is needed to raise an Ancient temple, my guess is that Brother Shanks was right."

"Okay, then," said Jack. "We'll just fly close enough to the temple to get a teleportation lock on her and zap her right out of there and back to the ship. Easy."

"Jack," said Mourdock, looking at the display of the console at which he was seated. "The Earthship's sensors are picking up something strange…"

"Strange?" asked Jack as he made his way back into the pilot's seat. "What kind of strange?"

"There's some type of sensor anomaly out in space, right above this location. And whatever it is, it's getting bigger."

Jack called up on the bridge's viewscreen the anomaly that the Earthship's sensors were picking up. Everyone gathered around his chair to look at it. There appeared to be a swirling ripple in the fabric of spacetime not far outside of the planet's atmosphere. Jack looked at it, curiously. "That… that kinda looks like a tether," Jack said. "Like the one that used to be in the Conclave, only – you know – way bigger."

"Fascinating!" said Green. "If it is indeed a tether, I wonder where it leads?"

Suddenly, the ripple oscillated and a tear began to form within it, slowly opening up a window into a different universe, one which had no stars. In fact, the only thing within it appeared to be a diamond-shaped temple, which was currently engulfed in a strange, ghostly energy being shot at it from another tether far above it.

Jack looked at the image on the viewscreen with a mixture of confusion and worry. "Is… is that the Conclave?" he asked.

"Why would a tether to the Conclave universe be opening up over Eionmeer?" asked Sawbones.

"And what is that energy that is engulfing it?" asked Boone.

Just then, a sensor alarm beeped. Mourdock looked back down at his console and frowned. "Something's happening with the corrupted temple below," he said.

Jack switched the image from the tether above them to the dark temple. Its flattened top was opening up into four parts that slowly slid down the sides to reveal a chamber glowing with an intense ghostly hue.

"Crap, that can't be good," muttered Jack.

"Energy readings from the temple are spiking!" warned Mourdock.

"Everyone, hang on," Jack said as he juked the Earthship away just as a beam erupted from the top of the temple.

The Earthship shook from the force of the beam as it raced by, rocketing up into the atmosphere and through the tether, hitting the Conclave and adding its power to that of the other beam that was already striking it.

Jack steadied the ship from the turbulence the death ray had caused, bringing it back around toward the temple. The image on the viewscreen showed the beam twisting and twirling as it emanated from the dark pyramid at the center of the destroyed colony. "What the heck is that???" Jack asked.

"It looks like the pillar of spirit energy we found trapped inside the temple," noted Sawbones.

"This must have been why the Deathlords had been harvesting all the life from this planet," Green said. "They needed enough souls to power some type of… weapon."

"Weapon?" said Jack, alarmed. "And they're firing it at the Conclave???"

"Whatever that beam is that's hitting the Conclave, it doesn't appear to be doing any damage to it," said Mourdock as he looked at his readouts.

"If it's from the Deathlords, it can't be doing anything good to it, either," said Jack. "We left everyone there without a way to escape the temple. There's no telling what that energy could be doing to them!"

"All the more reason to hurry and retrieve the Princess before any permanent harm can be done," said Seqis. "Can you get a lock on her position, Jack?"

Jack frowned. "No," he said. "That beam is messing with the ship's sensors. I can't get a teleportation lock on her."

"Then we shall have to go in and retrieve her," stated Seqis.

"Um, not that I'm not for rescuing the Princess," piped up Boone, "but there's nowhere to land, and the surface is crawling with those Deathstalker things."

"And I'm not going to be able to teleport us in, either," Jack said. "My ship can't get any readings from inside the temple."

"Then we shall need to teleport to the surface and fight our way in," said Seqis.

"Oh! I may have a better alternative!" chimed in Green as he pulled out his Imperius device. "The temple has a portgate within it! If we can get close enough so that my Imperius device can connect with it, we could use that to transport us inside."

"That is indeed a better alternative. Thank you, Professor," said Seqis. "Jack, can you bring us in close enough for the Professor's device to make a connection?"

"I'll try," Jack said as he brought the Earthship around to make another pass at the temple. As he did, a notification popped up on one of his holoscreens alerting him to an incoming message.

"Jack, are you seeing this?" asked Mourdock, also noticing the alert from his station.

"Yeah. Is it coming from the surface? Does someone else need help?"

"No," Mourdock replied. "It's coming from the Conclave."

Jack frowned. He called up the message on a holoscreen that appeared in front of his chair. His chest clenched when he saw the faces of Krupp and Scrappy, looking haggard and pale.

"Is it working?" Krupp asked. "Are we recording?"

"I think so," Scrappy replied. "The little light is blinking…"

"Would you two masculine meat-brains hurry it up!" came Morosa's testy voice from off-screen.

Krupp sighed before looking into the camera. "Guess we'll just have to pray it is," he muttered. "Jack, I hope you get this message. We're in desperate need of your help! Something strange is happening here at the Conclave! An unknown energy has infested it, and it's turning everyone crazy!"

"Like, murderously crazy!" chimed in Scrappy. "People's eyes are going black, and then they're turning evil!"

"Almost everyone we know in the temple has been affected by this," Krupp said. "It's bad, Jack. Real bad. Those affected are attacking anyone who hasn't been. They're tearing the Conclave apart from the inside! Me and the others are going to make our way to the outer ring, back to where you brought your ship to dock with it. We're going to try and rescue as many people as we can on our way there, but we don't have much time. Almost every Paragon in the Conclave has succumbed to this strange energy, and if they find us, I'm not sure how long we'll be able to hold out."

"They're coming!" came Morosa's voice. "We must move!"

Krupp nodded to her and looked into the camera one final time. "Jack, if you get this message, please – get here quickly! We need you!"

With that, the recording ended.

"So, the Conclave was the Deathlords' target all along," said Rionknidis.

"Time is of the essence," Seqis stated. "We must get to the Princess and stop that energy they are shooting at the temple before it is too late."

Jack frowned, his heart feeling like it was being torn in two. He didn't want to abandon Anna, but he knew he couldn't abandon his friends, either. "I can't go with you," Jack said, turning toward the Vanguard. "I know Anna needs help, but those at the Conclave need help, too. I can't abandon them."

"But you'll abandon the Princess?" asked Lugard.

"He's not abandoning her," Seqis said. "He's making the choice to do what we cannot."

"But if the Earthman flies his ship away, how will we get the Princess out of here?" asked Rionknidis.

"I'll come back," insisted Jack. "As soon as I get everyone I can out of the Conclave, I'll fly back here and get you guys. I promise!"

*He's… he's choosing the Conclave over Anna*, thought Mourdock with surprise. The memory of his vision where he killed Jack for betraying him flashed to his mind, causing him to feel pangs of guilt. *If he truly loved her, would he really abandon her to help those at the temple? Perhaps I was wrong about him and his intentions…*

Seqis nodded. "Very well," he replied. "Dahuud, accompany the Earthman back to the Conclave. Assist him in the rescue effort."

"But you guys need to focus on rescuing Anna!" Jack said. "It's your duty!"

"If what your friends informed us of is true, then what awaits you in the Conclave is just as dangerous as what awaits us in the temple below," replied Seqis. "You will need the help of a seasoned Paragon to rescue those trapped there. I will not send you back to that place alone."

"He won't be alone," said Mourdock, making his decision. "I will be at his side."

Jack looked at Mourdock, surprised. "But… what about Anna?" Jack asked.

Mourdock frowned. "I love Anna with all my being," he said. "More than life itself. But I can never forget when you came to me on Omnicron and I refused to help you when you most needed it. After that, I promised I would never let you down again. The Lord Commander is right, you're going to need help up there. That is help I can provide. Besides, I trust the Royal Vanguard to uphold their sacred duty. If there is anyone who can bring Anna back to us safely… I believe it to be them."

Mourdock gave Seqis and the others a nod of respect, which Seqis returned. "I swear to you, Ascendant," he said, "we will return the Princess to you, safely."

"See that you do, Lord Commander," replied Mourdock with a grin. "If you return her otherwise, I shall be very put out."

Seqis smiled at that, before placing his fist over his heart – a gesture the other members of the Vanguard performed also. "For Legacy Prime," Seqis said.

"For the blood of the Ancients," Mourdock replied, returning the salute. "May the Great Observer keep his eye always upon you."

"And you, as well," Seqis said before turning to the Professor. "Send us in."

Green looked down at his Imperius device, which had made its connection to the temple. He engaged the temple's portgate, and in a flash of light, the Royal Vanguard had disappeared.

“Good luck,” Green whispered softly.

Mourdock came up beside Jack, looking at the ship’s viewscreen as the vessel pulled away from the dark temple of Eionmeer. “Thanks,” said Jack. “You know… for sticking with me.”

“What are friends for?” Mourdock replied with a smile. “Now take us back to the Conclave. The Vanguard will save Anna. It’s up to us to save everyone else.”

Jack smiled at that. Though the Vanguard may have been gone, with his friend Mourdock at his side, he felt practically invincible. He glanced over toward Green, Boone, and Sawbones. “Everyone buckle in,” he said. “We’re off to save the day…”

And with that, the Earthship flew out of Eionmeer’s atmosphere, heading straight for the tether that led to the Conclave.

# CHAPTER 12

Anna couldn't stop screaming while using every ounce of what remained of her strength to fight against Verrutus. The Deathlord Supreme was exerting his will upon the slythru that controlled her, despite Anna's best efforts to resist him. Lightning flashed all around Anna in the darkness of her mental construct as the booming crashes of war drums rang out, echoing all around, mixing in with the haunting chants of distant voices.

*BOOM-DOOM-BOOM-DOOM*

*Mulloch! Hadda, hadda, mulloch!*

"Do you hear it, Princess?" asked Verrutus, gleefully, as Anna continued her struggle. "That is the sound of inevitability! That is the sound of the Lords of the Void! That is the sound of their will being made manifest! And the louder it grows, the closer our Lords are to returning to this universe, so that they may reshape it in their image!"

Anna screamed again. The pain was almost unbearable. She could feel a dark connection to an evil corruption. Something which had trapped thousands upon thousands of tormented souls. She knew Verrutus was using her to manipulate this dark power, and doing so only strengthened him while weakening her.

In the flashes of light created by the lightning sparking all around, she could see images from her own eyes. Images of her hands on a glowing access orb. Images of a horrifying ghostly tempest. Images of robed figures all around her, watching her as she unleashed terror upon the universe.

*I... I can't fight this... much longer...* Anna thought, lamenting the bitter realization that despite her efforts to fight back, this was a fight she was destined to lose.

"It is futile to resist any longer, Princess," gloated Verrutus. "You are mine, now! And there is nothing that can save you!"

Shanks' staff hit the ground with a dull thud as he made his way through the dark corridors of the temple. He could feel himself growing weaker by the minute, but he knew the Princess wasn't far. He could sense her, and had used that sense to guide him through the labyrinth that was the corrupted structure, drawing ever nearer to her location.

*I must not fail...* thought Shanks as he forced himself closer and closer to his destination. *I must keep going... I must do my duty...*

Shanks could see the opening to the central chamber of the dark monolith looming before him. The monk could feel his hands trembling as he walked, leaning heavily upon his staff as he did so. He felt colder the closer he got to the chamber in which the monolith ominously awaited. He could feel the fear rising within him, a tense sensation which caused him to clutch at his chest.

*My body is weak, my mind unfocused... but my spirit must remain strong!*

Shanks willed himself forward, despite the protests from his body. He opened his third eye as he approached the entrance to the monolith's chamber and saw the icy blue haze of the fearful energy hanging in the air within. He ventured onward, moving as close to the energy as he dared. Beyond the haze, he could see the two massive, open double doors, which revealed the soul vault. The Princess was standing there upon a platform, before the swirling, ghostly tempest. Four cloaked figures surrounded her, the terrible energy of fear radiating from them.

Shanks took a deep breath and tried to steady himself. "There is no pain, only peace," he whispered. "There is no hate, only serenity. There is no fear, only calm."

When last he'd seen this chamber, it had been filled with Deathstalkers. Those creatures were now gone, and save for the monolith, the chamber was empty. However, he could not get any closer to the Princess without having to fight the dark energy of the Terrormancers – something he knew he did not have the strength for.

The monk took a few steps into the chamber and slowly lowered himself to the ground. *The light give me strength*, he thought as he settled into his meditation position.

Shanks held his elderwood staff before him, opening his third eye to look at it. He could see the staff glowing, it having been infused by his spiritual energy after he'd mastered the art of imbuement at the Luminadric temple so long ago. Shanks knew if he were to have any chance of saving Anna, he would need to retrieve that energy. But once he did, there would be no going back. Whatever protection the staff offered him would be gone.

*Luminous beings are we*, he prayed, using the mantra of his order. *Embrace the light, and your mind shall be free…*

Shanks focused his mind as best he could and began pulling the energy from the staff back into himself. The smooth elderwood of the staff became dry and brittle as it was drained, until it disintegrated into dust. Shanks could feel the rush of spiritual energy surge through him, filling the gap that had been left behind when he'd transplanted a part of his soul into Jack.

With his renewed strength, Shanks closed his eyes and entered his meditative state. When he opened them once more, he sat in a desolate field. A violent storm raged all around him. Fire, brimstone, soot, and ash were everywhere. The grim landscape stretched out in all directions as the wind howled furiously around him.

Shanks brought the palms of his hands together in front of his chest as he entered his prayer mudra, focusing on his center.

*Peace, love, harmony. My body is prepared. My mind, focused. My soul, eternal.*

Around him, an oasis began to form, offering sanctuary from the raging storm. Green grass began to grow beneath him. The vile winds were diverted, unable to cut at him. Light began to emanate from his body, pushing away the darkness that surrounded him.

*Let my body, mind, and spirit work as one*, he thought. *Let them forsake the darkness. Let them embrace the light!*

Slowly, the oasis Shanks was creating began to grow. It fought back against the dark storm. The grass overtook the dirt. The clouds began to part. The light began to shine.

As Shanks sat, meditating, it was as though the dark monolith which lorded over the chamber could sense what he was doing. When it did, it sent out a call for help to its protectors.

In the soul vault where Anna stood manipulating the access orb of the death tempest, the Terrormancers all turned their attention away from the Princess, looking back toward the monolith's chamber.

"The monolith callsssssss," one of them said.

"An intruder hasssss returned," said another.

"What issss he doing?" wondered the third.

"Whatever it isssss," said the fourth as he began to descend the stairs to the platform which led back to the monolith's chamber, "he won't be doing it for very long…"

One Terrormancer stayed behind to guard Anna, watching his three brethren descend the stairs and make their way toward where Shanks sat, the monk completely exposed and vulnerable in his meditative state.

The storm around Shanks in his vision began to intensify as the monk could sense the growing sensation of terror being directed at him, yet his oasis held firm, keeping him safe for the time being. Shanks steeled himself, knowing that he did not have much time left.

"My whole life, I have dedicated myself to the pursuit of enlightenment," he said. "That pursuit led me to the Luminadric Order. To Legacy Prime. To the teachings of the Ancients themselves. I have studied. I have prayed. I have freed myself from all distraction in my quest to achieve enlightenment. And yet, it has always eluded me. I pray to you now, Great Observer… turn your gaze upon me. Grant me what I have strived to achieve for all these years. Not for my sake, but for that of the Princess. Grant this humble servant the strength I need to rescue her from her tormentors. Please… help me to help her. Help me to do my duty. Help me to fulfill my purpose…"

There has been much debate by historians as to what happened in this moment to help the Luminadric Monk Shank'asogla'phli do what he was about to do. Some claim that he was more skilled in the Paragon disciplines than any had previously believed. The more religious scholars claim that his prayers were answered by a higher being. Others believe that, more likely than not, he simply got lucky. But despite what theory one ascribes to regarding the Luminadric Monk and what he did next, there is something nobody can deny – and that is, when Shanks opened his mind to the universe for that brief moment seeking some type of miracle…

The universe answered him.

In the storm before his oasis, a vision started to appear. Shanks regarded it curiously as it took shape, forming into an image of a large closed eye. At first, Shanks thought that it was the All-Seeing Eye of the Great Observer come to answer his prayer. But as he studied it, he realized something, which surprised him.

He realized that this eye belonged to him. It was the eye of his soul, and it had been long hidden, deep inside him. This eye had always been under his control, he'd just never known it before. When he recognized this, he decided it had been closed long enough.

"Eldil meldilorn[10]," Shanks whispered.

With that final command, the great eye opened, gazing in all its wondrous glory upon Shanks. Its light shined with a brilliance the monk had never thought possible and filled him with a glow that permeated every fiber of his being with peace and harmony.

*I was blind…* Shanks thought to himself. *But now… I can see!*

That was when Shanks opened his actual eyes to see the three Terrormancers standing around him, having encircled him while he'd meditated, their deadly scythes in hand. The three creatures gazed down at him, curiously.

"Why isssss he not afraid?" asked one of the Terrormancers.

"Because there is no longer anything for me to fear," Shanks replied, serenely.

The Terrormancer standing before him hissed. "There will alwaysssss be something to fear…"

"Fear is an illusion," the monk replied.

"Then we ssssshall make it a reality for you!"

The Terrormancer to the right of Shanks swung his scythe, its ghostly blade impaling Shanks from behind and emerging from his chest.

Shanks did not react.

The one to his left did the same, running his scythe through the monk, two ghostly blades now protruding from him.

Again, Shanks did not react.

The Terrormancer standing before Shanks gazed down at him with his soulless black eyes. "Do you not fear death?" it asked.

Shanks smiled. "Life is also an illusion," he said. "You may strike down my body, but I can never truly die."

"Let ussssss see," said the Terrormancer with a sneer.

---

[10] In Old Solar, the language of The Ancients, Eldil Meldilorn means "Free Your Mind."

The Terrormancer raised his scythe over his head and swung. The ghostly blade took Shanks' head off with a single swoop. The other two Terrormancers jerked their blades from the monk's body and it fell over to the floor.

The Terrormancer who'd issued the killing blow smiled. "Looksssss like you were wrong, monk," he said, with a derisive chuckle.

The three creatures began moving back to the soul vault where Anna stood. They almost didn't notice when Shanks' body began glowing. It was a soft glow at first, but the glow began to brighten, growing stronger by the moment.

The Terrormancers turned back and looked at Shanks' body, their eyes wide.

"What issss happening?" asked one of them.

The glow from Shanks body rose from it, forming into a brilliant golden orb that hovered in the air. The three Terrormancers gazed at the orb, not knowing what to make of the sight. Then, the orb formed into the image of Shanks, a golden apparition which glared at the Terrormancers in serene defiance.

"I was not wrong," came Shanks' disembodied voice.

"He'ssss a… he'ssss a…" stammered one of the Terrormancers.

"*Sssssoulwalker!!!*" another hissed.

Before the Terrormancers could react, the visage of Shanks held out its arms, as if to embrace them. A brilliant flash of light emanated from the golden apparition, tearing through the dark chamber. The Terrormancers recoiled as they were hit by it, each one screaming in pain as their skin blistered and burned. They all turned and ran, disappearing out of the closest exits they could find to escape the light Shanks was emitting.

When they were gone, Shanks' soul hovered in the air, looking to the vault beyond the monolith where Anna stood. The final Terrormancer was next to the Princess, gazing upon Shanks with an expression of sheer disbelief.

*Time to fulfill my duty*, Shanks thought. *Time to end this!*

With that, Shanks' soul raced forward, like a rider on the wind, heading right for Anna.

Anna screamed as the agony Verrutus inflicted upon her intensified. *He's winning!* Anna lamented. *I can't fight him! He's too strong!!!*

Verrutus laughed as the drum beats quickened, the haunting chants from the darkness growing louder and louder. "It is over," he said. "Submit! Let the last part of yourself die, and your torment shall cease."

Anna gritted her teeth. "I will fight you to the end!" she cried. "If you want me – you shall have to kill me yourself!"

"If you insist," said the Deathlord.

Before Verrutus could overtake Anna completely, the lightning ceased to flash, the chanting faded away, and the beat of the war drums abruptly died.

The sudden, eerie silence which had settled in upon the mental construct distracted Verrutus as the Deathlord looked up in alarm, confused as to what was going on. That gave Anna some respite from his relentless torture, allowing her to regain some measure of strength.

"What just happened…" wondered Verrutus aloud, his fiery red eyes scanning the darkness.

Those evil eyes settled in on a glimmer of light in the far distance. The Deathlord squinted at the flickering golden flare, not knowing what it was. Then, as the light grew more brilliant, Verrutus's eyes widened in surprise as the golden beam raced right for him.

"NO!" he cried, right before the light made impact.

The golden beam hit him with forceful fury, ripping the tar-like entity away from the slythru it had formed around. Verrutus cried out, his shapeless avatar swirling as it tangled with the light, striking out at it as the golden glow fought back.

Anna gasped for breath. With Verrutus detached from her dark companion, she was no longer overwhelmed. Even the slythru seemed stunned and disoriented from the light that had struck it, giving Anna a desperately needed break from its influence.

Anna looked up to see the golden ray of light zooming around, twisting and turning along with the black muck that was Verrutus. The two entities danced like fighting snakes, each one striking at the other with vicious speed and fury.

The black tar reformed into the specter of Verrutus, the Deathlord's eyes burning bright red as he grabbed onto the light, struggling to keep it at bay. "What are you???" the Deathlord demanded.

The golden light formed into a familiar figure. It was that of Shanks, who stood defiantly against Verrutus, now on equal footing as he wrestled with the

Deathlord. "I am what *you* fear, Deathlord," Shanks replied. "I am the star that burns in the void. I am the flame that fights the night. I am the light that banishes the darkness. I am the spark that powers all life – and I have come to defeat you, once and for all!"

Verrutus's eyes burned with pure malice. "I am undying, you fool!" he growled. "I cannot be defeated!"

"Let us see if that is true," replied Shanks, before attacking the Deathlord once more.

Shanks and Verrutus continued to tangle with one another, the monk's golden glow dancing with the Deathlord's black tar, each one swirling around the other as they intertwined, neither side giving way.

Anna gazed at the scene before her as Shanks and Verrutus struggled, their forms twisting and grappling with each other. One was golden, the other was black. One was light, the other was dark. One was good, the other was evil. Each one had a strength unique to itself, powerful enough to cancel the other out. In a strange way, they were exactly alike.

"Light and dark… two sides of the same coin…" Anna muttered, remembering the words of Arcturus.

Memories flashed into Anna's mind. Memories of her ancestors. Good men, who'd chosen to embrace their darkness. Men who were willing to give in to their darker natures when they needed, but who always found their way back to the light.

Atashah appeared before her, looking up into Nameer's eyes as a planet died behind them. "I will be your anchor to the light," Atashah said. "I will be by your side to guide you back when you need it. I will be there to remind you of who you truly are. One man may not be strong enough to fight his darkness. But that is why we find others to love. For it is love that gives us the strength to be who we want to be."

"Love…" said Anna.

Suddenly, she was surrounded by those she loved – and who loved her. She saw the image of her father. Her mother. Shepherd. Jack. And she saw Shanks, who smiled down at her kindly. Arcturus himself appeared, gazing down on her with eyes which had been wizened from lessons hard learned. "Embrace both the dark and the light," he said. "But always remember to balance them."

"How?" asked Anna, her gaze drifting back to the furious struggle between Shanks and Verrutus. "How do I do such a thing?"

"By not being afraid of the dark," came a voice.

Anna looked up to see the image of herself as an Empress. It looked down upon her with strength and confidence. Emperor Tarrok was at her side, along with Nameer. Arcturus approached, joining them. "What is it you fear?" Arcturus asked.

"I… I don't know…"

"You do," insisted Anna's doppelganger. "You fear embracing your own darkness. You fear not being strong enough to balance it. You fear who you will become should you allow it in."

"You have been fighting all this time to keep it at bay," Tarrok said. "But how does one fight something that is already a part of them?"

A realization settled in on Anna, hitting her as powerfully as a lightning strike. She had been doing her best to fight the slythru – to resist its influence. She'd been seeking a way to defeat it, but the slythru had told her many times she could never do so. It was now a part of her. A part she had refused to accept.

It was then Anna realized why she'd been losing to the slythru. Verrutus had been right all along. Anna couldn't fight what was happening to her. Struggling against it was the very thing that was tearing her down. If she had any hope of regaining control, she had to do the one thing she'd feared more than anything else…

She'd have to embrace her own darkness.

"Now you are beginning to understand," her doppelganger said.

"But… if I do this… I'll die…"

"You'll change," Nameer said. "As we all did when we had to face this same choice."

"I'm afraid…"

"The key is to not be afraid of the dark, but to tame it," said Atashah. "To find a balance between each side, and to become whole by doing so."

"To control one's fear is to preserve one's spirit," said Arcturus. "Know your fear! Do not fight it! Face it! Embrace it! Only then can you conquer it!"

Anna knew what she had to do, but she could not bring herself to do it. Not until she saw the image of Jack, kneeling at her side, smiling at her warmly. "Don't be scared," he said. "You can do this."

"What if I can't?" Anna asked. "What if I let it control me? What if my darkness takes over?"

"It won't," said Jack, reassuringly. "I'll be there to make sure it doesn't."

"And if you aren't?"

"Then others will be," Jack replied. "But even if they aren't… he'll always be with you."

With that, Anna turned to see Shepherd kneeling at her side. He smiled at her and gently cupped her cheek with his hand.

"Be strong," was all he needed to say.

The apparitions which had surrounded her were suddenly gone. Anna could feel her dark companion stir, recovering from the stun of being hit by Shanks' light. It was rising up to reassert its dominance over her, just as Shanks and Verrutus reformed, grappling with one another.

"You cannot fight darkness, monk!" Verrutus hissed.

"You can," Shanks replied.

"Darkness is eternal!" insisted the Deathlord. "It is unyielding! Fighting it is impossible!"

"Anything is possible."

Verrutus tried to overtake Shanks with his tar-like form, but Shanks glowed brighter, keeping the Deathlord at bay.

Anna felt the slythru's claws dig within her. She took a deep breath and steeled herself for what she was about to do.

"VERRUTUS!!!" she cried.

The Deathlord looked at Anna, setting his fiery gaze upon her. Anna met that gaze with a defiant one of her own. She gritted her teeth and began to concentrate…

Suddenly, the figure of the slythru behind her jerked, its red eyes growing wide with surprise.

*What… what you do?* it hissed.

The slythru's arms sunk deeper into Anna's back. The creature looked confused as Anna pushed herself up, fighting to get off her knees and back to her feet. The slythru struggled, looking as if it were trying to yank itself away from Anna, but instead, its arms were pulled deeper into her back.

*Stop!* the slythru cried. *STOP!!!*

"What is happening?" Verrutus demanded. "What are you doing???"

"Embracing my dark side," Anna said with a sneer as she rose to her feet.

Anna closed her eyes as the slythru was steadily pulled into her. It fought for its very life, struggling frantically as it was drawn into Anna. But no matter how hard the slythru fought, it was not strong enough. Anna was absorbing it, little by little. When Anna had fully risen and was standing upright, the slythru cried out one final time as the last of it disappeared into the Princess.

Verrutus's red eyes were wide in shock at what he'd just witnessed, his distraction allowing Shanks to maneuver behind him, grabbing onto the Deathlord and holding him steady. Verrutus struggled but could not break free of the light which held him in place.

Anna breathed deeply, feeling transformed after absorbing her dark companion. She could feel the turmoil insider her – good and bad, light and dark – all whirling chaotically within as she accepted the slythru as a part of her.

*Find balance,* she thought as she concentrated. *Become whole.*

As she brought her dueling nature into alignment, the air behind Anna shimmered and rippled as the golden outline of a magnificent eye appeared. Verrutus's eyes were wide and confused as the great eye formed behind Anna, her arms outstretched as though she were waiting for an embrace as she floated in the dark void of the construct, a faint golden aura beginning to emanate from her.

"WHAT ARE YOU DOING???" the Deathlord cried again.

Shanks smiled. "She is about to do the impossible, Deathlord," he said. "She is about to fight you. And she is about to win."

Anna opened her eyes and glared at her tormenter as he struggled in Shanks' grasp. As Anna stood tall and proud and powerful before the shimmering golden eye she'd made manifest, she saw something in Verrutus's soulless eyes that the Deathlord had never shown before.

She saw fear.

"I am a Deathlord!" Verrutus cried. "You cannot kill me!!!"

"Maybe not," growled Anna. "But I can *beat* you!"

Anna summoned her power, and the great eye that had appeared behind her opened – bright and wide and all-seeing. The darkness that comprised her mental construct was instantly banished, replaced by a brilliant illumination. When that magnificent eye turned its gaze upon Verrutus, the Deathlord screamed as the tar-like substance he was comprised of melted away, consumed by the light which shined and shimmered all around.

Verrutus's anguished cry slowly died out as the final remnants of his avatar fluttered away, disintegrating into nothingness. When the last vestiges of the Deathlord Supreme disappeared, one thing became crystal clear…

Darkness only has power in the absence of light. And in that moment, nothing shined brighter than Princess Glorianna of Legacy Prime.

# CHAPTER 13

The Office of the Director was a scene of chaos when Alabaster and his team arrived. Obviously, he hadn't been the only official to receive the emergency alert when Uleeg Casgor's body had been discovered. The Director's personal security detail, along with the Imperial Investigative Service and at least four other agencies were all present, all having brought their own legions of personnel to try to claim jurisdiction over the investigation.

Agent Bob, who'd accompanied Alabaster to the scene along with a handful of other I.I.A. agents, frowned when he saw Casgor's body on the floor. "This is a most… unexpected development," Agent Bob muttered.

"Unexpected, and unfortunate," said Alabaster, only half-meaning it. "There hasn't been a successful assassination of a Directory member in over two hundred years, let alone one in the most secure office in the Empire."

"How could this have happened?" asked Bob.

"That is a good question, Agent. And by the looks of things around here, no one has an answer to it."

Alabaster approached a group of senior officials who were huddled together, engaged in a heated exchange. He recognized Commander Sorus, the head of the Director's Special Security Contingent of the Royal Guard, along with Deputy Director Hegglundz of the I.I.S. The two appeared to be arguing, making it impossible for the other four officials to get a word in edgewise.

"This is your mess, Sorus," stated Hegglundz, sternly. "You and your men were responsible for the Director's safety!"

"This is not on us!" sneered Sorus. "We've tripled security measures since the Earthman incident! Short of having an armed Alpha Force unit inside the Director's office at all times, we couldn't have done anything more to protect him!"

"Then how is he dead?"

"I don't know! None of the biometric sensors signaled any distress! We weren't aware the Director had been attacked until his assistant found him! None of our monitoring alerted us!"

"Gentlemen," Alabaster said as he joined the group. "Might I suggest we stop trying to assign blame for this tragic incident, at least for the moment, and focus on figuring out who did this and where they might be?"

Hegglundz gave Alabaster a frustrated look. "Chief Alabaster," he said. "The I.I.S. would like nothing more than to begin conducting our investigation, but Commander Sorus here is adamant that his team take the lead."

"Director Casgor was our responsibility," insisted Sorus. "His death falls under our jurisdiction. We can conduct our own investigation into this matter."

"Give me a break," groaned Hegglundz. "You're a bunch of glorified bodyguards, and judging from the state of the body on the floor, you're not even very good at that!"

"Why you son of a—"

Before Sorus's anger could flare further, Alabaster placed his hand on the man's shoulder to calm him. "Let us not forget, this is a galactic tragedy, gentlemen, and emotions are understandably running high," Alabaster said. "I do not see a reason why two independent investigations cannot be run simultaneously. The crime scene can be handled by the I.I.S. along with interviews of all external visitors to the office. The Royal Guard can look into all security footage and interview those who work in the building. Both investigations can be coordinated through my office, which will ensure each agency gets access to the intelligence it needs. Now is not the time for red tape and jurisdictional quibbling, compatriots. All our energies must be focused on apprehending whoever is responsible for this. Agreed?"

It was obvious neither man was happy with the suggestion, but regardless, they both nodded in acceptance.

"Good. Now, let's thin out the army of personnel each agency has milling about outside this office and do our best to preserve the integrity of the crime scene so the I.I.S. investigators can get to work. Commander Sorus, have your team start pulling footage from the security network and reviewing it immediately. Report to me if you should find anything that could identify the killer."

Sorus grumbled in displeasure but complied as he left to carry out his task. Alabaster then went about giving the other agencies assignments – at least enough to make them feel involved in what was, undoubtedly, the most high profile murder in the galaxy. Once the other agency heads had left, Alabaster turned to Hegglundz.

"So… what do we know?" Alabaster asked.

"Not much, thanks to that lughead Sorus trying to cover his sorry hide," Hegglundz responded. "We know the Director's assistant found him dead in this office about an hour ago. None of the security measures were tripped and none of the Director's bio-monitors indicated any distress. He could have been dead for hours before his assistant found him."

"Who was the last person to see him alive?"

"I have my men checking on that now," Hegglundz replied. "But according to the assistant, the Director's last appointment had been with Armonto Virtuoso."

"Armonto Virtuoso?" said Agent Bob, who'd been standing nearby. "Are you certain of that?"

"We'll need to check surveillance footage and visitor records to confirm, but so far, I have no reason to doubt it. But why would the head of the Maguffyn Corporation want to murder the Director?"

*Especially considering the two of them were working together with the Deathlords,* thought Alabaster. *Either this execution was carried out on Verrutus's orders, or Armonto Virtuoso decided on his own to end his association with this evil enterprise of theirs. Either way… it's a strange development.*

"Casgor had a knack for making enemies," Alabaster replied. "However, if anyone could bypass all the security measures in place to protect him, it would be Virtuoso."

"But to what end?" asked Hegglundz. "By all accounts, the two were close allies. What could Virtuoso possibly have to gain by Casgor's death?"

"That, Deputy Chief, is another very good question."

Alabaster sighed as he surveilled the crime scene. Something was nagging at him. It was very unlike Virtuoso to get his hands dirty, let alone perform such a risky deed in one of the most secure locations in the capital.

"What are you thinking, Chief?" Agent Bob asked.

"I'm thinking this wasn't just about killing Casgor," Alabaster replied. "Armonto Virtuoso is a man who methodically thinks twelve moves ahead. His actions are always geared toward multiple purposes. The question is not necessarily why he killed Casgor, but why he killed him here and now?" Alabaster turned to Bob. "Does any of your incarnations have sight of him?"

"Not as yet, Chief," Bob replied. "But rest assured, I am looking for him everywhe—"

Just then, Bob's gelatinous eyes went wide as he screamed in agony. The outburst was so sudden, Alabaster stepped back in alarm as everyone in the room turned their attention to the alien.

Bob stumbled backward, his body losing form as it devolved into a shapeless puddle on the floor.

Gasps could be heard as others in the room watched the sudden meltdown. Hegglundz rushed to the pink puddle of ooze that had once been Bob, kneeling beside it with concern. "Ambassador!" Hegglundz cried. "Blast it! Someone get a medic in here! Something's happened to Bob!"

"Sirs!" called out an I.I.A. agent who'd just gotten an alert on his datapad. "We're getting word from around the system! All incarnations of Bob have just melted!"

"All of them?" gasped Hegglundz. "But… how is that possible?"

Alabaster frowned, pulling out his datapad and checking the time on it. *No…* he thought. *This isn't right. It's too far ahead of schedule. Something is wrong!*

"Get away from him!" Alabaster snapped.

He quickly grabbed Hegglundz by the arm and pulled the man back to his feet.

"Alabaster, what the blazes do you think you're—"

"You!" barked Alabaster, pointing to the Agent who'd just informed them of Bob's status. "Contact all agencies and Peacekeeper forces! Have them isolate every incarnation of Bob that they can while he's incapacitated! Alert Megabase Cygnus and deploy all Alpha Force units to the city! Anyone who has a blaster, draw it! NOW!"

"Chief Alabaster!" cried Hegglundz, insistently. "Why are you acting like this? The Ambassador needs our help!"

"No, we are the ones in need of help, blast it!" Alabaster said, urgently. "Bob is not what he seems!"

"I don't understand!" said Hegglundz. "What is he?"

Then, the puddle of pink ooze bubbled. All eyes in the room turned toward it as the slime began to rise back up, growing in height and reshaping itself as it did so.

Alabaster watched, frozen, a sinking feeling of dread welling up in the pit of his stomach.

The figure that reformed before him wasn't the comfortingly generic visage of the Bob he'd known for years. Instead, this figure had long, sharp claws. It was tall and lithe and intimidating. Its face was entirely featureless, except for two fiery red eyes, which burned with unadulterated malice when they reopened.

"He's Verrutus…" Alabaster said, with a sneer.

Everyone in the office looked at the horrifying gelatinous visage of the Deathlord Supreme with shock and confusion. Verrutus chuckled. "It would seem my true identity is no longer a secret," the Deathlord said, his voice deep and ominous. "For that much, at least, I am grateful."

"And why is that?" asked Alabaster, fearing he may already know the answer.

Verrutus met Alabaster's gaze.

"Because now, Chief Alabaster... I get to show the universe what I am fully capable of!"

*****

According to the databanks of the Regalus Empire's xenobiology index, the entity known as "Bob" was actually something that could only be classified as an 'Autonomous Neurofibrilious Mass', which is simply a fancy way of saying he was just a gigantic brain.

How gigantic, one may ask? Well, in Bob's case, his brain was roughly 760 miles in diameter and surrounded by approximately 3,000 miles of protoplasmic gel, which that giant brain had generated around itself over the millennia. It was this gel that the neurofibrilious mass known as "Bob" controlled and sent out into the universe as tiny incarnations of itself.

What was not in the databanks of the Empire's xenobiology index was that this entity was actually named Verrutus, and it had adopted the innocuous guise of "Bob" only after coming into contact with civilization as a means to covertly insert itself into the fabric of Imperial society for the sole purpose of undermining it as an agent for the Lords of the Void.

Seeing as how Verrutus's brain was so large, it made sense that his mental abilities extended into the psychic realm, his neurons firing with such power that he was able to control his own protoplasmic muck across vast distances. But apparently, Verrutus's abilities to exert psychic control did not end there. Indeed, that ability allowed him to exert his influence over all those infected by the creatures known as slythru, whose psychic threads he connected together and managed as he saw fit.

Thus, between those infected by the slythru and the thousands upon thousands of incarnations of Verrutus himself, those that comprised the Secret Army were practically everywhere within the Empire.

But when Princess Glorianna used her powers to banish Verrutus from her mind, she had somehow disrupted the psychic control Verrutus had over his various incarnations, causing them all momentarily to lose their forms. For the span of a few minutes, the most powerful brain in the universe was knocked for a loop, losing its connection not only with its protoplasm, but also with every single slythru over which it had control.

When that big brain, which all this time had secretly been the most dangerous Deathlord Supreme in the galaxy, recovered, he was understandably quite upset.

And he was about to let the entire universe know it.

Starkeeper Cohaagen stood in the command center of Megabase Cygnus, listening to a briefing from the Chief of Station Security Commander Tesswahld and his Chief Engineer Mads Wilkuns. "What do you mean the planetary defense rings' safety protocols have been disabled?" Cohaagen asked upon the conclusion of the briefing.

"We don't know how to explain it, Starkeeper," Wilkuns replied. "We didn't spot the glitch until running a routine maintenance diagnostic on the rings. But my people have confirmed that all safeguards for targeting and firing of the defense rings' weapons have been completely removed from our systems."

"This means Senior Command-level permission for the rings' use is no longer required to operate them, Starkeeper," said Tesswahld. "All safeties and redundancies concerning their operation are gone."

"Which means what, exactly?" asked Cohaagen.

"That anyone can operate the rings, sir," stated Wilkins. "There are no longer any restrictions as to what they can target or hit."

"Great Observer," muttered Cohaagen in concern. "How is this even possible?"

"It shouldn't be, sir, short of the Directory using their Executive Overrides. But that type of thing would only happen in the event of an emergency where the Megabase would be unable to operate the rings."

Cohaagen looked to Tesswahld. "How many capital ships do we have in the area?"

"Four battlegroups, sir," Tesswahld replied. "Twenty capital ships in total."

"Bring them in around Omnicron," Cohaagen ordered. "Defensive positions. We'll use them to guard the planet while we shut down the rings until they can be fixed—"

Cohaagen's orders were interrupted by an ear-piercing scream. The men turned to see the handful of incarnations of Bob in the command center suddenly melting into puddles.

"What the blazes…" muttered Cohaagen as everyone looked at the pink puddles of ooze in confusion.

Various members of the command center personnel rushed to assist Bob, calling the base's medical center and fielding reports of other cases of the alien's abrupt devolution. Cohaagen walked forward, looking down at one of the puddles of Bob with worry. "Ambassador?" he said as he knelt down at the side of the pink puddle. "Ambassador, can you hear me?"

"Starkeeper, reports are coming in that every incarnation of Bob on the Megabase has lost its form," reported Tesswahld.

"First the defense rings, now Bob…" Cohaagen said to himself, a rising feeling of apprehension growing within him as his decades of battle experience told him something was terribly wrong. "This can't be coincidence. It must be the start of some type of attack! Quickly! Lock down the Megabase! Alert the fleet and Starbase Sirius to do the same! Enact emergency defensive protocols throughout the system! And shut down the defense rings before they can be used to—"

Without warning, a spiked rod made up of the pink protoplasm Cohaagen was kneeling beside abruptly shot forward, impaling the Starkeeper through his chest and emerging from the man's back.

Cohaagen gasped, caught completely off-guard by the vicious strike. He struggled for air, the rod having pierced his lungs, causing them to begin filling with fluid.

Everyone in the vicinity looked on in shock as the Starkeeper knelt, impaled on the gruesome spike, while the pink puddle formed into the figure of Verrutus, the Deathlord Supreme's evil eyes glaring at Cohaagen. "I'm afraid I must countermand those orders, Starkeeper," Verrutus said as his other incarnations rose up from the various puddles around the room.

Cohaagen gazed at the true visage of Verrutus, wide-eyed in surprise. "What… what are you?" he wheezed.

"Is it not obvious by now, Starkeeper?" Verrutus replied. "I am *death!*"

Verrutus then took his other arm and transformed it into a spike which he drove up through Cohaagen's head. Just like that, Starkeeper Cohaagen – a man who'd survived countless battles to become one of the greatest military commanders in the galaxy – died at the hands of a single being he'd thought was his ally.

Upon witnessing Cohaagen's death, someone screamed. Members of the Megabase security force who were present in the command center quickly pulled their blasters out, aiming them at the various incarnations of Verrutus in the room.

Engineer Wilkuns turned to Tesswahld, who had his sidearm out and trained on the Deathlord. "Don't just stand there!" shrieked Wilkuns. "Do something!!!"

"Yes," said Verrutus, turning his fiery gaze toward the Chief of Security. "Do something."

With that, Tesswahld turned and abruptly fired his blaster directly in Wilkuns' face.

Immediately, every slythru-infected member of the command center began attacking those who were not of their ranks, swiftly and brutally killing them. Any resistance was quashed before the uninfected knew what was even occurring. When the carnage was over, all that remained were the handful of incarnations of Verrutus and members of his Secret Army.

Tesswahld approached Verrutus. "What are your orders, Supreme?" he asked.

Verrutus turned and looked at the planet of Omnicron on the command center's viewscreen, gazing upon it as one would an enemy under the heel of his boot.

"Rain destruction down upon them," Verrutus commanded. "Make that world *burn*."

With that command, the Secret Army of the Deathlords finally struck at the Empire. The two massive defense rings which surrounded the capital planet of Omnicron turned their thousands of plasma cannons upon the surface and opened fire. Red streaks of death rained down on the planet from above. No area of the planet's face was safe as the heavy-duty plasma bolts hit, toppling supertowers, leveling cities, and scorching the surface.

Fires burned. People screamed. Destruction ruled. All the while, the rings meant to defend the planet continued to set about annihilating it.

As Omnicron was ravaged, Verrutus and his Secret Army took advantage of their presence on some of the capital ships in the system, taking them over and turning their weapons upon other ships in their battlegroups. Caught unaware, entire parts of the Homeworld Defense Fleet were destroyed as their sister vessels fired upon them without warning or mercy.

In every sector of space, every planet, colony, and outpost in which an incarnation of Verrutus and members of his Secret Army were present – they attacked. People were killed. Ships were destroyed. Civilizations were thrown into chaos.

The Empire trembled.

And as the attack commenced, Verrutus stood in the command center of Megabase Cygnus, basking in the glory of the type of widescale destruction he'd longed to unleash upon the galaxy.

"Begin charging the station's megalaser," he commanded. "It is time to put an end to the Galactic Regalus Empire, once and for all."

# CHAPTER 14

*he Reaver* shook as it absorbed another hit from *The Megavolt's* plasma cannons. "Shields at 68%, Cap'n," reported Tarkrane from his station. "That *Megavolt* hits like a hyped-up hornhog in heat!"

"Hyped-up hornhog?" said Dan. "I really must update my colloquial slang database."

Scallywag sat in the Captain's chair, looking at the ship's readouts. They'd been able to put some distance between themselves and Eisenwolf before *The Megavolt* had started giving chase. Since that time, they hadn't been able to pull far enough away from the vessel to get out of its weapons' range. Instead, they'd had to rely on evasive maneuvers to keep from getting blown to pieces by the capital ship's superior firepower. But as maneuverable as *The Reaver* was, Scallywag knew they wouldn't be able to keep this dance up much longer.

"Fire all rear plasma batteries," ordered Scallywag. "Keep needlin' them as much as possible."

"Aye, Cap'n," replied ReeRee. "But we ain't gonna make a dent in their shields."

"Eisenwolf is keeping pace with us," Glimmer reported. "They're fast for a capital ship. We won't be able to outrun them. Do you have a plan?"

"Yeah. Annoy tha snot out o' them," grumbled Scallywag.

"Is that seriously your plan?"

"It'll have ta do for tha moment," Scallywag replied as he looked at the sensor readouts.

*The Megavolt* was indeed a superior ship. Scallywag knew they couldn't outrun her, nor could they go toe-to-toe and outfight her. But it was a much larger ship than *The Reaver*, which meant their only other option was to outmaneuver her.

"Kapplan," Scallywag said. "Where are them Regalus vessels that were assigned to tha quarantine?"

"Couple thousand miles away, in orbit around tha planet," Kapplan replied as he checked his sensor console.

"Plot a course ta intercept 'em," Scallywag ordered. "Oy – you – tha one piloting tha ship…"

"Name's Tweak," replied the female Karkovian[11] who was busily maneuvering *The Reaver*.

"Right, bring us about," Scallywag said. "Take us right through tha middle o' them Regal cruisers."

Tweak gave Glimmer a skeptical look. Glimmer simply nodded, signaling for her to obey the command. Tweak appeared unconvinced that the maneuver was a good one, but she complied anyway.

"Mind if I ask why you're bringing us closer to military starships assigned to apprehend rogue vessels in the system?" asked Glimmer.

"We're gonna put 'em between us and *The Megavolt*," Scallywag replied. "Not even Eisenwolf is crazy enough ta keep firing and risk accidentally attacking a Regalus starship and sparkin' a possible war. It'll give us a bit o' breathing room to recharge our shields. He'll also need ta adjust course around the Regal battlegroup, which'll give us time ta pull away and escape ta hyperspace."

"That's actually a pretty good plan," said Glimmer. "You know… if the Regalus ships don't decide to disable us and hand us over to Eisenwolf."

"I'd rather tussle with three Regal cruisers than one *Megavolt* at tha moment," Scallywag said. "*The Reaver* is a tough old bird. She was designed ta stand up ta Regal vessels. That Terranda-class ship on our tail, however, is a whole other story."

"Never thought three against one would be preferable odds," muttered Glimmer. "Let's hope our luck continues to hold out."

"You mean tha bad kind?" said Scallywag. "No thanks. High time we started makin' our own luck. Far less opportunity ta screw up."

*The Reaver* rounded the planet and headed right for the Regalus cruisers, which were flying in a standard trinity formation, with two of the vessels side-by-side and one underneath in the shape of an upside-down triangle. Sure enough, the barrage of plasma blasts from *The Megavolt* died away as *The Reaver* came into alignment with the trajectory of the Regal ships.

"It worked!" said Glimmer. "*The Megavolt* has stopped firing!"

---

[11] Karkovians are humanoid aliens with six arms.

"They're still in pursuit, though," reported Gage. "Picked up a bit of speed. My guess is they diverted some power to their engines."

"They want ta catch us before we can squeeze by tha Regals, but we ain't gonna let 'em," Scallywag said. "Divert power from forward shields to tha engines. Get us a boost o' speed! Tweak, take us right through the middle o' tha Regalus ships' formation. The moment we're on tha other side, keep 'em between us and *The Megavolt.*"

"Lowering our forward shields would leave us vulnerable to an attack by the Regals, Cap'n," stated Tarkrane.

"We can take a punch or two, One-Eye," Scallywag replied. "Just so long as we ain't knocked out."

"Maneuvering into the Regalus formation… *now,*" stated Tweak.

*The Reaver* banked and corkscrewed as it pulled ahead, speeding toward the gap in the formation of the Regalus ships. *The Megavolt* was forced to alter its course as *The Reaver* shot between the Imperial cruisers before banking away, keeping the grouping of ships between it and *The Megavolt.*

"WOO-HOO!" cried Tarkrane. "We did it!"

"The Regals didn't fire on us at all," said Glimmer, somewhat surprised. "They let us waltz right past them."

"Never look a gift bova[12] in tha mouth, I say," Scallywag replied. "Kapplan, plot us a course to tha fastest route out o' tha system. I wanna jump ta hyperspace as soon as possible."

"Plotting course now, Cap'n."

"What the…" muttered Gage as he monitored his sensor station.

"What?" asked Glimmer. "What is it?"

"The Regalus vessels are preparing to fire…" Gage replied.

"Quick!" Scallywag cried. "All shields to full!"

"No – not on us," Gage said. "On *The Megavolt!*"

Glimmer and Scallywag exchanged confused glances. "On screen," Scallywag ordered.

---

[12] A bova is a large, hairy, buffalo-like animal raised by many primitive cultures to ride, use as pack animals, or as a source of meat.

The crew of *The Reaver* watched as the three Regal cruisers they'd just raced by spread out as *The Megavolt* attempted to maneuver around them. Without warning, the three vessels opened fire, peppering *The Megavolt* with their plasma batteries.

"By Osiris…" muttered Scallywag. "What tha squick are they doing?"

"They're… they're attacking Eisenwolf!" Glimmer said. "But why would they do such a thing?"

Scallywag continued to watch the scene unfold on the ship's viewscreen. It appeared *The Megavolt* was caught off-guard by the sudden attack, which allowed the focused fire from the Regalus vessels to quickly drain its shields. *The Megavolt* began to return fire, taking on all three ships at once. There was a heated exchange as the Regal cruisers struck at *The Megavolt*, but *The Megavolt* fought back. One cruiser fell to the Visini capital ship's firepower. Then, another. By the time the third Regalus cruiser was destroyed, *The Megavolt's* shields were completely gone and the ship had sustained significant hull damage, with one of its engines appearing to be completely disabled.

"Um… did we just accidentally start a war between the Regals and Visinis?" asked Tweak, sheepishly.

"That weren't us, lass," Scallywag said. "Whatever it is we just saw, them Regal cruisers were actin' totally on their own."

"Sensors show one of *The Megavolt's* engines is damaged," Gage reported. "They're not going to be able to keep up with us now. The Regals may have just started a war, but they also just saved our hides."

Glimmer turned to Scallywag. "What was that about you saying our luck was bad?" she teased.

Scallywag frowned. Something didn't sit right with him concerning what had just happened. But, then again, he wasn't one to turn away opportunity when it came knocking. "Kapplan," he said. "Ya got our escape route plotted yet?"

"Closest hyperspace jump point locked in, Cap'n," Kapplan replied. "E.T.A. thirty minutes, and we are good to go!"

"Right. Set course then," Scallywag said as he took his seat in the Captain's chair once more. "Get us tha squick out o' here."

"Master Scallywag, sir," Dan said, shuffling up beside him. "Forgive me, but I have a matter I believe requires your immediate attention before we make our getaway."

"What is it, Dan?" Scallywag asked.

"As you know, my previous body contained a subspace communicator which I used to exchange messages with Chief Alabaster back on Omnicron," Dan said. "As it so happens, I was able to salvage this, along with my other upgrades, after being installed in this new body. I did not believe the message I picked up on during our evasion of *The Megavolt* to be a priority, given the severity of our situation. But now that we are out of danger, I do believe this is something you should be made aware of."

Dan plugged himself into a console and began playing the message Professor Green had sent out on the bridge's viewscreen. Scallywag and the rest of the crew watched as the events of the recording played out.

When it was finished, Dan unplugged himself. "It would appear Master Green and Princess Glorianna are still in desperate need of assistance," he said.

"Don't matter. We can't help 'em anyway," said Tarkrane. "There be a Visini capital ship between us and that bloody planet. We just now got away because of a lucky break. If we head back there… we ain't getting' away a second time."

Glimmer looked at Scallywag. "The Professor saved our lives in the temple," she said. "We can't just leave him behind."

"We don't have a choice," Gage said. "Tarkrane is right. We get anywhere near *The Megavolt*, we're going to be blasted to bits. That ship may be wounded, but it's a long way from no longer being a threat."

Scallywag grimaced. *I owe Green a big one,* he thought. *But I can't risk me ship and the lives of all me crew ta try and rescue him.*

Scallywag knew the smart play was to run – to open a window to hyperspace and high-tail it away from the nightmare that had been Eionmeer as fast and as far as *The Reaver* could carry him. Though his head was telling him one thing, his heart was telling him another. Maybe all those times Jack had forced him to do the right thing instead of being his normal, selfish self had taken root within Scallywag. Maybe his feelings of loyalty and friendship with the crew of the Earthship were overriding his good sense. Or maybe he really was beginning to turn over a new leaf. Regardless of the reason, despite knowing he couldn't go back to help the Professor, he also knew he couldn't simply abandon him.

Scallywag pushed himself out of his Captain's seat and walked toward the bridge's viewscreen. "Hail *The Megavolt*," Scallywag ordered.

"But, Cap'n…" objected Tarkrane.

"Just do it, One-Eye."

Tarkrane sighed. "Aye, sir. Sending hail."

Scallywag stood before the ship's main viewscreen until the image of Eisenwolf appeared, gazing at Scallywag with malice. "Called to say good-bye before you scurry away like the cowardly bottom-feeder you are, Red?" asked Eisenwolf.

"As much as I enjoy our little chats, Wolfie, this ain't about you and me," Scallywag replied. "There be a broadcast goin' out over subspace. It ain't encrypted, so I take it ya've seen it."

"Yes, I'm aware of the message," Eisenwolf replied.

"Then ya know what's happenin' down on tha planet," Scallywag said. "Ya know tha Deathlords are there. That they're attacking tha Regals. That they've got their hands on tha Princess."

"What of it?"

"I need ta know what ya plan on doin' about it."

"Not that I am in the habit of sharing my plans with one such as you, but since you went through so much trouble to ask, I suppose I could make an exception just this once. I plan to do nothing."

"Nothing?" said Scallywag, somewhat surprised.

"It's the Regals' planet. It's the Regals' Princess. Therefore, it is the Regals' problem."

Scallywag stepped forward, his face hard. "Oy, what's goin' on down there is about more than rivalries between Empires," he said. "Ya got tha troops. Ya got tha firepower. Yer involvement could turn tha tide o' this thing. Yer tha only ship worth a toss in tha system, blast it! Ya need ta turn around and go help!"

"And break off our pursuit so you can get away to safety?" said Eisenwolf. "I don't think so."

"Yer engines took a hit, Wolfie. We've already gotten away. What ya need ta do now is yer duty!"

"Don't dare to lecture me about duty!" spat Eisenwolf. "You? The man who betrayed his House? His people? His empire? You stand there and have the gall to say I have a duty to protect our enemy?"

"The Regals ain't tha enemy! Tha Deathlords are!"

"In case you didn't notice, Red, my ship was just attacked by the people you claim aren't our enemy."

"I don't know how ta explain that. But I do know this… tha Deathlords don't differentiate between empires. They don't care about skin color or past transgressions. If yer alive, they want ya dead, and that's all they care about. Now pull yer head out o' your nethers, Eisenwolf! Right now, tha fate of the galaxy is hanging by a thread – and yer the only one powerful enough ta bring tha fight to the Deathlords and stop what's happening on Eionmeer!"

"I no longer care what happens on that forsaken planet," Eisenwolf replied. "The fall of the Regalus Empire only means an opportunity for the Visini Empire to flourish. Let the Deathlords have their Princess. Let them tear the Regals down piece by piece. After they are done, we shall be waiting to pick up what remains. Only then will I take action."

Scallywag clenched his hands in frustration. "I don't bloody believe this," he sneered. "Yer makin' *me* tha good guy in this situation!?"

Eisenwolf scowled. "You? A good guy?" he growled. "My ship was just attacked by Regalus vessels! They have just essentially declared war on the Visini Empire! And you, like the vile traitor you are, are now pleading for me to assist them. No, you red piece of filth… you are not a good guy – not in any scenario. The Regalus Empire can burn for all I care. And you can burn along with it!"

Scallywag gazed at Eisenwolf's image with steely resolve. "Blast it, Eisenwolf… yer gonna make me do somethin' I don't want ta do."

"Do what you will," Eisenwolf said. "But know this, Red. You can run. You can hide. But I will never stop coming for you. You may have slipped through my fingers this time, but when next we meet, I assure you I will bring this dance of ours to a swift and decisive end."

"When next we meet, this thing between you and me is definitely gonna end," replied Scallywag. "On that, we can agree."

Scallywag then killed the transmission. He stood still for a moment, his face dark and deep in thought. The eyes of all his crew were upon him as they waited for him to say something.

"Scally?" asked Glimmer. "What are you going to do?"

Scallywag turned and sat in his command chair, having come to his decision. He gazed at the image of *The Megavolt* on the ship's viewscreen like a hawk about to descend upon its prey.

"Tha right thing. Fer once," he said.

★★★★★

On the surface of Eionmeer, Commander Gunner and his men stood on the outskirts of the remains of the Twin Rivers settlement. He and his troops had been warned by their master to flee right before the dark temple had started to rise, and they'd barely had enough time to escape the settlement before the temple had destroyed it. What remained of the colony's Peacekeeper forces was with them, as well, having also escaped the destruction just in the nick of time.

Gunner gazed up at the ominous temple as the black rock from it reached the city limits, creeping into the dead fields surrounding the settlement and toward the distant mountains. Deathstalkers were crawling all around, with more growing from the black rock by the minute. However, the members of the Secret Army were safe. The Deathstalkers ignored them, thanks to the slythrus they all bore.

Governor Fetch came up to Gunner's side. "The Supreme has at last revealed himself to the Empire," the man said. "Our brethren rise up across the galaxy, and yet we are here twiddling our thumbs."

"We are exactly where the Supreme needs us to be," Gunner replied.

"Has he spoken to you?" Fetch asked. "Have you received any orders?"

"He is a tad preoccupied at the moment. The last I heard his voice, he said we were to wait."

"Wait? For what?"

Gunner's gaze drifted down from the temple to the rubble in front of them. "For this, I assume," he said.

The Deathstalkers parted as a robed figure with a staff emerged from the remains of the settlement. Behind him, a dark monolith followed, hovering horizontally over the ground as the Terrormancer shepherded it away from the temple.

The members of the Secret Army all stood still as stone while the Terrormancer approached. Gunner frowned as the robed figure neared, his black eyes and bone-white face becoming more visible the closer he came.

"Why have you removed the monolith from its chamber?" Gunner asked.

"The temple issssss no longer sssssafe," the Terrormancer replied. "The blood of the Ancientssss proved too ssssstrong for the Sssssupreme. And now, Paragonsssss have arrived to protect her."

"Paragons?" Gunner said. "You speak of the Royal Vanguard."

"My brothers sssssshall handle them," the Terrormancer said. "But jussssst to be certain of successsss, the Sssssupreme gave me orderssss for you."

"What is the Supreme's will?"

"You are to go into the temple. And you are to kill the Princesssss, along with any who may sssssstill try to protect her."

Gunner nodded. "The Supreme can rest assured. The last of Legacy Prime shall die this day."

"Make it sssssso," the Terrormancer said. "For the glory of our Lordssssss."

The robed figure then pushed past the group, which parted to allow him and the monolith to continue on toward the far mountains. Deathstalkers followed them obediently, acting as guard dogs for the evil slab of rock.

"Weapons ready, men," Gunner said as he unslung his blaster rifle. "Our mission is simple. Kill the Vanguard. Kill the Princess. Kill anything that gets in our way. Let's move."

The small army of slythru-controlled Royal Guard and Peacekeepers all took out their weapons, readying themselves as they began to venture toward the dark temple, intent on ensuring one thing and one thing only...

That Princess Glorianna would not survive the fight to come.

# CHAPTER 15

In the command center of Starbase Sirius, the hyperspace counterpart to Megabase Cygnus, Star Commander Qualen stood at his station, fielding numerous strange reports that were flooding in from outside of hyperspace.

"What the blazes is going on out there?" Qualen grumbled. "Operations! Report!"

"We're picking up multiple plasma exchanges, Star Commander," a sensor technician replied. "Both around the planet and within the system."

"Is Omnicron under attack?"

"Sensors show no hostile contacts. Hyperspace is clear, sir."

"Comms," barked Qualen. "Get me Starkeeper Cohaagen. Now!"

"Megabase Cygnus is not answering any of our hails, Star Commander," said the young, female communications technician. "I've tried all dedicated subspace channels. No one is responding."

Qualen scowled. As far as he was concerned, a firefight in the mother dimension coupled with a communications blackout was tantamount to an attack, despite hyperspace being completely clear of hostiles. "Move us to red alert," he commanded. "All hands at battle stations. Ready all drone wings and fighter squadrons. Contact battlegroups H5, H6, and H7. Have them all prepare to exit hyperspace. If Omnicron is under attack, we need to join in on the fight and quickly!"

Red lights flashed as alarms blared throughout the massive starbase, signaling to its personnel that this was not a drill and to report to their action stations. Drone fighters were launched as pilots scrambled to get ready to fly their aircraft. Alpha Force squadrons began suiting up, in case they were needed. Hyperspace patrols regrouped in preparation to join in with the starship deployment, and the capital ship battlegroups all prepared to exit the hyperspace dimension and to join the fight.

As Star Commander Qualen readied himself to have his forces deploy, his sensor technician called out. "Sir!" he said. "Megabase Cygnus is opening a hyperspace window!"

Qualen turned his attention to the command center's viewscreen as a window to the mother dimension opened, revealing Megabase Cygnus. His eyes widened as he saw the Megabase had angled its primary megalaser directly at Starbase Sirius, and its barrel was already glowing bright green with a charge.

"Star Commander!" cried the technician. "Cygnus's megalaser is charged! They're preparing to fire!"

As the barrel of Cygnus's megalaser grew more brilliant, Star Commander Qualen's breath caught in his throat. In those briefest of moments as he watched the superweapon that was meant to protect the home system from the greatest of threats bear down upon his station, a chilling realization settled in upon him.

An attack was, indeed, underway – and he was powerless to stop it.

Cygnus fired its megalaser, the powerful beam instantly cutting through Starbase Sirius. The station was violently ripped apart in a massive explosion that was both magnificent and horrifying in its scale. The station's destruction wiped out all nearby drones, defense matrix platforms, and fightercraft, which had managed to launch from it. Two capital ships from the closest battlegroup were badly damaged in the blast, as well.

Verrutus stood in the command center of Megabase Cygnus, gazing upon the fiery destruction he'd just unleashed with satisfaction.

"Starbase Sirius has been destroyed, Supreme," reported one of his thralls.

"Long past time someone put that dog down," Verrutus said. "Begin recharging the megalaser. Bring the station around to aim it at the planet. The megalaser is no Planetkiller beam… but it will do enough damage to make Omnicron uninhabitable for millennia."

"Recharging megalaser now, Supreme," his thrall responded. "Reorienting the Megabase toward the planet. Estimated time of reorientation, one hour."

Verrutus looked at the image of Omnicron on the display of the command console at which he stood. If the Deathlord had had a mouth, he would have been smiling.

In one hour, all life on the surface of that planet would be completely wiped out.

The Wild Ones were sharing a cell in the detention center of Megabase Cygnus. Buff was passing the time by (badly) singing some songs. Buchignani was lounging on one of the cots, his eyes closed and his feet kicked up. Siv sat stoically as Kamm paced around the cell, looking out of its shield wall into the corridor.

"How much longer do you think we're going to be here?" Kamm asked, looking restless.

"Don't rightly know," drawled Buchignani. "Boss said he needed us here. So we're here."

"I still don't understand why we had to let ourselves get arrested," grumbled Siv. "Moriarty knew we were gonna get nicked when he had us leave the planet. What good are we sitting in a cell?"

"I'm less worried about sitting here and more worried about staying here," grumbled Kamm.

"Relax, buckaroos," Buchignani said. "The boss-bot said that Alabaster fellow was in on this. He'd get us released when the time was right. All we need to do is sit tight. Easy money."

"Ee-yo," chimed in Buff. "What if… you know… Heckubus Moriarty isn't as smart as we think he is, and we just borked ourselves?"

"That thought has crossed my mind as well," said Kamm.

"Well, if'n that is the case, I suppose we'd just need ta break ourselves out of here," Buchignani replied, nonchalantly. "We still got our Ace-in-the-hole, after all."

Suddenly, the overhead light in the cell they were in turned blue. The group looked up with interest at the sudden change in the color spectrum of their enclosure.

"Greetings, Wild Ones!" the light said as it flickered.

"Ee-yo," said Buff in astonishment. "The light is talkin' to us!"

"A talkin' light?" said Buchignani. "Now I've seen everything."

"My name is #00B2EE$^{n}$. I am a sentient color and special agent with the Imperial Intelligence Agency, assigned by Chief Alabaster to assist and to watch over you."

"A sentient color?" asked Siv. "Do you have to be blue? I've always liked green better."

"Trust me, you do not want any shades of green here. They are incredibly lazy and unreliable colors," replied #00B2EE$^{n}$, snootily. "Regardless, I've come to warn you that you are in terrible danger!"

"Finally, something interesting," said Kamm.

Buchignani sat up, a curious look on his face. "Danger, eh?" he said. "What type of danger we talkin' here?"

"Long story short, the Deathlord Supreme Verrutus and his Secret Army have taken over the base and launched an attack on Omnicron. Members of his slythru controlled security force are on their way here now to torture you for information concerning the plans of Heckubus Moriarty, and when they are done, they will most likely kill you."

"Ee-yo. That *does* sound dangerous."

"And terrible," muttered Siv.

"Don't suppose there's anything you can do to help us out?" asked Kamm.

"Unfortunately, since I do not have a body, there is very little I can actually do other than observe and report," #00B2EE$^{n}$ replied. "I had hoped that by warning you ahead of time, you four would be prepared to defend yourselves when the Secret Army arrives."

"Thanks for the heads-up, little blue buckaroo," said Buchignani as he got back to his feet. "We'll take things from here."

"I must say, considering the incredible amount of danger you are all in, none of you seems very concerned at the moment."

"That's because there ain't nothin' to be concerned about," Buchignani said with a smile. "We still got an Ace to play, after all."

It was then Kamm heard movement from the corridor outside the cell. "Heads up," he said. "We have company."

"Oh dear," said #00B2EE$^{n}$, nervously. "I wish there were more I could do to help! These men are armed and well trained."

"Don't sweat it, talking blue light guy," said Siv as he rose to his feet, as well. "We got this."

Four armed security officers appeared, looking grim and malicious as they gazed into the cell. The Wild Ones all gathered in front of the shield wall. Buchignani crossed his arms, appraising the slythru-controlled assassins, smugly.

"Howdy, y'all," he said. "Heard yer here to kill us."

"Torture, first," replied the lead officer. "The Supreme wishes to know everything about your association with the robot Heckubus Moriarty. Then you die."

"Yeah, that ain't happenin'," stated Buchignani. "I suppose the sportsman-like thing ta do in this situation would be to give y'all the chance ta walk away peaceful-like. But, then again, seein' as how y'all are bein' mind controlled by an evil all-powerful Deathlord fella, I'm thinkin' it would just be a waste of both our times. So, what's say we just get right to it, shall we?"

The lead officer scowled. "Sounds good to me," he replied.

With that, Buchignani made an odd gesture with his hands. The security officers looked at him curiously, right before two of the officer's heads bashed together.

The dazed officers stumbled, grabbing their heads where they had hit each other. The other two officers looked at their companions in alarm, right before one of them was flung against the wall. He hit it hard and then doubled over as though he'd just been punched in the gut before he fell to the ground after looking like something had struck him across the face.

The Wild Ones all stood with amused looks on their faces as the four officers continued to suffer from the invisible assault. They flinched when one officer had his arm broken. Chuckled when another screamed as he was thrust into the wall head first. And high-fived when one officer tried to crawl away, only to be dragged back and his head repeatedly bounced off the floor.

The lead officer pulled his weapon, firing his blaster wildly, fear in his eyes as he was not even sure what he was trying to hit. His wrist twisted and snapped, before the blaster was pulled from his hand. Its butt was then used to smash the man across his face, knocking him out and sending him to the ground.

When all the officers had been dispatched, the Wild Ones all clapped and whistled in approval.

"Ee-yo! That's what I'm talkin' 'bout!" cheered Buff.

"That was good. You can tell he's been practicing," said Kamm.

"You guys see that one that tried to crawl away?" asked Siv with a chuckle. "They always try to get away! Classic!"

"I say…" stated #00B2EE$^{n}$, curiously. "What just happened?"

"Ee-yo! That's Aneel!"

"Aneel? What's an Aneel?"

"Our Ace-in-the-hole," drawled Buchignani. "Thing about Aneel is that he can't hear or speak, but his eyesight is pretty darn good. So when we need his help, we just use hand signals."

"Observe," said Kamm as he used two of his six hands to make a gesture. Not long after, one of the security keys was lifted from an unconscious officer and swiped through the cell's lock, lowering the shield wall.

The Wild Ones wasted no time in stepping out of the cell and collecting the weapons from the unconscious guards, before dragging them into the cell and raising the shield once more to ensure they wouldn't come after them. #00B2EE$^{n}$ hopped from the light in the cell to the light in the corridor as the Wild Ones regrouped.

"Though I commend you all on the expert and unexpected nature of your escape, I fear you are not out of danger quite yet," said #00B2EE$^{n}$. "The Megabase is filled with members of the Secret Army."

"Nothing we can't handle," said Siv.

"I clocked the route they took us from the hangar to the brig," said Kamm. "It's not far. We can be back on *The Shamrock* in no time."

"That is certainly one of your options," said #00B2EE$^{n}$. "However, I fear I must stress the severity of what is currently happening. The Empire's capital is under attack. Enemies are everywhere. Thousands are dying by the minute. As an agent of the I.I.A., I am duty bound to try and do something to salvage the situation and save Omnicron. However, I am limited in what I am capable of. With your assistance, we may be able to stop this attack."

"Ee-yo, I dunno," complained Buff. "Sounds like work."

"It could save countless lives!"

"Meh. We don't know anybody on the planet all that well," said Siv, with a shrug.

"You'd be celebrated as heroes!"

"Never been much for the limelight," replied Kamm. "Too many creditors and ex-wives I don't want knowing where I am."

"Surely, there is something that could convince you to step forward and assist me in this time of the Empire's greatest need?" pleaded #00B2EE$^{n}$.

The Wild Ones all looked at one another, thoughtfully. Buchignani smiled.

“Answer me this, little blue buckaroo,” Buchignani said as he checked the plasma clip on his blaster. “What kind of reward could one expect for savin’ the Empire?”

# CHAPTER 16

"Battlegroups 8 and 9 have finally arrived, my Lord," reported Commander Neelson from his station on the bridge of *The Shieldbearer*. "The entire Maxima fleet is now present. All fifty-one vessels."

Gebhard glared at the viewscreen, taking stock of the large number of enemy ships standing between him and his planet. "And what is the final tally of Deathlord fleet?" he asked.

"We're counting eleven battlegroups, my Lord," Neelson responded. "Fifty-five ships."

Gebhard scowled. "Well, if there were ever any doubt they were aware of the size of our fleet, I guess that answers the question," he said. "They came practically ready for a one-on-one engagement."

"Four more ships will not make much of a difference," General Wessux stated, confidently. "Our fleet is state of the art. Each of our ships is worth two of theirs, easily."

"Let us hope you are correct about that, General," replied Gebhard, not looking so sure.

At the back of the bridge, Wilvelm and Fredreek were huddled together with Alpha Force, listening in on the preparations for battle. "Fifty-five Dreadnaughts," Fredreek muttered. "You gotta figure each one is comparable to one of our own, with equivalent Dark Soldier brigades and starfighter squads."

"That's a lot of Deathlords," Roadblock grumbled as he pulled out his sidearm and checked it.

Copperhyde grimaced at him. "Ya expecting to fight many Deathlords here on the bridge, soldier boy?" the mercenary asked.

"Don't know about those Dreadnaughts, but the Planetkillers had some sophisticated teleportation technology," Roadblock replied. "They could beam entire boarding parties onto ships in a blink of an eye. Somebody needs to be prepared to defend this bridge. So yeah, I'm gonna play it safe rather than sorry."

The rest of Alpha Force nodded and pulled out their plasma pistols to make sure they were loaded. Copperhyde shifted uncomfortably on his feet as the wisdom of Roadblock's words settled in on him, prompting him also to draw his sidearm and check it.

Fred turned to Wil. "Do you think maybe we should…"

"Couldn't hurt," Wil replied, before heading to the bridge's weapons locker and unlocking it, pulling out two blaster pistols for him and his friend.

"The fleet has entered formation, my Lord," stated General Wessux. "All ships are networking with *The Shieldbearer* to coordinate our advance."

Gebhard nodded. "Very well," he replied. "Give the order. Have us move to engage the Deathlords."

"Advancing the fleet now," said Wessux.

An ear-piercing scream suddenly erupted on the bridge as all incarnations of Bob lost their forms, melting into puddles on the ground. The rest of the bridge crew all reacted in alarm to the troubling incident. Gebhard shot to his feet, looking over to where Ambassador Bob had been moments before, only to find a pink puddle in its stead.

"Bob!" Gebhard cried. "What's happened to Bob?"

Wilvelm and the others gazed around as the bridge team rushed to the puddles, trying to find a way to assist what amounted to half their crew.

"Is this some type of attack?" asked Roadblock in concern.

"If it is, it's a blasted brilliant one," replied Fredreek. "Bob is manning half the Maxima fleet. Without him, our numbers just dropped significantly."

"Someone call the infirmary!" Wessux barked. "Get a doctor up here, now!"

"General," said Neelson from his station. "We're getting reports from all across the fleet. Their Bobs have all lost form, as well."

Wessux frowned. "Without him, we'll barely be able to man *The Shieldbearer*, let alone the rest of our ships."

"How could this happen?" asked Gebhard as he knelt beside the puddle that used to be Ambassador Bob. "What could harm Bob in such a way?"

Wilvelm frowned as a sinking feeling began to take hold of his gut. "If the Deathlords somehow figured out a way to kill Bob, it could be the start of an attack against the fleet," he said, turning to Roadblock. "Maybe your worry about a boarding party wasn't so far-fetched after all."

Roadblock set his jaw, looking not the least bit happy at the prospect of being right. "We should suit up, in case this is the start of something," he said. "Where's the closest Alpha Force armory?"

"A couple levels down, toward the center of the ship," replied Fred.

"You guys keep an eye on things here," Roadblock ordered as he turned to his squad mates. "The rest of you, come with me. We need to get armored."

"Hoo-ah," the others replied.

As Roadblock and the rest of his Alpha Force squad made their way to the bridge's exit, the puddles of Bob began to stir.

"Look!" said Commander Neelson as he pointed to the pink ooze. "Something's happening!"

Gebhard got back to his feet and backed away as Ambassador Bob and his other incarnations began to take shape once more. Wilvelm stepped forward, looking at the shapes the ooze was forming into with concern.

"That doesn't look like Bob…" he said.

Roadblock and the others stopped at the bridge's exit, turning to see the ooze forming into the shape of Deathlords. The incarnation of Ambassador Bob finished its reformation right in front of Gebhard, its eyes flaring to life with fiery red light.

Before Wil knew it, a small army of Deathlord incarnations had formed on the bridge, glaring at the shocked and surprised crew, which they easily outnumbered.

Gebhard looked at the gelatinous Deathlord looming before him, an expression of abject shock on his face. "Bob…" he said. "What… what's going on?"

"My name is not really Bob," the Deathlord replied. "My true name is Verrutus. Deathlord Supreme."

"Verrutus!" hissed Fred, turning toward Wil. "That's the thing Jack warned everyone about! The Deathlord that controls the Secret Army!"

Wilvelm felt fear grip his chest as he looked around at the enemy that now surrounded them. "It was Bob all along…" he said. "And he's everywhere!"

"Everybody run!" Roadblock shouted, opening fire on the Deathlords.

Verrutus sprang into action, his many incarnations rushing forward. His arms morphed into blades, stabbing through General Wessux and Commander Neelson before the two men even had a chance to react.

The crew of the bridge all screamed as they began to be slaughtered. Some turned and ran for the exit as Alpha Force gave them cover. Wil, Fred, and Copperhyde also opened fire. Most of their blasts tore through the different Verrutus incarnations, their gelatinous ooze reforming before the plasma bolts could do any real damage. It was only when they were hit with enough bolts to keep them from healing that they melted. But for each Verrutus that fell, there were more that continued to tear through the bridge.

Verrutus reached out and grabbed Gebhard by the neck, gazing into the man's surprised eyes as chaos reigned around them.

"H-how is this… possible?" Gebhard asked.

"Through a great deal of planning and patience," Verrutus replied. "Admittedly, we had a different type of ambush in mind for your fleet, but now that I have been revealed, this shall have to do."

"But… I know you!" Gebhard hissed. "We're friends! Allies!"

"You never really knew me, you insufferable idiot. You saw what I allowed you to see, all the while granting me access to every corner of your little planetary system. Why do you think our raids here were so effective? But I couldn't have done this alone. Your wife was instrumental in setting the stage for our attacks."

Gebhard's eyes went wide with confusion. "My… my wife?"

"She disabled your entire communications network before raising that dark temple," bragged Verrutus. "Your planet will be destroyed, thanks to her. And many more will follow! It's a pity she's not here to see this. After all, your wife has been waiting for this to happen for a long, long time…"

Without further preamble, Verrutus stabbed Gebhard through the chest, the Deathlord's arm having transformed into a massive blade. Gebhard gasped in pain, clutching at the arm that had just impaled him. As the man stood, dying, Verrutus leaned toward his ear.

"She never loved you," he whispered.

That was the last thing Gebhard Skyborn heard before his life was extinguished.

"NO!" cried Wilvelm.

Verrutus yanked his arm from Gebhard's body, letting the man's corpse fall unceremoniously to the floor. He turned to face Wil and Fred as they both rushed forward, blasting away at him and dispatching that incarnation.

"Fools!" shouted another incarnation of Verrutus that stepped toward them. "I am a Deathlord! I cannot die!"

"Can you shut up?" shouted back Roadblock as he and his team blasted away at him.

The large number of Verrutus incarnations formed up and began marching toward Wil and the other survivors on the bridge. The group began to back away toward the exit.

"We gotta get out of here!" Roadblock cried. "There are too many of them!"

"There are even more Bobs deeper into the ship!" exclaimed Fred. "They were everywhere!"

"Well, we can't stay here!" snarled Copperhyde. "So what do we do?"

Wilvelm scowled at the encroaching army of Deathlords.

"We run," he said.

With that, the group turned and retreated from the bridge, pursued by Verrutus, and heading toward even more incarnations of him.

*****

*The Shieldbearer's* medical bay was in pure chaos as injured people poured in. Some were badly wounded. Others were scared, looking for a safe place to hide. It was clear that Doctor Samsers and his assistants were completely overwhelmed by the sudden influx of panicked people.

"Get this one a bed, immediately!" ordered Samsers as he caught a crewman bleeding from a massive belly wound. "Get some sealant foam on his wound! STAT!"

The ship shook from what could only have been plasma fire. The doctor had been alerted that the fleet was about to engage with Deathlord ships and to be ready for casualties, but surely the bridge would have alerted him before engaging the enemy? The alarms hadn't even rung to signal the crew for combat.

"What the blazes is going on?" muttered Samsers in frustration. "What's happening out there?"

"The fleet… we're firing on each other…" said the man with the belly wound.

"What?" asked Samsers. "Why?"

"Bob…" croaked the man. "It's… Bob…"

Samsers looked at the man in confusion. "Bob? I don't understand."

"He's a Deathlord… he's the one… who's attacking us…"

Samsers' eyes went wide. "Great Observer…" he muttered. "There are hundreds of him on the ship! If he's the one attacking…" Samsers turned to one of his assistants. "Quickly!" he barked. "Seal the doors!"

"But, Doctor, the wounded are still arriving—"

"We can't allow him in!" said Samsers, urgently, as he rushed toward the med bay's door to seal it. "We have to focus on saving those who are already here, before—"

Right as Samsers reached the door, it hissed open, revealing an incarnation of Verrutus, his eyes burning red. Doctor Samsers barely had any time to react to the Deathlord's appearance before Verrutus shot his arm toward the man, impaling him with its spiked tip.

The Doctor cried out, a feeble gurgle escaping from him before Verrutus yanked his arm back, allowing the man's body to fall to the floor.

The others in the med bay screamed in alarm. None of them was of the Secret Army, and therefore, there was no reason to allow them to live. Verrutus quickly dispatched each of them, manipulating his protoplasmic form into instruments of death which struck without mercy.

When all who'd been gathered in the med bay were dead, the Deathlord turned his burning red eyes toward a particular bed where Grohm lay. The Rognok's skin was almost completely charred off. Small black patches still held on to his fibrous dark red muscle. He was heavily bandaged, but bits and pieces of his tough grey hide appeared to have grown back sporadically.

Verrutus approached Grohm, looking down upon the massive alien who lay stoically on the medical examination table, the equipment monitoring him still not knowing what to make of his vital signs. Verrutus's fiery eyes narrowed as he gazed upon the Rognok.

"So, we meet again," Verrutus said. "You and your entire race have always been a thorn in the sides of those of us who follow the Lords of the Void. I'd hoped to rid myself of you back on Omnicron and again when the little Lordlings tried to take custody of you. But when the Maxima fleet came upon you in that mining colony, I knew I would never get a better opportunity. I convinced Lord Gebhard you were attacking your captors and fired the plasma battery that hit you myself. You cannot imagine the elation I experienced, seeing you burn and crumple from its impact. And yet, it's unclear as to whether or not you actually died from it."

Verrutus lifted his arm, forming it into a deadly blade.

"Your entire species has always been stubborn in that regard," he continued. "The Ancients designed you to be the ultimate weapon. And that weapon has been notoriously hard to kill. I do not wish to leave this to chance. I will make sure you are dead, Rognok. And it pleases me to no end that I am the one who gets to kill you myse—"

Before Verrutus could finish his sentence, Grohm's massive hand latched onto him and unceremoniously flung the Deathlord across the room and into the wall with such force, the protoplasmic ooze he was comprised of splattered in all directions.

Grohm then opened his eyes. He sat up, sneering. Though the Rognok's body may have been ravaged by the plasma blast the Deathlord had just confessed to firing upon him, one thing could be said for certain…

Grohm wasn't dead. But he was extremely pissed off.

# Chapter 17

The Earthship flew through the tether over Eionmeer and into the Conclave universe, heading straight for the temple as it was engulfed in the ghostly beams being shot at it from two different planets. Once inside the pocket universe, Jack was able to get a closer look at the other tether and the planet to which it led.

"That's… that's Maxima!" said Mourdock as he gazed at the image on the viewscreen.

"Oh, dear," lamented Professor Green as he looked at the scanner readings from his console. "I'm picking up multiple sensor contacts on the other side of that tether. There is a space battle going on over there, and a great number of Deathlord ships are present."

Jack frowned. "First the Conclave, then Eionmeer, and now Maxima…" he said. "What are the Deathlords up to?"

Jack turned and looked at Mourdock whose face was grim.

"I know Maxima is your real home, Mourdock," Jack said. "After we finish rescuing those in the Conclave, we can go check out what's happening over there."

Mourdock nodded. "I will have to trust that my father and his fleet are able to handle whatever is going on," he said. "Right now, our priority must be the Conclave."

"Whatever we're going to do, we need to be quick about it," said Boone as he gazed at the sensor readings of his station. "There appear to be Deathlord ships headed directly for the tether leading from Maxima. They'll be here very soon."

"Then there's no time to waste," Jack said. "Professor, can you begin locking onto the life signs within the Conclave and teleporting them onboard?"

Green frowned as he tapped away on the console at his station. "It would appear that whatever those beams are that are engulfing the temple are interfering with any attempts to scan it with our sensors," the Professor replied. "I'm afraid we cannot get teleportation locks on anyone in there."

Jack grimaced and looked toward Mourdock. "Guess we're going to have to go inside and extract everyone ourselves," Jack said.

"If that's what it will take," Mourdock replied. "But who knows how long we'll spend bringing every survivor we find back to the ship if we cannot teleport them directly."

"I may have a solution for that!" chimed in Green, cheerily. "The Earthship still has the specifications for the teleportation signal booster we used to rescue the Princess from the Sunshell. If you bring that with you, you should have no issues teleporting anyone you find back to the ship!"

"Sounds like a plan to me," said Jack.

"Agreed," said Mourdock. "Take us in."

Jack flew the Earthship toward the temple's outer ring, docking with the structure at the spot Krupp had specified. Those onboard quickly made their way to the docking hatch where a haggard group of survivors awaited them.

"Thank the Great Observer you came," said Krupp as he and the rest of the Unlikelies helped the others inside. "We weren't sure if you'd get our message."

"Came in loud and clear," Jack said as he looked at the group. Krupp, Scrappy, Snodgrass, Soundwave, and Morosa were all there. "Where's Flitter?" he asked.

"We could not find her," Morosa said. "We picked up as many as we could while making our way here. Unfortunately, we do not know where she is."

"She might be at the clinic," Scrappy said. "Or somewhere on the Water Ring level. I believe she had classes there today."

"<More likely, she's trying to help those who are being affected by that ghost energy>," Snodgrass stated. "<You know how Flitter is. If the world is ending, she'll be there trying to save everyone on it.>"

Jack nodded. "Okay," he said. "I'll keep an eye out for her when we go inside."

Krupp's eyes went wide upon hearing that. "Inside?" he said. "Jack, you have no idea how bad it is in there!"

"We don't have any other choice," Jack replied. "Our sensors can't get past the energy that's surrounding the temple. If we're going to rescue any survivors, we've got to find them and use a signal booster to get them out."

Krupp looked to the rest of the group, asking a silent question. Morosa and Snodgrass both nodded to him in agreement. "Then we'll come with you," he said. "We're not going to let you go in there alone."

“He won’t be alone. I’ll be at his side,” said Mourdock. “And no offense to you and your companions, but you’ll only slow us down.”

“Mourdock’s right,” Jack said. “Stay here. Help guard the Earthship and get the survivors we send your way onboard. You guys have been through enough already. Let Mourdock and me handle this.”

Krupp frowned but nodded. “If that’s what you think is best,” he said.

Jack waved his hand and a compartment on the wall of the Earthship’s docking bay flipped open, revealing a rack of plasma rifles. He grabbed them and gave each of his friends one. “If you need anything, just ask the ship to manifest it for you,” Jack said before handing a rifle to Agent Boone. “Since you’re the closest thing we have to a soldier here, do you think you could oversee everyone guarding the ship?”

Boone nodded as he accepted the weapon. “Compared to what I just went through on Eionmeer, this will be a piece of cake.”

Jack then looked to Sawbones. “Paragon MacCrusty, will you—”

“Tend to the wounded?” finished Sawbones. “Of course, man! That’s what I do.”

“She’s a doctor, apparently,” said Boone, wryly. “Has she mentioned that, yet?”

Jack then looked at Professor Green as he approached with the cylindrical metal signal booster, which he handed to Jack along with an earpiece communicator. “Radio in when you find survivors. I shall stay behind and operate the teleporter,” Green said.

“Thanks,” replied Jack. “Hold down the fort. We’ll be back as soon as we can.”

“Here,” said Krupp as he handed Jack and Mourdock some practice saber handles. “This is what we used to fight our way to the outer ring. Those inside who’ve turned… they’re not really evil. Just sick. These won’t kill them, but they will still protect you.”

“Good idea,” said Jack as he ignited the practice saber and looked at Mourdock. “You ready to do this?”

Mourdock activated his practice saber, as well. “Ready,” he replied.

With that, Jack and Mourdock exited the Earthship and took off down the corridor of the outer ring, using their enhanced speed to zoom away. Krupp watched them go, a worried look on his face.

"Don't look so glum, kid," said Boone, reassuringly. "A Hero of the Empire and the most famous Paragon in the galaxy just went off to save the day."

"Yes," replied Krupp. "But if they get into trouble… who's going to save them?"

It didn't take long for Jack and Mourdock to come to one of the access tubes leading toward the temple, its transportation pod appearing to have been destroyed. They hopped through the broken pod and began running down the tube, quickly reaching the inside of the Conclave. However, the moment they crossed the threshold into the temple, Mourdock cried out, grabbing his head and stumbling to the ground. Jack immediately stopped and came to his aid.

"Mourdock!" he cried. "Are you okay?"

Mourdock looked pale, a pained expression on his face as he cradled his head. "I'm fine… it's just my head. It feels like it's about to split open."

"Maybe… maybe you should go back?" Jack said, looking around at the ghostly energy seeping from the walls with concern.

"No. I'm fine," grunted Mourdock as he climbed back to his feet. "I just may not be able to keep pace with you as well as I thought I could."

Jack frowned. "Don't worry, we'll take it slower. But if you feel like it's becoming too much for you, I want you to teleport to the ship immediately."

Jack offered Mourdock the signal booster. Mourdock nodded and took the device, sliding it into his belt. "Agreed," he said.

Jack was concerned about how being inside the temple was affecting Mourdock. He, himself, didn't feel anything strange, but there was no telling how the ghost energy was infecting people. Regardless, Jack believed that if anyone could handle it, it was Mourdock.

The two immediately set out searching the temple, going room to room looking for any survivors. The ones they found, they teleported to the Earthship. But more often than not, all they came across were bodies. Some of them were people they knew, while others were nameless victims of the infected.

"All the dead are Initiates," Mourdock noted. "There's not a single Paragon among them."

"Me and my classmates weren't as affected as you seem to be," Jack observed. "Maybe the corruption is stronger among those who've spent more time in the Conclave for some reason?"

Mourdock frowned. "If that is the case, then those who have turned will be extremely dangerous, as they will be the most skilled."

"Well, then, I guess we should be careful," said Jack. "But either we've been really lucky, or all those who've been infected are hiding somewhere, because we've found nothing but bodies so far."

"Either way, we should remain on guard," Mourdock said as they continued on. "I do not wish to fight other Paragons if we can avoid it."

"Agreed," said Jack.

Whatever had happened in the Conclave had damaged a great portion of it. When Jack and Mourdock came upon the Workshop of Wonders, it had been completely ransacked and all its machinery smashed. An electrical storm was raging uncontrolled within the confines of Paragon Tessla's workshop, the Wezden's[13] fried remains at its center. Even Master Wallbeard's wall had been broken down, the Paragon's majestic beard now shredded and strewn across the floor.

With each grim discovery, Jack became more and more heartbroken. There was so much death and destruction in a place meant to foster the best in those who lived there. He simply didn't understand how such a thing could happen.

"Stay centered," Mourdock advised, noting Jack's reaction to the discoveries. "I know this is hard, but we must remain focused and not allow our emotions to get the better of us."

Jack nodded, trying to push aside his feelings. He glanced at Mourdock, who looked paler than he'd been previously, sweat collecting on his brow. "How are you holding up?" Jack asked.

"I am fine," Mourdock said, not sounding fine in the slightest. "I just need to keep moving."

Truth be told, Jack thought Mourdock looked like he was about to collapse. But he believed Mourdock would hold true to his word and teleport away if he were in danger of turning. Frankly, Jack couldn't think of a worse possible development than an evil Mourdock Skyborn.

As they continued their journey deeper into the Conclave, Jack and Mourdock heard screams coming from further down the hallway in which they were travelling. They both rushed forward, rounding the corner to see a group

---

[13] Wezdens are red-hued humanoid aliens with stout rounded bodies, big eyes, and antennae that sprout from their foreheads.

of children running down the corridor, tears in their panicked eyes as they were chased by Master Fareia. This wasn't the kind, motherly Master Fareia Jack had known. This woman's hair had gone as white as her skin, with ugly red, purple, and green veins bulging in her neck and cheeks. Her eyes were now completely black, and she had a look of pure malice on her face as she chased after the Boarders with a moonfyre dagger.

"Quick! Get behind us!" Jack ordered, rushing forward to put himself between the corrupted Paragon and the children.

"Master Fareia, stop!" Mourdock commanded.

Master Fareia halted her advance and gazed at Mourdock and Jack with disgust as her children cowered behind them. "Those kiddies are mine!" she hissed, pointing her blade toward the children. "They've been naughty. Oh, so naughty! And now they must be *punished!*"

"She's mad we didn't change, too," whimpered Xanpher, one of the Boarders. "None of us did! And now she wants to kill us!"

Mourdock glared at Fareia. "This isn't you, Master," Mourdock said. "You love these children. You're their guardian…"

"They are nothing more to me than a burden!" Fareia cried. "And the sooner they're dead, the sooner I'm free of them!!!"

Fareia let loose a blood curdling scream and launched herself forward. Jack reacted immediately, hurling his practice saber at her, the energy blade embedding itself in her chest and causing her to fall to the ground. Jack and Mourdock both looked at the woman as she writhed on the floor.

"What happened to her?" Jack muttered. "What could do this to someone?"

Mourdock frowned before turning his attention back to the frightened Boarders. "Everything's okay," he assured them. "You're going to be safe now."

The children sniffled. "What's wrong with Master Fareia?" asked Relli. "Why did she turn so mean?"

"She's just sick. But we're going to get her help, I promise," said Mourdock. "Right now, though, we need to get you all somewhere safe. Now huddle together. We're going to teleport you to Jack's spaceship and get you out of here, okay?"

The children all grouped together and quickly gave Mourdock a grateful hug. Mourdock took the teleportation signal booster and held it out, activating it. Jack notified Professor Green over his communicator, and immediately, the Boarders all teleported away. When they were gone, Jack pulled his practice saber from Master Fareia's chest, causing her to groan.

"What should we do with her?" Jack asked. "I don't know if teleporting her to the ship would be the best idea, even with someone as skilled as Paragon MacCrusty there to help her."

"Agreed," said Mourdock. "For now, keep your practice saber active to keep her incapacitated. We will figure out what to do with her later. But we will not give up on her."

"You… fools…" choked Master Fareia. "You… cannot… undo what has been done…"

"And what exactly has been done here?" asked Jack. "What's happened to you?"

Fareia chuckled. "I have been… reborn…" she said, a gleeful look in her dark eyes. "Transformed… into something… greater than I was! And this change… is permanent! There is… no coming… back from it!"

"I don't believe that," said Jack.

"Nor do I," replied Mourdock. "You are a good, kind woman, Master Fareia. Not this monster you have now become. I have faith you can fight this and return to us."

"The only thing… I wish to fight…" said Master Fareia with a sneer. "Is *you!!!*"

Master Fareia cried out, holding her hand toward Jack and Mourdock. Mourdock acted quickly, pulling Jack behind him and holding his hand out, as well.

"LOOK OUT!" Mourdock shouted.

Mourdock manifested a graviton wave just as Master Fareia's gravity pulse erupted. Though Mourdock's counter prevented them from being harmed, the force of the pulse still pushed Jack and him back, even as the pulse Master Fareia manifested crushed her to death.

Jack and Mourdock both frowned, looking down at the Paragon's mangled body. "Holy crap…" Jack muttered. "Why would she do that?"

"Whatever corruption had laid claim to her, it obviously made her act against her nature," Mourdock said. It looked as though Mourdock were about to say more when he started to collapse. Jack quickly caught him before he could hit the ground.

"Whoa!" Jack cried. "Dude! Are you okay?"

Mourdock shook his head, recovering and standing back up. "Yes…" he said. "Fending off that gravity pulse just took a bit of energy out of me."

"Mourdock, you're not looking so hot. Maybe you should go back to the ship…"

"I'm fine," Mourdock insisted. "And if I had not been here just now, you'd have been killed by that gravity blast. Do you really want me to leave you behind?"

Jack frowned. "No," he said.

"Then we keep going," stated Mourdock as he marched past Master Fareia's body.

Jack was still concerned about Mourdock's condition, but he followed his friend regardless. The two continued to search for survivors, making their way down a corridor when they heard voices in the distance. Jack and Mourdock slowed down, sticking close to a wall as they approached the Escrimar Arena of Fire Ring. The two peeked inside to see a group of infected Paragons gathered together, their skin all pale white and riddled with red, green, and purple veins. Their eyes were all completely black.

Krixus and Desmodus were among them, their appearance revealing they, too, were now among the corrupted. Tethers were opening up within the arena and the two Paragons directed the infected into them.

"I guess that's why we've run into so few of the corrupted," Jack said, quietly. "They're all leaving the Conclave through tethers!"

"That answers one question," Mourdock replied. "The question now is… where is it the corrupted are going?"

"Anywhere we can do the most damage," came a voice.

Jack and Mourdock both turned in alarm to see Tannyn standing a few feet away, having snuck up on them silently. The boy's skin was bone white, riddled with veins, and his eyes were black as tar. He stood, appraising Jack and Mourdock with a look of amusement as the two men slowly backed away.

"Tannyn?" said Jack.

"Heya, Hero," Tannyn replied. "Glad to see you came back. I was afraid I was going to have to hunt you down after I'd left. I've been itching for a rematch."

Jack frowned. "I don't want to have to fight you, Tannyn."

"I don't blame you. I wouldn't want to fight me either."

"You're not just taking on me," Jack cautioned. "You'll be fighting him, too."

Jack tilted his head toward Mourdock. Tannyn regarded Mourdock with his pure black eyes, not looking worried in the slightest. "The more the merrier, I say," he replied before snapping his fingers.

From adjoining corridors, more of the corrupted emerged. It was the rest of Tannyn's crew – Gunshow, Headbasher, the Femezon Ariandre, and the Karkovians Nix and Medkav. They all gathered together, facing off with Jack and Mourdock, grinning at the duo devilishly.

"Six against two…" muttered Jack as he held his practice saber at the ready. "I still think we can take you."

"You may want to begin rethinking," came Blackmane's voice as he emerged from behind the group, stepping to the forefront. Jack and Mourdock frowned at Blackmane's corrupted appearance. The Paragon smiled at the two men. "Ascendant. Earthman. Welcome back," he said. "I did not anticipate seeing the two of you again so soon. We gave you ample opportunity to get away."

Mourdock stepped forward, glaring at Blackmane. "What do you mean by that?" he asked.

"If it had been up to me, I'd have killed you both before you left on the Earthman's ship," stated Blackmane. "But our Master ordered we were to let you go. On the off-chance you both lived up to your reputations for fighting Deathlords, he did not want you around for… all this."

Blackmane gestured around him at the thin layer of ghostly energy that clung to the walls. Jack narrowed his eyes at Blackmane. "But… that was before the dark temples shot at the Conclave," Jack said. "You couldn't have been corrupted then."

"Oh, my colleagues and I were a part of this long before our transformations," Blackmane admitted. "As were you, Mourdock. Though you may not have realized it."

Mourdock scowled. "So… you, Krixus, and Desmodus… you were all in league with the saboteur?"

"Should have known," muttered Jack. "You were too big of a jerk not to be evil."

Blackmane chuckled. "Evil is simply a matter of perspective," he replied. "What I am a part of… what we are all now a part of… is something much grander. And I was honored to be approached and offered a role in the Great Rebirth. A chance to reshape this imperfect universe into something better than what it is. But in accepting that role, part of my responsibility was choosing who should be brought along with me. As you can see, I've already chosen…"

Blackmane gestured to the Initiates around him. His face then hardened, and he pointed toward Jack.

"And that choice does not include *you.*"

Blackmane manifested his red moonfyre sword, its tip directed toward Jack as the crimson blade hummed with stellar energy. Those around him stepped forward, the look on their faces almost feral as they prepared to attack.

Jack looked at the group nervously, taking a few tentative steps back. But whatever fear Jack was experiencing was obviously not shared by Mourdock who stood his ground. However, Jack knew if they were going to fight, practice sabers were not going to stop their opponents – particularly the highly skilled one with the moonfyre sword.

"Um… Mourdock," said Jack. "Maybe now would be a good time to retreat?"

"I think you're right," replied Mourdock.

Mourdock held out the teleportation signal booster, preparing to activate it… right before he gripped it with both hands and snapped it in two.

Jack looked at the remains of the device, stunned. "Dude!" he cried. "What did you just do?"

Mourdock then said something, his voice low and indistinct. Jack looked at him, confused.

"What did you say?" Jack asked.

"I said…" replied Mourdock as he turned to look at Jack, revealing his eyes to be pure black and his skin now chalky white with pulsing red, green, and purple veins beneath it. Mourdock's face was twisted in a sneer as he fought his losing battle with the corruption that was growing within him. And before the last vestige of the Mourdock Skyborn Jack knew was overtaken by the corruption, he gave Jack one final warning, and that warning was:

"*Run.*"

# CHAPTER 18

The Great Eye that had manifested closed, leaving the mental construct empty but for Anna and Shanks. The golden figure of the monk floated forward, smiling warmly at the Princess.

"Brother Shanks," Anna said, returning his smile. "How is it you are here?"

"In order to help you, I had to ascend to a different plane of existence," Shanks replied. "I had to be able to interact with you as Verrutus did. And doing so required me to shed the constraints of my body."

"Shed your body?" Anna asked. "You mean you're… you're dead?"

"In some ways. In others, I've never been more alive."

Anna frowned. "You died to help me. I'm so sorry."

"Do not be sorry, Princess. It was my duty to serve and an honor to fulfill that duty. Though I aided in this fight, it was you who finally tapped into the power of the Ancients and vanquished the Deathlord. I am proud of you, and you should be, as well."

"Verrutus is not vanquished," Anna said, looking troubled. "I pushed him out of my mind, but my slythru still feels his influence. I can sense Verrutus now. He is furious, and he is exerting control over his Secret Army to exact revenge. We must do something to stop him."

"I fear I have done all I can to aid in this fight," Shanks replied, smiling sadly. "I do not know how to describe it, but I feel as though I am being called away from this place. From this point forward, you will have to rely on yourself to defeat the Deathlord."

"But… I'm not sure I can do this alone."

"I did not say you would be alone," Shanks said, gently. "Just that you would have to rely on yourself. There is great power within you, Glorianna. Much of that power comes from you, not the Ancients. Remember, you are a *luminous* being. Do not be afraid to allow that light of yours to shine, big and bright and beautiful, now and forever."

Anna nodded. She could see the light of the mental construct fading and knew their time was growing short. "I wish I knew how to thank you for what you did for me," she said.

"No thanks are required," the monk replied. "But if you were so inclined, I would take one final embrace before I go."

Anna smiled. "It would be my honor, Brother Shanks," she said.

The Princess reached out and hugged Shanks' spirit, holding his glowing golden form close as the mental construct she'd been inhabiting faded away. But even as their surroundings darkened, the light from the two souls that held one another grew brighter and brighter.

*You are stronger than you know, Princess,* came Shanks' voice. *As long as you embrace that strength, you'll never have anything to fear.*

Anna gasped as she opened her eyes.

She felt disoriented, looking around at the dark temple she was in. The death tempest swirled before her. The platform she was lying upon was cold and hard. Her head hurt, and she felt dizzy. But as that disorientation cleared, she realized she was back in control of herself. Her mind was hers once more, as was her body. She looked at her hands, moving them as though she'd almost forgotten how.

*I'm back!* she thought with excitement. *I'm in control once more!*

Anna groaned as she pushed herself upright. Though her body felt strange, she was slowly returning to normal. Before she could get to her feet, she heard a voice cry out.

"Princess!"

Anna turned to see Seqis and the Royal Vanguard rushing up the steps leading to the platform, quickly coming to her side. Seqis knelt next to her, his light blue eyes gazing at her in concern.

"Princess, are you alright?" Seqis asked.

Anna smiled, glad to see the old Commander and his companions. "I am," she said. "Thank you."

"Careful, Lord Commander," Lugard said. "The slythru still controls her."

"It does not," Anna replied. "I was able to break its control."

"The slythru also lies," growled Rionknidis.

"Whether this is the Princess or the slythru is immaterial for the moment," said Seqis. "She is unharmed, and we must now get her to safety. Prepare to move out…"

"No," Anna said. "We can't leave. Not yet."

"This is not a discussion," Seqis replied, grabbing onto Anna's arm as though to force her to go along with him.

"You don't understand," Anna said, resisting. "Defeating Verrutus and pushing him from my mind caused him to be unleashed on the Empire. He's using his Secret Army to attack everywhere! But I think I might be able to stop him."

"And how would you do that?" asked Seqis.

"When I was his captive, Verrutus showed me how he controlled those infected by the slythrus," Anna explained. "I think I could also control them, or at the very least, disrupt Verrutus's ability to do so. But I need to interface with the temple's access orb and use its power to go back to the place he showed me."

"The access orb that controls the corrupted temple and the death beam it's firing?" said Lugard, unconvinced. "Yes, we're certainly going to let you do that. It's worked out so well, thus far."

Anna frowned. "Please, you must believe me," she said. "I am not under the slythru's control any longer. I control it, now."

"Princess, even if we did believe you, it makes no difference," Seqis said. "Our duty is to protect you, and that means getting you from this place as quickly as we can."

"Your duty is to protect Legacy Prime so that Legacy Prime can protect the Empire," stressed Anna. "And right now, the Empire is under siege, and I'm the only one who may be able to save it! Are you not soulbound to obey me if I were to order you to let me do this?"

"Not if the slythru is still pulling your strings," replied Rionknidis.

Anna then stood, and Seqis stood along with her. She gazed at her four sworn protectors. "I am Princess Glorianna of Legacy Prime," she stated. "Daughter of Emperor Tavlos IV. Heir of Arcturus, Tarrok, and Nameer. Ruler of the Galactic Regalus Empire, keeper of the sacred bloodline of the Ancients, and master of their forgotten technology. But above all, I am the protector of my people and all who put their faith in my Legacy! Now, look me in the eyes, and tell me… do you see one who is controlled by darkness?"

Lugard, Rionknidis, and Dahuud all glanced at each other in uncertainty. But when Seqis's eyes met Anna's, he did not see any sign of deceit. Nor did he see any hint of the quiet, timid, insecure girl who'd grown up under his protection. What he saw when he looked into her eyes was something pure. Something powerful. Something… good.

"No, I do not," Seqis answered.

"Begging your pardon, Lord Commander, but she's fooled you before," said Lugard, softly.

"She's fooled all of us before," Dahuud whispered.

"The slythru fooled us," Seqis said. "But I swore I would not be deceived in such a way ever again. When the slythru had control, there was a certain look in her eyes… but that look is gone now. I can see it."

"You're taking an awfully big risk trusting her," said Rionknidis.

"If you do not take my word for it, then listen to that of your own souls," Seqis replied. "Our oath to Legacy Prime is a part of our own being. When they speak, our spirits know it is them. Give us a command, Princess. We shall let our souls decide who is speaking – Legacy Prime or the slythru."

Anna took a deep breath. "I wish for you four to uphold your oaths to protect me," she said. "But I ask that you not protect me to simply keep me alive. I ask that you protect me so that I may do what I am meant to do. And at this moment, I am meant to make contact with that access orb, fight the Deathlord Verrutus, and save our Empire. All I ask is that you let me do that."

Lugard, Rionknidis, and Dahuud all stared at Anna for a pregnant moment. Then, Lugard nodded his head.

"As you wish," he said.

"As you wish," whispered Dahuud.

"As you wish," repeated Rionknidis.

"The Vanguard stands with you, Princess," Seqis said. "We shall watch over you as you do what you must. But I do ask that you hurry. There are enemies in this temple – ones that even we may not be a match for. The four of us would give our lives to protect you. But should we fall before you get a chance to complete your task…"

"I understand, Lord Commander," Anna replied. "You fight for me. I'll fight for the Empire. And may we all emerge victorious."

The Vanguard all raised their fists to their hearts in salute. "Hail, Legacy Prime!" they all said.

Anna nodded, then turned and walked toward the access orb. She gazed up at the swirling ghostly tempest of death that raged before her. For the briefest of moments, she was nervous and afraid – unsure if she could really do what was needed to fight Verrutus. But then she heard a voice in her head.

*Know your fear! Do not fight it! Face it! Embrace it! Only then can you conquer it!*

A steely resolve came over Anna as she acknowledged her fears before setting them aside. She knew what had to be done, and with two simple words, she said what she needed to do it.

"Be strong," she whispered.

With that, she placed her hands on the orb.

The moment she connected to the temple, she was back in the dark void of her mental construct. She could see the swirling tempest of death energy before her, still. She could sense the souls that were trapped within it, held together by a dark force of the purist tyranny. She could hear the screams of anguish, the cries for help, the pleas for release. The tempest was not just a weapon – it was also a prison.

*I must free them*, Anna thought. *I must free all of them!*

Anna made contact with the slythru that was now part of her. It tried to resist, but was now powerless to stop her. Anna looked down at the silver thread that connected at her chest. She followed it with her gaze as it rose up into the far distance of the mental construct.

Anna grabbed onto the thread and willed herself to follow it. Immediately, she began rocketing upward, sliding along the thread with incredible speed. Higher and higher she went, her grip never faltering, until the darkness of the mental construct gave way to an image of the galaxy spread out before her, with billions of silver threads all connected like a labyrinthine spider web.

There were so many threads, it was almost too overwhelming for Anna to comprehend. She followed her thread to its end, hovering over a cluster of silver strings which led all over the place. When she made contact with the cluster, it was as though she could hear and see the actions of all those connected to it.

Anna cried out in pain, the sensations of those connections too intense and unfamiliar for her to handle. But she forced herself to hold on – to try to understand the sensory overload from which she was suffering. She braced herself, trying her hardest to regain focus and to exert her control over the strings she now held in her hands.

Little by little, she began to quiet the voices and make sense of the images the threads allowed her to experience. It was as though she were in the heads of thousands of different people, all at the same time. And just like she could hear everything they could, she somehow knew they could hear her, too.

"All of you… listen to me!" she said as she tightened her grip on the cluster of silver threads. "This is Princess Glorianna of Legacy Prime…"

As Anna spoke, across the galaxy members of the Secret Army could hear her voice.

"I speak not to the slythrus who control you, but to that small part of you that still exists! That still fights!" she continued. "I know you are there because I, too, was overtaken by one of these creatures. I know the pain you are in. I know you feel scared, confused, and helpless. You are all slaves in a prison designed by a Deathlord. But I'm here to tell you there is hope! There is a way to escape your prison!"

The threads in Anna's hands began to vibrate. She immediately knew that she'd made a connection to those with whom she was speaking – not the slythrus, but that small piece that still existed of those they had overtaken.

"You cannot fight your dark companions. They are a part of you, now," she explained. "Fighting them only makes them stronger. But that does not mean you can't defeat them! To do so, you must accept that they are now part of who you are. You must embrace them – draw them into yourself – become one with them. I know that sounds scary, but I need you to believe in yourselves. Believe in your strength! Believe in your light! Just because they are a part of you, does not mean they control you! You are all luminous beings! And should you fear your light is not bright enough to balance out their darkness, draw upon mine! You are not alone! I am here! I am with you! And I will help free you!!!"

Anna called upon her inner light and sent it flowing down the silver threads. All across the galaxy, those infected by slythrus made contact with that light, immediately causing whatever consciousness still remained in those who had been infected – no matter how miniscule it was – to flare back up and to begin conquering the dark creatures controlling them.

"Rise up!" Anna commanded. "Take back your minds! Take back your bodies! Take back your lives!"

Anna could feel the turmoil of those whose threads she held. The dueling nature of all of them as their spirits struggled with their dark companions was palpable. But she could feel the growing awareness of those who'd been enslaved as they fed upon the light she was sending them. She could feel them regaining control.

"You are no longer prisoners! You are no longer slaves!" Anna cried. "Break your chains! Be free once more!!! BE FREE!!!"

And with that final command, Princess Glorianna had done the one thing the Deathlord Supreme Verrutus could never have anticipated.

She'd started a mutiny within his Secret Army.

# CHAPTER 19

A fierce battle was raging within the corridors of Megabase Cygnus as the station personnel fought against the legion of the Secret Army who'd overtaken it. But none of those fights was as frenzied as the blaster exchange between a small group of Regalus soldiers and some slythru-infected security officers who'd barricaded themselves before the door to the command center, safely planted behind thick cargo crates and portable shield barriers.

Sergeant Choronz flinched as a blaster bolt struck the wall not inches from his face, forcing him to duck back behind the intersection leading to the command center. He and his handful of men had been trying to take out those defending the room's entrance, but they were having little luck.

"Blast it!" Choronz cried. "There's no way past them!"

"We have to get to the command center, Sarge," one of his men said. "The defense rings are still firing! They're tearing the planet apart more and more every minute!"

"And the station has almost finished its reorientation," another added. "There's no telling what that megalaser will do to the surface!"

"You don't think I know that?" snapped Choronz. "Fat lot of good we'll be in saving Omnicron if we're cut to pieces before we can make it to the control room!"

"Howdy, pardners," said Buchignani as he and the Wild Ones approached, casually strolling toward them as though nothing serious were going on at all.

The soldiers all gave the new arrivals odd looks. "Who are you guys?" Choronz asked.

"We're the cavalry," Buchignani replied. "What's the situation?"

"We need to get into the command center, but they have a small army guarding the entrance. There's no way we can make it down there without getting torn to shreds by blaster fire."

"That is indeed a bit of a pickle now, ain't it," drawled Buchignani. "Mind if I take a gander?"

Buchignani shuffled by the soldiers, carefully peeking around the corner at the collection of slythru-controlled guards barricaded at the end of the long corridor.

"What we lookin' at?" asked Kamm.

"I count eight, all pretty well dug in," Buchignani replied.

"Like I said, any attempt at storming the command center will get us all killed," said Choronz.

"Well, maybe not *any* attempt," said Buchignani as he made some strange hand signals. "Y'all just be ready to charge when I give the go ahead."

"Charge?" asked Choronz. "Are you mad?"

"I'm actually quite happy, truth be told. Turns out bein' heroes pays extremely well."

"Eight's a lot. Even for Aneel," Kamm said. "You sure about this?"

"Pretty sure," Buchignani said. "As long as Aneel can keep 'em occupied long enough fer us to close the distance and get some shots in, we should be good."

The light overhead suddenly turned blue as #00B2EE$^n$ hopped into it. "And what if the guards couldn't see you coming?" asked 00B2EE$^n$. "Would that help?"

The soldiers all looked up at the talking light in confusion as Buchignani considered the option. "It certainly increases the odds of survival, fer sure," Buchignani answered. "Why? Ya got a way to hide our advance?"

"Sort of," the sentient color replied.

Buchignani shrugged. "Okay, little blue buckaroo. As soon as Aneel starts doin' his thing – you do yours."

"How exciting!" said 00B2EE$^n$. "I've never gotten to participate in combat before. I'm so glad I can contribute to the effort!"

The soldiers who'd been watching the exchange all looked at one another, none of them quite sure what was happening. "A talking light and four suicidal mercenaries," Choronz muttered. "I know I already asked this, but… who *are* you guys?"

"We're the Wild Ones," Kamm replied.

"And pardner, things are about ta get mighty wild 'round here," said Buchignani with a smile. "Y'all ready, little blue buckaroo?"

"And waiting!"

"Do yer thing in three… two… one!"

At the end of the corridor where the Secret Army was waiting, the invisible fifth member of the Wild Ones attacked, catching them all by surprise as Aneel sprang into action.

"Now!" cried Buchignani as he and the other Wild Ones rushed out from behind the corner and began sprinting down the hallway.

#00B2EE$^n$ hopped from the light and raced down the corridor in a blue streak, zooming past the Wild Ones as they advanced. He hit each and every Secret Army soldier in the eyes, blinding them, before hopping back up into one of the lights overhead.

Buchignani and the others charged forward, hopping over the barricade the guards had erected and joining in the fight, making quick work of the blinded slythru thralls as they knocked each one out. After seeing the successful advance, the soldiers came rushing up behind the Wild Ones, looking at the group in disbelief. "That was incredible!" exclaimed Choronz.

"Yep," replied Buchignani with a cocky twirl of his blaster. "That's why we get paid the big bucks."

"Not to cut this moment short, compatriots," said #00B2EE$^n$, "but we must breach the command center and stop the megalaser from firing. We only have a few minutes before the Megabase has successfully reoriented itself toward the planet."

"Well, let's not dilly dally then," said Buchignani. "Time to kick some rears and show no fears! Y'all with me?"

"Lead the way," replied Choronz as he and his companions held their weapons at the ready.

Buchignani turned to his friends, who were already itching for the fight. "Wild Ones," he said. "Let's get wild!"

"YEEEEE-HAW!!!!!" they all cried as they opened the door to the command center and charged inside.

The Secret Army was ready and waiting for them as the group rushed into the room, firing their blasters immediately. The Wild Ones and the soldiers barely had time to find cover so they could return fire.

An incarnation of Verrutus stood at the center of the fray, absorbing a few blaster bolts before his body melted. However, other versions of him were still operating and quickly joined the fight. The Wild Ones focused on hitting all versions of the Deathlord Supreme they could, but they were pinned down by the blaster fire from those Verrutus was controlling.

"You are too late!" taunted Verrutus. "You cannot stop the inevitable!"

"Ee-yo! I don't even know what that means!" called back Buff.

"Seriously?" muttered Kamm. "You don't know what 'inevitable' means?"

"Ee-yo, as long as he thinks I don't, he can't brag about winning, right?"

Buchignani frowned. "Well, spit," he muttered. "They got us pinned down somethin' good. Ain't no way we can stop that megalaser in time. And I was really looking forward to that reward, too."

"Maybe we still have a chance?" Siv offered as a blaster bolt sparked off the console he was using for cover.

"Maybe," drawled Buchignani. "But we've played our Ace already. Anything else would be a miracle."

An incarnation of Verrutus turned and looked at Commander Tesswahld. "Fire the megalaser!" the Deathlord ordered.

"As you command, Supreme," Tesswahld replied as he moved to the control panel, its readouts showing the planet of Omnicron directly in the targeting reticle for the superweapon.

Just as the Commander was about to fire the megalaser, his finger stopped right above the activation button. In fact, all blaster fire from the Secret Army suddenly ceased. Buchignani looked curiously at his companions before peeking his head over his cover to see all those who moments before had been firing on them were now still as stone. Their faces were drawn, their teeth were gritted, and their hands trembled.

"What's going on?" asked Kamm.

"Don't rightly know," said Buchignani. "They all kinda look like Buff when he's tryin' ta decide what to eat."

"Why have you all stopped?" demanded Verrutus. "Resume firing! Kill them all!"

None of the slythru-infected soldiers moved.

"I SAID FIRE!!!" the Deathlord cried.

Commander Tesswahld then turned toward Verrutus and scowled. "As you command, *Supreme*," he said before raising his blaster and firing upon the Deathlord.

Suddenly, all the infected turned and began attacking the closest incarnation of Verrutus. The Deathlord lost three versions of himself before he overcame his surprise and started fighting back, striking at his former thralls as they viciously attacked him in blind, vengeful rage.

"FOR THE PRINCESS!!!" they all shouted. "FOR LEGACY PRIME! FOR THE EMPIRE!!!"

All across the galaxy, members of the Secret Army began to revolt, turning on their master and fighting back. The destruction the Deathlord and his thralls were causing throughout the Empire suddenly ceased as more and more of the slythru-infected regained control of themselves.

Buchignani didn't question what was happening. Instead, he took the opportunity to hop over the cover he was hiding behind and run toward the command console where Tesswahld had just been. Buchignani quickly lowered the power output to the megalaser, dissipating its charge, before turning off the planetary defense rings.

The other Wild Ones and the soldiers joined in on the fight, helping to destroy any remaining incarnations of Verrutus alongside the former members of the Secret Army. Before long, there was only one incarnation of the Deathlord left, and he was surrounded by those he'd previously controlled.

"How is this possible?" the Deathlord sneered. "How are you free?"

"The Princess helped show us how to break our chains," growled Tesswahld. "We're not your slaves any longer!"

"It makes no matter," Verrutus replied. "This attack isn't over. All you have done is delay the inevitable. No matter how many bodies of mine you destroy, I will be back to finish what I've started. I am a Deathlord! You cannot kill me!"

"Maybe not," drawled Buchignani as he raised his blaster pistol. "But that don't mean we ain't gonna try."

With that, everyone in the room opened fire on Verrutus, melting away the last version of the Deathlord Supreme on the station.

On practically the other side of the Empire, an equally frenzied battle against Verrutus was raging as Wil, Fred, Copperhyde, and the surviving members of Alpha Force MX017 rushed down the corridors of *The Shieldbearer* while being pursued by a mob of the Deathlord's incarnations. Roadblock and Lucky covered their rear, firing at the encroaching gelatinous Deathlords as Missionary and Wilvelm covered their front, with Fredreek, Copperhyde, and Skeptic in the middle.

Everywhere they turned, incarnations of Verrutus were emerging, forcing them to either fight their way past him or find an alternate route. They could hear screams and cries of struggle as they made their way through the ship, all emanating from the attacks the Deathlord was perpetuating upon the crew.

"Blast it! That pink gob o' snot is everywhere!" cried Copperhyde as the group blasted their way through three incarnations of the Deathlord.

"Bob made up almost half the crew of the ship," replied Wilvelm. "Some ships in the fleet are almost entirely crewed by him!"

"You saying we're outnumbered?" asked Skeptic.

"Yeah, outnumbered by one guy. Will wonders never cease?" quipped Fred.

"Once we get to the armory, the odds will be a bit more even," said Roadblock. "That walking tub of ooze may be able to harden his arms into blades and spikes, but that ain't gonna do squat against Alpha Force armor!"

"And how much further is the armory?" asked Lucky.

"Not far!" said Wilvelm. "This way!"

The group turned a corner to find a small army of Verrutus incarnations marching toward them. Wil and the others skidded to a stop and turned back around, heading down another corridor as the incarnations of the Deathlord, which had been following them, came up from behind. The group didn't get very far before they turned down a hallway to find the blast door at its end had been sealed shut and three of Verrutus's incarnations were already there, waiting for them.

Wil and his companions stopped, some of them turning as they prepared to backtrack, only to find the two other groups of Verrutus's incarnations approaching from each avenue of escape.

"Blast it!" cursed Roadblock. "They herded us into a choke point! They've got us boxed in!"

"Everyone, back-to-back!" said Wilvelm. "Prepare to fight!"

The group immediately put their backs to one another, each one holding up a weapon and aiming it at an encroaching version of Verrutus. But then, the Deathlord stopped his advance, glaring smugly at the prey he'd just trapped. "Fighting is futile," the Deathlord said. "I have sealed off every pathway to the armory. Even if you should somehow survive this, there is nowhere for you to go."

"If we gave up every time a Deathlord threatened us, we wouldn't be here right now," growled Roadblock.

"This is not a threat. It is a fact," Verrutus said. "Lord Gebhard relied on me far too heavily. I hardly needed to infect any in the Maxima system with my slythrus because he invited me in and encouraged me to propagate the system with my incarnations. I have a bigger presence here in Maxima than anywhere else in the Empire. You may destroy a few of me here and there, but it makes no difference in the grander scheme…"

The Verrutus, which had been guarding the door leading to the armory, stepped forward, his fiery eyes burning.

"I am everywhere!" he said. "I am legion! And there is nothing that can stop me!!!"

Just then, there was the sound of screeching metal as the door blocking the corridor was ripped open, revealing a very angry looking Grohm.

Instantly, each and every version of Verrutus went wide-eyed in surprise.

Wilvelm smiled at the sight of the Rognok.

"I wouldn't say 'nothing'," he said.

"Uh oh," squeaked Verrutus, right before Grohm brought his hands crashing together over the Deathlord.

With a thunderous *CLAP*, the Deathlord splattered, its pink goo flying in every direction.

Grohm wasted no time in slamming another incarnation of Verrutus into the wall, splattering him all over the place, as well, right before he grabbed the third version and swung him over his head and smashed the Deathlord into the ground, dispersing its ooze everywhere.

"Run!" shouted Roadblock as he opened fire on the mobs of Verrutus when they started to advance.

The group all shot at the Deathlord as they made their way down the hall. Grohm was glaring at the approaching legion of pink protoplasmic assailants as the group ran by him. Wilvelm stopped at Grohm's side as the others went on ahead.

"We're coming back!" Wilvelm told him. "Think you can hold them off?"

Grohm sneered.

"Right, forgot who I was talking to…" muttered Wil before rushing back after his companions. As he ran, he heard Grohm roar and glanced behind him just in time to see the Rognok charge toward the army of protoplasmic Deathlords, goo splattering everywhere as the Rognok began smashing them left and right.

A side door in the corridor suddenly opened and another incarnation of Verrutus appeared, swinging his deadly sharp blade-arm at Wil. Wil barely had time to duck the swing, rushing past the Deathlord and firing his blaster at it, the bolts ripping through Verrutus, but not causing enough damage to dispatch him before the protoplasm reformed.

All the doors in the corridor began opening as incarnations of Verrutus emerged, trying to intercept the group as they ran. The group all fired, trying desperately to hold back the Deathlord as they made their mad rush for the armory.

"Over here!" cried Fredreek. "It's this way!"

Fredreek led the group to a sealed armored door. He immediately began entering his Legacy code into the door's access pad. The door slid open to reveal a large room with full suits of Alpha Force Armor hanging in hydraulic suspension rigs.

"Go!" said Wilvelm. "We'll hold them off!"

Roadblock and the rest of his squad wasted no time in rushing inside as Wil, Fred, and Copperhyde stood at the entrance, firing at the steadily encroaching army of Verrutus's incarnations.

"We ain't even makin' a dent in 'em!" cried Copperhyde as he fired, the Deathlord healing from the blaster bolts before they could have any lasting effect.

"We just have to slow them down!" Wilvelm said. "Hold them off as long as we can!"

"It isn't going to be very long!" replied Fred as he fired. "They're right on top of us!"

Indeed, the Deathlord continued his relentless march toward the armory, and no matter how much Wil, Fred, and Copperhyde fired upon him, it was not enough to slow him down.

"Fall back!" ordered Wilvelm.

"Fools," Verrutus said as he closed in on them. "Do you really think you can stand against me?"

Verrutus came to the entrance of the armory, only to see four fully armored members of Alpha Force MX017 standing there, defiantly, their charged graviton rifles aimed right for him. Roadblock sneered at the Deathlord.

"Yep," he said.

With that, he fired his rifle, the gravity pulse rocketing forward and tearing through the gelatinous assailants, splattering them all over in a hail of pink goo.

Missionary tossed Wil, Fred, and Copperhyde graviton rifles of their own as Roadblock advanced on Verrutus, firing the gravity pulses which hit with enough power to completely disrupt the cohesion of the ooze comprising the Deathlord.

Wil and the others followed Roadblock out into the corridor, firing their rifles and quickly dispatching all versions of Verrutus they saw. Within a matter of minutes, the corridor was dripping in pink slime and the group all stood together, victorious.

"What now?" asked Copperhyde.

"Now?" said Roadblock as he cranked up the charge on his rifle. "Now, we take back the blasted ship!"

With that, Roadblock began leading the group back toward the bridge, dispatching any incarnation of Verrutus they came across. Eventually, they reunited with Grohm, who had torn his way through his own fair share of Deathlords as he rampaged through the corridors. As the group turned toward the bridge, all the corridors' emergency blast doors closed, sealing off the way to the control center.

"The Deathlord is trying to keep us away from the bridge," Fredreek said.

"It'll take some time, but our graviton rifles should be able to break through these doors," Roadblock said as he cranked up the charge on his weapon.

"I've got a better idea," Wilvelm said. "Grohm?"

The Rognok looked at Wil. Wil pointed toward the doors.

"Smash."

The Rognok grinned, right before charging toward the closed blast door and punching it with all his might. The door ripped away, flying backward and landing with a heavy THUMP. Grohm ran down the corridor, slamming though the next door. And the next. And the next.

Wil and the others followed closely behind as Grohm tore a path to the ship's bridge. As they ran, alarms began to blare.

"What's happening? Why are the alarms suddenly going off?" asked Roadblock.

"Those are self-destruct alarms!" Fredreek cried. "Verrutus must be getting ready to destroy the ship!"

"We can't let that happen!" said Wilvelm. "We need to hurry!"

Grohm roared as he launched himself forward, slamming into the final blast door and tearing it from its rails, immediately attacking any and all versions of Verrutus he found on the bridge.

The rest of the group rushed in, firing their graviton weapons at the multitude of targets. Wilvelm saw one incarnation of the Deathlord at the bridge's command console and opened fire, splattering him everywhere.

As the rest of Alpha Force and Grohm cleared out the room, Wilvelm rushed up to the command console and began overriding the self-destruct sequence. The alarms stopped just as the last incarnation of Verrutus on the bridge was squished to pieces by Grohm.

For a brief moment, the group members all looked at each other, the queer peace at the end of a frenzied fight settling in upon them. Wilvelm laughed with relief.

"We did it!" he said. "The bridge is ours!"

"There are still a lot of Deathlords on this ship," Roadblock said. "We're going to need to go deck by deck and get rid of them."

"Grohm will handle that," stated the Rognok as he lumbered out of the bridge.

Roadblock turned to the rest of his squad. "Go with him," he ordered. "Go room by room. Dispatch any version of that walking tub of mucus you find. I'll stay here and guard the bridge."

"On it," Alpha Force replied as they filed out of the room to carry out their assignment.

Fredreek glanced at one of the sensor consoles and swore under his breath. "Quick! Copperhyde, I need your help!" Fredreek said as he rushed over to the ship's piloting station.

"Me? What ya need me for?" replied the mercenary.

"You're the only one here besides me with experience piloting starships," Fredreek said. "The ships Verrutus overtook are still attacking our fleet! I need you to maneuver *The Shieldbearer* while I target them and try to save what's left of our battlegroup."

"You're going to fire on our own ships?" asked Roadblock.

"They're not our ships anymore," Fredreek replied. "The ones Verrutus controls have already destroyed too much of our fleet. If we don't take them out now, we'll have nothing left."

"Do it," Wilvelm said.

"Already doing it," said Fredreek as Copperhyde took the seat next to him.

Wilvelm moved to one of the communications stations on the bridge and opened a channel to each Maxima vessel that was defending itself against attack. "Attention Maxima fleet," he said. "This is Lord Wilvelm Blackfyre. We are under attack by Bob, who is working for the Deathlords. He has overtaken some of our ships, but we've regained control of *The Shieldbearer*. We are preparing to launch a counterattack. Focus your fire on the attacking vessels, assist one another if you can, and hang in there!"

"Bring us into the center of the fleet," Fredreek ordered.

"Aye, bringin' us in," said Copperhyde.

"Locking onto targets," Fredreek stated. "Preparing to launch Deathscream missiles in three, two, one…"

Fredreek hit the launch button and *The Shieldbearer* fired its complement of Deathscream missiles, the deadly projectiles rocketing from the ship's missile tubes and arcing through space, impacting each and every ship under Verrutus's control.

Wil watched the bridge's viewscreen as magnificent explosions erupted all around, busting through the shields of the targets and inflicting massive damage on the vessels.

The defending ships wasted no time in taking advantage of the counterattack, firing upon the Deathlord controlled vessels with focused fury.

With their shields down, the ships controlled by Verrutus began to fall, breaking apart under the plasma batteries of the ships still loyal to Maxima.

"Firing second volley," said Fredreek. "Now!"

Again, a full complement of Deathscream missiles launched from *The Shieldbearer*, taking out the remaining enemy ships.

Everyone on the bridge cheered as the last of Verrutus's influence was wiped out. The communications console Wilvelm was at immediately lit up as he received reports from the surviving starships of the fleet, informing him of their status and their success at clearing away any incarnation of Verrutus onboard.

"We did it," Wilvelm reported. "The fleet's been saved."

"At the cost of almost all our Deathscream missiles," muttered Fredreek. "Lest we forget, we still got these kittens to deal with…"

Fredreek recalled the image of the Deathlord fleet of Dreadnaughts guarding Maxima. Any elation those on the bridge of *The Shieldbearer* had felt at defeating Verrutus immediately vanished as they gazed upon the massive fleet between them and the planet.

"How many ships do we have that are still operational?" Wilvelm asked.

"Aside from those too damaged to operate…" said Fredreek as he checked his console. "Seven."

Roadblock blinked dumbly upon hearing the number. "Uh… what was that?" he asked.

"Seven ships," Fredreek repeated, dourly. "Counting us. That's all that's left."

A heavy silence hung in the air until Roadblock pounded his fist onto a console in frustration. "Blast it!" he cursed. "We took out that big pink gob of snot, but not before he took out almost our entire fleet!"

"We need to retreat," said Copperhyde. "Take what ships can still fly and get out o' the system."

"We can't just surrender Maxima to the Deathlords," said Roadblock.

"Look at that viewscreen, soldier boy, and tell me what other alternative we have," argued Copperhyde.

Everyone looked at the bridge's viewscreen with the numerous Deathlord Dreadnaughts looming before them. A collective feeling of hopelessness gripped the group.

"It's seven ships against an armada," Copperhyde said. "How in the twelve systems are we supposed to fight all that?"

"We don't," Wilvelm declared.

All eyes turned to Wil, who was gazing at the viewscreen with steely resolve.

"Finally, the little Lord is talking sense," Copperhyde said.

"The Deathlord ships are a distraction," Wilvelm stated. "The real threat is the temple on the surface of Maxima shooting that death ray. If we can destroy it, we can wait out the Deathlord fleet until help arrives."

"Spoke too soon," muttered Copperhyde.

"Destroy the temple?" said Roadblock. "How? Our last missile strike had zero effect."

"We don't attack from orbit," Wilvelm said. "We use boots on the ground. We do a frontal assault and take that temple out from the inside."

"A ground assault?" said Roadblock, looking unconvinced.

"Of the seven ships we have left, each one has five complements of Alpha Force squads. *The Shieldbearer* has ten," Wilvelm said. "If we deployed all of their atmospheric entry pods, enough soldiers might make it through to the planet."

"There ain't no way anything is making it through all those Deathlord ships," Copperhyde said. "Setting aside their point defense arrays, they've got fightercraft which'll tear those Alpha Force pods to shreds before they even get close to the planet."

"Not if we engage their fleet," Fredreek said.

Copperhyde turned to Fredreek in disbelief over what he'd just heard. "Engage their fleet???" he cried. "That's suicide!"

"Only if we're trying to win the fight," Fredreek said. "If we group up our remaining ships into a tight formation, we can get close enough to the Deathlord fleet to launch the Alpha Force pods well within their point defense range. We can launch what fighters we have to give them cover, then pull back once they're through. I'm not saying it's perfect, but enough of Alpha Force may get to Maxima to make a difference."

"It's a risky plan. But it's the only one we've got," said Wilvelm, turning to look at Roadblock. "Assuming Alpha Force is up for such a dangerous mission."

"Alpha Force lives for danger, Lord Blackfyre," Roadblock replied.

Wilvelm nodded. "Very well," he said. "Let's coordinate with the rest of the fleet and prepare for the assault."

Wilvelm turned and looked at the image of the looming Deathlord ships.

"This battle isn't lost yet…" he said.

# CHAPTER 20

eqis gazed upon Anna as she stood before the access orb. Her eyes were pure white as she interfaced with the ancient construct, her face bathed in the ghostly illumination from the swirling death tempest.

"Is there any part of you that has doubts about her?" asked Rionknidis as he stood at Seqis's side.

"If there is, it is far too late to acknowledge those doubts," Seqis replied. "Her duty is to protect the Empire. Our duty is to protect her. Right now, it is imperative we all do our duty."

Lugard and Dahuud looked out into the central chamber of the temple, its dark shadows dancing in the faint light of the death tempest.

"Do you feel that?" Lugard asked.

Dahuud nodded. "Cold," she whispered.

"Our enemies return," Lugard announced, turning toward Seqis. "They are coming."

Rionknidis bared his fangs and punched his palm in anticipation. "Let them come!" he growled. "I'll rip out their throats with my bare teeth!"

Seqis placed a hand on Rionknidis's shoulder. "I need something else from you now, brother," he said. "Something more important than your prowess in battle."

Rionknidis raised an eyebrow. "And what is it you need?" he asked.

"Your fearlessness," Seqis replied. "At the Conclave, you were unaffected by the power of these robed figures."

"That is because nothing frightens me."

"Indeed. However, the same cannot be said for the rest of us. Though we now know what to expect from our enemy, the effort we will expend pushing past the fear they'll cause will put us at a disadvantage in battle."

"What are you saying, Commander?"

"I'm saying I need you to stay back from the coming fight," Seqis said. "I need you to engage in battle meditation so you may share your fearlessness with your sworn companions to help us resist this dark magic our opponents wield."

Rionknidis sneered. "You're asking me not to fight?"

"I'm asking you to fight in a way that benefits us all," Seqis responded. "You helping us maintain our focus through battle meditation will even the odds. And should the three of us fall, it will be up to you to defend the Princess. I know you are always one to jump into battle, my friend, but right now you have a far more important role to play. We are depending upon you. What do you say?"

Rionknidis snarled but eventually nodded. "Very well," he replied. "I will do what is required of me. But it has been a while since my last battle meditation. I may be a bit rusty."

"Do what you can. I have faith in you."

Rionknidis nodded at that and then knelt on the floor, entering his meditation position as Seqis joined Lugard and Dahuud.

"Are you two ready?" the Lord Commander asked.

The two Paragons manifested their weapons – two moonfyre daggers for Dahuud and the famous sword Starbeam for Lugard.

"I am eager for a rematch," Lugard replied. "These villains will find Dahuud and I are not such easy targets this time around."

Seqis manifested his hammer.

"We know what they can do," Seqis said. "It is time they learned what we are capable of."

With that, the three Paragons made their way down the steps of the platform, leaving the soul vault and walking into the central chamber. They stood in the middle of the room, their weapons at the ready. Seqis gazed into the darkness of the chamber's main entrance, waiting to catch sight of their approaching adversaries.

The feeling of cold in the room slowly began to intensify. Seqis could feel his body shiver in response as the sensation grew, travelling to his very bones. He gritted his teeth, steeling himself as he held his hammer Grapthaar before him.

He reached out with his senses, trying to make his connection to Rionknidis, but he was already finding it difficult to concentrate.

*Come on, old friend,* he thought. *Do not let me down…*

Suddenly, a surge of fear coursed through the three Paragons. Images of the most horrifying things imaginable flashed into their minds. Fears from childhood. Long forgotten nightmares. All the things they dreaded and were ashamed to admit they were afraid of.

Seqis, Lugard, and Dahuud all grabbed their heads in anguish as they tried to fight against the almost overwhelming emotions. Though Seqis had fought in many battles, he'd never had the urge to run away until that very moment. The fear he was experiencing was palpable – so intense he could hardly see straight.

He looked up as three Terrormancers emerged from the darkness, their hands outstretched as they projected their vile energy. They each wielded a long staff with a ghostly scythe at its top, and their bone-white faces seemed scarred, as though they'd all suffered from a burn, making their appearance only that much more ghastly.

The Vanguard stumbled as the Terrormancers neared, falling back a few steps as they struggled to hold onto their sanity. "RIONKNIDIS!" Seqis cried. "HELP US!!!"

"There isssss no help," one of the Terrormancers said.

"You will all die…" said another.

"And so will the Princesssss!" said the third.

The three Terrormancers fanned out, each one closing in on a member of the Vanguard, holding their deadly scythes at the ready.

Seqis fell to his knees, unable to keep his balance as he fought against the overwhelming fear being inflicted upon him. The old warrior was not afraid of much, but the thing he feared the most was failing to do his duty. To let any harm come to the Princess.

In that moment, as his enemy approached, ready to strike him down, that fear felt more and more like a reality.

As the Terrormancers neared the three members of the Vanguard, Rionknidis sat close to the Princess, his eyes closed as he entered into a meditative state, the burly Tygarian trying desperately to make a spiritual and mental connection with his companions.

Just as the Terrormancers raised their blades to deliver the killing blows, Rionknidis found the strength and focus to fight his way through the evil energy they were emitting and connected with his allies.

As the deadly scythes came crashing down, they were blocked by meeting Dahuud's moonfyre daggers.

They clashed with the humming blade of Starbeam.

And they met with the head of Grapthaar, a clap of thunder ringing out as the ghost blade collided with the hammer of legend.

The Terrormancers' pure black eyes widened in surprise as they met those of the Vanguard, who rose up to their feet defiantly. They could still feel the fear the Terrormancers were generating, but with the help of Rionknidis, they were able to ignore it.

They were now fearless.

"How is thissss possible???" hissed one of the Terrormancers.

"We are Paragons, you vile creature," sneered Seqis. "For us… *anything* is possible!"

With that, the Vanguard attacked, forcing their dark opponents back as they struck with their weapons. But the Terrormancers quickly recovered, counterattacking with their own weapons as they dodged and parried those of the Vanguard.

As the Royal Vanguard fought with the Terrormancers in a vicious and frenzied dance to the death, Princess Glorianna remained in her mental construct, trying her best to free as many under Verrutus's control as possible.

She could see the silver threads breaking as each slythru-infected being regained control of itself. She quickly reached out to more, grabbing onto clusters of the silver threads and telling those at their ends how to free themselves.

"Rise up! Break your chains!" she told them. "You no longer have to be slaves! You can be free! You can free yourselves!"

"WHAT ARE YOU DOING?" raged a dark voice.

Anna turned to see a massive, spider-like creature made of dripping black tar scurrying toward her, its sharp legs clicking away on the web of silver strings as it raced forward, its fiery red eyes burning with malice.

Anna turned and faced the creature defiantly. "I am freeing those you've enslaved, Deathlord!" she shouted back. "I will no longer allow you to torment these innocent people!"

"You will not *allow* me???" cried Verrutus, indignantly, as he approached the Princess. "Who are you to dictate what I may do?"

"I am Princess Glorianna of Legacy Prime! I am the blood of the Ancients! The protector of the Regalus Empire and its people! I've already beaten you once, Verrutus – and I will do so again!"

"Do not be so sure, you insolent child," Verrutus said, his dark voice echoing throughout the construct. "When last we met, we were in your domain. Now… you are in mine!"

Verrutus struck at Anna with two of his legs, their ends razor sharp. Anna fell backward, barely dodging the blow, and found herself falling through the void of the construct. She reached out, grabbing onto a nearby silver thread and using it to slide back up to Verrutus. She launched herself off the thread and held out her hand, shining a bright light from it and forcing Verrutus to flinch away.

"GRAAGHHHH!!!" the Deathlord cried.

"This may be your domain, Deathlord, but your weakness hasn't changed," Anna declared. "You are a shadow that only has power in the dark. And I am here to shine a light upon you!"

Anna held out both her hands and projected light from them, but the Deathlord did not flinch away again. He charged toward her, trying to overwhelm her as he stabbed at her with his many legs. Anna quickly called upon her spirit to shine brightly, her entire body glowing, keeping the black tar of the Deathlord at bay as it tried to consume her.

"Shine your light as brightly as you will, little girl!" sneered Verrutus. "Light dies! But darkness reigns eternal!"

"Look around you, Deathlord," Anna replied. "Every soul in this universe shines as brightly as the stars do! Once, darkness may have reigned, but if you ask me – it's the light that is winning!"

The Deathlord roared in anger, intensifying his attack as Anna fought back just as hard. And there, on a different plane of existence, over the entire galaxy, a struggle as old as time played out as Princess Glorianna and the Deathlord Supreme Verrutus tangled with one another.

Light against dark. Good against evil.

The fate of billions of lives hanging in the balance.

# Chapter 21

Mourdock had never felt anything before like what he was now feeling. He felt drunk on power. It was as though any trace of fear, doubt, or insecurity had been purged from him and all that was left behind in its place was clarity. He was the superior being. All who were not of his kind were beneath him and unworthy of favor, sympathy, or mercy. They were as insignificant as insects to be crushed under the heel of his boot.

The sensation quickly washed away the struggle Mourdock had been feeling since he'd entered the Conclave. He had resisted his transformation at first, but now that it had happened, he was glad that it had. He had been so wrong about it! This was not a corruption. No… this was a rebirth! He was something new. Something better. Something powerful.

Blackmane was standing before him. The man's skin was white and veined. His eyes pure black. But he was smiling broadly, his grin wide and welcoming. "Finally, now you see," Blackmane stated.

Mourdock nodded. "Yes," he replied. "I understand now."

"As do we all," said Blackmane, gesturing to Krixus and Desmodus who had emerged from the Escrimar Arena to join them. "We have been granted an incredible gift – one that has made us more powerful than any other Paragon to ever live!"

Blackmane grasped Mourdock by his arms and then embraced him.

"We are no longer rivals, you and I," he said. "We are brothers, as we were always meant to be. Both bound by the glory of our new master."

Mourdock returned Blackmane's brotherly embrace. "And who is this master who's granted us such a gift?" he asked.

"We shall take you to him," Blackmane said. "Come, Mourdock. Supreme Mellegogg is eager to receive you."

Jack's heart thumped in his chest as he frantically sped through the corridors of the Conclave, his pursuers practically on his heels. Jack had been in a mad scramble for survival since the moment Mourdock had fallen to the corruption. Tannyn and his mob of corrupted Initiates had engaged in pursuit almost immediately, using their enhanced speed to try to run him down. Jack had to channel every last ounce of speed and stamina he'd learned in his Fire Ring conditioning to stay ahead of them – and even then, it was barely just enough.

"Jack so nimble! Jack so quick!" shouted Tannyn mockingly, as he chased after his prey. "I want Jack's head impaled on a stick!"

"I could think of a few places you could shove that stick, Tannyn!" yelled back Jack.

"Here, Hero, Hero, Hero!" called out Headbasher. "Why ya gotta run away, Hero?"

"Stand and fight, you wimp!" heckled Gunshow.

"I want my rematch, Earthman!" yelled Medkav. "This time, we play for keeps!"

Jack could hear Ariandre and Nix laugh with the rest of the group as they all charged after him, enjoying their bloodsport like rabid dogs attempting to chase down their prey.

*I gotta ditch these guys! If only so I don't have to listen to their lame taunts anymore!* thought Jack as he turned and began heading toward the Crystal Concourse.

Jack emerged into the concourse, making a weightless leap from the platform and soaring through the air. His pursuers performed the same maneuver, following him as he sailed over the wide expanse toward the platform leading to the other side of the Conclave.

*I hope this works!* Jack thought as he turned in mid-air, manifesting some electromagnetic energy and sending an arc of electricity rocketing toward Tannyn's group. The electric tendrils hit every one of them and knocked each away mid-leap.

"Gravity pulses!" ordered Tannyn as he fell to the platform below.

"Oh, crap!" exclaimed Jack as he quickly erected an electromagnetic field around himself just as Tannyn and his henchmen unleashed a volley of wild and unfocused gravity pulses.

Jack was knocked off his jump as the pulses erupted all around, crashing into the various platforms of the Crystal Concourse with unrestrained fury, showcasing what little control Tannyn and his group had over the powerful force. Jack landed hard on the platform he'd been aiming for, his electromagnetic field having successfully protected him from the deadly explosions of gravity.

The same could not be said for the Crystal Concourse.

Jack heard a loud groan as the spinning gyroscope which lit the concourse was knocked loose by a stray pulse, falling down and crashing through any platforms in its path. Jack jumped aside just as the gyroscope tumbled downward, hitting the platform he was on and breaking it. Rubble began to rain down as the platforms above him started to collapse and break away, falling straight for him.

*CrapCrapCrapCrapCrap!!!* thought Jack frantically as he scrambled up the platform he was on, trying to keep from sliding down it as it broke apart.

Jack launched himself off the falling platform, making a weightless leap to the other side of the area, stepping on falling debris to help propel him forward.

"Follow him!" screamed Tannyn. "Don't let him get away!!!"

Jack saw Tannyn and the others also making weightless leaps, dodging the falling platforms as they all collapsed from above. Jack and his pursuers continued climbing upward, dancing between the destruction with weightless leap after weightless leap as the Crystal Concourse collapsed all around them.

Finally, Jack propelled himself toward the remains of a platform leading to the Water Ring level just as he ran out of falling debris to jump from. He came up just short of the broken platform, grabbing onto it and precariously dangling from its ledge.

Jack looked down to see Tannyn and his crew making powerful leaps toward him. He quickly pulled himself up and raced through the platform's exit and down a corridor just as Tannyn and his cronies landed.

"After him!" Tannyn ordered.

Jack sprinted around a corner and ran as fast as his enhanced speed could carry him. He knew he only had a few moments before his pursuers would be upon him again. He looked at his surroundings, quickly taking them in. The corridor was filled with doorways to medical chambers, most of them with their doors broken.

Jack turned and entered one of the chambers. It was an observation room filled with stadium seating, but dark enough to hide in. Jack leapt up into one of the far rows of the room, ducking down behind a row of seats and sticking to the shadows. He peaked over his hiding place, catching his breath as he saw Tannyn and his group pass by the chamber's entrance.

"Spread out!" he heard Tannyn cry. "He couldn't have gotten far!"

Jack knew it would only be a matter of time before the group entered the room and found him. He quickly crept along the row of seating he was hiding behind, making his way toward an office door at the back of the chamber. He dropped down and sneaked inside, quietly closing the door behind him. He was about to seal the entrance when he heard a gasp.

Jack turned, alarmed, to see Flitter there, cowering behind a desk. Her large eyes went even wider when she saw him. "Jack?" she whispered. "Is that you?"

"Flitter!" Jack replied, glad to have finally found his friend. "I've been looking everywhere for you!"

"Are you evil?"

"Do I look evil?" Jack asked, crawling toward her.

Flitter smiled when she saw his eyes and skin were still normal. She reached out and hugged him, holding him tight with relief. "Oh, thank goodness!" she exclaimed. "I've been so scared!"

"It's okay," Jack said, trying to console her. "I came back to rescue as many people as I could. I can get you away from the temple."

"It's not just me," Flitter said, pulling Jack back behind the desk to show Paragon Savage lying on the ground.

Savage was shivering violently. His green skin had grown pale and colored veins pulsed beneath it. Flitter quickly knelt by his side, placing her hands upon him to stop his trembling.

"Holy crap," muttered Jack. "What's wrong with him?"

"He's corrupted," said Flitter. "But he's fighting it. I was with him when the walls went ghostly and he started screaming and transforming before my very eyes. I used my healing powers to keep him from turning. It was enough so that he could regain control, but he's deteriorating. I need to get him out of here."

Jack frowned as he looked down at Savage's face. The Paragon opened his eyes, looking at Jack with a pained expression. "Earth… Earthman…" he said, his voice cracking.

"Don't worry, Master Savage, we're going to get you out of here," Jack said.

"No…" Savage replied. "Too far… gone. Take… take Flitter… get her to safety…"

"I'm not leaving you, Master!" Flitter insisted.

"You must!" Savage replied. "I… cannot… be saved…"

"I'm a healer!" Flitter said, stubbornly. "I can't leave behind someone in need. I won't!"

Savage smiled at that. "You always were… a good student…" he muttered. "Misguided… but good…"

"Master Savage, can you walk?" asked Jack.

"He can, as long as I can make contact with him," Flitter said. "I can keep the corruption at bay, take away some of his struggle, but I can't do it remotely. I'm not that advanced yet. Whatever this affliction is, it's too complicated."

"We've been teleporting survivors back to my spaceship, but the beams hitting the temple are blocking its sensors," Jack said. "I had a signal booster with me, but it was destroyed. Do you think you could get Master Savage to the outer ring from here?"

"I… I think so," Flitter replied. "Just so long as we don't run into anyone that's corrupted. I won't be able to defend Master Savage from them."

"It's okay, most of the corrupted have left," Jack explained. "They've been leaving through tethers that have been popping up everywhere."

"Where have they gone?"

"No idea. And frankly, at the moment, I don't really care. The only thing that matters is saving as many people as we can. Now, if you can make it to the outer ring, Krupp and the others on my ship can help you."

Flitter nodded. "Okay," she said, helping Master Savage to sit up. "We'll try."

Jack assisted in getting Savage to his feet, then led Flitter and the Paragon out into the chamber. He heard voices in the corridor and urged his companions to duck behind some seats just as Ariandre walked by, the large Femezon glancing into the chamber before moving on.

"Crap, I forgot," Jack muttered. "Tannyn and his goons are searching the level looking for me."

"They've all been corrupted?" asked Flitter.

"Yeah. And if you thought they were jerks before, you should see them now."

"There's no way we can get Master Savage past them to the outer ring," Flitter lamented.

"We can't, but you can," Jack said. "I'll draw them away. When I do, you take Savage and make a run for the outer ring."

Flitter grabbed onto Jack's arm. "No!" she cried. "Jack! You can't!"

"It's the only way to get you two to safety."

"But what about you?" asked Flitter. "They'll kill you if they can! I won't abandon you!"

Jack gently removed Flitter's hand. "Don't worry about me, Flitter. This is what I've been training for."

Flitter's lip trembled as her eyes became glassy with tears. "But… you're my friend! I don't want anything bad to happen to you!"

"I can handle myself," Jack reassured her. "Right now, Master Savage needs you more than I do. Focus on him, okay? Let me help the both of you get out of here."

Flitter lurched forward and embraced Jack, sniffling as she did so. "Please don't get hurt!" Flitter said. "I won't be around to heal you if you do!"

Jack returned the hug, patting his friend on the back to comfort her. "You've always been there when I've needed you, Flitter," Jack said. "Now it's my turn to be there for you."

Jack broke away and looked at his friend.

"As soon as they come after me, don't waste time. Get moving. You ready?"

Flitter grabbed Master Savage and slung his arm over her shoulder. "Yes," she replied. "Good luck!"

"You, too," said Jack as he turned and exited the chamber.

Jack walked down the corridor until he came across an intersection and saw Tannyn, Headbasher, and Gunshow at the other end.

"Hey, dumbnuts!" he yelled.

The men all turned and looked at Jack.

"You want me?" Jack taunted. "Come and get me!"

Jack turned and ran. "After him!" Tannyn yelled as they engaged in pursuit.

Once the corridor was clear, Flitter emerged, supporting Savage as they walked. The Paragon gripped at his chest, trembling as he shuffled along, the red, green, and purple veins beneath his skin bulging with each step. Flitter glanced behind her in the direction that Jack had run, a sad and worried look on her face.

"You're… afraid for him…" Savage said.

"He's my friend," replied Flitter. "He's brave, but even he needs help."

Savage nodded. "Indeed… he does…" he said. "Right now… we all do…"

Jack continued his sprint down the corridors with Tannyn, Headbasher, and Gunshow in pursuit. Jack glanced behind him just as he was about to turn a corner to gage how close his adversaries were, when suddenly, Nix appeared in his path. The Karkovian landed blows with three of his fists before Jack had time to react, causing Jack to stumble and fall, losing his practice saber handle in the process.

Ariandre and Medkav both came running up from adjoining hallways and before Jack knew it, the three Initiates had surrounded him.

"Keep him there!" shouted Tannyn as he approached. "I want a piece of him!"

Medkav, Nix, and Ariandre immediately started kicking Jack while he was on the ground. Jack covered up to block the blows, turning his attention away just long enough to see Tannyn manifest a sword, with Headbasher and Gunshow in tow, now wielding swords, as well.

Jack knew he didn't have much time. He kicked at one of Nix's knees, causing the Karkovian to cry out and fall close enough for Jack to gouge one of his eyes. He knew Medkav was too skilled at Escrima to take down, but Ariandre wasn't. Jack quickly grabbed onto her leg and pulled the large Femezon to the floor, rolling over her and elbowing her in the face as he put some distance between him and Medkav.

Medkav leapt over Nix to try to pounce upon Jack, but Jack kicked his feet up, hitting Medkav in the chest and knocking him back before Jack rolled to his feet.

With Tannyn and the others almost upon him, Jack sprinted down an adjoining corridor. He heard Tannyn shout: "Go around! Cut him off!"

As Jack made it to an intersection in the hallway, he turned to see Gunshow emerge from another corridor and speed toward him. Nix and Medkav, apparently having recovered from Jack's blows, ran close behind.

Jack went to turn in the opposite direction just as Headbasher and Ariandre rounded the corner and began heading for him.

Behind him, Jack saw Tannyn closing in, his sword at the ready.

"Nowhere left to run, Hero!" Tannyn yelled.

Jack looked at the wall before him and saw the various doors leading to healing chambers. *Maybe not, but there are places to hide!* he thought before racing into one of the chambers and sealing the door behind him.

Tannyn and his group all converged around the door to the chamber in which Jack had locked himself. Headbasher tried opening it, but when it did not respond, Tannyn simply laughed. "You think hiding in there is going to save you, Hero?" Tannyn shouted. "We're warriors! A locked door isn't going to stop us!"

Tannyn turned to his companions, his black eyes gleaming. "Break it down," he ordered.

Headbasher and Gunshow both manifested large sledgehammers and began striking the door. As they did so, the others manifested swords. Tannyn looked at his blade with loathing and tossed it aside.

"Been saving this for an actual battle," he muttered. "But I guess it's fitting my real weapon's first taste of blood will be yours, Hero…"

A moonfyre sword then appeared in Tannyn's hand, glowing bright red as the boy wielded the power of a star. Tannyn smiled, his face bathed in the red glow of his weapon. He looked at the chamber door in anticipation as it started to crack and crumble under the blows from Headbasher and Gunshow.

Inside the chamber, Jack looked around in desperation, a sinking feeling of fear growing in his gut. It was a circular chamber with white walls and no way out other than the door that was quickly beginning to break.

*Stupid!* Jack thought in dismay. *I trapped myself in a corner and now there's no way out!*

Booms rang loudly with each strike at the door. Jack turned and looked at it as cracks began to form in the stone from which the door was made, small puffs of dust emanating from it as it weakened more with each hit.

*What am I going to do?!* Jack thought as panic began to take hold of him. *I'm outnumbered! I don't have any weapons! There's nowhere left to run!*

Jack felt his heart thumping in his chest and realized that he was losing control. For some reason, it was that realization that made him remember something Ravencrow had told him in his training.

*In fighting, and in everyday life, your actions should be determined by calm,* Ravencrow had said.

"Calm…" Jack muttered.

*True calm can only be experienced when you surrender yourself to The Void,* said Ravencrow's voice in Jack's head. *To let go of all that seeks to control you and to hold you back. It is in this calm, this surrender, that you allow your mind to be free.*

"Surrender…"

Jack closed his eyes. He blocked out all the sensations that were distracting him and causing him to live outside the moment. He ignored his emotions. He ignored the sounds of the door being broken. He ignored all thoughts of the danger which lay just beyond that door. Jack blocked out everything that distracted him from that very moment. And with a deep breath…

Jack surrendered himself to The Void.

When he opened his eyes, he looked down and saw he was gripping two batons. They were the ones gifted to him by the Royal Vanguard, meant to mirror the weapons Shepherd had wielded. Jack looked at them, surprised to realize he had manifested them, but also, not surprised in the least.

"Sometimes you choose the weapon," Jack muttered. "Sometimes, the weapon chooses you."

Jack gripped the batons and used his skills with electromagnetism to funnel a charge into the sticks, causing them to crackle to life with power when he did so. Jack smiled and looked toward the door as it began to fall apart from the blows of those who meant to do him harm. And as the door started to crumble, Jack heard Ravencrow's voice one final time…

*When you free your mind, you allow yourself to react in such a way that nothing can harm you. No danger is too great. No obstacle too big…*

"Anything becomes possible," Jack said.

Gunshow and Headbasher pulled their sledgehammers back, winding up to deliver a final blow to the chamber door as Tannyn and the others readied to charge inside.

Just as the two men were preparing to swing, the door shattered, the stone from which it was made exploding outward and knocking them back as Jack came flying through it, his power batons crackling with electricity.

Tannyn and his group were caught off-guard, surprised by Jack's appearance. Jack wasted no time as he landed, throwing one of his batons forcefully and hitting Nix in the face, causing the Karkovian to cry out as he received a harsh electric shock that combined with the weapon's impact to instantly knock him out.

Jack rushed forward and struck Ariandre, sending a jolt through her right before he dropped down and swept Medkav's legs out from under him. Jack brought his baton swinging around, catching the Femezon at the back of her head as she doubled over from Jack's initial strike, rendering her completely incapacitated.

Tannyn prepared to swing his sword, but Jack quickly remanifested the baton he'd thrown and knocked aside Tannyn's strike, spinning on his heel and using Tannyn's momentum to push him away right as Gunshow and Headbasher rushed up to him with their hammers.

Jack ducked low and sprinted forward, ramming his batons into the two men's guts and sending as powerful an electric charge through his weapons as he could. Gunshow and Headbasher both cried out, dropping their hammers as Jack maneuvered between them.

Jack then turned and landed blows from his batons on the crook of each man's neck, shocking them into unconsciousness, their bodies dropping to the ground.

Medkav and Tannyn both leapt forward with a cry. Jack ducked past Tannyn, once more using his opponent's momentum to push him away. Jack engaged with Medkav, who had manifested a blade in each hand. Before the Karkovian could strike, Jack aimed one of his batons at Medkav's eyes and sent out a flash of light which blinded his attacker.

Medkav cried out, dropping two of his swords as his hands instinctively went to his eyes. Jack quickly struck at his knees, breaking them and sending the Karkovian to the ground. No sooner had he fallen than Jack jabbed him with both batons, shocking him into unconsciousness.

Jack heard a primal cry come from behind him and turned just in time to meet a powerful strike from Tannyn's moonfyre sword, the red blade sparking as it impacted Jack's baton.

Tannyn pressed his attack, sending a flurry of strikes Jack's way, which Jack countered and parried. The two rivals danced, bright yellow flares sparking each time their weapons met. They ducked and weaved and dodged, attacking and counterattacking one another until finally their weapons came together in a thunderous clash, the two men using their weight to press against the other while their weapons locked.

Jack gazed into Tannyn's soulless black eyes as the boy glared back at him with a scowl, the red and yellow glow from their weapons flickering across their faces.

"You are not a better warrior than me!" snarled Tannyn.

"No," replied Jack. "I'm just a different kind!"

Jack then used his batons to move Tannyn's sword aside, reeling back and slamming his forehead into Tannyn's nose. Jack heard a *CRUNCH* as Tannyn's nose broke, causing him to cry out, dazed from the unexpected blow.

Jack quickly dropped down and swung, landing a hard blow to the crook of Tannyn's knee, causing him to drop down, as well.

Jack spun to his feet, bringing both his batons down on Tannyn's shoulders while channeling as much electromagnetic energy as he could into the weapons, shocking Tannyn until the boy fell unconscious at Jack's feet.

Jack stood, surrounded by his defeated foes, breathing deeply as he caught his breath. He looked around, as though expecting to find more adversaries to fight, but to his surprise he had beaten them all.

"Wow…" Jack said, genuinely impressed with himself. "That was awesome."

# CHAPTER 22

Professor Green sat at his station on the bridge of the Earthship, watching the ship's internal security feed. He'd been teleporting the survivors Jack and Mourdock had been finding directly to the cargo bay where Sawbones had set up a small triage unit. There were some Initiates from the Water Ring who were now helping her tend to those who'd been injured.

The Professor nervously looked at his sensor readout, apprehension growing within him as he saw tiny blips indicating Deathlord Shards getting closer and closer to them.

"Oh dear, oh dear, oh dear..." he muttered before opening a communications channel. "Agent Boone! We have enemy spacecraft approaching the outer ring!"

Down at the Earthship's boarding hatch, Boone, along with Krupp and the other Unlikelies who were guarding it, looked up through the clear ceiling of the ring as the Deathlord Shards began their run toward it.

"Blast it!" grumbled Boone. "Everyone inside, quickly!"

The Shards opened fire, plasma bolts streaking across the void and impacting the outer ring structure, tearing through it. Boone had just barely gotten everyone inside and closed the hatch as the outer ring depressurized, its atmosphere violently sucked out through the damage the Deathlord plasma fire had caused. Immediately, emergency blast doors closed within the ring to isolate the damaged areas.

Green quickly raised the Earthship's shields as he spoke into the ship's intercom. "Everyone, brace yourselves!" he said. "We're about to take enemy fire!"

The Deathlord Shards zoomed by, strafing the Earthship as they passed. The ship's shields held, but the impact from the plasma blasts caused the ship to rumble and alerts to blare.

"Professor, the Deathlords fired on the ring," came Boone's voice over the comms. "It's not going to be able to take more hits like that. It's practically breaking apart already!"

*And we are far too easy of a target if we stay docked to it,* thought the Professor, grimly. "Seal the docking hatch, my good man," Green replied. "We shall be forced to leave soon."

"Roger that," answered Boone.

Green glanced at the sensor readout. The Deathlord Shards were coming back around for another pass, even as more Shards were approaching from the tether to Maxima. He quickly redirected energy from other ship systems to boost the shields, just as the Shards opened fire, hitting the Earthship again as they raced past.

The Professor frowned as he looked at the readouts on his console. There was no way for the Earthship to weather many more attacks such as that. They were going to need to leave, and soon.

★★★★★

Deep within the Conclave, Jack was still overwhelmed by his miraculous victory, surrounded by the unconscious bodies of Tannyn and his crew, when Green's voice came through his earpiece communicator. "Jack? Jack, my boy! Can you hear me?" the Professor asked.

Jack tapped his earpiece to activate it. "Yes, Professor, I'm here," he replied.

"Jack, you must get back to the ship immediately!" Green implored. "The Deathlord Shards are attacking! They're destroying the temple's outer ring! We must be away from here at once!"

Jack frowned as he realized the position the Professor and the other survivors currently found themselves in. "I… I can't make it back in time, Professor," he said. "The signal booster was destroyed, and I'm too far away to get to you before the Deathlords take out the ring."

On the Earthship, Green's eyes went wide with concern. "We… we could send someone in with a replacement signal booster," he said. "Someone who could meet you half way…"

"There's no time for that," Jack said. "You're going to have to pilot the Earthship again, Professor. Get the survivors away from the Deathlords and somewhere safe."

"Jack, I will not lose you!" Green exclaimed. "I was forced to leave Brother Shanks behind. I cannot leave you, as well!"

Jack smiled at the Professor's insistence. It made him feel good to know the old Trundel cared so much for him. But it also made him sad to know he'd have to let the Professor down. "Professor," Jack said, gently. "You have to start thinking about the lives of all the others on the ship. Right now… you're the only one who can save them."

Green's lips trembled as a tear welled in his eye. "And what of you, my boy?" he asked. "Who's going to save you?"

Jack smiled, sadly. "I'll be fine, Professor. Mourdock is with me," he lied. "There are tethers open within the temple. We'll find a way out of here through them. Don't worry about me. Just focus on protecting the others."

Green was silent for a moment. He did not want to leave Jack behind, but as his sensor readout showed more enemy Shards inbound, he realized he did not have any other choice. "Jack…" he said. "Should something happen, to either of us, I just want you to know… I'm proud of you, my boy. And if Shepherd were alive, I am positive he would be, as well."

Jack smiled at that, picking up on the unspoken good-bye. "Professor?" he said.

"Yes?"

"Thanks. For always believing in me. It's meant a lot."

Before Green could reply, the sensor alarms beeped at his console as the Deathlord Shards came around again, firing upon the Conclave's outer ring and causing the structure to break apart. The Earthship shuddered as the part of the ring on which it was docked tore away and enemy plasma fire rattled it.

"Go!" came Jack's voice over the comms. "Get to safety! Hurry!"

"Good-bye, my boy," Green said, sadly, before abandoning his station and moving to the pilot's chair.

In the Conclave, Jack turned off his communicator. He hoped the Professor and his friends would be okay. But at that moment, he realized there was nothing he could do for them. However, he might be able to do something for Mourdock. At the very least, he knew he could try to stop whatever it was the Deathlords had planned for the temple.

Jack took his leave, speeding away from the site of his battle with Tannyn. He moved quickly, disappearing down the corridor, never seeing the three shadowy figures who appeared shortly after he left.

★★★★★

The Earthship lurched as it moved away from the remains of the outer ring. Sections of the structure broke apart and drifted away from the temple. The new squad of Deathlord Shards approached, firing upon the vessel. Green clenched his jaw as he struggled to maneuver the ship away from the incoming attack. Once again, the controls felt sluggish due to his weak connection with the Earthship.

"Oh, dear," he muttered. "If I live through this, I really must take some piloting lessons…"

Alarms rang out as more Shards converged on the ship, firing upon it. Green began to sweat nervously as he looked before him at the holoscreens that showed the Earthship's shields falling dangerously low already. *There are so many systems to oversee!* thought the Professor with worry. *I cannot focus on piloting the ship, managing the shields, and fighting back against our attackers all on my own!*

As though to answer his concerns, Agent Boone appeared on the bridge's circular teleporter platform, accompanied by Krupp and the other Unlikelies. The group quickly bounded down the stairs to the different stations within the room.

"Professor! We need to get out of here!" said Boone as he slid into the chair at the ship's weapons console.

"Yes, yes, yes, I am in the process of doing precisely that, my good man!" Green replied. "But if you would be so kind as to shoot those Deathlord ships that are attacking us, that would very much assist me in doing so!"

"Wait, where's Jack?" Krupp asked.

"I fear he was not able to make it back to the ship in time," Green replied. "He ordered us to leave without him."

"But—"

"Kid," Boone said as he started targeting the incoming fightercraft. "The Earthman took on an entire fleet of Planetkillers. I think he can handle one possessed temple. Now make yourselves useful and man the ship's stations – unless you want us all to get blown to pieces."

Krupp frowned, looking at his companions. The others didn't seem to like the decision much either, but they also knew they didn't have any other option. The group quickly did as ordered and took their position at the bridge's different consoles as Green sped the vessel away from the Conclave.

Deathlord Shards moved to intercept the Earthship, but Boone and Morosa fired the ship's plasma cannons, forcing them to break away their attack run and even destroying one of the Shards.

"Good shot, lady," Boone said.

"Keep your compliments to yourself, manimal! I do not need any patriarchal validation of my skills!" Morosa snapped.

Boone gave Morosa a baffled look. Soundwave shrugged his shoulders and smiled. "That's her way of saying 'thanks'," he said.

"Sensors are picking up eleven Shards in the vicinity," Krupp reported. "They are all moving to attack us!"

"<We should probably run away from them,>" offered Snodgrass.

Green tended to agree with that sentiment. However, upon checking his holoscreens, he noticed the Entanglement Engine wasn't even close to being fully recharged.

"There are a number of Deathlord ships guarding the tether leading to Maxima, and more that look like they're headed this way," Scrappy said as he analyzed the sensor readouts. "But the other tether looks to be clear!"

"Then that is where we shall head!" said Green as he turned the ship toward it.

"Great, just when I thought we were done with Eionmeer," grumbled Boone.

The Earthship looped around and sped toward the Eionmeer tether, the dying planet looming largely just beyond it. The Shards all maneuvered to follow, loosing bolt after bolt of plasma blasts as they engaged in pursuit.

"Shields are down to 25%!" reported Krupp. "We're not going to hold out much longer if they keep attacking us!"

"I'll try to divert some power from non-essential systems to boost our rear shields," Scrappy said.

"And I shall try to vanquish more of our enemy!" exclaimed Morosa as she fired the Earthship's rear cannons. "Death to all men!" she cried, before turning toward Soundwave. "Except for you, my sweet. You're fine."

Even as two more Deathlord Shards fell to the Earthship's plasma batteries, their pursuers sought to overwhelm them with their firepower. Green increased the ship's speed, but even with his limited experience in space combat, he knew that unless he took action to avoid their adversaries, their chances of surviving were slim.

Green looked at the Earthship's viewscreen. The ghostly beam was still firing from the Eionmeer temple, travelling up from the planet and to the Conclave. "I think I have an idea!" he announced. "Everyone, hang on!"

The Professor quickly banked toward the beam, corkscrewing around it in an attempt to put something between the Earthship and its attackers. The beam of death energy appeared to react to the Earthship's presence, tiny tendrils of the energy licking out toward the ship as it maneuvered.

The tactic worked, forcing the Deathlord Shards to break their formation and to attempt to follow the Earthship as the ghostly beam absorbed the plasma blasts they'd fired. Green forced himself to concentrate, the corkscrew maneuver made more difficult by his sluggish connection to the ship.

Morosa and Boone continued to fire behind them at the Shards that were chasing the Earthship through the tether and back into the prime universe. Though the constant movement of the ship made it difficult for them to aim at their attackers, they were able to destroy two more of the Shards, which erupted in putrid green explosions.

"Seven Shards still in pursuit," Krupp stated.

"That's still seven too many," grumbled Boone.

"Our current strategy seems to be holding them off," Green said. "However, eventually, we will have flown all the way back to the dark temple and then we will no longer be able to avoid them."

"Jack used to tell us about his ship all the time," Scrappy said. "He told us it could fly really well within the gravity of a planet, almost like a smaller ship."

"What are you getting at, Scrappy?" asked Krupp.

"The Shards will be less maneuverable within the planet's atmosphere," Scrappy pointed out. "If we can get them to follow us down to the planet, it might even things up a little!"

"Since it appears as though we have no better option available to us, I believe that sounds like a fine idea!" replied Green. "Make sure you are all strapped into your seats! I am taking us toward the planet!"

The Earthship zoomed toward Eionmeer, continuing its corkscrew descent even as flames licked at its nose as it entered the planet's atmosphere. The entry made the Deathlord Shards break off as they, too, met with the friction. But such a reprieve didn't last long as the haze cleared and the remains of the Twin Rivers settlement appeared below.

"Here goes nothing!" Green said as he banked away from their descent, pulling up as the Shards were still in the process of following them.

The Shards were indeed less maneuverable within the confines of the planet's gravity, which gave Boone and Morosa the opportunity to shoot two more that spiraled away trailing smoke before they crashed into the ground.

"Two down, five to go…" said Boone.

The Earthship raced over the expanse of the Twin Rivers settlement, the area all around it covered with black rock and crawling with Deathstalkers. It flew toward the mountain range which butted up to the Twin Rivers territory, descending down into the valleys that dissected the hills as the Shards continued their chase.

Green found the Earthship controls to be even more sluggish as the craft now had to account for the increased gravity of atmospheric flight. His maneuvers were not nearly as effective as he'd hoped they'd be, with more enemy plasma fire finding their mark.

"Shields down to 9%!" said Krupp in alarm.

"Hold on, I'm going to head back to the settlement!" informed Green. "We shall try to use the dark temple to put some distance between us and the Shards!"

Green banked the ship back toward the settlement, the dark temple looming ominously before them. He began to circle around the structure as the Shards followed, two of them breaking away as they did so.

"Two of the Shards are maneuvering around the other side of the temple to cut us off," informed Krupp.

"So I see," replied Green. "I was hoping they'd do that."

"Why were you hoping for the bad guys to cut us off?" asked Boone.

"So that I might do… this!" the Professor replied.

Green had the Earthship pull upward, climbing in altitude just as the two Deathlord Shards came around the temple. The maneuver was so sudden that the three Shards following the ship did not react fast enough, and four of the ships crashed into each other, all of them disintegrating in a spectacular explosion.

Everyone on the bridge cried out in celebration. “Only one Shard left!” said Krupp with excitement. “We might actually make it out of this!”

“Where is it?” asked Scrappy as he looked at his sensor screen. “I don’t see it on my readouts.”

“It maneuvered away behind the temple,” Morosa said. “That ghost beam must be interfering with our sensors.”

“Get us back into space, away from the beam,” ordered Boone. “We can finish him off there.”

Before Green could comply, the Earthship rumbled as direct plasma fire impacted it. Too late, Green saw the final Shard emerge from the clouds, speeding directly toward the Earthship as it loosed its volley of blasts.

The Earthship rumbled. Alarms blared.

“Shields are down!” Krupp cried.

“LOOK OUT!” shouted Boone.

Green tried to maneuver the Earthship away from the incoming fightercraft, but the controls did not respond quickly enough. The Shard rammed into the vessel, hitting its side. Everyone on the bridge cried out as the Earthship was knocked off its trajectory.

Both ships tumbled toward the beam of death energy. The Shard hit it directly, disintegrating as it passed through. The Earthship just barely nicked the beam, but as it did, an explosion could be heard from the rear of the ship, alerts frantically flashing on each console in response.

The entire ship rumbled as Green struggled in vain to control their descent.

“We’ve lost one of our thrusters!” Scrappy cried.

“Engines are failing!” warned Krupp.

“Professor! Do something!” cried Boone.

Green frowned, fear gripping his chest as he looked at the bridge viewscreen. The mountain range beyond the settlement loomed before them as he fought to correct the ship’s descent.

“Everybody, prepare yourselves,” Green said. “We’re going down!”

The Earthship sped toward the ground, just barely correcting itself before it plowed into the black rock that covered the surface. Deathstalkers flew in every direction and were crushed as the Earthship sped through them, rumbling toward the mountains that stood awaiting the ship's inevitable impact.

Everyone on the Earthship held on for dear life as their surroundings shook violently. The high-pitched shriek of metal tearing rang out all around them as the ship's underbelly scraped against the jagged rock below it, the sound mixing with the cacophony of blaring alarms.

Finally, the Earthship slowed, having torn a scar through the land, and came to rest right before the mountains began. The ship bucked forward as it came to a stop, then collapsed back down on its belly with a groan. Its hull was ravaged. Its side was badly damaged. One of its engines bellowed smoke.

A Terrormancer finished his climb up one of the smaller summits before the mountain range, looking out into the distance to see the damaged Earthship lying on the ground. The dark monolith hovered beside him. He raised his staff and the monolith turned vertical in response. As the Terrormancer brought his staff to the ground, the monolith slammed into the top of the hill, black rock racing from it in all directions as it began to cover the area.

The Terrormancer turned and placed his hand on the smooth surface of the tall rock, then pointed his staff toward the Earthship far down below.

"Finish it…" was all he said.

With that command, there was a shift in the movement of the swarm of Deathstalkers around the vessel as the deadly creatures rushed toward it, like predators descending upon a wounded prey, closing in for the kill.

# Chapter 23

Alabaster couldn't feel his legs. He was lying among the rubble of the Capitol Supertower, a heavy structural beam on top of him. It was hard to breathe. His head throbbed. He gazed upward toward the sky. The planet's defense rings had stopped firing, but the assault from them was still having an effect. He could hear the despairing cries of the populous as the city continued to fall all around him.

*Something must have gone wrong,* he thought, sadly. *It was too early. It couldn't have happened yet. Somehow, the Deathlord knew to fight back… how could I have accounted for this?*

Alabaster heard a rustling sound of feet as they kicked aside debris from the floor. He turned and looked as one of the Bobs, now in the shape of Verrutus, approached him. "Are you still alive, Chief?" the creature asked, regarding him with a smug curiosity.

"Not for long… most likely…" Alabaster replied.

"You are probably correct," Verrutus said. The Deathlord gazed upward at the view Alabaster had been looking at, the planet's defense rings hazy in the distance. "You have no idea how long I've waited for this day. All the sneaking around… all the pretending… it can finally end. Now, I can stop hiding. Now, I can make the galaxy *tremble*."

"Why… now…" Alabaster asked. "What… happened?"

Verrutus looked back down at Alabaster. "Your precious Princess surprised me," he replied. "She figured out how to fight back in a way I hadn't anticipated. Once she hurt me enough to cause me to lose my cover, I decided it was time to act."

"The… Princess…" croaked Alabaster, smiling. "She beat you?"

"A momentary setback," Verrutus said. "I am currently in the process of dealing with her and fully intend to finish what I started. Of that, I can assure you."

"You shouldn't… make promises… you can't keep…" said Alabaster.

Verrutus chuckled. "Ah, you think something is going to happen to me, do you?" the Deathlord said. "You think that foolish robot is actually going to succeed in his hair-brained plan to kill me?"

Alabaster frowned. "You… know… about that?"

"Of course, I do," Verrutus said. "The robot isn't nearly as smart as he thinks he is. Nor are you, for that matter. I've been undermining him from the start. His missile will be quite ineffective, I assure you. And I have someone on his ship so that I can gloat about it to his face before I destroy him."

"The missile?" Alabaster said, his chest filling with relief. He sighed and then laughed, happy to know that despite how upside-down things had gone… the plan was still intact.

Verrutus stepped forward to loom over Alabaster, menacingly. "Why are you laughing?" he asked.

"Tell me, Deathlord..." croaked Alabaster. "Do you play... Optiass[14]?"

Verrutus glared down at Alabaster with smug distaste. "I do not concern myself with the mindless games of my inferiors."

Alabaster smiled a pained smile. "Pity," he said, coughing. "Then the irony… of the Swindle[15]… will be lost on you..."

Verrutus gave Alabaster a curious look. "What are you blathering about?" the Deathlord asked.

"You'll see," Alabaster said. "I'm just sorry... I won't be around... to see you die."

Alabaster looked up and met the Deathlord's gaze. And with his last breath, Phineas Alabaster spoke his final words.

"Game... over..."

The slythru that controlled Banjax didn't know what was going on, but it knew something was wrong. He'd heard the call of his master when Verrutus had revealed himself and ordered the Secret Army to attack the Empire. But Banjax had been in hyperspace at the time, travelling to the coordinates Heckubus Moriarty had set and then locked him out of. He'd asked his master what he

---

[14] Optiass is a chess-like game where players must convince pieces to move on the board rather than manually move them.

[15] A "Swindle" is an Optiass strategy of purposefully putting one's self in a losing position to trick one's opponent into allowing for a win or a draw.

should do, but it would seem Verrutus was too busy to respond. Thus, Banjax decided that, for now, he would simply stick to the plan unless directed otherwise.

Banjax checked his navigation computer and saw they were soon set to arrive at their mysterious destination. The security monitor in his ship's hangar bay showed Heckubus working on his missile. The robot hadn't left the blasted thing unattended for a second.

*If I'm going to make my move, it will need to be now,* Banjax thought.

Banjax left the ship's bridge and made his way to the small detention hold he used to ferry bounties for collection. Xao was inside, looking bored and miserable. He perked up when Banjax entered. "Finally!" Xao cried. "How much longer Xao have to be stuck in here?"

"Not any longer. I'm here to free you."

"About time! Now hurry and let Xao out! Xao getting claustrophobic in such teeny-tiny cell. Xao requires leg room!"

"I need you to agree to something first," Banjax said, trying to ignore his annoyance with the Izard. "I need a distraction to get the robot away from that blasted missile of his so I can disable it."

"You need Xao to create distraction? Xao can do that! Xao great at being distracting!"

"Obviously," muttered Banjax. "I need you to go to the escape pod and try to get away. You know how to work one?"

"Psh. Silly glitch," said Xao, bemused. "Of course Xao know how to operate escape pod! Xao was *born* on an escape pod."

"That explains a lot, actually," muttered Banjax as he opened Xao's cell. "Just wait for the robot to arrive and try to stop you. That'll give me the opening I need."

"*Then* can we kill him?"

"Yes, then we can kill him."

Xao clapped his hands, giddy with excitement. "Xao really hope robot programmed to feel pain! Xao want robot to suffer!"

"I think foiling his so-called brilliant plan will make him suffer enough. Now get going. And remember, don't eject the pod until he arrives. Understand?"

"This not Xao's first escape. Xao an expert on knowing how to run away!"

"Of that, I have no doubt," said Banjax. "Off with you. I'll pull the alarm once I'm in position."

Banjax let Xao slink off to find his way to the escape pod. The bounty hunter was sure Xao would screw up his assignment somehow, but it didn't matter at this point. All he needed was a little bit of time. Banjax made his way toward the cargo bay and then opened up an access panel on the wall, hitting the emergency alarm and calling the cargo bay's communication system. "Boss? Boss, you there?" Banjax asked.

"Of course, I am. Where else would I be?" snapped Heckubus. "What's going on? Why is the alarm going off?"

"It's Xao. Somehow the sniveling sewer farragut[16] escaped the holding cell. He's making his way to one of the escape pods now. You're closer to it than I am. I need you to go and intercept him before he gets away."

"That is Henchman work," stated Heckubus. "I'm busy doing evil genius things."

"If he escapes, you'll never get to properly punish him for betraying you."

Heckubus tapped at his metallic chin. "Hmmm. Fair point. Very well! I shall go and put a stop to this hair-brained escape then, if only to ensure that moron gets his appropriate comeuppance."

Heckubus left the cargo hold, marching off to attempt to intercept Xao. Once he was gone, Banjax made his way into the hold and opened up the missile, setting about to dismantle it and render it harmless.

Heckubus arrived at the escape pods just in time to see Xao close the hatch to one and seal it shut from the inside. Xao looked smugly out of the porthole of the tiny pod, which was big enough to only hold one person. As Heckubus approached, Xao laughed. "You too late, *muggahugga!*" Xao taunted. "Xao already seal the pod door! Xao gonna escape, and silly robot can't do anything to stop it! Nyah, nyah, nyah!"

Xao stuck his slithery tongue out at Heckubus. Heckubus narrowed his ocular orbs. "And why would I want to stop you?" he asked. "Go ahead. Eject the pod and be on your way."

---

[16] A farragut is an unhygienic animal that's a cross between a weasel, a rat, and a fox.

Xao gave Heckubus a funny look before his expression changed to one of suspicion. "Ah, ha! Silly robot try and use reverse psychology on Xao! But Xao too smart! Xao gonna escape anyway! Toodaroo, *roboboi!*"

"Far be it for me to lecture one as smart as you, your *Thugnificence*, but you do realize that if you eject now you'll be doing so from a ship travelling at the speed of light through hyperspace."

"What of it?"

"Oh, nothing. Except that based on our current trajectory and the fact that hyperspace contains no friction with which to slow you down, if you eject now, you'll most likely slam into the gravitational shadow of our destination before the escape pod has a chance to exit from lightspeed. And should you somehow miraculously miss said gravitational shadow, you'll most likely be stranded in hyperspace until you die a slow and agonizing death from thirst and starvation."

Xao's eyes went wide at that. "Say whaaaaaa?"

Heckubus twiddled his fingers, thoughtfully. "You know, come to think of it… that is an appropriately slow and torturous way to die. One I quite approve of, upon further analysis."

Heckubus then opened the escape pod's control panel and began tapping away at it. Xao looked through the pod's porthole with growing concern. "Hey!" he cried. "What you do?"

"Adjusting the pod's exit trajectory to ensure you miss the upcoming gravitational shadow," Heckubus said. "You'll be trapped, adrift in hyperspace, until you die. Sure, someone may pick up on your pod's emergency transponder, but quite frankly, the odds of that happening in this area of space are quite marginal, so I'm entirely happy with this decision."

"Wait!" cried Xao, looking panicked. "You can't—"

"Oh, but I can!" said Heckubus, gleefully. "Toodaloo, you moronic, spineless, jackanape."

Xao frowned. "Toodaroo? That Xao's line…" he said, sadly.

"Then allow me to use my signature line," Heckubus said as he gripped the ejection lever. "Mwuahahaha!"

Heckubus pulled the lever, ejecting Xao's escape pod from the ship and letting it twist off into the great empty void of hyperspace at the speed of light.

When the despicable Izard[17] was gone, Heckubus brushed off his hands, rather pleased with himself.

"And good riddance!" he said. "I do believe I've wasted enough of my time with this thinly-veiled little distraction."

Heckubus then made his way back to the cargo hold. When he entered, he found Banjax was waiting for him. "Ah! There you are, Henchman," Heckubus said. "You'll be pleased to hear the Izard will not be bothering us any longer…"

"Well, that's two things that will no longer be bothering me," Banjax said as he pulled his blaster from his belt and aimed it directly at Heckubus. "I think this little charade has gone on long enough."

Heckubus eyed the blaster in Banjax's hand. "Gasp! Oh, no! A double-cross? From you? Why… I would have *never* expected that!"

Banjax's eyes narrowed.

"In case you couldn't tell, that was sarcasm, you twit," Heckubus muttered.

"Yeah, I got it," sneered Banjax. "So you expected this to happen?"

"But of course I did," Heckubus replied. "In fact, I was counting on it. Why else would I keep around such an obvious slythru-infected minion such as yourself?"

"You know I'm being controlled by a slythru?"

"Indeed. I was there when they infected you, in fact. Well, not me, personally, but the security-bots, which I had hacked into to save that peevish Visini pirate, saw the whole thing. It was why I sought you out, in fact."

"Sought me out?" asked Banjax, confused. "But you came to Xao…"

"Only because you were working for him," replied Heckubus. "I was never interested in anything Xao had to offer, you see. My entire purpose of dealing with him was so you could keep tabs on my movements and report them to Verrutus."

"I'm tempted to ask about your reasoning behind doing something so stupid," said Banjax. "But I think it best to just kill you right now and save me the headache of having to listen to you drone on."

---

[17] Izards are a serpentine race that very closely resemble Earth's depictions of Oriental Dragons.

"Before you kill me, I'm going to require some time to sufficiently monologue about my brilliance."

"No."

Banjax pulled the trigger on his blaster, but nothing happened. Banjax looked at the blaster in confusion and tried to fire it again, but it would not work. Heckubus glared at the bounty hunter, smugly. "Did I neglect to mention that when I gave you your new armaments, I'd programmed in safeguards to them so that they would not work against me?"

Banjax sneered and tossed away the weapon before reaching behind him with his cybernetic arm and pulling out a different blaster. "I guess it's a good thing I kept my old one then," he said, aiming it at Heckubus.

Again, Heckubus looked unconcerned. "But me revealing the genius of my plan is half the fun!" he said, twiddling his fingers. "Don't you want to know how I'm going to blow up your master?"

"Sorry, robot. You won't be blowing anything up today."

"Oh, don't be so sure," Heckubus replied, holding up a tiny detonator switch. Banjax barely had time to register what it was before Heckubus clicked it.

Suddenly, Banjax's robotic arm exploded, the blast hitting him squarely in his chest and shoulder, knocking him back. Banjax screamed out in pain as the smoking ruin of his robotic arm hung limply at his side, burns raging across his chest. Heckubus strutted up to him and glared down triumphantly.

"I suppose that's one of the disadvantages of carrying a tiny missile in your arm," the robot said. "That an enterprising evil genius might tune into its detonation frequency and blow it up at some opportune time. Luckily, you made it easy when you loaded it with one of the missiles I gave you."

Banjax clutched at his serious wound, glaring up at Heckubus with malice. "You… you… deceitful… little…"

"Oh, pish-tosh!" mocked Heckubus. "You just tried double-crossing me, you dolt. Don't be upset that I double-crossed you better. It's *extremely* unprofessional."

"I'll… kill you!" Banjax grunted as he tried to get back to his feet, but Heckubus promptly grabbed a small tubular device that was hidden nearby and fired it upon the bounty hunter. An electro-net flew out, wrapping itself around

Banjax and pinning him to the wall. Banjax cried out as the net shocked him into submission.

"Now, now, not so fast," Heckubus admonished. "I'm the only one in a position to be doing any killing around here."

"Then… get it over with!" said Banjax through gritted teeth.

"Sadly, killing you accomplishes nothing, especially since I still have use for you," Heckubus said, casually. "Now, do me a favor and let your master know I wish to speak with him."

"And what makes you think he'll care to hear what you have to say?" asked Banjax.

"Oh, trust me. He'll want to hear this," Heckubus replied. "He's going to want to know what it was that ultimately defeated him."

Banjax chuckled derisively. "Defeated?" he growled. "Verrutus is orchestrating attacks all over the Empire this very moment. He's destroying Omnicron, laying waste to entire fleets of spaceships, and murdering anyone he can lay hands on. He's anything but defeated!"

"Oh, he is. He just doesn't know it yet," Heckubus said. "Would you care to tell him that?

Banjax was silent for a moment, simply glaring at Heckubus with loathing. Then, he closed his eyes, and when he opened them back up, they were pure white. "So, we meet again, robot," Verrutus said.

"Indeed we do," Heckubus replied. "Your minion tells me you've been busy, recently. Something about attacking the Empire?"

"I'm currently at odds with the little Princess," Verrutus said. "But it is not an issue. The bulk of my Secret Army is still intact, and between Mellegogg and me, we will tear her pathetic Empire to shreds."

"That is unfortunate," commented Heckubus. "I'd hoped to destroy you before you could do any widespread damage. Not that I'm against widespread damage, mind you – what self-respecting evil genius would be? Just that I did not want you to have the satisfaction of partaking in such a thing before I had the opportunity to annihilate you."

Verrutus chuckled. "Many have been trying to kill me, today. But I cannot be killed. I'm a Deathlord. Killing me is impossible."

"So you say, but I beg to differ. You see, once I figured out who you really were, I came up with a plan to *do* the impossible."

"You figured out who I was?"

"Indeed, I did," Heckubus replied. "That is why I brought us to the destination at which we should be arriving just about… now."

Banjax's ship then dropped out of lightspeed and exited hyperspace. Heckubus called up an image of their destination on a monitor in the cargo bay, showing a large pink sphere in orbit around a distant sun.

"And there you are in all your glory," Heckubus commented. "The planet Bob – thousands of miles of protoplasmic goo wrapped around an impressively large neurofibrilious mass. In hindsight, who you truly were was rather obvious, actually. The concept that you would be able to exert control over so many beings at the same time was quite extraordinary. A colleague of mine commented on it, and I realized there was only one other being in the known universe which had the ability to process sensory data on such a wide scale. And once I realized that only Bob could possibly do such a thing, all the rest became completely clear to me."

"I suppose it doesn't matter, now," Verrutus said. "The Princess forced my hand and I had to reveal myself. Everyone now knows what you apparently figured out."

"Ah, that may be so. But such a revelation caught them all by surprise! Whereas I had time to prepare!"

"Yes, your so-called *Deathkiller* missiles," mused Verrutus as he looked at the missile in the cargo bay. "A doomsday weapon meant to, what? Destroy me?"

"Is that not the function of a doomsday weapon?" asked Heckubus. "To destroy?"

"Your efforts have all been for naught, machine," Verrutus said. "I've been watching you at every turn. I knew exactly what you were doing every step of the way. I confiscated your primary cache of those missiles. Then I took your back-ups. And now, the very last one, which you have been working so diligently on, has been completely disabled. My servant here made sure of that while you were taking care of the Izard."

"Yes, I figured as much," Heckubus said. "And that would certainly be a cause for concern, had I ever actually intended to use the missiles."

Verrutus looked at Heckubus with suspicion. "What do you mean by that?" he asked.

"Ah! The perfect segue into my monologue!" Heckubus exclaimed. "You see, I knew you'd be keeping an eye on me after I left my companions at Port Somewhere. I had no way of knowing who you controlled. But I did have a way of knowing who you didn't! So after hacking into the Empire's xenobiological index and learning everything I could about you, I approached Chief Alabaster about a special project designed specifically to destroy you – one which would be worked on only by hand-picked Paragons, which we knew your slythru couldn't infect!"

Verrutus's eyes narrowed. "Paragons?" he said.

"Yes, a whole group of them, working in secret with the assistance of my own minion – an annoying but dependable little robot which you also could not infect. But even with entrusting my brilliant scheme to those I knew you couldn't control, I could not discount the notion that you might discover my plans to undo you by some other means. So, while Chief Alabaster set up the construction of the real doomsday device, I sought out someone I knew, for a fact, you controlled, and then proceeded to use him to feed you false information about my activities! For I knew if you believed you were keeping tabs on me and my machinations, you would not be looking closely elsewhere, thus giving the Chief and I the freedom we needed to create the instrument of your destruction!"

"And what might that be, exactly?"

"So glad you asked," replied Heckubus. "After analyzing the xenobiological data about you in the Empire's databases, I designed a special *death laser*, which I intend to destroy you with."

"A death laser?"

"A laser which causes death, yes."

"You cannot hope to defeat me with a mere laser…" Verrutus growled.

"Oh, this is not just any death laser…" Heckubus said, giddily. "It's a GIANT FREAKIN' DEATH LASER! MWUAHAHAHA!"

On the viewscreen, a hyperspace window opened and out flew a large, cylindrical structure close to the size of a Regal capital ship. It appeared to already be powered up, with chaotic red energy visibly roiling in a myriad of exhaust ports located along its body.

Verrutus's eyes went wide at the sight of it.

"More specifically… a giant freakin' death laser that is specifically attuned to the molecular structure of that gelatinous mess you've surrounded yourself with. When fired, it will cut through that protoplasmic ooze as though it didn't even exist. However, just to be on the safe side, I've gone a step further and ensured that the blast will cause a chain reaction that will make the ooze unstable enough to destroy itself, just to ensure that there is no part of you left. At all."

"No…" choked Verrutus. "It's… it's not possible!"

"Actually, it's quite possible, as evidenced by the ginormous weapon of destruction I have currently aimed directly at you."

"You couldn't have built something that big!" Verrutus said, his voice panicked. "I'd have known!"

"Yes, you would have if there had been any materials required to build it," Heckubus replied. "But the Chief wisely used the Royal Corps of Paragon Engineers to create it. Working off my designs, they manifested the entire thing, piece by piece, in secret. No materials were required to be shipped anywhere. All we needed was time. Thus, I simply had to keep your attention focused on what you *thought* was our real plan in building this ridiculous and completely impractical missile. A simple use of misdirection, which you fell for hook, line, and sinker."

Heckubus then turned to a nearby panel and opened a video channel to the giant freakin' death laser. The image of Hunchy appeared on the screen.

"Minion! Minion, can you hear me?"

"Yes! Yes, former Master!" the tiny robot said. "Hunchy hear you loud and clear!"

"I don't know what is more degrading," Heckubus mused, glancing back at Verrutus. "The fact that you were so obviously out-played by me, or that you're going to be killed by a thing called 'Hunchy'. You may fire when ready, Hunchy!"

"NO!" Verrutus cried. "DON'T!"

Heckubus turned and regarded Verrutus with amusement. "What's that?" Heckubus asked. "Is it possible that the mighty Deathlord Supreme suddenly knows the fear of impending doom?"

"You think defeating me will stop us?" Verrutus sneered. "You have no idea what's in store for you and your friends! Our plans are already in motion and in the end – *you* will be the one who's destroyed!"

"Oh, you think so, do you?" snooted Heckubus.

"I *know* so!"

"I think we both know that in the eternal struggle between good and evil, good is always destined to fail because... well, good is stupid. Which means the real fight, when it comes down to it, is between those who aren't bound by pesky things such as morals or ethics, which you and your lot clearly aren't. But no matter how carefully you've planned and how far ahead you think you may be, I can say with absolute certainty that I will never be defeated by the likes of you. And would you like to know why?"

"Why?" asked Verrutus through gritted teeth.

Heckubus approached and leaned toward the Deathlord Supreme, the robot's large ocular orbs gazing directly into his white, soulless eyes.

"Because you may be evil, Deathlord," Heckubus said. "But I'm *eviler!*"

At that very moment, outside the spaceship on which Heckubus and Verrutus had their final exchange, a massive red beam of destruction blasted forth from the gigantic cylindrical weapon floating close by, speeding toward the planet Bob with the fury of a thousand suns. The beam shot across thousands of miles in an instant, impacting the pink gelatinous surface of the large sphere and burrowing though it to its core.

The massive brain-like organism that was Verrutus could do nothing to protect itself as the laser raged toward it. In the end, the being that could control billions of minions through the sheer will of his thoughts could not stop the machinations of a single megalomaniacal robot.

A mournful groan emanated from the spherical body as Verrutus was consumed by the laser beam, the gelatinous ooze curling in on itself as the planet slowly imploded. Layer after layer of the ooze roiled and bubbled as it consumed itself, the planet decaying like a piece of rapidly rotting fruit. The chain reaction from the laser continued to do its dastardly work, until finally, the largest and most sinister threat the Regalus Empire had ever known was snuffed out of existence forever, its death knell ending with a pathetic, quiet little *PLOOP* sound.

Nothing was left of the planetary body once known as Bob. And in the silent, empty void of space where it had once existed, the only thing that could be heard, if one listened closely enough, was a fleeting sound. And that sound went rather something like this:

"Mwuahahahaha."

# Chapter 24

Anna grappled with Verrutus, using her light to fight back the many tar-like legs striking at her. The two tangled above the galaxy as their consciousnesses clashed, fighting for the fate of the universe. Though Anna did not yet fully understand her power, she had learned enough to know how to use it against the Deathlord, despite his being stronger than her.

Verrutus lashed out at Anna with his spindly legs, striking her ferociously. Anna took the blows, refusing to let them banish her from this construct where the Deathlord controlled his slaves. Anna knew she wasn't just fighting for her own life, but for the lives of all those Verrutus had robbed of their freedom.

Then, something quite unexpected happened.

Verrutus suddenly cried out and his body began to burn, the tar-like substance he was comprised of fluttering away like embers in the wind. The Deathlord writhed and churned in agony, his fiery red eyes wide with shock and pain.

Anna watched as Verrutus, the Deathlord Supreme, disappeared before her very eyes. When the creature she'd been battling was gone, Anna looked around, confused and worried it was some type of trick. She moved to a cluster of silver threads and made contact with it, receiving images from those they were connected to.

Across the galaxy, all the incarnations of Verrutus were losing their forms, falling to the ground in puddles of ooze. One by one, they all lost their shape. The chaos and destruction they'd been causing ceased, disappearing along with them. Anna had no way to know if it were something she did that destroyed the Deathlord. But she did know one thing…

Verrutus was gone, and he would not be coming back.

Anna gazed back down upon the image of the galaxy. There were so many psychic threads still connected to the spider web the Deathlord had created. So many people still yet to be freed from the influence of the slythrus. But there was a more pressing battle which needed to be fought, and as she gazed back down at the planet of Eionmeer, she saw the swirling tempest of trapped souls there, still writhing in agony in their prison.

*I cannot allow those poor souls to suffer any longer!* Anna thought. *Time to finish this!*

Anna grabbed onto her silver thread once more and began sliding down it, racing toward the swirling ghostly tempest. She released herself and fell toward the tsunami of death, gathering all her light within her and harnessing its power.

"BE FREE!" she cried as she fell into the tempest, her light exploding with the power of a thousand suns, destroying the vile prison once and for all and allowing the souls trapped there to finally escape.

Anna opened her eyes, tasting the tangy flavor of copper on her lips as her nose bled. She felt dizzy and disoriented as she released her hold on the dark temple's access orb and fell to her knees, a wave of exhaustion washing over her.

She looked up in time to see the massive pillar of death energy die, individual souls escaping from it and disappearing as they flew away. The beam stopped firing and the ghostly illumination it emanated faded.

Only then did she become aware of the sounds of battle. She turned to see her protector, Rionknidis, kneeling nearby with his eyes closed. In the chamber beyond, the three other members of the Vanguard were fighting with robed figures, the clashing of their weapons casting the only light in the darkness.

Anna forced herself up, crawling to the edge of the platform and looking down on the battle raging below her. Her protectors moved with speed and skill, but those they fought matched them in every respect.

*I must do something!* Anna thought. *I must help them!*

But outside of the mental construct that the access orb had allowed her to enter, she did not know how to use the power of the Ancients. Thus, all Anna could do was watch, helpless, as those who'd sworn their lives to her put them on the line in a deadly dance with the servants of the Deathlords.

Seqis hopped back to avoid a strike by his opponent's scythe and held out Grapthaar, aiming it toward his assailant. Lightning burst forth from the hammer, but the Terrormancer morphed his scythe's blade into a shield which absorbed the energy.

Dahuud flung her daggers at her attacker, who twirled his scythe and deflected them. As quickly as she threw her weapons, Dahuud manifested new ones and attempted to strike, but the reach of her enemy's armament kept her at a distance, preventing her from getting close enough to inflict any real damage.

Lugard skillfully fenced with his opponent, using Starbeam to strike out and needle the Terrormancer with which he fought. But despite the Paragon's speed and prowess with his blade, the Terrormancer kept Lugard busy dodging his counterattacks, never allowing the swordsman enough opportunity to land a decisive blow.

The Terrormancer Seqis was facing brought his scythe down in a powerful overhead swing, which Seqis blocked with Grapthaar. Sparks flew as the hammer met the blade of ghost energy, the two weapons locked together as the Terrormancer pressed his weight against the clash.

"I sssssense your fear, Paragon…" the Terrormancer hissed.

"And yet you have no measure of my courage!" replied Seqis.

"You are brave. This issss true," said the Terrormancer, his forked tongue flicking out as he spoke. "But it issss fear which drivessss you – and I know what you fear the most!"

"You know nothing of me, vile creature!"

"Oh, but I do!" the Terrormancer said. "I know you are bound to the fate of the Princessssss! And your greatest fear is failing to protect her!"

"I will not fail to do my sacred duty."

"Be you ssssso sure, Paragon?" asked the Terrormancer, his gaze travelling behind Seqis. "Becausssse you are about to!"

Seqis glanced behind him to see the Terrormancer was staring at Anna, who had crawled to the edge of the soul vault's platform and was watching the battle. Seqis's eyes widened as he immediately realized what the Terrormancer intended to do.

"No!" he said.

"NOW BROTHERSSSS!" the Terrormancer cried.

With that command, each Terrormancer leapt backward, disengaging from their fights. They each swung their scythes, the ghostly blades at their ends launching off, spinning toward the Princess.

"VANGUARD!" shouted Seqis.

Without wasting another moment, all three of the Royal Vanguard sprang into action. Lugard hurled Starbeam at one of the ghost blades, knocking it off course. Dahuud leapt up into the air, flinging a volley of moonfyre daggers at another of the ghost blades, sending it off its mark. Seqis stepped forward and held his hammer out, firing lightning from it.

Anna cried out as she flinched away, the third ghost blade barely missing her as the lightning from Grapthaar just barely knocked it away in time.

The momentary distraction gave the Terrormancers the opportunity they needed. They immediately rushed forward, striking their adversaries with their staffs. One blow landed on Lugard's throat, causing him to stumble backward, choking. Another hit Dahuud in the chest as she was landing from her leap, sending her flying backward. And the last blow hit Seqis in the base of his skull, forcing him to fall to the ground.

The ghost blades that had been thrown returned to the Terrormancers, who caught them at the end of their staffs, forming scythes once more. Seqis scrambled to his knees, trying to recover from the vicious blow he'd received. He turned just in time to see the Terrormancers launch their blades once more.

Each blade rocketed toward a member of the Vanguard, hitting them square in the chest and sending them flying backward with extreme force.

"NO!!!" Anna screamed.

Lugard, Dahuud, and Seqis all landed at the base of the stairs to the platform Anna was on, large dents in the front of their ultanium[18] breastplates from the impacts of the ghost blades. They all gasped in pain, the force of the blows powerful enough to have knocked the wind out of them.

Seqis gritted his teeth and looked at the Terrormancers as their ghost blades returned to them once more. Before they had a chance to attack again, Seqis pushed himself forward, holding his hammer out, and shouted:

"OYARSA GRAPTHAAR!!![19]"

Thunder boomed as arcs of lightning shot from the Paragon's hammer, multiple strands of energy blasting toward each Terrormancer.

The Terrormancers formed their ghost blades into shields, which protected them from the wrath of Grapthaar. The robed figures braced themselves as the lightning continued to strike against their cover, pushing them back with the intensity of its impact.

Seqis slowly rose to his feet, continuing to concentrate as he unleashed the elemental power of his hammer upon his enemies. Lugard and Dahuud rose to

---

[18] Ultanium is the strongest known metal in the universe, and one of the rarest.

[19] In Old Solar, the language of the Ancients, "Oyarsa Grapthaar" means "Hope Is The Power."

their feet, as well, remanifesting their weapons and coming to Seqis's side. When his sworn companions had joined him, Seqis ceased fire, lowering his hammer.

The Terrormancers stood with their shields up, unaffected by the attack with which Seqis had bombarded them. They lowered their shields to reform their scythes and stood in a mirror of unity to that of the Vanguard – three against three, facing down one another.

"As I said," Seqis stated. "I will not fail."

The Terrormancer at the center of the group stepped forward, his burned face twisted into a scowl. "Your skill in battle issss impressive," he said. "The ssssssix of us could fight all day to a ssssstand still. But when our powerssss are combined with that of an army, you have no hope to sssssurvive!"

"Then I suppose it's a pity you have no army."

"Oh, but we do…"

From the dark entrance into the chamber, men with blaster rifles emerged. Dozens of them, all lead by Commander Gunner, who slowly fanned out within the room, their weapons trained upon the Vanguard.

Seqis, Lugard, and Dahuud immediately held up their weapons in a guarded stance, looking at the new arrivals in surprise. The Terrormancers all smiled. "We have a Sssssecret Army, Paragon!" the Terrormancer proclaimed. "And they give usssss the advantage we need to defeat you!"

Seqis, Lugard, and Dahuud all looked around, nervously, waiting for the barrage of blaster bolts to begin. But the slythru-infected soldiers did not attack. The Terrormancers glanced back at their allies.

"Don't jusssst stand there!" hissed the Terrormancer. "Kill them!"

"You heard him, men," Commander Gunner said. "Kill them."

Suddenly, each soldier turned his weapon on one of the Terrormancers and opened fire. The unexpected blaster bolts ripped through the creatures, causing them to scream and cry out. The Vanguard watched in surprise as their opponents were cut down, their bodies eventually turning to smoke and drifting away, leaving only their charred black robes behind to fall to the floor.

"Good riddance," sneered Gunner as he spat on one of the robes.

Despite their recent stroke of fortune, the Vanguard did not let their guard down as the soldiers approached them.

"There is no need to fear us," Commander Gunner said, holding up his hands. "We are on your side."

"You are of the Secret Army," Seqis said. "How are you not controlled by the slythru?"

"Because of her," Gunner said with a nod.

The Vanguard all turned to see Anna coming down the stairs, escorted by Rionknidis. Immediately, all the soldiers knelt, placing their fists over their hearts.

"Hail, Princess Glorianna!" they all said. "Hail, the breaker of chains!"

Anna smiled as she came forward toward all the men. "I am glad to see you have all been freed," she said.

Gunner got back to his feet. "I can still feel the slythru inside of me," he said. "It still tries to command me. To control me. To bend me to its will."

"I know the feeling," Anna replied. "I still sense mine, as well. But by accepting its darkness, we take away its power. We can control it with our light, and so long as we surround ourselves with those we love, and who love us, we will never fall back under its influence."

"Your Highness," said Gunner. "I think it's safe to say that I, and all the men here, were forced to do terrible things under the influence of the Deathlords. Things which will haunt and shame us to the end of our days. But if what you say is true, and light and love are the key to never again falling prey to these vile creatures… then it is your light we shall pledge ourselves to, and your love that we will work to earn until our dying breaths."

All the men stood and nodded toward Anna.

"We pledge ourselves to you and Legacy Prime, Princess," Gunner stated. "We may no longer be members of the Secret Army. But we are now members of your army."

"I accept your pledges of service, my friends," Anna said. "And I thank you. For I fear that in order to survive what awaits us outside this temple, we shall indeed need an army."

# Chapter 25

The Alpha Force armory on *The Shieldbearer* was bustling with activity when Wil and Fred arrived. The remaining Alpha Force units had helped to purge the ship of any trace of Verrutus and were now readying for the upcoming assault on Maxima. It didn't take long for the two men to find what remained of Alpha Force MX017 re-enforcing their suits with some of the equalarium plates confiscated on Essox.

"Lord Blackfyre, Lord Goldstone," Roadblock said as they approached. "Come to wish us luck?"

"Indeed we have," said Fredreek. "We would have thrown you all a going away party, as well, but it would seem Verrutus destroyed all the good booze in his rampage throughout the ship. Just when you thought that Deathlord couldn't be any more evil, right?"

"Actually, I'm not just here to wish you luck," Wilvelm said. "I'm here to join you."

Everyone gave Wil a curious look.

"Join us?" asked Roadblock.

"This was my plan," Wilvelm said. "It's not right to send you guys into harm's way while I stay behind."

"With all due respect, Lord Blackfyre, this is our job," said Missionary.

"Missionary is right," Skeptic said. "We're front-line fighters. This is what we're trained to do."

"I understand. But I'm still going with you."

"My Lord, we train for six months, minimum, to learn how to operate Alpha Force armor," Roadblock said. "Someone with no experience can't do what we're about to and hope to survive."

"I trained in power armor usage at the academy. It's not that different from what you guys go through in Alpha Force training," Wilvelm said. "I know enough to get by."

Roadblock looked at the rest of his squad, who all shrugged. "He proved himself on Essox," Lucky said.

"He's cool under fire," added Skeptic.

"And he's gotten us this far," stated Missionary.

Roadblock nodded. "Okay, then," he said, looking at Wil. "Welcome to MX017, Lord Blackfyre. Looks like you and the Rognok are our latest additions."

Wilvelm turned to see Grohm being fitted by technicians with some makeshift armor. He smiled. "We do make a good team," he said.

"Wil, can I talk to you for a moment?" whispered Fred, pulling Wil off to the side before snapping at him. "Have you lost your mind? These guys are going to be flying through a blasted shooting gallery where the Deathlords will be using them for target practice! And the ones who make it past the Deathlord ships win a trip to the surface filled with feral monsters and a dark temple of doom! Wil, if you do this… you won't make it back!"

"You never know. I might," replied Wilvelm.

Wil meant his response as a joke, but it was obvious Fredreek didn't find it funny. "I'm not going to let you throw your life away," he said.

"Look around you, Fred," Wilvelm said, gently. "All these men, they're getting ready to fly through that shooting gallery and take on that planet full of monsters because right now, that's what needs to be done. How can I ask them to do such a thing if I'm not willing to do it myself?"

"Because that's their job!" emphasized Fred. "That's what they're trained to do!"

"I've trained to do it, too," Wilvelm argued.

"Wil, you're not a soldier!" Fredreek cried. "You're the heir to a blasted Legacy! You're not meant for this type of thing!"

"I'm a Blackfyre. My family has a long history of exactly this type of thing."

Fredreek's face darkened. "So you think getting yourself killed will, what? Somehow make you worthy of being Torboron Blackfyre's descendant? That's what this is about?"

"This is about giving what's left of our soldiers a leader," Wilvelm said. "They need someone who knows what we're up against to tell them what to do. I've seen what those monoliths are capable of. I've fought those Deathlord monsters and whatever the blazes that… that Terrormancer thing is. They need me, Fred."

"*I* need you!" Fredreek replied.

The emotion with which Fredreek spoke took Wilvelm aback. Fred's lip trembled as he appeared to be barely holding himself together.

"You're my best friend," Fredreek said. "Without you, I… I don't know what I am."

Wilvelm frowned. He placed his hand on Fredreek's shoulder, trying to comfort him. "You're stronger than you know, Fred," he said.

"I'm really not."

"You *are*," Wilvelm insisted. "I know you are. And you know I have to do this. It has to be me. There is no one else."

Fredreek nodded, reluctantly. His eyes were getting red as he struggled to hold back his tears, but he still met Wilvelm's gaze. "Fine," he said. "Then I'm going with you."

"No, you need to stay here."

"If you're going, I'm going."

"Your place is here on the ship."

"My place is by your side."

"There's no sense in both of us dying," Wilvelm said, sternly. "Besides, I think my odds of coming back are much higher with you up here."

Fredreek raised an eyebrow. "Why would you think that?" he asked.

"Because, dummy," Wilvelm said with a smile. "There's no one I trust more to have my back than you. And once I destroy that Deathlord temple on Maxima, I'm gonna need someone I can depend on up here to take out those Deathlord ships. Otherwise, I don't have a way back home."

Fredreek looked unconvinced, but he nodded. "Fine," he replied. "If that's what you need… I got your back. Always."

"I knew I could count on you."

"What you said before was right, you know," Fredreek muttered, looking at Wil, sadly. "You're not the smart one."

Wil chuckled at that. "Guess I'll just have to settle for being good looking, then," he replied.

It was then that Fredreek embraced Wilvelm, as both a brother and a friend. Wilvelm returned the hug, knowing full well this could be the last time the two saw one another.

"You come back," Fredreek whispered. "Mourdock's not nearly as fun as you are."

That made Wilvelm smile. "I'll try my best," he replied. "Good luck to you."

"And to you," said Fredreek.

Fredreek then broke off the embrace and sulked out of the room. Wilvelm watched his friend go. He knew, deep down, Fred was right. Chances were he was throwing his life away, and the last thing he wanted was to take Fred with him. But Wil felt this was something he had to do. After all, it was his plan.

Wil turned and saw Roadblock staring at him. "You ready to suit up, my Lord?" he asked.

Wilvelm nodded. "Lead the way," he replied.

Roadblock took Wil to an Alpha Force suit hanging in one of its hydraulic rigs. "Step on in," he ordered.

Will stepped into the suit and Roadblock began closing it up around him. "You know, when I first met you, I was convinced you were some spoiled little Lordling looking to pad your resume by doing busy work in warzones."

"If we're being honest, that wasn't far from the truth," Wil replied.

Roadblock smiled at that. "Well, I was wrong, Lord Blackfyre," he said. "If your ancestor Torboron was half as brave as you, it's no wonder Edvard the Undying never stood a chance."

"Are you getting sentimental on me, Sergeant?" ribbed Wilvelm.

Roadblock chuckled. "Don't read too much into it," he said as he finished locking in the Alpha Force armor. "Swap the word 'brave' with 'crazy' and what I said still holds true."

"Nevertheless… I appreciate it."

Roadblock nodded and pulled the lever releasing the armor from the rig. Wilvelm stepped forward, moving around to get a feel for it. "You said you trained in the use of power armor," Roadblock said. "Alpha Force armor is similar, but it has a lot more built-in systems. Some are more responsive than others and all have to be managed, but here are the basics – this controls your lethal ordinance, this controls your non-lethal ordinance, this controls your jump jets and zero-g thrusters. Anything more than that will require six months of training."

Wilvelm nodded. "I think I've got the gist of it," he said. "The rocket launchers still stick, right?"

"Look at you, talking like a real Alpha," mused Roadblock. "Yeah, they do. Each suit can have its own quirks, seeing as how they're all so complicated. But if anything doesn't ever work right, just try hitting it until it does. That's what the rest of us do, anyway."

"When in doubt, hit the suit. Got it."

Roadblock nodded. "See you in the pod, my Lord," he said, walking to his own suit of armor. "We drop in thirty."

Wilvelm turned and looked at Grohm as he was finishing being strapped into armor which looked to be far too small for him. Wilvelm approached and looked to one of the technicians. "Is this the best we can do?" he asked.

The technician shrugged. "Frankly, I'm amazed we were even able to do this much," he replied. "You see how big this Rognok is? I'm not even sure if his jumpjet will support his weight."

"Well, at the very least, try and armor his exposed wounds," Wilvelm said. "The big guy is tough, but considering what we're going to be facing on the planet, I don't want to take any chances."

"We'll try our best, my Lord."

Wil looked up at Grohm, who returned his gaze. "I never got a chance to ask you how you knew Deathlords were on Essox," he said.

"How does Regal know when hungry?" Grohm responded.

"Um… I just know, I guess."

"Same," the Rognok replied. "Grohm just know."

"Yeah, but… how? I don't understand."

"Long time ago, Rognoks were made. Made to fight a great enemy. Deathlords were made to fight us. Deathlords and Rognoks… similar, but different. Weapons in a war that never ended. Deathlords now winning that war. Kill all Rognoks. But Grohm still alive. And so long as Grohm lives… Grohm fights."

Wilvelm smiled at that and nodded. "So long as we live, we fight," he repeated. "That I completely understand."

The bridge was full of activity when Fredreek arrived. As soon as order had been restored, they'd made a call for any crewmen with operational experience to report to the bridge to assume the duties of the crew that Verrutus had killed. Fredreek was happy to see that it appeared that call had been answered.

"You there," Fredreek said as he approached a young Ensign. "Where's the acting Captain?"

The Ensign looked at Fredreek in confusion. "My Lord?" he asked.

"The acting Captain, I need to speak with him," Fredreek replied. "We need to go over the plan to deliver Alpha Force to the surface."

"The acting Captain, sir… is you."

Fredreek blinked at the Ensign, dumbly. "Me? What are you talking about?"

"*The Shieldbearer* is a Legacy ship, my Lord," the Ensign replied. "That means command reverts to the ranking Legacy member onboard. That's you."

"Me?" said Fredreek, aghast. "Surely, you can't be serious."

"It's the protocol, my Lord. You can, of course, appoint a new captain to take command if you wish, but… all the senior officers are dead."

"And there's no one else with command experience here?"

"Just enlisted members of the crew, I'm afraid," the Ensign replied. "The Deathlord attack took out all our commanding officers."

Fredreek grimaced. He looked at the empty Captain's chair on the bridge with a mixture of fear and uncertainty. "Well, I always did want to command my own Legacy ship," he muttered. "Have enough non-essential personnel come to the bridge to man the empty stations. We're going to need all hands on deck if we're going to give Alpha Force the cover they need to make it to the planet."

"I'll get right on that, my Lord," the Ensign said. "But… there aren't many onboard who are trained to pilot a capital class ship. We may have trouble in that department."

Fredreek sighed. "Don't worry, I'll take care of it," he said. "Just get as many stations manned as you can."

The Ensign nodded. "Right away, my Lord," he replied before going off to enact his task.

Fredreek glanced over to where Copperhyde, looking beyond grumpy, was leaning against the wall. He approached the mercenary who met Fredreek's gaze as he approached. "Whatever it is yer gonna ask me, the answer is 'no'," Copperhyde grumbled.

"I know you didn't sign up for any of this, Copperhyde," Fredreek said. "None of us did. But we're all in the muck together now. So you've either got to help out or get out."

Copperhyde raised an eyebrow. "I can get out?" he asked.

Fredreek nodded. "Yeah, through an airlock," he replied. "Because as of right now, that's the only way off this ship."

Copperhyde scowled. "I ain't gettin' paid enough to be a hero," he said. "But I might be tempted ta be paid enough to help out."

"After this is all over, I'll make sure you're well compensated," Fredreek assured the man. "My Legacy has paid out far more to people who haven't helped saved the galaxy. I promise to see to it that you'll never have to work again."

Copperhyde smirked. "Very well," he said. "What do ya need me to do?"

"You're a rubbish pilot, my friend. But you're the only one we have at the moment. If you'd be so kind to take the pilot's seat, I'd much appreciate it."

"Guess this means you'll be takin' the Captain's seat, eh?"

Fredreek frowned as he looked at the Captain's chair. He didn't know why, but something about sitting in Lord Gebhard's seat just felt wrong. Despite the fact that Fredreek was now apparently in charge, he certainly didn't feel like he deserved to be. "I'll be at the command console, actually," Fredreek stated, referring to the station usually manned by the ship's Executive Officer. "It'll be easier to oversee things from there."

"Whatever you say, yer Lordship," Copperhyde replied. "You're in charge now."

Fredreek sighed, nervously. "Yeah, I guess I am," he muttered.

Fredreek stepped up to the command station, opening up a signal to the fleet.

"Attention, Maxima fleet. This is Lord Fredreek Goldstone, acting commander of *The Shieldbearer*," he said. "All ships, prepare to get into formation for Alpha Force deployment. We are about to take the fight to the Deathlords."

The inside of the Alpha Force drop pod was quite cramped as Wilvelm was locked into his station between Missionary and Lucky. Skeptic was there, as well, as was Grohm, clad in a makeshift harness that gave him jumpjet capabilities. The Rognok was so large he was taking up two slots in the pod and had to stand hunched over. Roadblock entered the pod and sealed the door before locking himself into his station where his armor attached to the drop pod's ejection mechanism.

"Alright, people, listen up," Roadblock said. "In a few minutes, we and every other Alpha Force squad in the fleet are going to be shot out into space, through a kitten-ton of Deathlord spaceships, all so we can have the good fortune of crashing onto a planet that's full of Deathstalkers. Drop pods are armored, but that don't mean they'll survive direct hits from capital-class starships. If we're damaged en route, we follow emergency protocol and initiate an early eject sequence, using our armor to carry us the rest of the way. If we're destroyed en route, well… it was an honor serving with you all."

"Hoo-ah, Sergeant!" Missionary, Skeptic, and Lucky all replied.

Wilvelm looked over to Grohm, who seemed even more uncomfortable than Wil felt. The Rognok still appeared to be in bad shape, despite his ability to battle Verrutus earlier. Much of his skin was still missing, with only exposed muscle in its place. "Grohm, are you sure you're up to this?" Wil asked. "You still look very rough…"

"Only flesh wound," the Rognok replied.

"Um… you literally had all your skin burned off you."

"Well then, I guess technically he's right," Roadblock mused. "It is only a flesh wound."

"I'm just saying… you've already almost been killed twice since we met you," Wilvelm said. "No one would blame you if you wanted to sit this one out."

"No sitting when battle is waging," Grohm replied. "Deathlords destroy Grohm's planet. Grohm go to Maxima. Grohm destroy them."

"He doesn't say much," said Skeptic. "But when he does… I like what I hear."

"As do I," said Roadblock. "The Deathlords ain't gonna know what hit 'em. Helmets up! Get ready for deployment."

All those in Alpha Force armor closed their helmets, engaging their suits' life support systems. When everyone was situated, Roadblock entered the 'allready' code into the small command console nearby. The light inside the pod switched over to red as the pod was loaded into its launch tube, jerking as it was locked into place.

****

On the bridge of *The Shieldbearer*, Fredreek stood at the command console, directing the fleet toward the awaiting armada of Deathlord Dreadnaughts. "Boost power to the forward shields," Fredreek ordered. "Keep formation. Have all fightercraft on stand-by."

"Sir, yes, sir," replied the technicians in the operations stations.

"Take us toward the gap in their blockade, Copperhyde," Fredreek said.

"Taking us in," replied Copperhyde. "We'll be in range of their point defense arrays in five minutes."

"Prepare to return fire when we are."

As the ships of the Maxima fleet drew closer to the Deathlord blockade, the Dreadnaughts began firing, sending a wall of plasma bolts toward Fredreek and his ships. The fleet's shields took an immediate pounding as they returned fire and continued to close the distance.

"Forward shields holding," reported Copperhyde. "For now, anyway."

"We don't need long, just enough time to launch the drop pods and cover their landings," said Fredreek. "Prepare to launch starfighters."

"Starfighters ready to launch upon your orders, my Lord," replied an Ensign.

Fredreek took a deep breath. He knew the moment he gave the command that many of those pilots would not be coming back. Regardless, he also knew he had a mission to complete.

"Launch fighter squadrons one through four," Fredreek ordered.

Fightercraft flew from *The Shieldbearer's* hangar bays, right into the fray of blaster fire. They immediately scrambled, targeting any missile projectiles the Deathlords fired. In response, the Dreadnaughts launched their own squadrons of Shards, and before long, the space between the capital ships was filled with dogfights as the fighters zipped around like angry insects.

Fredreek kept his eyes on the readouts at his station, tracking the distance between the opposing fleets. "C'mon, just a little closer," he muttered.

"Those plasma blasts are more powerful the closer we get," said Copperhyde. "If you take us in any further, they're going to melt our shields!"

"They'll melt Alpha Force, too," replied Fredreek. "We gotta get right up in their faces. Our shields can take it."

"And what of the shields of the other ships?" asked Copperhyde.

Fredreek frowned. "Guess we'll find out," he said. "Have all ships focus fire on the targets surrounding our gap. Let's keep them occupied."

The Maxima fleet began firing volleys toward the four Deathlord ships they were approaching, peppering the large vessels with plasma fire and forcing a few of them to adjust their position, giving the fleet a larger window for their launch.

"It's not going to get much better than this," said Fredreek. "Prepare to deploy Alpha Force."

"All Alpha Force drop pods ready to be deployed, my Lord," replied a crewman.

"Good luck, buddy," whispered Fred before he looked up at the crewman and gave the order: "Launch Alpha Force."

In the drop pod, the red light began to blink. Wil looked up at the light, nervously, the sound of his breath in his helmet as loud as the banging of drums. Roadblock held onto the handgrips at his station, as did all the other members, except for Grohm, who was also looking at the flashing light with interest.

"Prepare for launch," Roadblock said.

With that, the blinking light turned green.

Suddenly, there was a gut-wrenching lurch as the pod was jettisoned out the launch tube. There were no windows in the drop pod to see what was happening, but Wil could certainly *feel* what was happening. The pod accelerated, its engine burning at full. The remotely piloted pod spun as it maneuvered, jerking to and fro.

Wil felt the chassis of the pod rumble from the stress of the maneuvers. Despite the protection from his armor, he still felt the g-forces pulling on him, making him feel as though he were being crushed inside a large tin can. Wil gripped the handholds at his station tightly, his heart pounding in his chest.

Without warning, the pod rumbled as one of its sides was ripped off by a plasma blast. What little air there was in the pod was sucked out into space, and

Wil could see the chaos outside flying by the opening. The pod spun as dogfights and blaster bolts zoomed by all around. The light in the pod started blinking red again, and an alert appeared in his helmet's HUD warning him of damage to the pod.

"We've been hit!" came Roadblock's voice over the helmet comms. "Pod integrity is deteriorating! Enact emergency protocol! Prepare for ejection!"

Fear gripped Wil's gut as he released his handholds, preparing to be ejected from the pod.

*This was a bad idea!* Wil thought in a panic. *This was so stupid! How could I have been so stupid???*

Wilvelm Blackfyre did not have time to linger on his regrets as Roadblock hit the pod's eject button. Instantly, the pod's walls broke away, and each of its sections blew outward, propelling each Alpha Force soldier forward.

Before Wil knew it, he was flying through space, the large orb of Maxima displayed before him as chaos raged all around. Bright red plasma blasts streaked by from every direction. Deathlord Shards zoomed past, either firing at Imperial starfighters or being fired upon by them. Massive capital ships loomed everywhere, firing relentlessly at what remained of the Maxima fleet far behind him.

And throughout it all, the only sound Wil heard was that of his rapid, panicked breathing.

Roadblock and the other members of Alpha Force quickly disappeared from sight as their armor's maneuvering thrusters moved them out of the way of debris and blaster fire. Wil grabbed onto his suit's jumpjet control, trying to also maneuver out of harm's way. And though he was able to accomplish that, doing so also served to make him lose awareness of his surroundings.

In a flash of red, a large blaster bolt clipped his armor, sending Wilvelm spinning in an uncontrolled spiral toward Maxima. He quickly lost his bearings as he spun head over heels so rapidly he thought he was going to be sick.

Alarms blared on his helmet's HUD, alerting him to damage from the blast and a breach in the heatshield of the suit. Wil desperately tried to gain control and right himself, but he had no way of knowing which thrusters to fire.

Flames appeared in his vision as he entered the friction of the planet's atmosphere, and more of his suits alarms went off. Wil knew he was falling toward the planet and that with his heat shield damaged, chances were he'd burn up before landing.

"Help!" Wilvelm cried into his radio. "My heat shield's been damaged! Someone? Anyone! HELP!"

Suddenly, Wil felt something grab onto his arm. Whatever it was had stopped his uncontrolled spin. He looked up just in time to see Grohm had taken hold of him. The Rognok quickly pulled Wil toward him, hugging him close and shielding the damaged part of his suit with the Rognok's own body.

Flames erupted around Grohm's back as the two fell through Maxima's atmosphere. Wil could see Grohm grunt in pain as the heat intensified. As soon as the friction of entry subsided, Grohm's eyes closed and his grip went slack. Wil drifted from Grohm as the Rognok fell away, tumbling through the air as the ground began to grow larger.

"Grohm!" Wil cried out. "GROHM!"

Wilvelm tried firing his suit's grappling cable to save the Rognok as he fell. However, Wil's aim was off and he missed. There was no time to try again as Grohm fell out of range, tumbling off unconscious, the armor on his back having melted onto him.

Alerts blared inside Wil's helmet, telling him his altitude and that he needed to engage his jumpjets to slow his descent. All thoughts of Grohm quickly fell away as Wil tried to ignite his jets and discovered, to his horror…

They weren't working.

Wil tried again, but whatever plasma blast had stripped his armor's heat shield must have impacted his jumpjet as well. Wilvelm engaged the suit's diagnostic tool and tried resetting the armor's jets, frantically trying to fire them as he continued to plummet.

"FIRE!" Wil cried out as he pounded on his suit. "FIRE, DAMN YOU!"

As the ground came rushing up to meet him, Wilvelm felt his jump pack rumble to life as its jets fired up at the last minute. Even within the insulation of his Alpha Force armor, Wil could feel the pressure of the deceleration hit him, making him feel as though he were being crushed as his jump pack fought to slow his descent.

Wilvelm landed hard, the boots of his armor absorbing what impact they could as he hit the ground, causing it to crater with the force of his impact. He felt a jolt travel through him, then stumbled and fell as his jumpjet disengaged. Wil groaned in pain as he flailed about on the ground, like a tortoise flipped on its back, struggling to get upright once more.

Wil eventually managed to turn himself over and push himself back up to his feet. He disengaged his helmet, retracting it and gratefully breathing in the fresh air of the planet. His hair was matted with sweat and his entire body shivered with nervous energy.

He looked up into the sky from which he'd just fallen. In the hazy distance, he could see small blips of light as the space battle continued to rage above him. Though flying through it seemed terrifying and overwhelming, from the surface it looked insignificant and small.

*I'm lucky to be alive*, Wil thought, gratefully.

After taking a minute to recover from his deployment, Wil did a quick diagnostic of his Alpha Force armor. Despite his harrowing trek to the planet, Wil was surprised to find his suit was still almost fully operational. He quickly opened up a comm channel to see if anyone else had made it.

"This is Wilvelm Blackfyre of Alpha Force MX017," he said into his radio. "I have successfully landed on the surface of Maxima. I estimate my position to be sixty miles southeast of the target area. Can anyone read me? Please respond."

Aside from the snap and crackle of radio interference, Wil received no reply.

"This is Wilvelm Blackfyre of Alpha Force MX017," he repeated. "If you are part of the assault force that made it to the surface of the planet, please respond!"

Again, nothing.

"Roadblock, come in," said Wilvelm, hoping against hope to make contact with someone. "Lucky? Skeptic? Missionary? Is anyone reading me?"

The only reply Wilvelm received was garbled static in his earpiece. A sinking sensation gripped his gut as a grim realization settled upon him.

*Forty-Five Alpha Force squads launched, and I may be the only one who made it*, he thought with dismay.

Wilvelm looked off into the distance toward where Grohm had fallen. He could see no sign of the Rognok anywhere. Though the hulking alien was resilient and had survived the impossible already, even Wilvelm had his doubts that the injured Rognok could withstand the stress of entry into the planet's atmosphere, as well as the impact from a fall from orbit.

He then turned his gaze toward the dark temple, which loomed in the far distance. He was miles away from the intended drop zone and he could see the landscape moving with the activity of Deathstalkers as they made their way across the land, the vile dark rock of the Deathlords spreading out along with them. Though the specter of the task before him was daunting, if Wilvelm really was the only one to have made it to the planet, it was up to him to carry out the mission. But before he began his advance, Wil took a moment to say a quick prayer to his ancestor.

*Torboron, you once did the impossible*, he thought. *Please… help me to do the same.*

Wilvelm pulled his graviton rifle from the back of his suit and readied himself. He sprinted forward, engaging his jumpjet as he did so, which propelled him far into the air, covering a great distance before he landed and jumped again. And thus, Wilvelm Blackfyre proceeded toward the dark temple of Maxima…

One man, against an army.

# CHAPTER 26

igh above the planet of Maxima, the Maxima fleet continued to clash with the superior numbers of the Deathlord ships. Not a single Imperial vessel was being spared from the onslaught of powerful plasma fire from the enemy.

*The Shieldbearer* rocked as a missile from a Deathlord Dreadnaught evaded the ship's point defenses, impacting its shields. However, the Legacy capital ship had strong shields and stronger armor, and was faring far better than the rest of the ships in its battlegroup. Fredreek stood at the ship's command console, monitoring the condition of his fleet and the maneuvers they found themselves in the middle of.

"Operations, report!" ordered Fredreek. "What's the status of the Alpha Force deployment?"

"Sensors have lost contact with almost all Alpha Force drop pods, my Lord," reported the sensor technician. "We're showing five have gotten through to the planet, but they have all landed far outside the target area."

"Only five?" muttered Fredreek with disappointment. That was not a good sign, considering the tens of thousands of Deathstalkers that were crawling around on the surface. "What of MX017? Any word on if their pod made it?"

"I'm sorry, my Lord. We lost sensor contact with them. There's no way to tell."

Fredreek frowned. *Blast it, Wil!* he thought. *Please don't be dead! Not after everything we've just been through!*

Just then, *The Shieldbearer* jostled as it absorbed more hits from the Deathlord Dreadnaughts. "Oy, my Lord," grumbled Copperhyde. "Seein' as how we're done here, might I suggest executing a hasty retreat before what's left of our fleet is blown ta bits?"

"Yes, good idea," Fredreek said with a sigh. "Signal the other ships. Have them all start to withdraw. Tell them to lend cover fire to one another to ensure a safe retreat."

"My Lord!" cried one of the sensor technicians. "Sensors are picking up multiple new anomalies!"

"What kind of anomalies?"

"Signatures match those of the tethers that appeared along with the Deathlord fleet!"

"On screen."

Fredreek looked at the ship's viewscreen as more tears in the fabric of reality formed around Maxima. More Deathlord cruisers flew through the openings, but one vessel, in particular, stood out among the new arrivals.

It was unlike any ship Fredreek had ever seen before. It was big – not as big as a Planetkiller, but slightly larger than a typical capital ship. The black rock which covered its surface looked wild and overgrown, not as sleek as was the case on the other Deathlord vessels. Large spikes jutted from the ship's hull, giving it a look similar to that of a porcupine. All-in-all, Fredreek knew the intimidating ship's appearance did not bode well for him and what remained of his fleet.

"What the blazes is that thing?" Fredreek asked.

"Unclear, my Lord," one of his sensor technicians replied. "There are no matches for it in our Deathlord database."

"The ship appears to be headed toward the tether the dark temple is firing into, my Lord," said another technician at the navigation station. "It's moving there along with its escorts."

"Good," said Copperhyde. "Means we won't have to fight 'em."

"As much as I love things that are new and exciting, that sentiment does not extend to things that come from the Deathlords," Fredreek said. "Proceed with the retreat. Get us out of here and away from… whatever that is."

"My Lord!" cried the sensor technician once more. "Multiple anomalies detected, again! They're appearing behind us!"

"You've got to be kidding me," grumbled Fredreek. "On screen!"

The ship's viewscreen switched to a rear view of the vessel, showing multiple Deathlord Dreadnaughts emerging from the tethers which had suddenly opened behind the Maxima fleet. Fredreek cursed and slammed his fist on the command console.

"Blast it!" Fredreek said. "They've surrounded us and cut off our escape route!"

"So much for the hit-and-run strategy," muttered Copperhyde.

*The Shieldbearer* was rocked once more from the plasma fire of the Deathlord ships. "What are your orders, my Lord?" asked the crewman at the operations station.

Fredreek frowned. *Like I bloody know. I'm a functioning alcoholic, not a starship captain!* thought Fred, bitterly.

Fred glanced down at this console's readouts. There was no clear way out of the trap. The Deathlords had them boxed in. The only way out was to fight through their blockade. But Fred didn't need years of command experience to know that was going to be costly.

"Bring the fleet into cluster formation," he ordered. "Group us up, tight. Have all fightercraft fly in escort protocol. We're going to have to punch our way out of here."

"And if the Deathlords punch back?" asked Copperhyde.

"Then pray to your buddy RNGsus we don't get knocked out," replied Fred.

The Maxima fleet reversed itself, firing back upon the Dreadnaughts that were harassing them as they positioned themselves in a cluster formation, surrounded by swarms of fightercraft that gave them cover from Deathlord Shards and missiles.

But as the Maxima fleet made its maneuvers, the Deathlord ships made theirs, as well. Their Dreadnaughts had completely encircled the fleet in every direction, closing in on them as they pulled their noose tighter. As the Deathlord ships converged, their point defense networks began to overlap, hitting the Maxima ships on all sides and from all fronts.

*The Shieldbearer's* hull rumbled as they began to take more and more fire. "Shields are down to 65% and falling!" stated Copperhyde. "We're not going to be able to take much more of this!"

"We don't have much choice," snapped Fredreek, fully aware of how dire their situation was. "Have all ships return fire! Keep pushing!"

"There ain't nowhere to push to!" replied Copperhyde. "Unless you want ta run the risk of ramming them, they got us completely boxed in!"

"My Lord, *The White Mountain's* shields have failed!" reported a sensor technician. "Sustaining massive hull damage! She's not going to make it!"

"*Winter's Peak* and *Sky Barron's* shields are both critical, as well!" stated another.

"Fighter wings Blue and Yellow have almost been completely wiped out!"

Fredreek frowned. *My first command and I get every ship in my fleet killed,* he thought, sadly. *Guess you were right all along, father… I am a disappointment.*

Fredreek watched helplessly as *The White Mountain* blew apart, the Maxima vessel erupting in a hail of Deathlord plasma fire. Then, *The Sky Barron* followed suit, its destruction so spectacular that it caused *The Shieldbearer* to violently lurch, due to the proximity of the explosion.

Another explosion occurred. At first, Fredreek thought it must have been *The Winter's Peak* which had fallen. But as he looked at the sensor reports at his station, he saw that it was a Deathlord Dreadnaught that had just been destroyed.

"What the…" Fredreek muttered.

He looked up at the bridge's viewscreen just in time to see twelve Deathscream missiles impact three Dreadnaughts, breaking through their shields and inflicting massive hull damage. The sudden attack sent the Deathlord vessels scrambling.

"What just happened?" Fredreek asked.

"My Lord! Multiple sensor contacts!" said a sensor technician in excitement. "Hyperspace windows are opening up everywhere, sir!"

"On screen!"

Fredreek watched in amazement as he saw one hyperspace window after another open, with Imperial ships flooding through. Many were marked as battlegroups of the 3rd fleet, while others bore the eight-pointed star of Redwater vessels. At their head flew *The Colossus,* firing complement after complement of Deathscream missiles at any Deathlord ship within range.

The crew on the bridge cheered as more Deathlord Dreadnaughts received direct hits and the Imperial fleet continued to arrive, immediately fanning out and engaging with the enemy. In almost an instant, the odds had been evened as the combined might of the 3rd fleet and the Redwater militia appeared to match that of the Deathlords.

"My Lord, we are being hailed by the 3rd fleet flagship," reported the comms technician.

"Put it through," said Fredreek.

The image of Amadeus Evenstar, standing side by side with Starkeeper Drucker, appeared on the viewscreen. "Hello, Fredreek," Amadeus said. "We heard you needed some help."

Fredreek couldn't help but laugh, relief washing over him like a warm shower. "Amadeus Evenstar," he said. "I never thought I'd be glad to see you!"

"You sound like every girl I've ever dated," quipped Amadeus.

"What's your status, Lord Goldstone?" asked Starkeeper Drucker.

"Shields are at 50%, but *The Shieldbearer* is holding up," Fredreek replied. "Our fleet's been decimated. We only have four other ships operational. Lord Skyborn was killed when Ambassador Bob was revealed to be the Deathlord Supreme Verrutus in disguise, and we have Alpha Force soldiers on the surface of Maxima trying to assault the Dark Temple down there, which seems to be spawning creatures we're calling Deathstalkers to attack the planet's population centers. Deathlord ships keep appearing from mysterious tethers to ambush us, and… oh! A big, scary looking Deathlord vessel we've never seen before just showed up and is heading toward the tether the dark temple is firing its death ray into."

"I see…" said Drucker, looking a tad overwhelmed. "That it?"

"I think that about covers everything."

"Very well," Drucker said. "I'll take things from here, my Lord. Standby for orders."

"Standing by," replied Fredreek, relieved he didn't have to be in charge anymore.

"Oh, and Fredreek," Amadeus said. "Good job keeping your fleet alive until we could arrive. What you guys were doing… it took a lot of guts."

"Thanks, Amadeus, that means a lot," he said. "Now, do me a favor… let's blow these Deathlords back to oblivion where they belong and retake this system, yeah?"

Amadeus smiled. "Consider that a favor I'm more than happy to grant," he replied, just before the transmission ended.

Fredreek looked at Copperhyde and smiled. "Looks like Wil was right," he said. "This battle isn't lost yet!"

With that, what remained of the Maxima fleet joined with that of the 3rd fleet and the Redwater militia and re-engaged the Deathlords, the crews of the beaten and battered starships bolstered by the knowledge that maybe, just maybe…

This was a fight they could now actually win.

# CHAPTER 27

Scallywag checked his weapons, ensuring they were all charged and ready to go. His stun pistols were at full, but he'd also equipped his trusty blaster pistols, as well. He'd hoped he wouldn't have to use them, but he wasn't about to make the mistake of going anywhere without them again.

Once his weapons were equipped, Scallywag surveilled his assault force. He'd raided with Tarkrane, Kapplan, and ReeRee before. Glimmer's security muscle – the Rattan[20] thug named Smash – seemed like this wasn't his first time doing such a thing either. Gage was big, and Recklec's could usually handle themselves in a fight. But it was Betran and his men who made up the bulk of the party and gave them the numbers to do what Scallywag had planned.

Betran and the other Yellow Visinis were all checking their plasma rifles, which Scallywag had issued them from *The Reaver's* well-stocked weapons locker. "Y'all set ta use those?" Scallywag asked.

"I think so," replied Betran. "It's just point and shoot, right? Simple."

"Do me a solid, lads," Scallywag said. "When we get on tha ship, aim fer the knees and shoulders if'n ya can. Try not ta kill anybody ya don't have to."

"Are you being serious?" asked Betran. "That dirty Blue browner not only betrayed us, he'd have killed us all! As far as I'm concerned, he and everyone who follows him deserves what they got coming to them!"

"Maybe so, but you lot are in a very precarious situation right now," Scallywag said. "Ya don't have a House, and yer about ta do something that – while justified – goes against the Visini Empire and the teachings of the Great Whites. Ya got a fine line ya all gotta walk, lads, lest yer skin end up being as crimson as mine."

"I'd rather be alive and Red than Yellow and dead," replied Betran.

"Trust me, I know tha sentiment," Scallywag said. "I ain't sayin' don't defend yerselves. But only kill if it's a last resort. Murder is a gateway to tha Red, lads. And despite what we're about ta do, we're the good guys. We should hold ourselves to a higher standard, savvy?"

---

[20] Rattans are a large, rodent-like alien species.

Betran nodded, despite looking like he still had his doubts. "I should have listened to you about Eisenwolf," he said. "I'll make sure my men and I listen to you now."

Scallywag gave Betran a pat on the shoulder. "Good lad," he said. "Now make yer way down to tha hatch. Me and tha others will join ya as soon as we complete tha maneuver."

Betran and the rest of the boarding crew filed out, leaving just those on the bridge needed to execute the risky maneuver Scallywag had planned.

"Are we ready to go?" Scallywag asked.

"Almost in position," Tweak reported.

"Can I just go on record as saying this is a terrible plan?" grumbled Gage.

"'Course it is," replied Scallywag. "That's why it's gonna work."

"What you want us to do, I ain't never heard of before," Gage said. "How do you know it will even work?"

"I seen it done once," said Scallywag. "Worked out fine then."

"Can this ship even handle performing this maneuver?"

"Guess we're about ta find out. Danny-boy, ya all plugged in?"

"I am indeed, Master Scallywag!" replied Dan from the console with which he was interfacing. "Though my processors aren't as fast as those of Master Moriarty's, I do believe I shall just be able to meet the minimum requirement to make the calculations you have requested. That being said, I feel I should warn you that we will only have about 90 seconds before the strain of this maneuver overloads the ship's brane accelerator. If we have not cleared the hyperspace windows by then, the ship will be destroyed."

"Noted," replied Scallywag. "Tweak, what's our position?"

"We're right where we need to be, Captain."

"Then bring us around," Scallywag ordered. "We're only gonna get one shot at this. So let's make it count."

Glimmer came up to Scallywag and took him by the hand. They looked into each other's eyes. Glimmer smiled. "No matter what happens, I just want you to know… I'm proud of you for doing this," she said.

"I appreciate that," Scallywag replied. "But at the end o' tha day… it still don't change me color."

"Frankly, my dear, in situations like this… I think we need a bit of red."

Scallywag smiled at that. He turned his attention to the viewscreen where the image of *The Megavolt* loomed, the far superior ship practically daring him to turn and face it.

"Bit o' red or no… Eisenwolf is about ta get all o' it!" stated Scallywag.

On the bridge of *The Megavolt*, Eisenwolf stood, hands clasped behind his back, dourly looking at the image of *The Reaver* as it continued its escape.

"The pirate vessel has reached safe hyperspace distance," Rintin reported. "They should be jumping away any minute, Captain."

Eisenwolf scowled. "Have navigation plot out all possible hyperspace routes from their trajectory," he ordered. "We shall follow them as soon as possible and try to catch up with them at their destination, wherever that may be."

Before he could carry out his orders, Rintin looked at the readout on his console with confusion. "Captain," he said. "*The Reaver*… it's turning."

"Turning?" asked Eisenwolf. "On the screen. Magnify."

Rintin zoomed in on the image of *The Reaver*. The ship appeared to be turning around to face *The Megavolt*. Eisenwolf looked at the maneuver with interest.

"What the blazes are you up to?" he wondered aloud.

Then, *The Reaver* rotated, angling its starboard side toward the ship as it blew off the last remaining vestiges of its *Bluebell* façade, revealing the pirate ship in all its intimidating glory.

"Captain!" exclaimed Rintin. "Sensors indicate the ship is powering up its plasma batteries! I think they mean to fight us!"

Eisenwolf smiled at that. "Battle stations," he ordered. "Set condition to alert one. Power up all plasma cannons."

As *The Megavolt* went to full battle readiness, Rintin gave his Captain a questioning look. "Sir," he said, "this does not make sense. Why engage in a fight they know they cannot win when they were free to escape?"

"I do not know what they think they are doing, Lieutenant," Eisenwolf replied. "But I am not about to pass up the opportunity to punish them for it. Full speed ahead! Close the distance! Prepare to fire everything we have at them the moment they are within our range!"

On the bridge of *The Reaver*, Glimmer monitored *The Megavolt's* response from her station. "Eisenwolf's taking the bait," she said. "They're speeding toward us. All their plasma batteries are charging."

"Are we lined up?" Scallywag asked.

"Our broadside is in-line with the ship's command deck," Tweak replied.

Scallywag nodded. "Engage port-side thrusters," he ordered.

"Thrusters engaged," replied Tweak as the ship began moving its starboard side directly toward *The Megavolt.*

"Danny-boy," said Scallywag. "Do yer thing."

"Opening dual hyperspace windows now, Master Scallywag," replied Dan.

Just then, *The Reaver's* brane accelerator, with the assistance of Dan's sentient processing power, opened two hyperspace windows approximately 20 micrometers apart from one another. The double-opening of the hyperspace windows instantly negated the distance between *The Megavolt* and *The Reaver*, with each ship speeding toward the other.

"Thrusters to full!" barked Scallywag. "Snare winches! Now!"

Gage fired the topside and bottom snare winch lines of *The Reaver*, the cables rocketing through the hyperspace opening and latching onto the hull of *The Megavolt.*

"Reel us in!" Scallywag ordered.

The spools of the snare winches spun to life as they reeled *The Reaver* toward the capital ship.

"What the blazes?" said Eisenwolf in disbelief, not fully understanding what he was seeing.

"Captain!" cried Rintin. "They've latched onto us with snare winches! They are reeling themselves directly toward the command deck!"

"Fire at them!" Eisenwolf shouted. "All weapons, fire!"

"We can't, sir!" replied Rintin. "One side of the hyperspace window is inside our range, while the other side is still too far away! We can't hit them!"

Eisenwolf watched in abject disbelief as *The Reaver* pulled through the dual hyperspace windows, passing them right before they collapsed in on themselves.

★★★★★

"We made it through, Master Scallywag!" cheered Dan. "Oh, how exciting!"

"Ya ain't seen nothin' yet, robot," Scallywag said. "Starboard thrusters at full! Open fire!!!"

The thrusters on the side of *The Reaver* which faced *The Megavolt* fired, slowing the ship's speed even as it continued to be reeled in by the snare winches. The pirate ship fired, peppering the rapidly approaching face of the Visini capital ship now that it was inside its shields, disrupting any and all operations those on the command level of the ship could perform.

"Brace fer impact!" shouted Scallywag.

The crewmembers on *The Reaver* readied themselves as their ship crashed into the command deck of *The Megavolt*, the impact only slightly cushioned by the thruster burn they'd executed. A violent lurch reverberated throughout the ship, but it quickly passed as the snare winches held the vessel steady against its prey.

"Right on target!" said Gage, looking at his readouts. "Boarding hatch engaged. We're locked onto the ship!"

Scallywag pulled out his blasters. "Right," he said. "Time ta go say hello."

Alarms blared on the bridge of *The Megavolt*, the impact from the pirate vessel having caused everyone who was not strapped in to fall to the ground. Eisenwolf sneered as he struggled back to his feet. "Someone!" he barked. "Report!"

Rintin scrambled back to his station, looking at its readouts. "The pirate vessel has latched onto one of the command deck's emergency airlocks!" he said. "A breach has been reported! They're… they're boarding us, sir!"

Eisenwolf blinked in disbelief. "Boarding us?" he said, indignantly. "Just who does that Red think he is???"

"Captain!" cried one of the security officers from his monitoring console. "Reports of shots fired in the corridors outside the airlock! Armed assailants are heading right for the bridge!"

"Seal the bridge blast doors!" ordered Eisenwolf. "Teleport in security personnel and any available soldiers, immediately!"

"Communications are down and teleporters are not responding, Captain," said Rintin as he frantically tapped at his console. "We've been hacked again!"

Blaster fire could be heard from the corridor leading to the bridge. Eisenwolf sneered. "Quickly!" he said. "Open the weapons locker! Prepare to defend the bridge!"

Before anyone could move, the entrance to the bridge opened. Dan stood there, blaster cannons extended from his arms. He launched two stun disks into the room, which went off with flashes of light and loud sonic cries, incapacitating everyone within range.

Scallywag and his crew stormed in, quickly fanning out. Anyone who appeared ready to put up resistance, Scallywag shot with his stun pistols, while the others secured the crew.

After the last of Scallywag's men were inside, Dan closed the blast doors and sealed off the bridge. "Bridge is now secure, Master Scallywag," he reported. "I have used my connection with the ship's systems to lock down all avenues to the command deck and to shut down the ship's teleportation network. No one will be able to get to us."

"Great job, Danny-boy," Scallywag said as he sauntered up to Eisenwolf, who gazed at him with sheer malice. "Hey ya, Wolfie. Miss me?"

Eisenwolf glanced around at the small army of pirates, outcasts, and spacers who now held his crew hostage. He rose up to his feet, glaring at Scallywag defiantly. "When I imagined our next meeting, I had something quite different in mind," he said.

"I'm sure ya did."

"So, you've come to kill me, have you?" Eisenwolf said. "Come to finish what you started with my father? Very well. Go on. Have your revenge. But do not think this is over, pirate. House Maestro is strong. You may kill me… but others will come for you."

"Believe it or not, I ain't here fer you, Wolfie," Scallywag replied. "See, I ain't the scoundrel ya think I am. I'm here ta help people. We need yer ship ta stop the Deathlords and rescue whoever is left down on Eionmeer."

Eisenwolf's eyes narrowed. "So that is why you've come? To take one of the most advanced capital ships of the Visini Empire and use it to assist our enemies? I should not have expected anything less from a vile traitor like you."

"Fer once, Eisenwolf, I'm askin' ya… no, I'm *beggin'* ya… look at tha bigger picture here. After this is all over, you and me can go back ta bein' at each other's throats. But right now, I need the help of you and yer crew ta operate this ship. I'm askin' ya ta be worthy of that blue skin of yours and help us save tha day. So what do ya say?"

Eisenwolf glared at him. "I'd rather die than assist you," he sneered.

Scallywag frowned. He turned and saw Rintin watching the exchange as Glimmer held her weapon trained on him. "You agree with him?" Scallywag asked.

"It doesn't matter if I agree or not," replied Rintin. "He's my commanding officer."

Glimmer lowered her weapon and moved in front of Rintin, looking into the Lieutenant's eyes. "You know he's not right about this," Glimmer said. "The people on that planet need your help. The fate of the entire galaxy hangs in the balance. How can you just stand by and allow this to happen?"

"My loyalty is to my Captain, my House, and my Empire," stated Rintin. "Captain Eisenwolf is a Blue. I trust in his decisions."

"I'm a Blue, as well."

"But you stand with a Red," Rintin replied. "And not just any Red, my Lady. Scallywag the Red. The great traitor. Harkon the Black's right hand. How could you ever expect us to trust the word of one such as him?"

Scallywag looked around at all the Yellow crewmen on the bridge. Their gazes were not something he was unfamiliar with. Those with red skin were always distrusted by those within his culture. But the fate of the galaxy – and his friends – relied on Scallywag somehow changing that perception. With that, Scallywag took a step toward the center of the bridge, gazing at all of its crew in turn as he spoke.

"Oy. Ya all know me," he stated. "It's true what he says. I am Scallywag the Red. And yes, I did betray everyone I ever loved and cared about. I stood by Harkon's side as he nearly destroyed the Visini Empire. But that ain't the full story. I wasn't always a Red. And Harkon wasn't always a Black. In fact, it weren't long ago Harkon was a bloke just like him..."

Scallywag pointed at Eisenwolf.

"He was a Purple, Harkon was," Scallywag continued. "But more than that, he was a man I believed in. A man I trusted. A man I followed, even though I knew every order he gave was wrong. But I never questioned his commands. I just did me duty. Even when that man's skin turned black as night, I continued ta do me duty, 'cause by then it was the only thing I had left. That didn't make it right. That don't offer much in the way of an excuse, but that's the bloody truth of it all. But what you all just saw me do wasn't about duty. Flying me ship against a superior one like yours… blasting me way in here… I didn't do any o' that for the reasons ya might think. I'm not here for revenge. I'm not here for plunder. I'm not here to murder each and every one o' ya and steal yer blasted ship. I'm here because there are people down on that planet that need help. And like it or not, we're the only ones in a position ta help 'em. Now, yer Captain here thinks it's acceptable ta let 'em die because it will benefit his House. He thinks it's okay to watch the galaxy burn because it's fer the greater glory o' our Empire. I understand his reasoning, because it was the same thing Harkon and I told ourselves every time we killed in the quadruple digits. So take a good, long look at yerselves, lads. What's it say about the lot o' you, when a Red is willing to lay down his life fer the sake of doin' what's right… while you all stand around and do nothing?"

There was a deafening silence which hung in the air after Scallywag finished his speech. The looks in the eyes of the ship's crew were confused and unsure. Despite the odds, Scallywag knew he'd reached them. But they wouldn't rise up against their Captain. Not without the permission of a Blue to do so.

Scallywag turned and looked to Rintin, whose face was also full of doubt. Scallywag pointed to him. "You," he said. "Yer a Blue. What does yer gut tell ya?"

Rintin frowned before looking to Glimmer, who gave him a nod. "It tells me… it tells me we need to help," he said.

"Have you lost your mind?" snapped Eisenwolf in disbelief.

"Apologies, Captain," Rintin said. "I understand your reasoning for not trusting the Red, but… I fear your hatred of him has clouded your judgement. If the Deathlords truly are attacking, then we should be doing something about it."

Eisenwolf looked at Rintin, stunned, as his X.O. turned toward the rest of the crew. "For the time being, I am relieving Captain Eisenwolf of his command," Rintin stated. "Everyone, resume your stations. We will be returning to the planet to assist the Regals."

"Belay that order!" shouted Eisenwolf. "You bloody traitor! Anyone who complies with this madness will be court-martialed for treason, so help me—"

Scallywag promptly approached Eisenwolf and punched him in the face, shutting him up and sending him to the ground in a daze. Scallywag turned to Rintin and nodded.

"As you were," Scallywag said.

Rintin sighed but acknowledged the pirate. "Hop to it, men," he said. "We do not have time to waste."

Scallywag's group lowered their weapons as the ship's crew went back to their stations, preparing to return *The Megavolt* to Eionmeer. As they did so, Glimmer approached Scallywag.

"So, how's it feel to do the right thing for once?" she asked.

Eisenwolf groaned and started to climb back to his feet, right before Scallywag blasted him with his stun weapon. Scallywag smiled.

"Pretty good, actually," he said.

# Chapter 28

Jack raced through the empty halls of the Conclave. The ghostly energy was still seeping from the walls, faces in the haze moaning at him as he sped by. Jack ran through the destruction and desolation, weaving his way through the temple – the place he'd called home – as it burned and collapsed. But Jack knew he couldn't stop to focus on such things. Right then, he only had two objectives:

Save the Conclave. Save Mourdock Skyborn.

Jack had no way of knowing where Mourdock was, but he did know where he could go to try to save the temple. The Great Seal was responsible for the Conclave's very existence. If there were any hope of stopping the corruption from completely overtaking everything, Jack guessed that hope lay with the seal.

As he got closer to the Chamber of the Great Seal, he slowed his advance to a more cautious walk. Jack stalked silently down the hallway, eventually coming to the entrance to the chamber. To his surprise, Mourdock was there, standing before the double doors that led inside.

Jack stopped and hugged the wall, looking around for any sign of other threats. Mourdock simply stood, looking at the doors, as if trying to decide whether or not to enter. Jack was torn. He knew Mourdock was corrupted and that he would most likely attack him if Jack tried to approach. But if Jack did nothing, how was he to save his friend?

Jack frowned. He knew that in a fight he would probably be no match for Mourdock. But there was no other way into the chamber than through the doors that Mourdock was now blocking. Jack either had to try to save Mourdock, or he would not be able to do anything else. Jack remembered his conversation with Savage and how Shepherd had guided the Paragon back from his corruption by reminding him of who he was and what he cared about. Jack could only hope that he could rescue Mourdock the same way Shepherd had rescued Savage.

After a deep breath, Jack gingerly stepped forward, approaching Mourdock quietly while still keeping a safe distance from him. "Mourdock," Jack said.

Mourdock turned his head and looked at Jack, his pure black eyes gazing at him. Jack held up his hands, signaling he meant to harm.

"It's okay, buddy. I'm not here to fight you," he said.

A chuckle escaped from Mourdock, who seemed amused by the proclamation. "As if you could ever put up a fight against me," Mourdock replied. "I am better than you in every respect, Earthman. Always have been. Always will be."

"Yeah, you're probably right," Jack admitted. "You're Mister Perfect, and you know what? I'm totally fine with that."

"Lies," snarled Mourdock. "You've always been jealous. Resentful. I can sense it whenever I am with you. You covet what I have and seek to take from me what you can…"

"The only thing I'm seeking is to get you out of here and away from this crazy death energy that's making you evil," said Jack as he gestured around him. "So what's say you and me take a trip to the outer ring, huh? There's no bad magic there, buddy."

"The outer ring is no more," said Blackmane as he emerged from down a corridor, looking bemused. "It's been destroyed, along with your ship."

Jack scowled at Blackmane. He immediately backed up, even as he saw Desmodus emerge from an opposite hallway. Jack turned to run, but found Krixus had come up behind him, blocking off all avenue of escape.

"Crap," muttered Jack as he manifested his batons, backing away as the four corrupted Paragons slowly surrounded him.

"You never did mind your surroundings, Earthman," noted Blackmane. "One of the many, many flaws you displayed in your training."

"Yeah, well… with teachers like you three, it's a wonder I don't have more flaws than I do," Jack grumbled.

"Petulant to the end, I see. Even now, when all hope is lost and all avenue of success is closed to you, you cling to the delusion that you can actually make a difference. I would find that somewhat admirable if it weren't so pathetic."

"Excuse me for not buying into your bullcrap, Blackmane," Jack replied. "If I had a nickel for every time a bad guy lied about my situation being hopeless, I'd have… like… a whole lot of nickels by now."

"You face four of the most skilled and deadly Paragon Warriors ever to come out of the Conclave, Earthman," Blackmane taunted. "How else would you describe your current situation?"

Jack looked around at the faces of his adversaries, all their eyes black and cold.

"Normally, I'd say you were right, and it is totally hopeless," Jack replied. "But since I quit Fire Ring, I've learned all sorts of really cool ninja stuff you guys aren't expecting. So I'm going to upgrade my situation to only *slightly* hopeless."

The corrupted Paragons all chuckled.

"After seeing what you did to Tannyn and his group, I must admit, you've proven more resourceful than previously believed," said Blackmane. "We came across them after your battle and sent them away through the tethers. They will all be punished for their failures later. But for now… let us see how you hold up against us!"

Blackmane held out his hand toward Jack who immediately reacted by also holding out his hand. A graviton pulse erupted just as Jack pushed out an electromagnetic pulse. Though the EM pulse was strong enough to keep the graviton one from seriously harming Jack, it wasn't strong enough to completely dissipate Blackmane's attack, the gravity wave hitting Jack like a dropkick and sending him stumbling back, causing him to drop his batons.

Blackmane raised a curious eyebrow. "Well now, it would appear you did learn something new," he said. "But seeing as how you are such a terrible student, I doubt you learned it very well…"

All four Paragons held out their hands to unleash more gravity pulses. Jack quickly raised his hands again and created an electromagnetic field around himself just as the pulses of gravity erupted all around him.

The area before the chamber quaked, craters appearing all around Jack as the floor was ravaged from the pulses. Dust and small pieces of stone fell from the ceiling as Jack gritted his teeth, feeling the harsh tremors of the gravity pulses shoot through his protective field, rattling him to the bone.

But even as one of nature's most primal forces erupted all around him, Jack stood his ground, standing defiant against his attackers until they all stopped their assault. When they did, Blackmane looked at Jack with a hint of surprise. Jack smirked.

"Learned it well enough to handle you, jerkwad," Jack said.

"No, Earthman, you did not," replied Blackmane, right before shooting an electrical charge at him.

The electrical strike was intensified by the field Jack had created around himself and hit Jack straight in the chest, knocking him back a number of feet to the ground, where Jack lay still, his chest smoking where the blast had made contact. Jack's body was rigid from the electricity before going limp as the charge escaped him.

"Ugh. I so despise using electromagnetism," muttered Blackmane, brushing his hand on his thigh like it was dirty. "It's such a pedestrian skill."

"Is he dead?" asked Mourdock.

"He is," said Blackmane. "No one could have survived that. Now, come. The Supreme awaits."

Krixus and Desmodus joined Mourdock and Blackmane as they turned toward the entrance to the Chamber of the Great Seal. However, they all stopped short when they heard Jack gasp for breath.

The group turned and looked with curiosity as Jack sat up, clutching his chest and coughing. Though they were surprised, none was as surprised as Jack. The electric blast had hit him full on. Even Jack knew he should be dead. Though his chest did feel like it was on fire, by some miracle, not only had Jack survived, he felt as though he were recovering from the attack very quickly.

Blackmane scowled at Jack. Desmodus looked up at his companion. "How is that possible?" Desmodus asked.

"It doesn't matter," stated Blackmane. "If an insect survives the heel of your boot, you simply step on it again, only harder. Mourdock..."

Mourdock looked at Blackmane. "Yes?" he said.

"Strike him down," ordered Blackmane. "Kill him and complete your transformation into one of us."

"With pleasure," replied Mourdock as he manifested his sword.

Fear gripped Jack's chest as he saw Mourdock's murderous black eyes set upon him. Though he was alive, Jack's body was still rattled from the jolt he'd received and he could not get up to run away. He knew the only chance he had was to remind Mourdock of who he really was – and pray Mourdock was strong enough to regain control of himself.

"Mourdock, this isn't you!" insisted Jack. "You can fight this, Mourdock!"

Mourdock sneered as he stepped closer, the humming of his moonfyre blade growing louder as he approached.

"Think of the people who care about you!" Jack said. "Think of your parents! Think of Wil and Fred! Think of Master Hasatan!"

Jack pushed himself back as Mourdock came closer, a feeble attempt to put some distance between himself and Mourdock's weapon.

"Think of our friendship! You're my friend, Mourdock! I believe in you! You're stronger than this corruption!"

Still, Mourdock advanced.

"Think of your love for Anna!" Jack pleaded. "Think of how she makes you feel! She loves you, Mourdock! She wouldn't want you to give into this! She'd want you to fight!"

Mourdock stopped walking. He loomed over Jack, his jet-black eyes completely soulless and gazing at him with malice.

"She loves you," Jack Insisted. "I know she does!"

Laughter erupted from the other Paragons. Desmodus and Krixus looked beyond amused at Jack's attempts to redeem his friend.

"That's your strategy? Use the power of love and friendship?" mocked Blackmane. "You are wasting your breath. Once touched by the corruption, there is no coming back. We have all been reborn – better and stronger than before. The Mourdock Skyborn you knew is dead. No one is coming to save you."

Jack scowled. "I'm not the one who needs saving," he said. "You all do."

"You always were an annoyance, Earthman," said Blackmane, smugly, as he manifested his red moonfyre blade and twirled it with a menacing flourish while approaching. "Forget letting Skyborn kill you. I wish to eliminate you myself, once and for all."

Jack felt his chest return to normal, as though the injury he'd suffered had been completely healed. He looked for a way to get up and run away, but he was unable to do so before Blackmane was upon him.

"You can't run, Earthman," Blackmane stated, as though reading Jack's mind. "Not from this."

"Then let me stand," growled Jack. "Let's have a fair fight. Just you and me."

"You should know by now, Earthman, there is no such thing as a fair fight. A true warrior uses every advantage at his disposal to win."

"What's the matter Blackmane? Afraid I'd beat you?"

"I must admit, you are more skilled than I'd have given you credit for. But that is one fear I could never harbor."

Blackmane raised his sword, holding it at the ready.

"You may put up a fight, but you could never hope to defeat me alone."

Jack looked up at Blackmane, helplessly, as the Paragon raised his sword overhead, ready to strike the finishing blow…

Just as the sword was swung, a melodic clash rang out as Blackmane's red blade met with that of a blue one, stopping it cold.

Blackmane's eyes went wide as he turned and saw the steely face of Mourdock Skyborn, all darkness banished from his eyes as he gazed at Blackmane with gritty determination.

"He is *not* alone," growled Mourdock.

Mourdock quickly raised his hand and shot a gravitational wave toward an equally surprised Krixus and Desmodus, the two Paragon's barely having time to react before the gravity pulse hit them and sent them flying backward.

Mourdock then swung his blade at Blackmane, who narrowly parried it before dropping back into a defensive stance and clashing with Mourdock as the Paragon drove his opponent back with unrelenting attacks. A bright flash flared each time the blue blade met its red counterpart, the zapping sound it made singing out in the hallway as the two Paragons engaged in their deadly dance.

"What? How!?" snarled Blackmane.

"Turns out there's something to the power of love and friendship," replied Mourdock. "Which you might know if you ever had either."

Jack was so ecstatic to see he had somehow reached his friend and Mourdock had overcome his corruption that he almost didn't see the massive warhammer that was descending upon him.

Jack immediately rolled to the side just as Krixus brought his warhammer crashing down on the floor, cratering it as it demolished the stones where Jack had been lying only seconds before.

Just as Krixus lifted the massive weapon back up, Jack sprung off his hand and back to his feet, quickly remanifesting his batons to face off with the imposing Paragon. Before Jack could react, a chain wrapped itself around him, pinning his arms to his sides just as Desmodus landed a hard dropkick to his back, propelling him forward as Krixus was pulling back for a crushing swing.

Jack quickly dropped to his knees, falling backward as Krixus swung, the Paragon's deadly hammer whizzing by just inches from Jack's head. Jack hit the ground and rolled to the side, shrugging off the weighted chain when Desmodus came flying at him.

Jack raised his baton to knock the Paragon away, but Desmodus spun and dodged Jack's block, landing a vicious kick to the side of Jack's face.

"That all you got, maggot?" yelled Desmodus as Jack stumbled backward. "VIETNAM!!!"

The kick felt like it had broken Jack's jaw at first, but the pain suddenly disappeared and Jack's jaw was set. Though he was surprised by his miraculous recovery, Jack didn't have time to think about it before Krixus attacked again, forcing Jack to maneuver away from the swings of the warhammer.

Jack threw his electrified baton at Krixus, but the large Paragon took the blow with his forehead, not even slowing down from the electric shock that was administered to him.

Jack dropped and tumbled forward, rolling past Krixus and grabbing his fallen baton as he did so. He quickly turned and struck the back of the Paragon's knees and legs, causing Krixus to grunt and stumble from the blows.

Before Jack could press his advantage, however, he felt the weighted chain of Desmodus wrap around his neck and forcefully yank him backward. Jack stumbled, choking, and fell to the floor. The RooRoo leapt up into the air and came crashing down on Jack's chest.

Jack cried out as he felt some of his ribs break from the harsh impact. Desmodus leapt up again, yanking on the chain around Jack's neck just as he reached his jump's apex, and zoomed back down, landing on Jack's chest once more.

Jack felt his breath knocked out of him as more ribs broke. Desmodus prepared to perform the maneuver again, but just as he was about to yank on the chain one last time for a killing blow, Mourdock disengaged from his duel with Blackmane and hurled his moonfyre sword directly at the RooRoo.

Desmodus twisted in the air, letting go of his chain as the sword spun by, missing the corrupted Paragon by a hair's breadth.

Blackmane wasted no time in seizing upon his opportunity and struck out at Mourdock, his red moonfyre blade slashing across Mourdock's chest. Mourdock cried out as the blade opened a wound, but quickly remanifested his sword to fight Blackmane off.

Jack clutched at his chest, unable to breathe, his sides searing with pain from his broken bones. He felt them snap back into place just as Krixus rushed up to him, his warhammer high overhead. Before he knew he could breathe again, Jack rolled away as the hammer came crashing down.

Likewise, Mourdock's chest wound instantly healed, allowing him to recover and begin driving Blackmane back, just as the corrupted Paragon sneered at him. "How are you doing this?" Blackmane demanded. "You and the Earthman should be dead by now!"

"Guess we're just tougher than you think!" quipped Mourdock as he pressed his attack.

Jack twirled away, spinning in the air as Krixus attempted to land a blow. The end of Desmodus's weighted chain came shooting toward Jack, but Jack was ready for it this time. He dodged the weight, grabbing onto the chain as he landed. He saw Desmodus flying toward him and jabbed the chain with one of his batons, channeling electricity through it and up the metal weapon. Desmodus cried out as he received a shock, and Jack moved to the side as Desmodus collided with Krixus, sending them both to the ground.

Mourdock punched Blackmane across the face and landed a blow to the Paragon's shoulder. Blackmane cried out and swung wildly at Mourdock, catching him off-guard and slashing the top of Mourdock's arm.

Mourdock stumbled back, but his arm immediately healed. Blackmane snarled and looked around. "They're getting help!" he shouted. "Gravity pulses! Everywhere!"

Jack and Mourdock both dodged away as Blackmane, Krixus, and Desmodus unleashed gravity pulses all around them. Jack quickly erected an electromagnetic field encompassing both him and Mourdock as the corridors around them trembled and walls exploded as the gravity pulses tore through them.

Jack heard a scream as someone flew onto the floor from one of the hallways, accompanied by bricks and debris. Jack's eyes widened as he looked at Flitter, who struggled back to her hands and knees.

"Who's that?" asked Mourdock.

"It's Flitter!" Jack said. "She's been healing us all this time!"

Flitter looked up and met Jack's eyes. She smiled at him. "I couldn't leave you, Jack!" she said. "I had to come back and help! I—"

"Flitter, look out!" Jack yelled as he started to move toward her.

But he was too late. Blackmane had spotted her and rushed up from behind, moving at a speed faster than Flitter could react.

Before Jack even had time to realize what was happening, Blackmane had driven his sword into Flitter's back, the raging red blade protruding from her chest. A cold feeling of shock and horror gripped Jack as he saw Flitter look down at the sword sticking out of her, a feeble gurgle escaping from her lips.

"NO!" Jack cried out.

"Go ahead," whispered Blackmane to Flitter. "Try and heal with a blade piercing your heart."

Flitter's large, dark eyes met Jack's gaze one final time, a single tear escaping them and rolling down her cheek. She looked like she wanted to say something, but before she could, her body went limp.

Jack collapsed to his knees as Blackmane withdrew his sword from Flitter's body, allowing it to slump onto the ground. Tears stung Jack's eyes as he looked at his fallen friend, his chest tight with emotion. The sight of Flitter's lifeless body filled Jack with anguish, which he quickly channeled into anger. Jack set his gaze upon Blackmane, his teeth clenched, determined not to have Flitter's sacrifice been in vain.

Blackmane, Krixus, and Desmodus all regrouped, glaring over at Jack and Mourdock as they both got to their feet and faced off with them.

"You're going to pay for what you've done," Jack said, scowling.

Blackmane smirked. "Are we?" he asked. "You and Skyborn could barely stand against us, even with your little healer helping you out. With her gone, what chance do you think you have against we three – the chosen of the greatest Paragon Warrior in the universe?"

Jack channeled more energy into his batons, making them crackle to life. Mourdock held his sword at the ready, its blue blade humming.

"Let's find out," Jack said with a sneer.

Blackmane chuckled. "Very well," he said. "It is time to finish this."

"Agreed…" came a hoarse voice.

Before anyone could react, Blackmane, Krixus, and Desmodus all cried out and dropped their weapons as the ghostly specters of their souls suddenly sprung from their bodies. Their spirits fought briefly to hang on, but were forcibly ripped from them, flying through the air as they wailed in agony, shooting past Jack and Mourdock and into the hands of Master Savage.

Jack and Mourdock watched in shock as the spirits of their adversaries swirled into a ball between Savage's hands. The Paragon gazed down at the ball of ghostly energy he held, sneering, before ripping it apart and letting it trail off into the ether.

The bodies of the Paragons all fell to the ground and Master Savage himself slumped to his knees as his skin turned paler and the red, purple, and green veins beneath it bulged fiercely. His face was drawn and taught as he gazed over at the body of Flitter, a look of sadness in his pained eyes.

"Blast it…" he said. "I told her… not to come back…"

Jack rushed to Savage's side, accompanied by Mourdock, who looked at him with concern. "Master Savage!" Jack said. "We… we need to get you some help…"

"I am… beyond help…" Savage replied, weakly. "Using Servuchur again… I can feel the corruption taking over… I will not be able to… retain control much longer…"

"You can," Mourdock insisted. "You must! We need your help, Master!"

"I fear… I am of no help to you. When I turn… I will kill you both without hesitation," Savage replied. "You must… you must kill me before that happens…"

Jack's eyes went wide. "No!" he said. "No, we're not going to kill you!"

"*You must!*" insisted Savage. "I do not have the strength to… do it myself."

"But… there's got to be some other way!" Jack argued.

Savage looked at Jack, the green color of his skin so faded it was almost white. His face was riddled with the spiderwebbed veins of the corruption. But despite all that, the Paragon simply smiled. "I was… wrong about you, Earthman…" Savage said, his voice strained as he struggled to hold onto control. "You are… the very definition… of what it means to be a Paragon…"

Jack felt his chin tremble with emotion at Savage's words. The Paragon's gaze then moved to Mourdock.

"Strike me down! Quickly!" Savage ordered, his whole body beginning to tremble as the veins of corruption grew beneath his skin. "Before there is nothing left of me to save! DO IT!"

Mourdock frowned, but raised his sword nonetheless, driving it through Master Savage's chest. Jack turned away as Savage gasped, Mourdock's sword remaining in his heart so that he could not heal the wound. Savage met Mourdock's sad gaze, a weak smile growing on his lips. And in a whisper, Master Grendal Savage spoke his final words.

"Thank you…" he said.

As the life drained from Savage's eyes, Mourdock withdrew his sword, allowing the Paragon's body to slump onto the floor. A sob escaped from Jack before he wiped his eyes of tears. He looked up at Mourdock, who gazed back at him, sadly.

"It had to be done," Mourdock said.

"I… I know it did…" Jack said before climbing back to his feet. He looked from Savage, to Flitter, to the bodies of Blackmane, Krixus, and Desmodus. "So much death," Jack muttered.

"And more to come, most likely," Mourdock said. "Blackmane and the others were here because whoever is behind all this is inside the Chamber of the Great Seal. And like it or not, we're the only ones left who can do anything about what's going on in there. Are you ready for what lies beyond that door?"

"You asking me if I'm scared?" Jack responded.

"Are you?"

"I'm a Paragon," Jack replied. "I've stormed Ghost Planets. I've fought Deathlord Supremes. I've had the entire galaxy come after me, and I'm still standing. With you at my side, I'm not afraid of anything."

Mourdock smiled at Jack. "Then let's go save the day," he said.

Jack nodded and gripped his batons as Mourdock brandished his sword. The two turned toward the towering doors to the chamber, which rumbled open as they approached. Inside, the two could see a shadowy figure standing before the access orb of the Great Seal, which was completely riddled with the red, green, and purple veins of corruption that glowed and pulsed, making the carved eye that adorned it look sick and ominous.

Jack and Mourdock marched down the stairs of the large amphitheater-like room, finally setting foot on the floor in its center, gazing at the back of the robed being as he let go of the access orb.

"It's over, jerkface," Jack said.

"Your thralls are all gone," Mourdock stated. "Show yourself. Let us end this."

"End this?" came a dark voice, echoing throughout the chamber. "But this is just the beginning!"

The figure turned, shrugging off the black robe it had been wearing to reveal none other than Master GorJiro, looking at Jack and Mourdock with a mixture of smugness and loathing.

Jack and Mourdock both took a step back in surprise. "Master GorJiro?" Mourdock said in disbelief.

"So…" GorJiro said, eyeing the two men in amusement. "My greatest student, standing side-by-side with my worst. This is what comes to stop me?"

"Stop you?" Jack asked. "How are you even here? You died!"

GorJiro chuckled. "Death is no obstacle for one such as I," he said. "You called me GorJiro. But you were correct when you said Cormac Braen GorJiro is dead. I killed that version of myself, long ago. What stands before you now is the Herald of Annihilation. The Bringer of Corruption. The Enslaver of the Free Mind. I am the darkness that shall extinguish the light. The shadow that enshrouds the universe. The incurable disease that shall spread across all creation. I… am *Mellegogg!* Deathlord Supreme! And I shall consume all who stand against me. Starting with *you!*"

Jack and Mourdock both gazed at their former teacher. The man who'd taught them everything they knew about being a warrior. The man who was proclaimed to be the greatest fighter in the entire galaxy. The man who'd never lost a duel and had slain opponents by the thousands.

"Mourdock," whispered Jack. "I'm scared."

"Yeah," answered Mourdock, grimly. "Me, too."

Jack looked at his friend. Mourdock hadn't said it to be comforting or ironic. It was just a statement of fact. And it didn't make Jack feel any better.

Mourdock returned Jack's look and smiled sadly, silently communicating that he knew what Jack was feeling. He nodded his head, as if to ask if Jack were ready for what would come next.

Jack nodded in response. And without another word, the two of them marched toward their adversary to face their destiny...

Together.

# CHAPTER 29

Zarrod stood at the entrance to the Equinox Temple in the guise of Paragon Hasatan. Panicked people – men, women, and crying children – were rushing by him as they fled for sanctuary. In the distance, Zarrod could see the city of Highpoint being overrun by Deathstalkers. The creatures overwhelmed the city, scurrying through its streets, stalking and killing any they could.

*Oh, how glorious!* thought Zarrod. *It really is a shame this cannot continue. But my plan requires this all to end.*

"Quickly! Run!" shouted a group of Peacekeepers as they covered the evacuation. "Get inside the temple! Hurry!"

"Great Observer!" gasped the High Pontifex as he stood at Zarrod's side, gazing at the carnage the Deathstalkers were perpetuating. "I have never witnessed such evil!"

*Then you haven't been looking hard enough*, thought Zarrod.

The Peacekeeper Lieutenant came rushing up to the High Pontifex. "Your Holiness," he said, "are the temple's teleporters working? Can we evacuate the civilians somewhere safer?"

"I… I fear the teleporters stopped operating around the same time the communication network failed," the High Pontifex replied.

"Get everyone inside," Zarrod ordered. "Seal the entrance and have your men guard it from within. The temple is built into the mountains. These creatures will have a hard time finding a way into it."

"But the temple's entrance will not hold out forever, especially not in the face of *that*," the Lieutenant responded, gesturing toward the Deathstalkers. "If they break down the front doors, those inside will be trapped! Everyone will be killed."

"They will not break down the doors," Zarrod said. "I shall stay out here and fight them off."

The Peacekeeper Lieutenant's eyes went wide. "But… that's suicide!"

"Perhaps," said Zarrod as he manifested a moonfyre sword. "But I am a Paragon. It is my duty to defend those who cannot defend themselves. I will hold these evil creatures at bay to my dying breath, if need be. Hopefully that will buy you all enough time for help to arrive."

"Let me give you some men to assist you—"

"No," replied Zarrod. "They would surely be killed. They are better off keeping those within the temple safe. Now go, all of you, before they arrive."

The Lieutenant frowned, but nodded. "Thank you, Paragon, for your sacrifice."

The Peacekeeper then ordered his men to fall back into the temple and began shepherding the last of the civilians inside. The High Pontifex placed a hand on Zarrod's shoulder. "Your bravery and courage are a thing of inspiration, Paragon Hasatan," he said. "May the Great Observer watch over you and grant you luck."

*I won't be needing any luck*, mused Zarrod to himself. "Thank you, your Holiness," he said. "Now go. Watch over your flock. I shall stay here and do my best to ensure you remain safe."

"Blessings shine upon you," the High Pontifex said before running away to the safety of the temple.

When the doors to the temple had been sealed shut, Zarrod stood alone, patiently waiting as the horde of Deathstalkers approached. He held up his sword, looking as though he were getting ready to do battle.

Then, as the Deathstalkers neared him and the temple's entrance, they stopped. Zarrod smiled, lowering his sword and stepping forward, reaching out and petting one of the Deathstalkers on its head.

"Yes, that's right," he said. "I am one of your masters, and you will obey my commands."

The Deathstalkers all snorted and bobbed their heads in response to the Deathlord Supreme.

"Continue your rampage," Zarrod said. "But leave this entrance untouched. No one inside is to be harmed. Now go."

With that, the Deathstalkers dispersed, moving on to continue their attack, but completely ignoring Zarrod and the entrance to the temple. Zarrod demanifested his sword and smiled, pleased with himself.

*So, this is what it's like to be a hero,* he mused.

★★★★★

Wilvelm fired his graviton rifle downward, the massive ball of directed, focused gravity smashing any Deathstalkers in his landing zone and driving the surrounding creatures away. Wil landed and immediately jumped again, his jumpjet carrying him high into the sky and ever closer to the looming dark temple.

The process had almost become routine for Wil in his long trek toward his target. Jump. Shoot. Clear. Land. Repeat. And though he was making good time and closing the distance to his objective, the HUD of his Alpha Force helmet began to warn him that he didn't have much more fuel left with which to make his jumps.

Wil was so close to the temple's entrance, he knew one last good jump would carry him there, but it would mean burning through the rest of his fuel. He cranked up his jumpjet output and made one last leap, burning the last of his fuel reserves and landing right in front of the temple's opening.

Though his graviton blast had cleared the landing area, now that Wil wasn't jumping away immediately, he realized the Deathstalkers were going to regroup quickly and attack. Wil immediately holstered his graviton rifle on his back and pulled the blaster carbine from his thigh, opening fire on the surrounding Deathstalkers as his weapon unleashed rapid bolts of superheated plasma upon the creatures, sending them off in puffs of dust.

But even with the automatic carbine, the Deathstalkers grouped at the temple entrance were too numerous to hold back for long. They rushed forward as a group, closing in on Wil faster than he could dispatch them.

*There are too many!* Wil thought, starting to panic. *Just too blasted many!*

Then, explosions of gravity erupted around him, dispersing all the Deathstalkers in Wil's vicinity. Wil looked up to see four Alpha Force soldiers descending from their jumps, landing close to him.

"Lord Blackfyre," said Roadblock. "Good of you to join us."

"Join you?" said Wil in relief. "I was here first!"

"And how was that working out for you?" joked Roadblock as he holstered his graviton rifle and pulled the two pieces of his gatling weapon from his thighs, quickly locking them together and popping the muzzle out. He then turned and began unleashing a relentless stream of blaster fire, arcing his weapon left and right so as to keep the encroaching Deathstalkers at bay. "All of you, get moving!" he ordered. "Shut this temple down! I'll stay here and make sure these Deathstalkers don't come after you!"

"I'm staying with you," said Lucky. "You can't hold off this many of them on your own."

"Watch me."

"I will, while I watch your back," Lucky replied, turning to Missionary and Skeptic. "You guys go with Lord Blackfyre. Take out the monolith and that death ray."

"Roger that," Missionary and Skeptic replied.

Lucky then pulled out her carbine and began giving Roadblock cover as the man and his impressive weapon continued to hold the Deathstalkers back. Wilvelm turned to Missionary and Skeptic. "On me," he ordered, leading the group through the entrance.

The three men made their way through the temple, the lights from their graviton rifles illuminating the way. "Stay frosty," Missionary said. "There's no telling what's in this place."

"You think there's another Terrormancer in here somewhere?" asked Skeptic.

Then, as the trio arrived in the temple's central chamber, they saw the large black monolith at its center, standing before them ominously.

"I'd say that's probably a good bet," muttered Wil.

Missionary looked down at the readout on his armor's gauntlet. "My suit is picking up massive energy spikes beyond those doors," he said, gesturing toward the two massive double doors on the other side of the chamber. "Think that might be where the death ray is coming from?"

"Only one way to find out," said Wil. "Skeptic, plant some explosives on that monolith. Missionary, you're with me."

"Acknowledged," both men replied.

The group slowly made their way into the chamber, keeping their rifles at the ready and fully charged. When they were within a few feet of the monolith, a voice emanated from the darkness.

"Trespasserssss!"

The trio stopped and looked around, aiming their rifles toward every dark corner of the room, instantly on alert.

"Well, I guess that answers the question about the Terrormancer," grumbled Skeptic.

"Missionary, go to heat vision. Skeptic, switch to infrared," ordered Wil. "If you see anything that's not us, shoot it."

"Roger that," both soldiers replied.

Each man slowly looked around, scanning the room for any sign of the Terrormancer. But everywhere they shined their lights, there was nothing.

"I don't see him…" said Skeptic.

"Where could he be?" asked Missionary. "This room is empty! There's no place for him to hide!"

Wil froze, a terrifying thought coming to him upon hearing Missionary's words. "Oh, no," he said. "Above us!"

The group all turned their weapons upward just as the Terrormancer came swooping down, landing in their midst and swinging his scythe, its ghostly blade striking each man in the chest and sending him flying backward.

Wil hit the ground hard, his armor alerting him to minor damage. He looked down at the equalarium plate on his breast and found it had blocked the scythe's strike.

Wil quickly got to his knees and aimed his rifle at the Terrormancer's location, but the robed figure had disappeared. Missionary and Skeptic also recovered, their equalarium plating having protected them, as well. The soldiers brought their weapons to the ready.

"Where is he?" asked Skeptic, frantically. "Where did he go???"

"You think you are ssssafe," the Terrormancer's voice said, carrying through the darkness of the chamber. "But you cannot hide from your fear!"

Before Wil could react, he felt something grab him from behind and rip his helmet off. Instantly, Wil felt a wave of terror wash over him as his mind was assaulted with the most horrific images he could imagine. He grabbed his head and screamed, falling to the ground.

As he struggled to regain his focus, Wil saw the Terrormancer speed behind Missionary and rip his helmet from him, before speeding toward Skeptic and doing the same. Both men cried out and fell to the floor, writhing as they wrestled with the overwhelming fear the Terrormancer was inflicting upon them.

Wil tried to regain control. He tried to push past the terror roiling in his gut. He tried to ignore the horrific images that sprung to his mind. But even as he struggled to hold onto his sanity, a real-life terror was playing out before him as the Terrormancer used his scythe to lop off Skeptic's head as he lay helpless on the ground.

"NO!!!!" Wil heard himself cry.

"It isssss uselessss to resissssst," the Terrormancer said as he moved toward Missionary, the soldier screaming uncontrollably as he flailed about on the ground. "Fear isssss the most powerful of all emotionssss. And of all fearsssss, fear of death isssss the most terrifying…"

The Terrormancer swung his scythe again, killing Missionary while he was vulnerable. Wil could do nothing but watch, helpless, as the Terrormancer then turned toward him, his black eyes filled with murderous intent.

"And in thissss place – I am the grim reaper!!!" the Terrormancer hissed.

Roadblock screamed as he continued to unload his weapon on the masses of Deathstalkers rushing toward him, cutting them down before they could get close to attacking. Lucky was at his back, firing expertly with her carbine at any Deathstalker that somehow got past Roadblock's weapon. For a glorious few minutes, Roadblock thought they might actually be able to keep the Deathstalkers at bay indefinitely.

Then, he saw in his helmet's HUD that Missionary's and Skeptic's armor readings had gone dark.

"Oh, no," Roadblock muttered. "Lucky! Are you seeing this?"

"What do you think happened?"

"Nothing good!" Roadblock replied. "Quick! Get inside! Give them backup!"

"I can't leave you here alone, Sarge!"

"You have to! Don't worry, I can—"

Suddenly, Roadblock's gatling weapon stopped firing, even though its muzzle continued to spin. Roadblock gasped. He'd been so distracted, he'd forgotten to keep an eye on his ammo. He'd blown through all the plasma canisters in his weapon.

"Oh, kitten," he cursed.

Without his gatling blaster to maintain a perimeter, the Deathstalkers surged forward. Roadblock quickly dropped his weapon and pulled his carbine out, firing on anything that moved as Lucky joined him.

Even the combined fire from the carbines could not keep the Deathstalkers at bay as they overwhelmed the two soldiers. Before Roadblock and Lucky knew it, they were beset on all sides by the creatures, slashing and clawing at their armor.

The two Alpha Force soldiers quickly resorted to every last trick they had available to them. They shot out their electro-nets. They used stun grenades and incendiary grenades. They fired their missiles. They did anything they could to desperately attempt to clear away the creatures that assailed them.

But it was not enough.

No matter how many Deathstalkers the two dispatched, more were taking their place. Before long, there were so many atop of Roadblock he stumbled and fell to the ground, having to resort to using his hands to fight off the creatures as they tore away at his armor.

"Sarge! SARGE!" he heard Lucky cry as she, too, was overwhelmed.

"Come on you pieces of squick!" shouted Roadblock, defiantly, as he wrestled with the creatures. "I ain't goin' down without a fight!!!"

A Deathstalker began clawing at Roadblock's helmet, forcing him to turn his head away. It was then he saw something strange. In the far distance, Deathstalkers were being flung aside, as though something were knocking them away while charging through them.

Then, something flew into the air, soaring high overhead and landing right in front of the temple's entrance with such force all the Deathstalkers nearby were knocked away or destroyed from the impact.

Grohm stood up and roared. His makeshift armor was dented and marred. His jumpjet was melted to his back. His exposed muscle was littered with cuts and scrapes. But despite all that, the Rognok was still fighting. Grohm quickly pulled the Deathstalkers off Roadblock and Lucky and threw them far away before whirling on the surrounding mob and lashing out, his strikes sending any Deathstalker he made contact with into puffs of dust.

Roadblock didn't waste any time. He grabbed his gatling blaster and ejected the plasma canisters. He quickly reloaded, scrambling back to his feet and rushing to the Rognok's side, opening fire and establishing the perimeter around the temple's entrance once more.

"Get inside!" Roadblock yelled to Grohm. "They need you!"

"We'll handle this!" yelled Lucky as she rushed up to fight alongside Roadblock. "Go! GO!"

Grohm growled, but turned and rushed into the temple's entrance, leaving Roadblock and Lucky behind. The two soldiers continued to fire, keeping the overwhelming swarm of Deathstalkers at bay.

"There's so many of them!" cried Lucky.

"What are you worried about?" laughed Roadblock. "The Deathlords may have an unending legion of Deathstalkers – but we got ourselves a ROGNOK!!!"

★★★★★

Wil felt his whole body trembling as he feebly struggled to push himself away from the encroaching Terrormancer. He wanted to scream. He wanted to cry. He wanted to run away and keep running and never ever stop. But despite those feelings, Wil dug down deep, desperately looking for something to hold onto – something to give him strength.

*Torboron would not have been afraid!* Wil thought. *He'd have fought! He'd have never given into his fear!!!*

Wil cried out, as though to expel the fear that was crippling him. Despite still feeling the terror, he was able to look past it, staring up at the Terrormancer who loomed over him menacingly. The black robed figure cocked its head curiously at Wil, almost looking bemused by Wil's efforts.

"You are not sssstronger than your fear," the Terrormancer hissed. "It isssss a weakness all of your kind share."

The Terrormancer loomed over Wilvelm, glaring down at him smugly, the blade of his scythe shimmering with a sickly glow.

"I'm not afraid of you..." Wilvelm said through gritted teeth.

"Then I shall give you ssssomething to fear..." the Terrormancer replied.

The Terrormancer lifted his scythe high overhead, ready to lower the killing blow. Wilvelm steeled himself, glaring at his foe with as much defiance as he could muster.

*If I'm to die, let it not be as a coward!* he thought.

The Terrormancer swung downward.

Wilvelm flinched, but the blow he was expecting did not come. When he looked back up, he saw the deadly blade of the scythe inches from his face, stopped only by the grip of a large, meaty hand.

Grohm stood by Wilvelm's side, the Rognok's exposed muscles tense as steel wire, despite being marred by many cuts and scratches. Grohm's red and black eyes seemed to glow with fury in the darkness as the massive alien looked down at the Terrormancer who gazed at the sudden appearance of the new arrival in shock and surprise.

"Want something to fear?" Grohm grumbled, his voice raspy and guttural.

The Rognok looked the Terrormancer dead in the villain's solid black eyes and sneered.

"Fear Grohm."

Before the Terrormancer could react, Grohm yanked the weapon from the creature's hands and swung it, the ghostly blade passing through him. The Terrormancer's eyes grew wide as he screamed, his skin smoking before melting away into a wisp of smoke, his dark robes crumpling to the floor.

Grohm looked at the scythe with distaste before breaking it in two over his knee, the ghostly blade fading away, leaving nothing but the worthless, gnarled wood of the handle, which Grohm promptly tossed aside.

As soon as the Terrormancer was dead, Wilvelm felt as though he could breathe again. The searing feelings of panic that had gripped him moments before began to subside and his wits returned to him. He lay on the ground, exhausted from the effort of fighting the fear that had been overwhelming him. Despite everything that was happening, Wilvelm took a moment to simply relax and try to recover. Grohm walked up and stood over him, looking down at Wilvelm with a curious gaze.

"Anyone ever tell you… you have impeccable timing?" Wilvelm said with a relieved smile.

"No," grunted Grohm.

"Happy to be the first, then," Wil responded as he raised his hand toward the hulking alien.

Grohm grabbed Wilvelm's forearm and helped him back to his feet. Wilvelm looked at the bodies of Missionary and Skeptic and frowned. He then brought his fist up to his chest in a final, silent salute to his two fallen brothers in arms.

"Looks like it's up to just you and me now, big guy," Wilvelm said.

"Battle," Grohm said with a nod.

"Couldn't have said it better myself," Wilvelm replied as he picked up a dropped graviton rifle. "You take care of the monolith. I'll handle the death ray."

Grohm nodded. Without wasting another moment, Wilvelm ran toward the large, ornate double doors. He charged his graviton rifle, pumping it up to a full 100%. The rifle hummed a high pitch whine, which steadily grew louder as it powered up its blast.

Wilvelm hefted up the rifle, leveled it at the doors, and fired. A rippling ball shot forth from the rifle's muzzle, slamming into the two large doors with its full force, causing them to crack and crater inward at the point of impact.

As Wilvelm charged his rifle again, Grohm lumbered to the monolith that stood tall and imposing in the open chamber, veins of glowing corruption extending from its base and into the floor. The veins pulsed, as if sensing the Rognok's approach.

The black rock covering the floor began to form into hands, which formed into arms, which formed into Deathstalkers that began to rise from the rock. They grasped at Grohm, trying to slow him, but the Rognok stomped on them, crushing them as he continued his relentless path forward.

Wilvelm fired his rifle again, and again, the doors withstood the blow, but just barely. They were hanging on by their hinges. In the crack of their openings, Wilvelm could see the room just beyond. The chaotic tempest of death energy twisted in the distance.

More Deathstalkers rose from the floor, hissing and snarling, focused on Grohm as the Rognok lumbered toward the monolith. The Deathstalkers pounced at him, but Grohm knocked them aside, hitting some so forcefully they turned to dust. More formed, rushing forth to protect the vile structure that created them. But Grohm paid them no mind. He was focused on one thing and one thing only – destroying that monolith.

With one final blast from the graviton rifle, the doors to the next chamber collapsed open. Wilvelm rushed through, dropping the heavy rifle in favor of his plasma carbine. The floor of the chamber extended outward to a circular area, which was suspended above a cavernous pit from which the death energy spewed forth, rising up to the sky.

A raised platform was at the area's center and at the top, a figure stood, clutching a glowing access orb that hovered above a stone kiosk. Wilvelm raced up the stairs, aiming his weapon at the figure and firing. One of the blasts hit the figure in the back, causing it to cry out and drop to the floor.

Back in the central chamber, Grohm was being swarmed by Deathstalkers. They scratched and clawed at him, biting down with their sharp teeth and slashing at him with their talons. But Grohm pushed through, screaming loudly as he finally reached the monolith and punched it with all his might. As though the impact had been inflicted upon them, as well, the Deathstalkers all cried out before doubling their efforts to tear the Rognok apart to prevent any more damage.

When Wilvelm reached the top of the platform, he kicked the figure over, ready to deliver a killing blast when he froze. He looked down at the face of the figure in shock. Her skin had turned bone white, her hair ashen grey, and her previously brilliant blue eyes had become black… but there was no mistaking her.

"Lady Skyborn?" Wilvelm said in surprise.

"You… pathetic… boy…" Judyth snarled. "How dare you interfere with my ascendancy!"

"You mean… you're behind all this?" asked Wilvelm in disbelief. "The death ray – you were the one controlling it?"

"I'm doing more than controlling it," Judyth sneered. "I am giving birth to a new universe! A new reality!"

Wilvelm's mind raced. It didn't make any sense. Maxima was Judyth Skyborn's home! She was part of the Legacy that controlled the star system! Why would she want to tear it all apart? Wilvelm was convinced she must not be in control of herself. "Lady Skyborn, the Deathlords have done something to you," he insisted. "We're going to get you help, but for now, I need you to fight it and tell me how to stop this thing!"

Judyth hissed and jutted her hand toward Wilvelm, a small ball of ghostly energy shooting forth and slamming Wilvelm square in the chest so hard it dented the breastplate of his armor and sent him flying backward.

Wilvelm cried out, the attack causing him to drop his gun before landing hard at the bottom of the stairs leading up to the platform. His head spun from its impact with the floor, and his chest burned from the force of the blow. When he looked up, the room was moving at odd angles as his head swam. He could see Lady Skyborn getting to her feet and slowly making her way down the stairs toward him, her steps wobbly as she clutched at her wound.

"No one controls me!" she said. "This is my destiny! My birthright! You will not take this from me!"

With that, she manifested another ball of death energy and flung it toward Wilvelm who had gathered just enough of his wits to barely dodge it.

In the opposite chamber, the Deathstalkers swarmed at Grohm. The Rognok thrashed about, flinging his attackers off him as he endured their assaults, continuing to punch the monolith with all his might as soon as he had an opening to do so. The face of the monolith was cracking with each successive blow, and the Deathstalkers cried out in pain as the Rognok inflicted his damage.

"Lady Skyborn, please!" begged Wilvelm as he dodged another death blast. "I've known you most of my life! This isn't you!"

A wicked smile grew on Judyth Skyborn's face. "You've never known me, you pathetic fool!" she hissed. "No one has! I am a part of something so much greater than any of you can possibly understand! I was the one who raised this temple from the ground so that I may finally embrace my destiny! I am endowed with the true Royal Blood! The blood of Halcyon! I am the progeny of the Void Lords! I am the Queen of Souls and mother of the Great Death!"

Wilvelm's eyes narrowed as Judyth Skyborn hobbled toward him, her words convincing him that whatever had happened to her, she was a willing participant in it.

"None shall stop me from fulfilling my sacred duty!" Judyth cried as she gazed upon Wilvelm with murderous intent. "Least of all *you!*"

"I wouldn't be so sure about that…" growled Wilvelm as he slammed his arm onto the ground, popping out a small launcher from the gauntlet of his armor and pointing it directly at Judyth. Judyth Skyborn's eyes widened in surprise just as Wilvelm fired, three explosive mini-rockets blasting forth, catching her directly in the chest and leaving a rather unsightly mess behind.

Thus ended the ascendancy of the Queen of Souls.

As he struggled back to his feet, Wilvelm could hear Grohm's cries from the opposite chamber. He glanced behind him to see the swarm of Deathstalkers clustered around the monolith. Wilvelm hoped that the Rognok could handle whatever was happening beneath that fray. He picked up the carbine he'd dropped and lumbered back up the stairs leading to the access orb, his chest burning with every step.

Wilvelm stood before the twisting tempest of ghost energy, dwarfed by its terrifying magnificence. He looked at the access orb that Judyth had been holding when he came upon her.

*If that's what's controlling this thing,* he thought, *then maybe that's what will stop it!*

Wilvelm raised his weapon and fired upon the orb, peppering the kiosk with plasma blasts.

Grohm hit the monolith again, even as the Deathstalkers tore away at his wounds, ripping bits of flesh and muscle from him.

Wil's blasts began to chip away at the black rock of the kiosk, the access orb flickering as he damaged it.

Some of the Deathstalkers broke away, racing up the stairs to attack Wil to stop his assault.

Grohm landed another hit, this one deepening the cracks of the obsidian surface of the monolith.

Wilvelm continued firing, even as the Deathstalkers rushed forward.

With a powerful cry, Grohm slammed his fist into the monolith one last time, breaking it apart, sending the ghost energy trapped inside it rocketing away with an eerie wail.

All the Deathstalkers screamed before disintegrating into dust, just as they were about to attack Wil.

And just as all that happened, the kiosk broke, and the access orb disappeared. The ghostly death tempest churned, roiling briefly before it broke apart, the souls trapped within it breaking away and escaping until there was nothing left.

Wilvelm stood for a moment, watching as the last of the tempest faded away. The light from the sky above filtered down from the chamber's opening, granting an almost peaceful aura to the room that had housed horrors only moments before.

Wil turned and saw Grohm kneeling in the central chamber, slumping to his knees after destroying the monolith. Wilvelm raced down toward him, coming to his side.

"Grohm!" he said.

The Rognok's back and arms were littered with deep lacerations. There was no blood, but the exposed muscle was badly shredded. From the Rognok's appearance, Wil couldn't imagine the type of pain Grohm must have been in. He knelt by Grohm's side, looking at the Rognok's face, which appeared tired.

"Grohm, are you okay?"

Grohm smirked. "Only flesh wound," he said.

Wilvelm couldn't help but laugh at that, despite the severity of the Rognok's injuries. "Come on, big guy," he said. "Let's get you some help."

Wilvelm slung Grohm's arm over his shoulder and used the power of his Alpha Force armor to heft the Rognok to his feet. He led the massive alien out of the chamber, leaving it as it deserved to be, as barren and empty as a tomb.

When Wil and Grohm emerged from the temple. Roadblock was still alive and was tending to Lucky. Both their armors had been badly damaged, and it appeared as though Lucky had been wounded, but they were both well enough to smile at Wil as he strode forward with the Rognok.

"You did it, my Lord," Roadblock said, looking relieved. "Perfect timing, too. We were just about to be overwhelmed."

"I couldn't have done it alone," replied Wil as he gently set Grohm down beside Lucky, the Rognok grunting in pain as he did so. "Grohm saved the day, yet again."

"What of Missionary?" asked Roadblock. "Skeptic?"

Wilvelm frowned. "They didn't make it," he replied.

Roadblock nodded, sadly. "I'm surprised any of us made it," he said. "Considering what we had to face… it's a miracle we're still breathing."

"We did the impossible, Sergeant," Wilvelm said. "Time to let everyone know about it."

Wilvelm checked his suit's radio. Now that the death ray had been stopped, it appeared communications were working once more.

"Attention Maxima fleet, this is Wilvelm Blackfyre of Alpha Force unit MX017," he reported. "The temple's monolith has been destroyed. All Deathstalkers have been dispatched. The death ray has been eliminated. The threat on Maxima's surface has been neutralized. Chalk one up for the good guys. Over and out."

"So, what are we supposed to do now?" asked Roadblock.

Wilvelm looked up at the sky. "We did our part," he answered. "Now let's just hope they can do theirs."

# Chapter 30

Jack and Mourdock stood side-by-side, facing down GorJiro with their weapons at the ready. Mourdock's moonfyre blade hummed. Jack's electrified batons crackled. But GorJiro didn't appear the least bit intimidated. In fact, the Paragon looked amused. He simply stood with his hands clasped behind his back, gazing at his two former students expectantly.

Jack looked over and saw a body lying on the ground, not far away. It was twisted and mangled beneath its white robes, the unmistakable fur of Master Highclaw visible, despite it being matted and bloody. GorJiro followed Jack's gaze over to the fallen Paragon and chuckled. "Ah, yes, Master Highclaw," GorJiro stated. "I admit, he put up more of a fight than I had expected. Tried to stop me, the old fool, as though he were any match for my abilities."

Jack and Mourdock both frowned at the sight of the dead Master. "So you killed everyone from the Order?" Jack asked.

"Just Hodapp and Highclaw," GorJiro replied. "I'd hoped to claim Savage when the corruption was unleashed. He'd have been a powerful thrall, and he was already so corrupted, I expected him to turn immediately. The other two, they were far too powerful to allow the corruption to take root in them, so they had to be dispatched."

"What did you do to everyone?" asked Jack. "How did you turn them all evil?"

"It was a long and arduous process," GorJiro replied. "I spent what felt like lifetimes corrupting the Conclave's Great Seal. And as it became more corrupted, I was able to spread that corruption to all who lived here. Those within the walls of this temple were exposed to the seal's influence, and the longer they stayed here, the more the corruption took root within them. But those in the Fire Ring were the easiest to corrupt. Each guided meditation I led instilled my corruption deeper and deeper within them, ensuring that I would have control over the deadliest warriors in the galaxy when the time came."

"So that's why everyone in Fire Ring was a jerk!" exclaimed Jack.

"They were simply being prepped for their eventual transformation," GorJiro said. "Once the death energy from the dark temples assaulted the Conclave, exposure to it brought out the corruption, and like butterflies emerging from their cocoons, the best this universe had to offer were transformed into the ultimate weapons for the Deathlords."

"Not for long," growled Mourdock. "We'll save them. I was able to fight my way back. So will others."

GorJiro looked bemused at Mourdock's proclamation. "Yes, you turned out to be a great disappointment, Skyborn," he said. "You, more than anyone, had the corruption rooted deep within you. By all rights, you should be standing by my side rather than against me. It must have taken a great deal of willpower to return from such a thing. But once one has been corrupted, there is never any coming back. You will eventually join me again, and when you do, it will be for good."

"Not if I have anything to say about it," snarled Mourdock.

"Or me!" chimed in Jack.

"You, Skyborn, will not have a say. As for you, Earthman, you'll be too dead to do anything about it."

"Scarier dudes than you have threatened to kill me before, GorJiro," Jack replied. "And I'm still here!"

"You have yet to see how frightening I can truly be, child," stated GorJiro. "But I shall be more than happy to show you. Come…"

GorJiro stepped forward and opened his arms, smiling defiantly at his two former students.

"Let us dance."

Jack and Mourdock looked at one another.

"You go right, I'll go left," Mourdock said.

"You go high, I'll go low," Jack replied.

And with a nod of their heads, Jack and Mourdock attacked.

The two men wasted no time assaulting their opponent, rushing forward and sending flurries of blows against him. But rather than fight back, GorJiro simply dodged each and every strike aimed his way, expertly maneuvering between the deadly slashes from the moonfyre blade and the electrified batons. Though Jack and Mourdock were channeling as much enhanced speed as they could to try to hit GorJiro, the Master Paragon was faster, and after three minutes of uselessly trying to hit their opponent, Jack and Mourdock broke away and regrouped.

GorJiro looked at the two men with a smug smirk. He wasn't even breathing heavily. "Is that all?" he asked. "I haven't even summoned my weapon, yet."

Jack and Mourdock scowled at the Paragon. "Okay, new plan," whispered Mourdock. "You distract him, and I'll try to close in for a killing blow."

"Distract him?" grumbled Jack. "I can barely get close to him!"

"You will," replied Mourdock. "Just get ready to attack on my signal. Are you ready?"

Jack tightened his grip on his batons. "As I'll ever be," he replied.

"Now!" cried Mourdock.

Mourdock quickly moved to the left as he flung his sword toward GorJiro, the blue blade spinning with incredible speed, appearing to be nothing more than a shining blue disk as it rocketed toward the evil Paragon.

GorJiro dodged the blade as it hummed by him, but the brief distraction allowed Jack to rush forward and attack.

Caught off-guard by the thrown sword, GorJiro was not able to avoid Jack's series of rapid blows. Instead, he struck out his hands, hitting at Jack's wrists and arms, knocking away each swing to ensure the batons never came close to touching him.

Jack grunted with each painful strike GorJiro landed to counter his hits, but he continued to press the attack to attempt to occupy the Paragon long enough for Mourdock to make his move.

Mourdock quickly made his way around GorJiro, rushing up in the Paragon's blind spot and remanifesting his sword...

As Jack pressed his attack, GorJiro knocked his hands away and delivered a solid blow directly to Jack's chest, sending him flying backward.

Mourdock raised his sword, rapidly approaching GorJiro, poised for a killing blow...

*CLANG!*

Just as Mourdock brought his sword down, GorJiro turned and manifested his own moonfyre blade, raising it just in time to meet that of Mourdock's. GorJiro's arm stood strong and firm, not even flinching as his blade met the full force of Mourdock's, the glowing red and blue swords shrieking and sparking from where they touched.

Mourdock tried to press his blade against GorJiro's, but it did not yield an inch. He looked past the crimson glow of his opponent's weapon and into GorJiro's dark eyes, which gazed back at him menacingly.

Mourdock immediately hopped back, assuming a more stable fighting stance. GorJiro slowly lowered his blade, one hand behind his back as he angled his body to meet the stance of Mourdock's. "You are, indeed, a good fighter, Skyborn," GorJiro said. "One of the best I have ever trained. But your best is not good enough. Despite your skill, you are still the student, and I am still the Master."

"Only a Master of evil, GorJiro," Mourdock replied.

"I am a Master of many things. Whereas you are a Master of none."

"You are wrong. There is one thing I am far better than you at."

GorJiro raised his eyebrow in curiosity. "And what might that be?" he asked.

A sly smile grew on Mourdock's lips. "Stalling," he replied.

The hum of Jack's energized batons crackled as they were hurling toward GorJiro's back. GorJiro's eyes went wide as he spun and struck them with his sword, swatting them away a mere instant before they were set to impact him.

Not far behind the thrown weapons came Jack, flying through the air. In hitting away the batons, GorJiro had left himself open to a kick to the chest from Jack, which caused the Paragon to stumble back.

Before GorJiro could recover, Mourdock rushed forward and lashed out with his blade, giving GorJiro little time to raise his sword in defense.

As soon as Jack hit the ground he re-manifested his batons and rushed forward, joining Mourdock in the assault.

GorJiro fell back, quickly recovering and fending off the two-pronged attack with his blade, striking away both Mourdock's sword and Jack's batons before either could land a blow. But despite his expert defense, GorJiro's two assailants were still pressing their advantage.

Just as it seemed Jack and Mourdock might have gained the upper hand, GorJiro hopped backward and thrust his open palm downward. The gravity pulse he created hit the ground, cratering it slightly and causing both Jack and Mourdock to stumble as the sudden move caused them to lose their footing.

With a twirl, GorJiro aimed his hand between the two attackers. Jack barely had time to raise his own hand to manifest an electromagnetic field to counter the incoming gravity pulse. Though he was able to create the field in time, it was not strong enough to entirely counter GorJiro's gravity wave, which plowed into both Mourdock and him.

Jack felt himself lifted off the ground and violently flung backward, the force of the gravity pulse hitting him like a speeding freight train, breaking his ribs and his limbs as he hit the floor and tumbled, losing his weapons and coming to a hard stop as agony washed over him.

Mourdock had begun to dodge the gravity pulse the instant he saw GorJiro move to manifest it, and he, too, manifested a gravity pulse to counter that of GorJiro's. This softened the blow far more than the one Jack received, and Mourdock was able to recover his footing quickly, despite being dazed by the impact of the gravity pulse.

Mourdock looked over and saw Jack writhing on the floor some distance away, but he could not help his friend with GorJiro now approaching him, the Paragon's crimson moonfyre blade at the ready.

"I have allowed you two to distract me long enough," GorJiro stated. "It is time to finish this."

Mourdock gritted his teeth, shifting his feet as he committed to a risky new strategy.

"I couldn't agree more," Mourdock replied.

With that, Mourdock leapt forward, the sudden frontal attack taking GorJiro by surprise.

GorJiro and Mourdock both swung their swords as GorJiro danced to the side to avoid Mourdock's leap, his blade slashing at Mourdock as the Paragon flew past.

Mourdock stumbled as he landed, clutching the wound he'd received from GorJiro's blade which had cauterized a long slash across his chest. He turned and looked at GorJiro, who gazed at him with malice.

"That was a foolish maneuver," GorJiro said.

"It worked, didn't it?" said Mourdock, smugly. "When was the last time a blade kissed the skin of the mighty Master GorJiro?"

GorJiro reached up and touched the side of his neck, feeling the small cauterized cut where Mourdock's blade had made contact. He grimaced and stared at his adversary with disdain as Mourdock resumed his combat stance, holding his moonfyre blade before him while ignoring his own wound.

"A little maneuver I picked up from Blackmane," Mourdock said, with a sly smirk. "Said you taught it to him. Something about being a double-edged weapon?"

"Foolish boy," said GorJiro with a snarl. "How can one who knows so much understand so little?"

"I understand everything, now."

"No, you do not," stated GorJiro. "But I shall see to it you learn these hard lessons."

"I am through learning from *you!*" growled Mourdock before charging forward.

GorJiro raised his sword to meet Mourdock's as the two clashed, red and blue blades sparking off one another as the stellar material they each harbored kissed. Mourdock channeled all his energy into his speed, furiously striking at his former Master, who seemed to easily keep up, deflecting each blow. And it was because Mourdock was so eager to find an opening in GorJiro's defense that he left himself open…

And that is when it happened.

GorJiro struck out, hitting Mourdock in the face with his palm, stunning the boy and making him stumble.

With a graceful twirl, GorJiro spun and swung his deadly blade.

Mourdock screamed as the arm that was wielding his sword flew through the air, completely severed from his body.

His arm had no sooner hit the floor than GorJiro was once more upon him, his hand outstretched, a mere foot from Mourdock's throat. Mourdock's breath caught in his chest and his body went rigid as the ghostly image of his very soul was pulled from it, flirting with being ripped away entirely as GorJiro used Servuchur to grab hold of Mourdock's spirit. Mourdock cried in agony, but could do nothing but twitch and endure the unimaginable pain as GorJiro loomed before him, threatening to rip the very essence of life from his body.

"You may be through learning from me, Skyborn," GorJiro said. "But pain is the ultimate teacher, and you have many more lessons yet to learn before you embrace your destiny."

GorJiro tugged on Mourdock's soul, causing the boy to scream loudly.

"How I wish I could kill you for your insolence," GorJiro muttered as he continued to torture Mourdock. "I have killed for far less, I assure you. But you still have a role to play in the grand plans of our Lords..."

The last bone in Jack's body snapped back into place as he finished healing himself. He'd been concentrating so hard on fixing his wounds, he hadn't noticed what dire straits Mourdock had been in until he heard his screams. Jack turned and looked at his friend, hanging helplessly inches off the ground as GorJiro toyed with him, ripping away at Mourdock's soul and inflicting wave after wave of pain.

Jack scowled and clenched his teeth as a single thought went through his mind...

*No.*

Jack felt the calm feeling of resoluteness settle over him. He wasn't going to stand by and watch his friend be murdered. He instinctually focused on his Source, despite its chaotic nature which had plagued him ever since his accident at Port Somewhere. In that moment, Jack found the strength to force his Trinity back into alignment, and when he did, time seemed to slow.

Jack became hyper-aware of his surroundings as he entered into Equilibrium. Before he knew it, he'd sprung to his feet, racing toward GorJiro with steely purpose.

Each footstep that landed rang out as loud as a drum beat. Jack could feel his energy coursing through him, making him stronger and faster.

GorJiro and Mourdock seemed to stand as still as statues as Jack raced up behind GorJiro, well within his blind-spot...

Jack sprung up into the air, making a weightless leap forward, manifesting his batons and channeling a surge of crackling energy into them.

Jack sailed toward his adversary, weapons raised, ready to strike...

Suddenly, a ghostly apparition emerged from GorJiro, racing toward Jack faster than even he, in his Equilibrium state, could react.

The apparition struck Jack full-on, hitting him with incredible force. Jack cried in pain as he was knocked out of Equilibrium, dropping his weapons while hurled backward.

Jack hit the ground hard and tumbled, feeling his legs break as he landed, coming to a painful stop as he clutched at his chest, laboring just to breathe. He heard GorJiro chuckle as the Paragon released his hold on Mourdock, letting him collapse to the floor.

Jack looked up in time to see the ghostly apparition return to GorJiro's body. The Paragon turned and smiled at Jack, wickedly.

"What… how???" Jack grunted as he struggled to breathe.

"Sorry, Earthman," GorJiro said as he started to stroll toward Jack. "There will be no sudden bout of heroics here. No last-minute rally. No unexpected reversal to grant you victory. You are far too outmatched for such things. I may not be allowed to kill Skyborn, but you on the other hand…"

GorJiro manifested his sword once more as he approached Jack.

"It is long past time someone put you down for good."

Jack struggled to get back to his feet, but the blow GorJiro's apparition had delivered had too much of an effect on him. His entire body ached, his legs wouldn't work, his chest felt as though it were on fire, and he was having trouble concentrating enough to heal himself before GorJiro would be upon him.

But before GorJiro could close the distance, a voice rang out.

"All hail Cormac Braen GorJiro, the mightiest Paragon Warrior to ever live," it said, echoing throughout the cavernous chamber.

GorJiro stopped his advance, looking around for the source of the voice, his gaze eventually settling at the entrance to the room, the small silhouette of Moon Ravencrow framed in the doorway at the top of the stairs.

"Picking on children, no less," Ravencrow said as he started to waddle down the stairs to the floor below. "No surprise. You always did prefer the easy targets."

GorJiro's eyes narrowed as he focused in on the Harvshodd, the hint of a smile growing on his face. "I had hoped you'd still be alive," GorJiro said.

"And I had hoped you were actually dead," Ravencrow responded, his walking staff clicking on the floor with each step he took. "But you never fail to disappoint, now, do you?"

GorJiro turned away from Jack, forgetting about him, completely fixated on Ravencrow. "So… you knew I'd faked my death."

"I had my suspicions," Ravencrow said. "The scene of the battle didn't quite add up. And it would be so unlike you to take such a severe wound to the chest without losing a limb or two, first. I must admit, it was unusually smart of you,

GorJiro. No one ever suspects a dead man. If I had been able to figure out how you were able to produce a dead body that exactly matched you, I'd have sounded the alarm immediately. How were you able to accomplish such a thing, by the way?"

"It was a clone," GorJiro said, with just a hint of bragging in his voice. "Created by the Ancient Medical Regeneration Chamber relic."

"Of course, it was," muttered Ravencrow. "It makes sense now. You destroyed the Sacred Vault to cover your tracks. No doubt you were able to bypass all its security by creating a tether directly into it, using the corrupted seal. And the reason you haven't killed everyone in the Conclave was so that you could have an army of corrupted Paragons under your command."

"It is the dawn of a new world, you twisted little imp," GorJiro said. "One in which I will have a part in forging. And ironically, it is you who are responsible for my role in it."

Ravencrow finally reached the bottom of the stairs. He breathed a sigh, as though the journey to the floor had taken a great deal of energy from him. "Is that so?" he replied.

"The day we met in that jungle on Torrobah has haunted me for what seems like an eternity," growled GorJiro. "I can remember how disappointed I was when I first saw you. The stories I'd heard of this great warrior, hidden away in a cave, able to defeat any man or beast that crossed his path had given me such hope. I'd sought out what I thought would be an honorable battle. What I got, was a small, twisted troll who wouldn't know honor if it bit him on his hideous face."

"Ah, yes," responded Ravencrow with a smirk. "I do so like your definition of honorable battle. Apparently, it's only honorable if you're the one who wins."

"I did not lose!" screamed GorJiro in anger. "Our contest did not count! You *cheated*."

"You're the one who picked a fight with a stunted hermit half your size, and you're upset when you underestimate him so badly that your perfect dueling record is broken?" mocked Ravencrow. "Where I'm from, that's referred to as being a 'sore loser'."

"You have no idea what that experience did to me!" snapped GorJiro. "It shattered my perception of who I was! What I was capable of! I had faced worthier opponents than you. Warriors of great stature and renown, all felled by my hand! But then you come along. And *you* are the one who claims to defeat me? Worse yet… you let me live so that I would have to bear that shame for the rest of my days?"

"I let you live because I wanted to teach you a lesson," replied Ravencrow. "I can see that lesson didn't take. But then again, I've never been much of a teacher."

"Oh, but I learned plenty from you," GorJiro said. "In my quest for answers, as to how one with no honor could cheat me out of victory, I came upon a new path that had been closed to me before. One that has taught me things I never before believed to be possible. One that has brought us to this very moment. A glorious rebirth, both for me, and the universe. It has been a long time in coming, but I have been patient, and my patience has finally paid off. I can now embrace my new destiny! For I am Mellegogg! Deathlord Supreme! Harbinger of the new world to come!"

Ravencrow yawned. "Yes, please, do explain your evil plan to me in excruciating detail," he muttered, his voice thick with sarcasm. "I am sooooo interested in your motivation for becoming a monster."

GorJiro's face turned hard. "You are right. We've talked enough…"

GorJiro held out his sword, pointing its tip toward Ravencrow, the blade glowing bright red, thirsty for blood.

"I have waited for this since the moment you first returned to the Conclave," he said. "You have no idea how badly I've wanted to kill you."

"If it's anything close to how I'm feeling about you right now, I think I have a pretty good idea," Ravencrow replied.

"You had your chance to kill me before," sneered GorJiro. "But you didn't. You made a grave mistake, sparing my life that day."

"Fear not, GorJiro. That is a mistake I am about to correct."

"Do not be so confident!" GorJiro snapped, anger rising within him at Ravencrow's condescending attitude. "I am not the same man you faced all those years ago. I have learned many new things since we last danced, troll. And I am eager to show them to you…"

Jack gritted his teeth in pain as he focused on healing the damage GorJiro had inflicted upon him. He gazed with concern at the two Paragons as they faced off. GorJiro stood tall and strong, a stark contrast to the tiny, hunched over, fragile-looking Harvshodd. GorJiro appeared every bit the powerful menace, while Ravencrow was dwarfed by the warrior's intimidating presence.

But Ravencrow did not appear intimidated in the slightest. In fact, as he leaned upon his walking stick, a chuckle escaped from the tiny alien.

"Aye," Ravencrow said, a broad smile growing on his face. "And I am eager to see them."

With that, Ravencrow dropped his staff and reached up behind his head. With a tug of the knot, his blindfold fell off, fluttering to the floor below like a leaf on the wind.

Jack watched, his gaze transfixed on the Harvshodd's eyes, which were pale and white, their irises an icy blue hue. For the briefest of moments, they appeared to shine, right before tendrils of electricity began to snake around Ravencrow's body, the air around him shimmering as reality shifted. Bits of metal armor started to manifest, growing around him, morphing as their pieces began to interlock. The pieces began to encase Ravencrow, forming into the shape of a body, until Ravencrow had completely disappeared and a new figure rose up, standing taller and stronger than GorJiro, its armor sleek and powerful and the red visor of its face glowing bright crimson as the transformation completed. Jack felt his breath catch in his throat as he realized what had just happened.

Moon Ravencrow had just transformed into Stalker Crux.

GorJiro looked at Ravencrow's Stalker Crux form with concern on his face, causing him to take a step back in surprise. Now, it was GorJiro who was dwarfed by the imposing cybernetic opponent.

"I've learned a few things myself since we last clashed," Stalker Crux's robotically augmented voice said, right before two shoulder cannons popped up and began firing plasma bolts at GorJiro.

GorJiro quickly raised his sword, concentrating as the blaster bolts from Stalker Crux bent around him, not even coming close to hitting him. But even as Stalker Crux continued to fire, he ran toward GorJiro, manifesting a moonfyre sword in each hand that burned bright orange with the fury of a raging star.

GorJiro immediately fell back and manifested another moonfyre sword himself, meeting each strike from the ones wielded by Stalker Crux, all the while the onslaught of plasma bolts the bounty hunter was rapidly firing bending around him. The two Paragons engaged in a deadly, violent ballet, moving so fast, they almost appeared as a blur.

Jack had never seen anything like the spectacle raging before him. The two Paragons were flipping through the air, striking at each other with incredible speed. Stalker Crux manifested a blaster cannon to fire at GorJiro only to have

GorJiro slice it off the exoskeleton. Sparks flashed like lightning strikes whenever the moonfyre blades clashed, as though two gods were battling in the cavernous chamber.

Stalker Crux flipped backward as GorJiro pressed his attack, but the cyborg's body was able to allow him to contort and maneuver at odd angles, making it hard for GorJiro to pin him down.

GorJiro swung his blade, cutting off one of Stalker Crux's hands, but before he could press the attack, Stalker Crux had manifested a new hand with a new sword and was able to continue fighting.

One combatant manifested a gravity pulse, and instantly a counter pulse met it, the power of their collisions rippled out between the two combatants and shook the entire floor. More gravity pulses emanated and were countered as the two Paragons furiously struck at each other, making it feel as if the entire temple itself were at the epicenter of an earthquake.

Stalker Crux flipped to the side, simultaneously lashing out with a strong kick that landed across the side of GorJiro's face. But the evil Paragon took the opportunity to swing his blade and sever the leg Stalker Crux had used to strike him. However, within seconds, a new leg had manifested, and Stalker Crux continued to battle without missing a beat.

*It's because he's using a robotic exoskeleton!* Jack thought. *He can afford to lose limbs because the robotic stuff is easier to manifest! It allows him to keep GorJiro off guard!*

Finally, the two combatants broke away from one another, quickly facing off once more as each slowly stalked around the other, weapons at the ready.

"Well, well, well," said Stalker Crux. "You weren't kidding. You have learned some new tricks…"

"It took me what seemed like hundreds of years to figure out your secret, imp," GorJiro said. "To figure out the secret of how you were able to cheat in our duel. But figure it out, I did! I discovered that you'd learned how to enter into Equilibrium!"

"Took you that long to figure it out, eh?" Stalker Crux said. "You never were the coldest Fizzy-Pop in the fridge."

GorJiro snarled. "It took me what felt like many hundred more years to discover how to utilize it myself. To hone my Trinity to work in harmony. But now I, too, can enter into Equilibrium. Your advantage has been erased!"

"So we have ourselves a fair fight, then?" Stalker Crux replied. "Oh, well."

With that, Stalker Crux dropped one of his swords and fired a grappling cable from his gauntlet, which latched onto GorJiro's shoulder and yanked GorJiro toward him. Stalker Crux leapt forward to kick GorJiro, but the Paragon twisted in the air, lopping off Stalker Crux's leg and severing the grappling cable in one swift stroke.

GorJiro tumbled onto the ground and back to his feet, but had to quickly deflect some blaster bolts as Stalker Crux manifested a new leg and rushed toward him. The two clashed with their swords until the blades became locked as the two men braced against the other's guard. Though Stalker Crux's face was a mask behind his helmet, GorJiro had his teeth gritted as he pushed back against his attacker.

"You are mistaken," GorJiro growled. "You of all people should know, imp – if you ever find yourself in a fair fight, you are doing something wrong!"

With that, the ghostly apparition GorJiro had used against Jack sprung from his body, slamming into Stalker Crux and knocking him back. The apparition zoomed off as Stalker Crux stumbled, looking around in surprise, right before the ghostly form slammed into him again from the side.

The ghost moved so fast, Stalker Crux had no time to react before it hit him again and again, tearing bits of armor from him as it did so.

GorJiro stood stoically, watching with malicious glee as Stalker Crux struggled with the apparition, firing his weapons at it and swinging at it with his swords, all to no avail.

The ghostly figure ripped off every cannon that fired at it.

It tore away the limbs that struck at it.

And finally, it hurled itself directly into Stalker Crux's chest, passing directly through it.

The sound of Ravencrow screaming could be heard as the chassis housing him crumpled, ghostly tendrils of energy snaking throughout his cybernetic exoskeleton that was hurled backward onto the ground, sparks flying from the numerous wounds as the armor shorted out.

And as the red light of Stalker Crux's visor died, Jack realized, to his horror…

GorJiro had won.

# Chapter 31

Anna, the Royal Vanguard, and the former members of the Secret Army emerged from the entrance of Eionmeer's dark temple to find the area infested with Deathstalkers for as far as the eye could see.

"There are even more of the creatures than when we arrived," noted Seqis, gazing out into the distance to see it covered by the feral Deathlords.

"So long as the monolith is on this planet, it will continue to spawn them," Gunner said. "The monolith is the vessel that harnesses the spiritual energy required to grow the black rock and the Deathstalkers. It is the virus that will not stop infecting the planet until it is overrun."

"Then we should destroy the blasted thing," growled Rionknidis.

"I did not see it in the temple," noted Lugard.

"A Terrormancer removed it," informed Gunner. "We saw him when we were ordered to kill the Princess. He was taking it up into the foothills of the mountains, that way."

Gunner pointed to the distance. Past the edge of the settlement was a large empty field now covered with black rock, and beyond that stood a mountain range. One of the steep hills leading up the mountain had black rock covering its face.

"How much you wanna bet that's where the Terrormancer took it?" grumbled Rionknidis.

Smoke was billowing from the field toward the start of the mountain range. Anna shielded her eyes from the sun, looking in its direction. "What is that?" she asked.

Commander Gunner climbed atop some rubble, pulling out a pair of binoculars and looking toward the smoke. "It looks like… it looks like the Earthman's ship," he said.

"Jack!" said Anna, quickly climbing up to join the Commander. Gunner handed her the binoculars and she zoomed in on the area with the smoke. Sure enough, the Earthship was there, its hull crawling with Deathstalkers.

"That is most unfortunate," said Seqis. "The Earthship was to be our ride off this planet."

"We have our shuttle not far from here, on the outskirts of the city," Gunner said. "We can use it to get away."

"If we aren't overwhelmed by these Deathstalkers on our way to it," Lugard noted.

"They won't harm us or the Princess," Gunner said. "The slythrus let them know not to attack us, just as the slythrus prevented us from experiencing the fear of the Terrormancers. So long as the monolith's guardian does not know where we are, we can make it through the Deathstalkers safely."

"And if the Terrormancer sees us?" asked Rionknidis.

"Then he will order the Deathstalkers to attack, and we're most likely good as dead."

"Very well," Seqis said. "We shall make our way to your shuttle then."

"Lord Commander!" Anna cried. "You can't expect us to simply leave the Earthship behind!"

"Right now, Your Highness, my priority is getting you to safety," Seqis replied. "Once we are aboard the shuttle, we may be able to come back and rescue whoever's aboard the Earthman's vessel. But until then, we must remain focused. Your safety is of the utmost importance."

Anna frowned. "That ship out there is a wonder of the Ancients," she said, pointing toward the Earthship. "It possesses great power, Lord Commander. Power I might be able to use to aid in this fight. Verrutus might be dead, but the Deathlords are still attacking the Empire. Look above us!"

Anna directed everyone's attention to the tether high overhead.

"That portal is still open! There are Deathlord ships within it! You can see the battle raging in the tether beyond the Conclave! If we are to have any hope of stopping this attack, we are going to need the Earthship!"

"Your Highness," Commander Gunner said. "I'm sorry to say there is no way to recover that vessel. As soon as the Terrormancer guarding the monolith sees us, we will be overwhelmed by the Deathstalkers. That ship has crashed at least ten miles outside the city. The distance between it and us is filled with enemies. There is no possible way we can ever make it there alive."

"As the Paragons are fond of saying, Commander, anything is possible." Anna said.

"What is it you are asking us to do, Your Highness?" asked Seqis.

Anna gazed out at the infestation of Deathstalkers that roamed the land between her and the Earthship. The black rock leading from the temple had already overrun the ground and the buildings of the settlement. On the hills in the far distance, Anna could see the monolith, standing tall and ominous as it continued to transform the land around it, sending more and more Deathstalkers clawing their way across the ground with each passing moment.

She glanced up at the sky, the massive portal leading to the Conclave shimmering in the distance, as big as a moon. Somehow, deep down, she instinctively knew Jack was up there. She knew he needed her help. She knew the entire universe needed her help. And just like her ancestors before her…

She was determined not to let the universe down.

"Lord Commander," Anna said, turning to look Seqis in the eyes. "Get me to that ship."

There were many things Lord Commander Seqis of the Royal Vanguard could have said to the Princess upon hearing that command. He could have argued with her. He could have tried to talk sense to her. He could have ignored her and forcibly dragged her to safety. But as he looked upon the Princess, he recognized the look in her eyes. It was not the look of a child making an unreasonable demand. It was the steely resolve of a leader, asking those who followed her to do what was required of them for the greater good.

Thus, Seqis did not flinch. He did not hesitate. He simply nodded and said:

"As you command."

Seqis turned to his companions.

"Vanguard!" he cried.

And just like Seqis, the other members of the Royal Vanguard answered the Princess's call without hesitation. They all manifested their weapons. Seqis stepped before the group, moving toward the seemingly unending mob of Deathstalkers that swarmed throughout the settlement and beyond. He stopped, his red cloak billowing as the wind picked up. He lifted his great hammer over his head, the distant sound of thunder booming as though in response. The air crackled with electricity as he gazed out into the distance at the crashed Earthship, determined to fulfill the Princess's command.

"Oyarsa GRAPTHAAR!" Seqis cried.

Lightning crashed down into the head of Grapthaar, imbuing it with raging power. Seqis aimed the hammer in front of him and unleashed the energy it had just collected, a powerful jolt of lightning barreling forth, annihilating all Deathstalkers in its way, sending them off in puffs of black dust and clearing a path toward the fallen vessel.

Seqis then turned to his companions. "FORWARD!" he cried.

The Vanguard let out a cry as they charged into the fray, Anna running along with them. Gunner and his men hesitated for the briefest of moments, exchanging bewildered glances with one another before Gunner unslung his plasma rifle and shouted:

"FOR THE PRINCESS!"

And with that, the Royal Vanguard charged forward, forming a protective formation around Anna as they entered the swarm of Deathstalkers that stood between them and the Earthship, with the men of the Royal Guard and the survivors of Eionmeer bringing up the rear.

*****

High on the hill at the base of the mountains, the Terrormancer stood next to the monolith, looking out over the view before him as he saw the charge of the Princess and her protectors. They cut through the settlement, emerging onto the field and fighting their way through any Deathstalker in their path. From his vantage point, the Terrormancer could see they were trying to make their way to the crashed spacecraft. He turned to the monolith and placed his hand upon its smooth surface.

"Kill all who ssssstill draw breath and destroy that ship," he commanded.

The dark monolith vibrated in response and immediately the landscape before the Terrormancer shifted as every Deathstalker received a new mission. A tidal surge was underway as the creatures all moved to focus their attack on the Princess, her companions, and the Earthship.

*****

Seqis saw the shift in the swarm as he led the charge through their ranks. He held out Grapthaar and fired more bolts of lightning from it, continuing to cut a path for the group to run through. Lugard was to the right of the Princess, striking at any Deathstalker he could with his sword as Dahuud covered the Princess's left side, flinging her moonfyre daggers at any enemy who neared. Rionknidis ran around Anna, striking at any Deathstalker who got past his companions with his claws and dispatching them before they could reach the Princess. And the former members of the Secret Army all followed, blasting away at the Deathlord creatures with their plasma rifles, giving the Vanguard the cover they needed to continue advancing.

As they ran, Seqis spotted the Terrormancer and the dark monolith on the hill. The old warrior knew that so long as the Terrormancer controlled that rock, the Princess would not be safe. Thus, he did the only thing he believed would save them all.

He called upon the most fearless warrior he knew.

"Rionknidis!" barked Seqis. "Get to that monolith! Turn that blasted thing into dust!"

"With pleasure…" growled Rionknidis before breaking off from the group, charging forward with a ferocious roar and taking a flying leap into the air.

No longer held back to protect the group, Rionknidis soared with his massive leaps, covering large distances with each one, briefly pausing to dispatch any Deathstalker that tried to accost him as he made his charge to the monolith.

As the Tygarian advanced toward the Terrormancer, the Vanguard continued leading the charge through the sea of Deathstalkers, fighting ferociously to get to the Earthship before they were overwhelmed by the Deathlords' superior numbers.

★★★★★

Alarms were blaring on the bridge of the Earthship as Professor Green frantically rushed from station to station, fielding the damage reports that were flooding in. "Oh dear, oh dear, oh dear," he muttered. "This is not good! We're in even worse shape than when we crashed!"

"What's wrong?" asked Krupp. "What's happening?"

"The outside of the ship is being overrun by those creatures," Green lamented. "They're damaging the hull quicker than the Earthship can repair itself! If this keeps up, we'll never be able to salvage it!"

"What the…" muttered Boone as he looked at his console.

Green looked up in alarm. "Oh, no! Is there another crisis?" he asked.

"I don't rightly know," replied Boone as he called up what he was seeing on the Earthship's main viewscreen. All on the bridge turned and looked at the image of Anna and her protectors fighting their way through the surging swarm of Deathstalkers.

"Is… is that…" said Krupp, not sure what he was seeing.

Green's eyes went wide. "The Princess!" he exclaimed.

"What the blazes are they doing?" asked Boone.

"It looks like they are trying to fight their way to the ship," said Krupp.

"More like they're trying to get themselves killed!" stated Boone. "Professor, can we lock onto them? Teleport them to us?"

"A very good idea, Agent Boone," Green said as he rushed to the teleportation console. He tapped away at it before his look turned to one of frustration. "At least, it would be if the teleporter arrays were operating! The ship has sustained too much damage! They're currently inoperable!"

"What does that mean?" asked Krupp.

"It means that until the teleportation arrays are fixed, we can't teleport anybody," said Scrappy. "According to the ship's schematics, the arrays are right under the hull on the top and bottom of the vessel. The Deathlord creatures are currently tearing away at everything they can reach. If we can't repair those arrays, then we can't help the Princess."

"What would it take to repair them?" asked Krupp.

"Aside from the Earthship's natural repair capabilities?" replied Green. "A lack of those creatures damaging us, someone with basic knowledge of matter traversal machinery, a toolkit for repairs, and enough time to enact them."

"So in other words, a miracle," grumbled Boone.

Krupp turned to Scrappy. "You don't happen to know anything about matter traversal machinery, do you?" he asked.

"Are you kidding? It's one of my hobbies!" Scrappy replied.

"Really? Mine too!" said Green, cheerily.

"Jack told us the ship can manifest anything we need," Krupp said. "Does that include the tools to make those repairs?"

"Why, I believe it would," Green replied.

Krupp turned to Scrappy. "If we could get you to one of the arrays, could you repair it in time to save the Princess?" he asked.

Scrappy looked nervous. "Um… you mean… go outside? With the monsters?"

"Yes, Scrappy. With the monsters."

Scrappy frowned but nodded. "If the Earthship really does repair itself, then that would speed up the process of fixing the array. Assuming those Deathlord things don't kill me first."

"You let us worry about that," Krupp said, gesturing to himself, Morosa, and Snodgrass.

"What does your puny man-brain have in mind, Scofeld?" Morosa inquired.

"Either a really good idea or a really terrible one," Krupp replied. "Come on. We need to go to the cargo hold."

"Wait! I should go with you," Green said, starting to follow them when Boone got up and stopped him.

"No," Boone said. "If they plan to do what I think they're going to do, we need you on the bridge. You not only know this ship inside and out, but you're also the only one who can fly it. You must stay here and oversee things."

Green frowned, looking at Boone with concern. "But… they're only kids," he said.

"Trust me, they're about to grow up real quick," Boone replied. "But don't worry. I'll go with them and watch their backs."

The Professor looked like he wanted to object, but instead, he simply nodded. "Do what you can for them, Agent Boone," he said. "Keep them, and yourself, safe."

Boone winked at Green. "Hey, you only live twice, right?"

With that, Boone turned and joined the group of Initiates on the bridge's teleporter platform. When they all arrived in the cargo bay of the Earthship, they found it filled with scared and injured people. Sawbones and a handful of survivors from the Water Ring were there healing the wounds of those who'd been hurt in the Conclave attack and the crash.

Krupp looked around at all the Initiates who were there. Some were children, no older than eight or nine. Others were musicians, engineers, scientists, spiritualists, and researchers. None of them were fighters. Of those who'd trained in the Fire Ring, the only ones who remained were himself, Morosa, and Snodgrass. But despite having nothing but the wrong types of people available for the task at hand, Krupp knew he had to make do with what was available.

"Everyone, can I have your attention, please?" he said, stepping forward.

All eyes in the bay turned to him.

"We need your help," Krupp said. "We have a situation outside. The Princess, along with the Royal Vanguard and a small group of soldiers, are trying to make their way to this ship. But they are being overwhelmed by the creatures who are trying to tear this vessel apart."

"Is that what those noises are?" asked a scared looking Ground Ring Initiate. "The scratching on the hull?"

"I'm afraid so, yes," replied Krupp. "Our only hope of saving those people is to fix the teleportation arrays on the outside of the ship."

"On the outside?!" cried another Initiate in a green robe. "Anyone who goes out there is going to die!"

A murmur of fear spread through the group as everyone reacted. Krupp frowned.

"I know you're all afraid," he said over the noise of the commotion. "Believe me, I am, too. But we are no safer inside the ship. Not for long, anyway. Even now, the Deathlord creatures are ripping away at the ship faster than it can repair itself. If we don't do something about it, they will eventually breach the hull. When they do, none of us will survive what comes after that."

"What are you asking us to do, man?" asked Sawbones.

"I'm asking for you all to stand with us as we venture outside and attempt to repair the ship," Krupp stated. "Scrappy here knows how to fix the teleportation arrays. If we can hold the Deathstalkers off long enough for him to repair the arrays, we can teleport the Princess to us and the Royal Vanguard can help us fight the creatures."

"That's suicide!" exclaimed a white robed Initiate. "Look at us! We're not warriors! We wouldn't last two minutes against those things!"

The panic and fear the Initiate expressed began to spread to the others. They all began arguing amongst themselves, voicing their worries about such a course of action. Krupp could feel the situation slipping away from him. He dug down deep for the confidence he knew they all needed, stepping forward and speaking loudly.

"BE SILENT!" he shouted.

Immediately, everyone quieted down, looking at Krupp in surprise. Krupp eyed them all, one by one.

"Center yourselves," he instructed. "Find your Source, just as you were taught in meditation classes. Find your calm. Find your peace. Open your ears. Free your minds. Do so now!"

Despite some harboring reservations, the Initiates all obeyed Krupp's instructions, using their training to calm down and center themselves. When all the Initiates appeared to have regained control of their emotions, Krupp spoke again.

"You all know of our reputation," Krupp said, gesturing to himself and his friends. "They call us the Unlikelies. They called us this because we weren't supposed to succeed. We weren't supposed to make it. From the beginning, the deck has been stacked against us. But somehow, someway, we haven't let that stop us. We've fought back. We've stood strong. We've proved – not just to others, but to ourselves – that we can succeed despite everyone telling us we can't. Being an Unlikely used to be a label of shame, but we've turned it into a badge of honor. To be an Unlikely means that no matter the odds, no matter the obstacle, no matter the adversity… we'll find a way to overcome. By standing together. By working with one another. By refusing to give up, we've shown the universe our best. We've shown it why we deserve to be Paragons. But most of all, we've proven to everyone that no matter how unlikely it may be… *anything* is possible."

Krupp pointed to the rear door of the ship.

"Out there, right now, is what we've been training for," he stated. "It's moments like this which are why we've fought so hard. Why we've endured so much. These are the moments that demand we be at our best. So let us not run from it! At this moment, we are all Unlikelies. Let us prove, once and for all, what that means. Let us show the galaxy that the impossible can be done. And let us prove, to each other, that we are all worthy of being Paragons!"

A silence hung in the air as everyone gazed at Krupp, letting his words settle in upon them. Then, one of the Initiates stepped forward and nodded.

"I'm with you… Paragon Krupp," he said.

Then, another Initiate stood. "As am I," he stated.

"Me, too," said another.

One by one, each and every Initiate rose to his and her feet, accepting the call Krupp had put forth. When everyone had agreed, Krupp nodded in approval.

"Then let us begin," he stated.

"Ethermincers!" said Soundwave. "To me!"

"Any of you with healing experience, gather here," called Sawbones.

"The rest of you, come with me," stated Boone. "I'll show you how to use a blaster."

The wall of the cargo bay morphed into an armory, filled with weapons and armor. Boone immediately began dispensing the equipment, showing all the Initiates how to operate the weapons. Krupp, Morosa, and Snodgrass all took vibro-swords from the racks, the blades humming to life with an electric charge.

"That was quite the speech, mansplainer," Morosa said. "It stirred something in my loins."

"<I just hope we can live up to it,>" Snodgrass said.

"We will, or we'll die trying," stated Krupp, trying to feel as brave as he sounded. "Do you have what you need, Scrappy?"

Scrappy was assembling a mobile toolkit from the devices the Earthship had manifested for him. "I believe so!" he said as he attached a communicator to his ear, a visor extending from it over his eye. "Professor, are you reading me?"

"Loud and clear, my boy!" Green responded. "Your visor's video transmission is coming through perfectly! I'll be able to walk you through any problem you may come across."

Scrappy gave Krupp the thumbs up. "Good to go!" he stated.

Krupp nodded. He moved toward the rear door of the Earthship, the rest of the Initiates all gathering behind him as he did so. The faint sound of snarls and scratches could be heard just behind the hydraulic ramp, a grim reminder of what awaited them on the other side. Krupp gripped his sword as nervous energy shot through him.

*Great Observer, I hope this works,* he thought.

"Everyone, ready yourselves!" ordered Morosa.

The group all brought their weapons to the ready.

"As soon as we open that hatch, those creatures are going to come flooding in," warned Scrappy.

"No, they won't," stated Soundwave as he stepped forward, cracking his knuckles. "Everyone, cover your ears."

The group all did as they were told, and Soundwave gave Krupp a nod telling him to open the hatch. Krupp hit the button and the rear door to the Earthship began to lower. The Deathstalkers instantly seized upon the opportunity and began to flood into the ship.

Soundwave extended his arms before him and unleased a wave of sound so powerful, it knocked back every single one of the Deathstalkers, hurling them back out of the opening they'd just poured through. Soundwave moved forward, projecting the compressed sound vibrations as the other Ethermincers joined in, pushing the Deathstalkers away and creating an opening off the ship.

Morosa smirked and leaned in toward Sawbones. "That's my boyfriend," she bragged.

As soon as the way was clear, Krupp turned to his companions.

"NOW!" he cried.

The Initiates all charged down the ramp to the outside, Morosa leading the way. She screamed as her sword met with a Deathstalker, turning the creature to dust. Krupp and the others quickly joined the fray, slashing at any Deathstalker that got near them while Soundwave and his fellow Ethermincers covered them by unleashing sound blasts that kept the Deathstalkers at bay.

"GO!" ordered Boone. "Form a perimeter around the opening! Don't stop firing!"

The agent led the Initiates outside, quickly fanning out and opening fire at the mobs of Deathstalkers all around. With the swarm of targets in all directions, none of them needed to be an expert marksman to be effective. They were able to assist in destroying the Deathstalkers and in guarding the opening to the Earthship.

Despite the efforts of the Initiates, some Deathstalkers were able to breach their perimeter, leaping through the air and attacking the students. Some suffered slashes from the creature's claws, others vicious bites. The Deathstalkers were dispatched, but not before they inflicted their damage. However, every time an Initiate fell from a wound, they'd find themselves suddenly and miraculously healed and able to get back into the fight.

Even Agent Boone suffered a terrible slash across his back while trying to save an Initiate from having his throat ripped out by one of the creatures. Before Boone had even dropped to his knees, the pain had disappeared. He looked over in surprise to see Sawbones and a small number of blue robed initiates standing at the base of the Earthship's ramp, aiming their hands at any Initiate who suffered injury as they remotely healed them. Sawbones caught Boone's gaze and smiled.

"Why ya acting so surprised?" she bellowed. "I'm a doctor, daggit!"

Boone smiled and got back to his feet, firing again upon the Deathstalkers. Krupp broke away from the fight just long enough to survey the situation. The Initiates had successfully pushed back the Deathstalkers from the ship's rear entrance, but the top of the ship was still crawling with the creatures who were tearing away at the hull with their razor-sharp claws.

"Snodgrass! Soundwave!" Krupp cried, pointing toward the top of the Earthship. "We need to clear those creatures away!"

Snodgrass nodded. "<Everyone, form up!>" he ordered, quickly moving past the group and toward the Earthship.

"This is so exciting I think I'm about to wet myself!" exclaimed Scrappy, his eyes wide with the thrill of the situation as he lined up with his friends.

"I know the feeling," Morosa stated before grabbing Soundwave and giving him a kiss. "Your prowess in battle has pleased me greatly. You are a shining example of your otherwise pathetic gender."

Soundwave blushed. "You say the sweetest things, babe," he replied.

"<Ready?>" asked Snodgrass as he turned to face the group.

Krupp looked at the others standing beside him. They all gave him a nod.

"Forward!" Krupp cried.

The four friends all sprinted toward Snodgrass, who lifted his hands upward as they approached. He used his prowess with the weightless leap to propel all four Initiates up into the air, soaring toward the top of the Earthship.

Soundwave blasted a wave of sound toward their landing area, pushing a cluster of Deathstalkers away. The second Krupp and Morosa landed, they rushed forward and hacked and slashed at the creatures, cutting a way toward the area where the Earthship's teleportation array was located. Scrappy followed close behind, clutching his toolkit as Soundwave took up the rear, blowing back any Deathstalkers that got too close. Snodgrass followed, leaping up onto the ship himself and joining the fight.

The instant they reached the exposed array, Scrappy hopped into the open hull breach and began surveying the damage. "Yikes! These things tore up the array something good!" he said as he inspected the equipment.

"Can you fix it?" asked Krupp.

Scrappy cracked his knuckles. "Piece of cake," Scrappy replied. "You know… if cake was incredibly complex and required a couple of certifications in the quantum sciences to eat."

"Just fix it!" snapped Morosa.

"Fixing!" replied Scrappy as he went to work.

Krupp, Morosa, Soundwave, and Snodgrass all surrounded Scrappy as the plucky Trundel went to work in a desperate attempt to save the Princess. Across the way, separated by thousands of deadly creatures, Princess Glorianna and her group struggled for their lives as the small assembly of Paragon Initiates fought valiantly to save their ship and their allies…

However unlikely the possibility of success may have been.

# Chapter 32

*No! He can't win! He can't!* thought Jack as he struggled to concentrate enough to heal his wounds. He'd been so distracted by the duel between GorJiro and Ravencrow that he'd neglected healing himself, and now that it seemed GorJiro had emerged victorious, Jack was desperately trying to repair his broken bones.

GorJiro took no notice of Jack. Instead, the evil Paragon approached the sparking remains of Stalker Crux, looking down at his defeated opponent with satisfaction. As GorJiro loomed over the exoskeleton, he used his sword to carve through the crumpled chassis of the torso, then ripped it away to reveal Ravencrow inside.

The Harvshodd appeared pale and wounded, his stunted legs pinned within his enclosure from the impact of GorJiro's attack. Ravencrow gazed up at GorJiro with his light eyes and scowled, not liking the smug look of his adversary one bit.

"You are no doubt wondering how I beat you," GorJiro said. "It is because you made a grave error, imp. For all your talk of channeling The Void, you failed to realize that even Equilibrium can be countered by the one thing that is impossible to perceive until it is too late! In my time planning my revenge, I learned the spirit is the most powerful force in the universe. And when it is honed as a weapon, not even Equilibrium can defeat it! Yes, Ravencrow… I discovered your weakness! The same weakness the Ancients you so respect shared. That weakness is… Servuchur!"

Ravencrow snarled. "You blind, bloody fool…" he muttered. "You learned Servuchur just to defeat me?"

"I did not simply learn Servuchur, imp. I *mastered* it!" GorJiro boasted. "What you just experienced is known as soulstepping. It is where one's spirit steps from the body and acts independently, yet in unison, with the mind. I used my own soul as the ultimate weapon – a weapon even Equilibrium is no match against."

"No wonder you've become such a vile, evil gob of grumpleguts," Ravencrow said, coughing. "Don't you see what's happened? The Servuchur corrupted you! Twisted you! Turned you evil! Just as it does to all who use it!"

"That is one way to look at it," mused GorJiro. "Another way is to say that it made me more powerful than any Paragon in history. With Servuchur, I defeated my greatest adversary, brought the Conclave to its knees, and will help to reshape the universe for all time."

"I always knew you were a moron, GorJiro. But you've truly raised stupidity to an art form."

GorJiro scowled. "There is something else I have raised to an art form, imp," he said. "And that is the ability to inflict pain!"

With that, GorJiro reached out and began to pull Ravencrow's soul from his body. Ravencrow screamed as his ghostly image struggled to stay with him. GorJiro smiled maliciously and laughed as he tugged away at the Paragon's spirit. Then, he let go of it, allowing it to snap back into Ravencrow as the Harvshodd wheezed weakly.

"Excruciating, isn't it?" GorJiro taunted. "There is nothing more painful in this life than a soul severance. It can make the mightiest of us weep like a child. And before you die, imp, I shall enjoy seeing you weep!"

Ravencrow screamed in agony as GorJiro once more tried to pull his soul from his body. Jack's heart was breaking as he watched his mentor tortured. He looked over and saw Mourdock writhing on the floor, struggling to regain his strength, but he was badly wounded, as well. The entire situation seemed hopeless.

Jack took a breath. Despite all that was happening around him, despite the sound of Ravencrow's screams as he was being tortured to death, despite all the pain that was coursing through Jack's own body – he pushed away everything and simply existed in that moment, placing his trust in The Void, the great unknown.

Once Jack's mind was empty, something made him think about the words GorJiro had just spoken. About how the spirit was the most powerful force in the universe. His mind flashed back to the moment where he'd manifested the knowledge of Servuchur himself. The image of Zarrod hurling a ball of death energy at him, and the invincible suit of armor that had encased him, made entirely of light.

*"There is great power in surrender,"* Shanks' voice said in Jack's mind.

*"What must I surrender to?"* Jack asked.

*"Yourself."*

And that is when he began to heal.

GorJiro released his hold on Ravencrow's spirit once more, allowing the tiny alien to gasp pathetically. "You are holding on to your soul tightly, imp," GorJiro said. "Such is the problem with trying to harvest a Paragon. Their mastery of the spirit can prevent a true culling. Though I would have liked to have absorbed your skills and have added them to my own, I grow tired of dragging this out. So I fear I shall have to resort to killing you the old-fashioned way…"

GorJiro manifested his sword.

Jack pushed himself up, struggling to once more make connection with his Source and align his Trinity. He knew he needed to do something to save Ravencrow, but he was struggling to enter back into Equilibrium.

*"Surrender,"* came Shanks' voice once more.

GorJiro loomed over Ravencrow, gazing down at the Harvshodd with his soulless black eyes, his smile twisted and devilish. "Now, I get to say to you the words I've been waiting for decades to speak…" GorJiro said, lifting his fiery red sword high overhead, poised to strike.

His eyes seemed to gleam with the impending victory over his opponent, as he said:

"I WIN!"

Jack forced himself to let go of his thoughts and his struggle to try to enter back into Equilibrium. A strange emptiness then took root within him, as though everything that had been holding him back had vanished. He had no thoughts. He had no emotions. He had completely surrendered his mind, body, and soul to The Void.

And when that happened, Jack could do nothing else but react.

He sprung forward, his weightless leap carrying him across the room as GorJiro brought his sword down.

Jack hit the ground, sliding across it on his knees, his hand reaching out…

…and catching GorJiro's blade, inches from Ravencrow's chest.

GorJiro's eyes went wide with surprise as he looked down at Jack, who held the blade, which wielded the power of a star, firmly in his grasp, protected by a gauntlet of spiritual energy that had formed around Jack's hand. For the briefest of instants, time seemed to stand still as GorJiro and Ravencrow looked at the sight in abject astonishment.

"It's… it's not possible!" GorJiro said.

Jack looked up at GorJiro, defiantly.

"Anything's possible, jerkwad!"

With that, Jack extended his other hand toward GorJiro, shooting a blast of his own spiritual energy directly into GorJiro's chest.

GorJiro cried out as he was flung backward through the air from the impact of the blow, just as the ball of spirit energy was pulled back to Jack, who reabsorbed it into his body.

GorJiro hit the ground hard. He clawed at his chest, the blow having broken some of his ribs. He quickly healed himself as he saw Jack rise to his feet, the boy's jaw set in determination, his eyes steely and focused. And in that moment, GorJiro realized he was no longer facing a former student.

He was facing a warrior.

Jack gripped his fists and manifested his batons in them, sparking them to life as he channeled newly ferocious electricity through them.

GorJiro rose to his feet and recalled his sword, brandishing the fiery red blade, ready to engage with Jack.

"I am through toying with you!" GorJiro growled. "Now, I shall kill you quickly!"

"Funny," came Mourdock's voice. "I was just thinking the same thing."

Before GorJiro could glance behind him, Mourdock reached out his hand and used his training in Servuchur to try to tear GorJiro's soul from his body.

The ghostly form of GorJiro wailed as it struggled to stay attached to its host, the physical body of which was fighting to keep hold of it.

Jack used the opportunity to rush forward and attack. Though in incredible pain, GorJiro was forced to turn his attention back to defending himself as he engaged Jack with his weapon. Jack drove GorJiro back, furiously attacking with his batons, striking so quickly that GorJiro could barely block the blows. GorJiro's eyes were wide with both pain and confusion as he tried to split his attention between fending off Jack and preventing Mourdock from harvesting his spirit.

Then, a plasma blast streaked by, and another caught GorJiro in the shoulder. He grunted in pain as he looked over to see Ravencrow. The Harvshodd's blackened and rotting teeth were gritted as he'd somehow found, in his exoskeleton's chassis, a working plasma cannon, which he fired at GorJiro.

Cormac Braen GorJiro suddenly found himself assaulted on all fronts. Jack was relentlessly attacking him with his weapons. Ravencrow was firing at him with hot plasma bolts of death. And Mourdock Skyborn was using Servuchur to attempt to rip GorJiro's life force directly from him.

*This cannot happen!* thought GorJiro, frantically. *This will not happen!!!*

Ravencrow's blasts continued to fly by, GorJiro's concentration so split that he could not protect himself from all of them. Some of the blasts curved around him, harmlessly, while others found their mark, forcing GorJiro to heal and further break his concentration as Jack pressed his attack.

GorJiro clinched his teeth, waiting for his moment as he felt Mourdock pull his spirit away from his body, his spiritual essence struggling to keep from falling completely under Mourdock's control as the Paragon pulled it closer and closer toward his outstretched hand.

Then, Ravencrow fired once more, his blast aimed right for GorJiro's face.

GorJiro moved his sword away from Jack's attack and instead deflected the blast. The plasma bolt shot directly back at Ravencrow, hitting the Harvshodd square in the chest, causing him to cry out.

The momentary change of his sword's position allowed Jack to finally make contact with GorJiro, hitting him in the knee and the chest, sending jolts of electricity through him, which disrupted his concentration enough to allow Mourdock to pull the ghostly apparition that was GorJiro's soul toward him.

GorJiro grunted in pain, but rather than re-engage Jack, he closed his eyes, raising his sword above his head.

Just as Jack was about to strike him again, GorJiro's body suddenly shot backward, moving directly toward his spirit, which was almost in Mourdock's grasp.

GorJiro's body rejoined with his spirit, just as he thrust his sword through his own chest, driving it out his back and directly into Mourdock's gut.

Mourdock's eyes went wide with surprise as he felt the pain of the blade enter him, completely blindsided by GorJiro's unexpected maneuver.

Without wasting another second, GorJiro's spiritual form rocketed forth from his body, shooting toward Jack and hitting him with its full force.

Jack cried out, losing his batons as he was flung backward, spinning in the air as he hit the ground. Jack tumbled end over end until he hit the floor and lay still.

GorJiro's spirit returned to him, and he turned his head to look into Mourdock's surprised eyes.

"*This* is how we wield a doubled-edged weapon…" GorJiro said, right before jerking his sword from his chest.

Mourdock fell to the floor and GorJiro demanifested his blade, clutching his wound as he desperately tried to heal himself.

All three of his opponents had been dispatched, but his self-inflicted wound was most dire. He turned all his focus toward healing. So concentrated was he, that he did not hear the sound of the blaster firing before it was too late.

The blast struck him across the face, taking out his right eye. GorJiro screamed as he fell back. He quickly looked up to see Ravencrow holding a newly manifested blaster pistol in his hand, scowling at the Paragon as he, too, clutched the wound at his own chest.

"You haven't won anything yet, GorJiro," Ravencrow snarled as he opened fire once more.

GorJiro quickly held out his hand, using all his concentration to shift the trajectory of Ravencrow's blasts around him as the Harvshodd emptied his clip. When the blaster had run out of ammunition, Ravencrow tossed it aside and manifested his staff. He slammed the butt of it into the ground and pulled himself out of the remains of his exoskeleton, standing up on his two twisted legs and gripping his staff with both hands in steely determination.

"Time to end this…" Ravencrow growled.

Ravencrow flipped into the air, swinging his staff around. GorJiro rolled to the side just as the staff impacted the floor where he'd been with such force that the bricks there shattered.

GorJiro held out his hand to shoot a graviton wave toward Ravencrow, but the Harvshodd countered with his own, sending both combatants backward as the space between them rippled from the meeting of the two gravity pulses, cratering the ground and causing the whole room to quake.

GorJiro attempted to get back to his feet, but Ravencrow used his staff to vault forward, kicking GorJiro in the chest and causing him to stumble.

GorJiro manifested his sword, but Ravencrow wasted no time in striking out, a flare erupting as the staff met with the moonfyre blade and knocked the sword aside. Ravencrow quickly used the opening to strike GorJiro's wrist, the sound of the bone snapping loudly ringing out.

Ravencrow spun, his staff swinging around, striking GorJiro's blind side where the plasma blast had cauterized half of GorJiro's face. GorJiro cried out as Ravencrow dropped to the ground and swept GorJiro's legs out from underneath him with his weapon, taking his opponent to the floor.

The Harvshodd hopped into the air, raising his staff above his head and swinging downward, the staff crashing down onto GorJiro's chest as the Paragon yelled in pain. Ravencrow twirled his staff overhead and then struck out, aiming the butt of his staff right at GorJiro's throat, but GorJiro was able to grab onto it inches from its mark to prevent the fatal blow.

GorJiro used his free hand to manifest his sword once more, jabbing it toward Ravencrow, the fiery blade hitting the Harvshodd in the shoulder. At the same time, Ravencrow manifested a blaster, and shot GorJiro right in his arm.

Both Paragons grunted in pain as their blows landed. Ravencrow hopped back, beyond the reach of GorJiro's blade and fired his weapon again as GorJiro feebly deflected the blasts and attempted to crawl backward, away from his attacker.

Ravencrow then threw his blaster at GorJiro. When GorJiro swatted it away with his sword, Ravencrow spun and brought his staff around in an arc, knocking GorJiro's blade away. He began to pummel GorJiro with his staff as the Paragon defensively raised his arms, absorbing blow after vicious blow from the Harvshodd.

Finally, Ravencrow stopped and looked down with disgust at his opponent. GorJiro lay on the ground, wheezing for air, his arms broken. His one remaining eye looking at Ravencrow in disbelief as he helplessly shuffled his feet, as though he could somehow escape the Harvshodd's wrath.

Jack groggily looked up from his position on the ground, just in time to see Ravencrow and GorJiro staring each other down.

"And now, you die, GorJiro," Ravencrow said. "Even after all your planning and preparation, you still don't get to win."

GorJiro smiled at Ravencrow, bitterly. "Very well," he said. "We will call this a draw…"

With that, GorJiro's shattered arms snapped back into place, just enough for him to lift them. The air behind him rippled and swirled as a tether opened, revealing two Dark Soldiers on the other side, their rifles at the ready.

Before Ravencrow had time to react, the Dark Soldiers opened fire, their blasts hitting him dead on. Ravencrow dropped his staff, stumbling back and falling to the ground.

The Dark Soldiers then grabbed GorJiro, dragging him back into the tether. GorJiro laughed, triumphantly, as the tether closed. That vile laugh lingered after the Deathlord Supreme had gone, echoing throughout the chamber before it faded away completely.

When it did, the only things that remained in the Conclave, were three fallen heroes.

# CHAPTER 33

A Deathstalker roared as it pounced at Anna. Though Dahuud was able to dispatch the creature before it could harm the Princess, the feral Deathlord had succeeded in causing Anna to trip and fall, just as the Deathstalkers surged around the group.

"To the Princess!" Gunner cried.

The Royal Guard and Eionmeer's Peacekeepers quickly encircled Anna, desperately firing their rifles all around them to keep the Deathstalkers at bay. The Princess's fall also forced the Royal Vanguard to halt their advance as the three fought back against the vicious creatures that had them surrounded.

"Everyone, gather together!" Seqis cried as he fell back toward the group.

The Deathstalkers pushed forward just as everyone had gathered around the Princess. Right before they were about to be overwhelmed, Seqis held up his hammer, a golden dome springing from it and encasing the entire group. Tendrils of electricity snaked through the dome as Grapthaar electrified the shielding, causing any Deathstalker that came into contact with it to disintegrate into dust.

"Princess, are you okay?" asked Gunner, helping Anna back to her feet.

"I'm unharmed," Anna replied. "Can we continue to the ship?"

"I fear we are trapped, Your Highness," Seqis replied. "The second I lower this shield wall, we'll be overrun."

Anna looked around, desperate for a way out of their current predicament. *It can't end like this!* she thought to herself. *The Empire needs me! Jack needs me! I cannot allow the Deathlords to win!*

But despite her determination not to give up, Anna could see no way out of their dilemma. The Deathstalkers were practically crawling over each other as they swarmed toward the group, unafraid of the deadly shock they'd receive from Seqis's shield. And as stalwart as the Paragon was, even he would not be able to hold his concentration forever. Eventually, the shield would fall, and when that happened, Anna knew she and all her companions would be killed.

At the Earthship, the Initiates defending it were slowly being driven back, unable to handle the ever increasing number of Deathstalkers that rushed at them. Sawbones and her healers did their best to keep the group fighting, but between injury and exhaustion, the Initiates weren't going to be able to last much longer.

As Krupp and his friends continued to defend Scrappy, he looked out in the distance and saw the shield dome Seqis had erected, knowing immediately that the Princess and her companions had been pinned down.

"Scrappy!" Krupp cried. "The Princess is in trouble! We need to get that teleporter working now!"

Though Krupp's words carried a great deal of urgency, Scrappy was oblivious to them as he worked on the Earthship's teleportation array. "Okay, that goes there… I think this needs to be replaced… hmmm… what the blazes is that thing? Oh well, I'll get back to it…" he muttered as he tinkered with the machine.

"There are too many of these abominations!" exclaimed Morosa as she diligently cut down the attacking Deathstalkers. "We cannot keep this up much longer!"

"We must hold!" Krupp replied. "Keep fighting! Just keep fighting!!!"

While the Princess was pinned down and the Paragon Initiates fought for their lives, Rionknidis continued his relentless trek toward the dark monolith, making incredible leaps and bounds toward his target. The Tygarian landed and began charging through the Deathstalkers, using his hands and hind legs to speed through them on all fours, his cloak billowing in the wind as he did so. The Paragon was practically a blur, moving so fast the Deathstalkers could not even react to him. Then, as he approached the base of the hill, Rionknidis launched himself upward, soaring through the air and landing right in front of the monolith and its Terrormancer protector.

The Terrormancer held out his hand, projecting a concentrated wave of fear toward Rionknidis. The Paragon did not react. Instead, he simply snarled and bared his teeth.

"Why are you not afraid?" the Terrormancer demanded.

"You obviously don't know the meaning of a silent 'K'," Rionknidis growled.

The Paragon then manifested power gauntlets over his fists. They crackled to life with a surge of energy as the Tygarian attacked.

The Terrormancer held out his staff, transforming his ghostly blade into a shield into which Rionknidis slammed his power gauntlet, creating a massive shockwave that rippled outward. The Terrormancer's shield absorbed each blow Rionknidis tried to land, the power gauntlets booming as loudly as thunderclaps as the Paragon tried to get past the monolith's protector.

As the battle between Rionknidis and the Terrormancer raged upon the hilltop overlooking the area, Anna and the others remained pinned down, overwhelmed by the enemy. Anna looked out, past the swarm of Deathstalkers and the golden dome which surrounded her, toward the Earthship. She could see the desperate battle playing out in the distance as the Paragon Initiates fought valiantly to repair the vessel. Her heart sank as a grim realization settled upon her.

*I am responsible for this,* she thought. *I led everyone into this mess. Now, they're all going to die because of me.*

The hopelessness of their situation appeared apparent on the faces of all those around her. Commander Gunner's face was grim. Lugard and Dahuud looked somber. Even Seqis appeared resigned to their fate. His gaze met that of Anna's, and despite her desire to appear strong for the others, she couldn't help but voice her regret for not paying heed to the council of her protector.

"I'm sorry…" Anna whispered.

Just then, in their darkest moment, a ray of light appeared.

Quite literally, as a matter of fact. Not far from the shield the group was huddled under, a blast of searing light striking with power and fury, shot down from the sky and evaporated any Deathstalker it touched.

More blasts began to rain down all around the group, destroying the Deathstalkers in an ever increasing radius. Anna looked up to see the clouds parting as a massive ship descended, firing down upon the sea of feral Deathlords from high above like an angry god coming to pass judgement.

The group all gazed upward, wide-eyed in amazement. "It's… it's the Visinis!" Gunner exclaimed.

On the bridge of *The Megavolt*, Scallywag stood, arms crossed, a pleased smile on his face as he surveyed the battle below on the ship's viewscreen. "There's yer lolly, Princess," the pirate mused. "Oy, X.O., what say we clear tha way fer tha poor sots, eh?"

Rintin nodded as he tapped away at his command console. "Plotting firing solutions," he replied. "Clearing a path to the downed ship."

Far below, Anna and her companions all cheered. Anna's spirits instantly lifted as she gazed upon the miracle that would not only save her friends but her Empire, as well.

"Look!" said Lugard. "They are clearing us a path!"

The group turned and saw the plasma blasts from *The Megavolt* firing in front of them, clearing out the surge of Deathstalkers between them and the Earthship. Seqis smiled.

"Everyone, prepare to advance!" he ordered.

The group all got into position, getting ready to run as soon as Seqis dropped his shield.

"NOW!" the Paragon cried.

The shield dome disappeared, and the group resumed their race toward the Earthship, immediately attacking any surrounding Deathstalkers as *The Megavolt* gave them cover from above.

While the Princess and her protectors resumed their advance, those at the Earthship were faltering. Soundwave was blasting waves of sound as quickly as he could, trying desperately to keep his friends safe while Krupp, Morosa, and Snodgrass dispatched any Deathstalker that came close.

Then, plasma fire peppered the ground around the ship, dissipating the push the Deathstalkers had been making. Krupp glanced upward as Visini shuttlecraft descended, firing upon the area and clearing it as they came in for a landing.

Agent Boone watched in joyous surprise as the doors to the shuttlecrafts opened and Visini soldiers flooded out, firing their weapons as they did so.

"Give me a perimeter around the ship!" ordered their Lieutenant as he led the assault. "Push these creatures back! Show them what it means to tangle with a Visini!!!"

His soldiers all cried out as they obeyed their directive, quickly forming up around the Earthship as they fought back against the Deathstalkers. As soon as the shuttles were empty, they lifted off from the ground and began to fire down upon the feral Deathlords, offering air support while the ground troops solidified their defense.

"<I don't believe it!>" exclaimed Snodgrass. "<Where did these guys come from?>"

"Who cares!" replied a relieved Soundwave. "They're here now!"

"They're keeping the Deathstalkers at bay," Krupp said. "Quickly! Clear those that remain on the ship!"

Krupp and his companions pressed their attacks, actually able to thin the amount of Deathstalkers on the Earthship while the Visinis and the Initiates all held the line against the encroaching creatures. As the group fought, Scrappy continued to work on the array, so focused on his task that he was completely oblivious as to what was going on around him.

"Okay, um… I think all that's left to do is reconnect the particle scrambler to the main power emitter," Scrappy said.

"Excellent work, my boy!" came Green's voice over Scrappy's earpiece. "I believe that should do it."

"Yeah, but is the main power emitter the blue wire or the red wire?"

"I believe it's the yellow wire."

"Well then what do the blue and red wires do?"

"We'll review that later, my boy. For now, let us just focus on getting the teleporter operational, shall we?"

"Humph," said Scrappy, crinkling his face. "Nothing like a life-or-death situation to make one realize he needs to brush up on his Intermediate Matter Traversal textbook."

With that, Scrappy stripped the yellow wire and connected it to the array, which promptly began to whir and hum.

"You did it!" exclaimed Green. "Teleporters are back online!"

Scrappy hopped up and cheered. "I did it!!!" he cried, right before he became aware of the raging battle that surrounded him. "Oh…" he muttered. "What did I miss?"

On the bridge of the Earthship, Professor Green tapped away at a console, locking onto Anna and her group as they made their way through the army of Deathstalkers.

"Teleporters locked on," he muttered to himself. "Engaging… now!"

As Anna and her companions fought their way toward the ship, in a flash of light, they all suddenly found that they were now right in front of its rear entrance, well within the perimeter being held by the Initiates and the Visini soldiers.

As the group looked around, surprised by their sudden rescue, Krupp and the others hopped down from the top of the Earthship, landing beside the Vanguard. "Princess!" Krupp said as he approached. "Thank the Great Observer you all made it!"

"You're okay, right?" asked Scrappy. "I mean, all your appendages and internal organs are where they're supposed to be, aren't they? I'm a little rusty on my particle reconversion calculations…"

"Yes, I'm fine," Anna said. "To whom do I owe my thanks?"

"Oh, I'm Krupp. Scofeld Krupp. And this is Scrappy, Snodgrass, Morosa, and Soundwave. We're Jack's friends."

"Of course, you are," said Anna with a smile. "Jack has a knack for befriending both the courageous and the resourceful."

"Behind you!" cried Morosa as she leapt forward, just as a Deathstalker charged past the perimeter, pouncing right at the Princess. The Femezon hacked the creature into dust just as the other Initiates sprang into action, rushing forward to protect Anna as more Deathstalkers breached the area.

"Quickly, men! On me!" barked Gunner as he led his troops charging into the gap the Deathstalkers had created, filling the hole in the defenses and joining the Earthship's defenders.

"Lugard, come with me, we must assist them in keeping these creatures at bay," said Seqis. "Dahuud, you stay with the Princess."

Dahuud nodded as the other members of the Vanguard and Krupp's group charged forward to assist in the fight. Anna turned, looking at the battle, which raged around her. "This is madness," she said. "How long can we keep this up?"

"If I had to guess, Your Highness," whispered Dahuud as she looked off into the distance at the shockwaves emanating from the far hilltop, "we won't have to much longer."

On that hilltop, the Terrormancer spun as Rionknidis moved in for another blow, morphing his ghostly shield back into a blade and slashing it across the Tygarian's back. There was a *screech* as the weapon slid against Rionknidis's ultanium armor, his majestic cloak cut away and fluttering off from the strike. Just as Rionknidis turned to hit his opponent, the Terrormancer redeployed his shield and absorbed the blow.

Rionknidis roared, speeding around the Terrormancer to try and get past his shield. But as fast as the Paragon was, the Terrormancer kept pace, not allowing for Rionknidis to get an opening.

"I can ssssssense your fear!" the Terromancer hissed. "You sssstill feel it! You cannot ignore it forever!"

"Watch me!" snarled Rionknidis as he broke off his assault and slammed his power gauntlet into the ground.

The blow made the ground tremble, causing the black rock beneath their feet to shatter and kick up in a concentric shockwave from the point of impact. The Terrormancer lost his footing and fell backward onto the ground.

Rionknidis seized on the opportunity and leapt into the air, raising his power gauntlet as it crackled with energy, ready to deliver a killing blow as he descended upon his enemy.

The Terrormancer swung his scythe, sending its blade rocketing upward and hitting Rionknidis directly in the chest. The blow sent the Tygarian spinning backward, head over heels, landing hard on the ground with a massive dent in his breastplate.

The Terrormancer kicked back up to his feet and caught his ghost blade as it returned to his staff. He rushed toward the dazed Paragon and swung his scythe overhead, the deadly blade racing down right for Rionknidis's head.

The Paragon barely had time to react as he raised his hands and caught the blade of death energy in his grip, the ultanium power gauntlets shrieking as the blade dug into them, slowly lowering its tip mere inches from Rionknidis's face.

The Terrormancer leaned in, leveraging his weight against his weapon, trying to push his blade down through the Tygarian's skull as it slowly cut through the protection the gauntlets offered.

"Even the fearlesssss die, Paragon," said the Terrormancer with a sneer as he pressed down on his weapon.

"They do," snarled Rionknidis. "Just not today!"

With that, Rionknidis moved the blade aside, the maneuver cutting through his gauntlets and severing his hands. The scythe impacted the ground right beside his head, causing the Terrormancer to fall forward as he continued to apply his weight to the weapon.

Rionknidis sat up, his muzzle locking around the Terrormancer's throat as his sharp canine teeth tore into the being's flesh. The Terrormancer gasped, right before Rionknidis jerked his head, tearing away what he'd latched onto.

The Terrormancer disintegrated into wisps of smoke as Rionknidis struggled back to his feet, spitting on the ground.

"You even taste terrible, you evil kitten," the Tyrgarian growled.

Rionknidis set his eyes upon the monolith. He could see it vibrate as it called upon its Deathstalkers to come to its aid, sending the creatures scrambling up the hill to attack. Rionknidis looked down at his hands which had been cut off in his desperate maneuver to kill the Terrormancer.

"With these hands, I accept the sacrifices involved in my duty…" he muttered.

The Paragon concentrated and manifested new power gauntlets, with massive pistons in the place of his hands. The gauntlets roared to life with energy as the Paragon rushed forward, howling with rage as he slammed one of them into the monolith.

Rionknidis continued to punch the monolith, his power gauntlets sending out a massive shockwave with each blow. Every strike created a high-pitched whine, as though the monolith were crying out in pain. Every Deathstalker screeched, each feeling the blows, as well. Those that had made it to the hilltop in time tried to attack Rionknidis as he focused on the monolith, but he'd shrug them off or quickly dispatch them with a tap of his gauntlets before hitting the monolith again and again.

Cracks began to form in the smooth obsidian surface of the rock, growing larger with each fierce blow from the Paragon. The ultanium gauntlets were also taking damage with each impact, but Rionknidis kept his focus, manifesting fixes as he continued his relentless assault.

With one final, powerful strike, a sphere of energy radiated outward, shaking the very ground for miles. The black rock of the monolith shattered, the death energy inside looking as though it had a face full of anger and anguish before it tore apart as the souls trapped there broke free, flying away and dissipating into nothing.

For miles and miles, the overwhelming swarm of Deathstalkers all cried out before crumbling to dust, disappearing as though they had never been there. Those defending the Earthship cheered as the sudden defeat of their enemy settled in on them.

Rionknidis stumbled backward, what was left of his power gauntlets demanifesting as he dropped to his knees, exhausted. He looked down at his missing hands, the pain from them being severed still lingering in him. But despite that, Rionknidis smiled as he looked up from his wounds, gazing at the vast, empty field before him that had once been crawling with Deathstalkers.

"Now that's what I call a critical hit…" he said, feeling rather pleased with himself.

# CHAPTER 34

The Chamber of the Great Seal was quiet as the aftermath of the battle with GorJiro lingered. Jack stirred, forcing himself to his hands and knees as every muscle in his body protested. Jack tried to get to his feet, but he stumbled and fell. He then crawled over to Ravencrow, looking down at the Harvshodd, whose wounds were still smoking from the impact of the Deathlord plasma blasts. Ravencrow's eyes were closed, his mouth hanging open. He looked lifeless.

"No… no, no, no, no, no…" Jack said as he reached out and placed his hands on the Paragon. "Don't be dead! Please, don't be dead!"

Jack concentrated and attempted to heal Ravencrow's wounds. He wasn't familiar with Harvshodd physiology, but he knew enough about how to fix injured tissue to repair some of the blaster damage. As the wounds began to close, Ravencrow's eyes opened. He gasped for air and then coughed up some blood before looking up at a relieved Jack.

"Ugh," Ravencrow muttered. "You again."

Jack couldn't help but laugh at that. "Please… don't make me laugh," Jack begged. "It hurts too much."

Ravencrow weakly grasped at his many wounds, flinching as he did so. "GorJiro…" he said.

"He escaped. The Deathlords dragged him through a tether of some type."

"Pity," growled Ravencrow. "I was looking forward to killing him. But it seems he's learned to utilize The Void a bit too well since he and I last clashed…"

Ravencrow coughed again, looking pained as his small body spasmed.

"Are… are you…"

"I'll live," Ravencrow muttered. "For all the good it'll do. Believe it or not, I've suffered worse."

"So, all this time, you were some kick-butt warrior who had beaten GorJiro in one-on-one combat, and you never told me?" asked Jack.

"There was nothing to tell. The Harvshodd that defeated that idiot lived a lifetime ago. I am nothing like he was. Not anymore. In case you didn't notice, I just got my hide handed to me."

"Not from where I was sitting," said Jack. "You stood toe-to-toe with the greatest warrior to ever live, and you made him run away."

"Not that such a thing does us any favors," muttered Ravencrow, coughing more. "GorJiro would never have left if he weren't confident in his victory. He may have run, but his plan – whatever it may be – is still in motion."

"Then we'll just have to stop it, won't we?"

"I'm barely hanging on by a thread, boy," Ravencrow muttered. "And the Emperor Ascendant over there looks like he may already be dead. Do you think you have the strength to do what it takes to put an end to GorJiro's plan?"

Jack frowned as he glanced over at Mourdock, who was lying still on the ground. Regardless of his emotion over seeing his friend in such a state, Jack nodded. "What do I need to do?" he asked.

"You've broken a Great Seal before. Think you can do it again?"

"You… you want me to break the Great Seal?" asked Jack. "But, if it's destroyed…"

"The Conclave's pocket universe will collapse, yes," replied Ravencrow. "But GorJiro has a plan for this place, boy. He has opened all these tethers for a reason and that seal is the only thing keeping them open. If we wish to stop GorJiro, we must destroy those tethers, and the only way to do that is to destroy the Great Seal."

Jack frowned, the weight of what Ravencrow was asking him to do settling in upon him. "Last time I destroyed a Great Seal, it was already breaking, and I had grenades…"

"Look at the seal," instructed Ravencrow. "The corruption has weakened it. You have learned to use electromagnetism, have you not?"

"I have."

"Then you don't need grenades. If you were to run enough current through it, the blasted thing should shatter like glass."

Jack hesitated. "If I do this… none of us will make it out of here," he said.

Ravencrow nodded. "Tell me, boy… what is life about?"

"Life is about believing in and standing for something greater than yourself," Jack responded.

"And why do we fight?"

"We fight the fights that deserve to be fought, for no other reason than we may be the only ones with the strength to do so."

"And what is the purpose of a fight?"

"To manifest what I believe to be right."

"So, you were paying attention in class," mused Ravencrow as he coughed. "Tell me… what do you want to manifest now?"

Jack smiled at the crotchety old alien. "I want to save the universe," he said.

"Then you know what you have to do."

Jack nodded and took the Harvshodd's hand, giving it a gentle squeeze. "Thank you, R.C. For being my teacher."

"You're welcome," Ravencrow replied. "And don't call me that."

Jack and Ravencrow both smiled at one another – an unspoken good-bye. Jack forced himself up to his feet and faced the corrupted seal. He approached it, limping as he did so, its great eye infected with veins of red, green, and purple. Jack stood before the Great Seal, gathering his courage for what he was about to do. He looked up at it, and though the eye was simply an image carved into the stone, Jack felt as though it were glaring down at him.

"Here goes nothing," Jack whispered before reaching out and placing his hands on the seal.

Upon contact, it immediately felt as though Jack's hands were being stabbed by thousands of razor-sharp needles. He cried out as the corruption began to seep from the seal, veins of red, green, and purple snaking through his hands and to his wrists, infecting him.

*No*, thought Jack as he gritted his teeth. *You can fight back all you want… but I'll beat you!*

Jack concentrated, slowing the advance of the corruption as he tapped into his Source and pushed his energy back into the seal. He could feel the corruption fighting against him, lashing out at his energy like an attacking snake. Jack braced himself against the large circular stone and began channeling electromagnetic energy into it.

The seal started to rumble, vibrating slightly as Jack forced more and more electricity through it. Particles of dust arose from it as Jack struggled to break it, but whatever had infested the Great Seal was determined not to go quietly.

Jack cried out as he felt the evil energy within the seal push back against him, the skin of his arms turning white as the hideous veins of corruption continued to spread up his forearms. The pain it was inflicting was interrupting Jack's concentration and he could feel himself weakening as the corruption spread deeper into him.

*I… I can't fight it!* Jack thought in despair. *It's too strong!*

Jack felt his knees tremble as his legs weakened. It took all the energy he had to keep himself upright, his hands now stuck to the seal, sewn to it by the vile veins of the corruption now trying to overwhelm him.

A tear escaped from Jack's eye as he tried to push back the pain that was being inflicted upon him. His skin felt as though thousands of angry insects were crawling all over it as the corruption continued up his arms and toward his shoulders.

*Please…* Jack thought, not exactly sure to whom he was praying. *Help me… give me the strength… to do what is needed…*

Then, another hand reached out and placed itself on the Great Seal, the corruption around it screeching as it started to crawl away from what had just made contact. Jack turned his head and looked beside him. He wasn't sure if he was hallucinating from the pain or if some mystical force had answered his plea. But regardless of the reason, he knew what he saw.

Shepherd was standing beside him, tall and strong, his face focused in determined concentration. He turned and looked at Jack and nodded, as if to say: "*Don't worry. You are not alone.*"

A second hand reached out on Jack's opposite side, causing the corruption to shriek and retreat also. Jack turned to see Shanks standing there. The wise monk turned and nodded his head, as well.

More hands appeared, bracing against the seal. The hands of Master Highclaw. Of Master Savage. Of Master Hodapp. Pennywise reached out, as did Frenesca, and Flitter, and the hands of all the Paragons who'd lost their lives there in the Conclave, appeared one by one to come to Jack's aid.

Jack could still feel the corruption worming its way through him, but he could also feel it weakening with the touch of each spirit that appeared to assist him. Whether they were real or not, Jack didn't know. But he did know that their presence made him stronger.

Jack bore down and funneled as much electrical charge as he could into the seal, which began to crack as he did so. Jack could feel the corruption which had infected it twisting and turning within the rock as it was assaulted on all sides from the spirits of those who'd sworn themselves to the tenants of everything the corruption stood against.

As more cracks began to appear on the seal's face, Jack could hear voices from all around him. They were faint at first, but grew louder as the seal slowly started to break. They were voices of young and old. Of past and future. Of all species, races, and genders. They spoke over one another, their voices obscuring what each was saying.

The carved eye of the Great Seal seemed as though it were gazing down at Jack as chunks of the seal began to break away, its surface trembling as electricity coursed through it. The discolored veins which riddled its surface appeared to be throbbing as they struggled to survive.

Jack felt the corruption spreading through his chest, down his legs, and up his neck. He fought it as best he could, but he knew if he were going to break the seal, he had to remain focused on doing that and not on saving himself. With a defiant scream, Jack manifested as much energy as he could and shot it through the stone.

The specters of those around him disappeared as the seal crumbled, breaking apart into dust and debris. Jack stumbled backward, clawing at his skin as the corruption overtook him, ravaging his body with an angry vengeance, as if to punish him for what he'd just done.

Jack fell to his knees, his vision starting to blur as it felt as though his insides were being torn apart. The voices he'd been hearing had grown louder and louder, each of them slowly converging in what they were saying...

Jack looked up toward the exposed vault that the seal had protected. A spark of light flashed there, blinking as it started to grow. And as that spark morphed into the image of a great, all-seeing eye, it gazed upon Jack just as the voices all came together to speak as one. And those voices said:

"Eldil Meldilorn."

With a powerful fury, the image of the eye transformed into a beam of energy and rocketed forth. Jack gasped as he felt the energy pass through him, its current so strong it lifted him off his feet and into the air.

Jack dangled from the beam as he felt the corruption within him wither, dying under the intensity of the force that coursed through him. He felt a vitality surge through his body, making him aware of every atom that comprised it. With that awareness, Jack's consciousness was set free, flying from his body and out into the universe.

Jack then saw many things at once, yet he was able to make sense of it all. He saw the grand majesty of the universe laid out before him. He saw each and every star in existence and the particles which made them shine. He saw the planets and all the life they harbored. He saw a vast array of beings and all the wondrous things of which they were capable.

And while he was seeing this, he also saw more specific things, such as Anna on the surface of Eionmeer. He could see her clutch her chest and look up into the sky, gazing at the Conclave, and somehow Jack knew she was aware of what he was experiencing.

On the surface of Maxima, he saw another man – one with a false skin, standing before an Ancient temple. This man also cried out and clutched his chest, dropping to his knees and gazing upward, confused as to what he was feeling.

Both these people were connected to Jack. But then, Jack realized his connections extended to so many others. In fact, *everything* was connected. And as the realization of these connections grew, a haze began to form around Jack, until he was standing in a pure white void.

And his father was standing there with him.

"Dad?" Jack said.

"Hey, kiddo," his father replied, smiling at Jack, warmly.

Jack looked around, confused. "Am... am I dead?" Jack asked.

"No, but you're very close to moving to a different plane of existence."

Jack raised his eyebrows. "Really?"

"Yep," his father said. "And as tempting as it may be to allow it to happen, I have to ask you not to."

"Why?"

"Because, a lot depends on you continuing to exist in your current reality."

"I... I don't understand..."

"I know you don't," his dad said. "But don't worry. Eventually, you will."

Jack frowned. "But... it's calling to me, dad," he said. "It wants me to join with it. Mom's there. And my friends. And people I care about... they're all there."

"They are," his dad replied. "But there are others who aren't, and they need your help. And by helping them, you're going to be helping your mom and everyone else, too. Professor Green needs you. Scallywag needs you. Mourdock needs you. Even Grohm and Heckubus need you. And Anna needs you most of all."

Jack felt torn. He knew what his father was telling him was right. But he also desperately wanted to see where all those connections he'd glimpsed were leading him. "I feel like you're asking me to turn my back on enlightenment," Jack said. "How… how do I know this is the right thing to do?"

"Because," his dad said with a loving smile. "It's what you told me to tell you."

Jack gave his father a confused look as the void around him began to dim and clouds started to appear once more.

"You must make your choice, son," his dad said. "I know you'll make the right one."

Jack's father disappeared. Jack then found himself flying through the clouds, emerging over the vast universe once again, looking down upon it like an all-seeing deity. The universe gazed back at him, as though it, too, were an all-seeing eye, asking Jack what it was he wanted.

"I want to save you," Jack replied.

With that answer, Jack began to fall, speeding toward the pupil of the universal eye and crashing through it.

In the span of a second, Jack was back in the Conclave, the last tendrils of the blast from the Ancient vault snaking through him. And when it did, Jack hovered in the air for the briefest of moments before falling to the ground.

Jack lay on the hard sandstone floor, completely unconscious. He'd made his choice.

Now, he'd have to deal with its consequences.

# CHAPTER 35

Anna gazed up into the sky, looking at the tether above the planet. She was unsure what she had experienced, but somehow, a part of her knew something had just happened to Jack. It was a strange sensation – as though a part of her were connected to him through some unseen force and she could tell he needed help.

"Princess Glorianna," said a Visini Lieutenant as he approached her, breaking Anna out of her trance, "may we be of any further assistance?"

"Yes, you may," Anna replied. "We shall need your help for repairs and also for your ship to follow us to engage with the Deathlords."

The Lieutenant frowned. "Apologies, Your Highness," he said. "My men are soldiers, not technicians. We will not be of much use in repairing your ship. And as far as *The Megavolt* joining you in battle… well, let's just say that from my understanding, things are a bit too complicated at the moment to permit such a thing."

"I see," said Anna, disappointed. "Very well. You and your men have done more than enough already. Please, extend my thanks to your captain and your enlightened Emperor. I am in their debt."

The Lieutenant nodded. "I shall be sure to do so, Your Highness," he said, bowing before taking his leave.

As the Visini shuttles began to depart, the Royal Vanguard watched them go with dismay. "That's Visinis for you," said Lugard with disapproval. "Reliably unreliable."

"And yet, without them, we would never have made it," Seqis said.

"Without a lot of things, we would not have made it," stated Anna, looking at all the Initiates and former Secret Army members who surrounded her. "Lugard, oversee the ship's repairs. Dahuud, have Rionknidis teleported back to the ship. Lord Commander, please escort me to the bridge. This battle is not over yet."

"As you wish," the Royal Vanguard all replied.

As Anna and Seqis made their way toward the bridge of the Earthship, Dahuud used the ship's teleportation array to lock onto Rionknidis and transport him back. When the Tygarian appeared in the cargo hold, he looked haggard and drained, cradling his missing hands.

Dahuud frowned when she saw her sworn companion in such a rough condition. Sawbones quickly rushed to the Paragon's side. "Mighty Alcazar's Axe!" Sawbones exclaimed. "What the blazes happened to ya, man?"

"You should see the other guy," responded Rionknidis.

"Quickly, come this way," said Sawbones, urging Rionknidis to follow her to the med bay. "We need to get ya treated immediately!"

"I'm fine," grumbled the Paragon as he struggled back to his feet, wobbling unsteadily as he did so.

"Fine? FINE? Are ya out of your Tygarian mind? Ya ain't got no hands!"

"I ain't got time for hands," growled Rionknidis.

"Ya got time for not being a blasted idiot?" snapped Sawbones. "Now get to the med bay before I take out your legs, too, you mangy flea-bag!"

Rionknidis blinked at the gruff Stonehooligan. He'd just faced down a Terrormancer and a monolith of pure evil, but for some reason, Sawbones MacCrusty intimidated him far more than either of them had.

"Go," whispered Dahuud. "Join us on the bridge after you get patched up."

Rionknidis growled but nodded. "How fares the Princess?" he asked.

"Oddly enough… better than I've ever seen her," replied Dahuud.

On the bridge of the Earthship, Professor Green's eyes lit up when Anna entered. He rushed toward her, arms outstretched. "Your Highness!" he exclaimed.

Anna gladly embraced the Professor, feeling as though she hadn't seen him in years. "Professor Green, it is so good to see you again!"

"And you, my dear!" Green said, his voice emotional. "I am so relieved to see you are safe and back to your old self! I can only assume Brother Shanks is the reason you've returned to us!"

"He is indeed," Anna replied, sadly.

Green pulled back and looked at Anna, taking note of her sorrow. "I take it he… he didn't return with you?" the Professor asked.

"No," she replied. "Though he may no longer be with us, he does live on… here." Anna touched her chest above her heart. "I don't quite know how to explain it, but I can still feel his presence."

"Ah! No doubt due to his spiritual energy having been imbued into you!"

Anna looked at Green, confused. "Come again?" she asked.

"It's quite fascinating, actually," Green said. "And quite a tale concerning Brother Shanks and how he helped both you and Jack. I suppose it all started back after we rescued you from the Sunshell—"

"I should like to hear all about it, Professor, but at another time," interrupted Anna. "Right now, we have more pressing matters to attend to."

"Oh! Yes, of course!" said Green, before a curious look settled upon him. "Um… what matters might those be?"

"The Deathlords attacking the Empire?" stated Seqis, looking at the Professor as though he couldn't believe the Trundel could forget such a thing.

"Oh! Right!" said Green, apparently having actually forgotten.

"And Jack," Anna said. "I don't know how to explain it, but I know he is in trouble. We must depart this planet immediately and retrieve him from the Conclave."

"Yes, yes, of course!" Green replied. "We should do all we can to help Jack as soon as possible."

"Not soon. Now," stated Anna.

Green twiddled his fingers, nervously. "Um… yes… I understand time is of the essence, Your Highness, but… it will take hours for the ship to be repaired enough to fly once more."

"We don't have hours."

"I fear we don't have much choice, either," said Green, sadly.

Anna looked around the bridge of the Earthship. She'd come to know it well. In an odd way, it had become more of a home to her during her month-long trek back to Omnicron after the events of the Ghost Planet than anywhere she'd ever lived. But something was different now. *She* was different.

Her experience with Verrutus and the temple had changed her in ways she had yet begun to understand, but for the moment, she felt more in-tune with her Ancient powers than she ever had before. Because of that, she could sense something within the Earthship she'd never noticed previously. A hum. A vibration. A pulse. Something that resonated with her. Something she inherently knew she could tap into. She couldn't quite explain it, but somehow she knew the key to saving Jack lay with this new connection she sensed.

"Professor," Anna said. "How is it you are able to fly the Earthship?"

Green's eyes widened. "Oh! That's right, you were possessed when last you were here. Funny story… well, maybe not so funny… but funny in the interesting sort of way—"

"Professor."

"Right, sorry. I discovered that the ship is able to identify individuals based on their bio-signatures. Because I spent time on Earth, I emit a small amount of radiation that was inherent to that planet, thus giving me a marker the Earthship can use to receive commands. I simply needed to adjust the sensitivity of its identifiers so that the amount of radiation I emit is enough to grant me the ability to access its flight controls."

"I spent time on Earth, as well," Anna said. "Could you recalibrate the ship's systems to allow me the same level of control?"

Green scratched his chin. "You would have a far weaker bio-signature since you spent less time on Earth, but, yes, I should be able to—"

"Do it," ordered Anna. "Now."

Green nodded. "Right away, Princess," he replied before going to one of the Earthship's consoles to carry out his task.

As the Professor went about adjusting the Earthship's identification protocols, Anna turned to Seqis. "Lord Commander," she said. "Get everyone on-board the ship."

"But… we've just barely started repairs," objected Krupp, who'd been eavesdropping nearby. "How will we be able to save Jack if we pull everyone back inside?"

Seqis placed a hand on Krupp's shoulder. "Legacy Prime just gave an order, son," Seqis said. "Have some faith."

Krupp frowned but acquiesced. He followed Seqis off the bridge to retrieve the others. When they had gone, Anna took a deep breath. She looked at her surroundings, gazing at all aspects of the room. Its design. Its systems. Its utter uniqueness among any starship she'd ever been on before. But more than that, the ship didn't just feel special to her in the sense that it was a wonder of the Ancients. It felt special to her because it felt like Jack – and that made her connection to it even stronger than she had ever realized. It was then she heard the voice of Emperor Tarrok in her head as she remembered her vision of him.

*There is an invisible thread that connects all things to one another,* he'd said. *From a blade of grass, to a hunk of metal, to a cell of flesh, to the particles of a star. All are entangled. All are one.*

Anna felt something stir deep within her as she remembered those words. It was a strange, unfamiliar feeling that somehow also felt natural to her. It was a feeling that had coursed through Arcturus's veins, just as it had with Emperor Youngblood and Emperor Tarrok. A feeling of deep, powerful connection to all things, everywhere.

She remembered how Emperor Tarrok had looked, a golden aura emanating from him as he made a connection with the starships of the Brightshade fleet, lightyears away. And as that image played out in Anna's mind, she heard Tarrok's voice one last time.

*Whether built by the Ancients or by man, it is all part of a whole.*

That is when Princess Glorianna of Legacy Prime realized what she had to do.

Anna was unsure of how long she'd been standing there in her trance, but she was suddenly aware of the commotion around her. The bridge was now full, its different stations manned by the Paragon Initiates, Agent Boone, and the former members of the Secret Army. Commander Gunner and his men from the Royal Guard were there, as well, as were Lugard, Dahuud, and Rionknidis. Seqis entered the room and approached her.

"Everyone is aboard, Your Highness," Seqis said.

Anna nodded. "Professor," she said as she moved in front of the pilot's seat. "Prepare for take-off."

"Me?" asked Green. "But… aren't you—"

"No, you will need to pilot the ship," Anna said. "I will be otherwise occupied."

"With what?"

"This."

Anna closed her eyes and held her hands out by her side. She could feel the vibration of the ship intensify as she tapped into it, now that the Professor had attuned the ship to receive her commands.

*You are of Ancient design*, Anna thought. *So am I. The blood that runs through my veins is no different from the electricity that runs through yours. We are the same. Right now, we need one another. Please… for Jack's sake… let me help you, so that you can help us all.*

As if in response, a hatch on the floor before Anna opened and a metallic kiosk housing an access orb at its top rose. Anna looked down upon it and smiled.

"Here we go," she said.

Anna placed her hands on the access orb and immediately felt her connection to the Earthship intensify. It was as though she could sense every part of it – every room, every system, every nook and cranny. She could see what was damaged and what needed to be fixed. She closed her eyes and focused, funneling her own energy through the access orb as the connection between her and the ship solidified.

All around her, the bridge began to come alive as the ship's systems rebooted. Scrappy looked at the readouts from his console with wide eyes. "I don't believe it!" he cried. "The damage is being repaired! It's like the ship is manifesting itself back into working order!"

"It's not the ship, my young friend," Seqis said with a smile as he gazed at Anna. "It's the Princess."

Aided by the Princess's power, the hull of the Earthship began to mend itself; all its systems and machinery became renewed as the energy from the blood of the Ancients flowed through it. The hum of the ship's thrusters sounded out and the Earthship jerked as it rose up from the ground. Green quickly clasped onto the control domes of the pilot's chair to control the lift-off.

"Great Scott!" Green exclaimed. "The ship is reporting all systems are functional! Hull integrity back to 100%!"

The tether into the Conclave universe appeared in the viewscreen on the bridge as the Earthship turned toward it. The image became magnified to display the tiny spec that was the Conclave temple. Anna looked at the image, well aware that Jack was there and that he needed her help.

"Professor," she said. "Take us to the Conclave."

"Right away, Your Highness!" Green replied as he accelerated the ship away from the planet's surface and toward the looming rip in time and space.

*Hang in there, Jack,* thought Anna. *For once, I'm coming to save you!*

# CHAPTER 36

The Earthship flew through the tether above Eionmeer and into the pocket universe of the Conclave, speeding toward the temple. High above it was another tether leading toward Maxima where a massive space battle was raging. As those aboard the Earthship entered the pocket universe, it became clear that was not the only tether that was open. All around them, tethers littered the edges of the pocket universe, each one of them open to a different star system with a different planet squarely in its sights.

"What the blazes?" muttered Krupp as he gazed at the strange sight on the viewscreen. "What is all this?"

"They're tethers!" exclaimed Scrappy from his sensor console. "According to sensors, each one is open to a different planetary system in the Empire!"

"Fascinating," noted Green. "I suppose that makes sense. Because the Conclave's pocket universe lies within our own, it could be used as a central hub to open tethers anywhere within the prime universe."

"But why?" asked Morosa. "For what purpose?"

"Whatever that purpose is, I'm sure this has something to do with it," said Boone from his station as he called up an image of the massive Deathlord vessel that was moving to the center of the pocket universe, escorted by two smaller Deathlord cruisers.

"Oh, dear," said Green, not liking the look of those ships one bit.

"The Deathlords are launching fightercraft to intercept us!" squeaked Scrappy as a sensor alarm went off at his station. "We don't have much time!"

"Professor, bring us in toward the temple," Anna ordered. "Scan it as soon as you can and try to find Jack."

"Sensors are picking up three life signs remaining within the temple, Princess," reported Boone. "All of them weak."

"And according to the Earthship, one of them is Jack," said Green, looking concerned.

Anna frowned. "Weak doesn't mean gone," she replied. "Lock onto them and teleport them directly to the med bay. Have Paragon MacCrusty standing by to tend to them immediately."

As those on the bridge carried out her orders, Anna gazed at the image of the Conclave temple on the ship's viewscreen. She'd visited the Conclave in the past and had always marveled at how wondrous it had been. Now, the light from its bricks was fading, and its outer ring lay in ruin. It was obvious the temple was dying, which could only mean one thing…

Its Great Seal was no more.

*Could that be what happened?* Anna wondered. *Did Jack break the Great Seal to try to stop the Deathlord attack? Is that the cause of the strange feeling I had?*

"Sensors are picking up three Deathlord Shards, incoming," Krupp announced.

"Oh dear, we still need to get closer to the temple!" said Green with worry. "Everyone hang on! I'm going to try something, and I'm only about 67% sure it's going to work!"

The Earthship sped toward the Shards that were bearing down on it, rolling on its axis and corkscrewing through the fighters' formation as they fired. The maneuver worked, allowing the Earthship to zoom by its attackers, even if it did absorb a few plasma blasts in the process.

"We're in range!" said Scrappy. "Locking onto the life signs. Teleporting… now!"

Green held the Earthship steady as the teleporter engaged. The moment he got the confirmation Jack and the others had arrived in the med bay, he quickly banked the ship just as four more Shards swooped toward them.

"Jack and the others are onboard!" Green announced. "Might I suggest we now make a hasty retreat and put some distance between us and those Deathlord ships?"

Anna looked at the sensor readout on one of the Earthship's holoscreens. She was tempted to agree with the Professor, wanting to join the rest of the fleet in Maxima, when her focus narrowed in on the large ship which was still making its way toward the center of the pocket universe. Something about that vessel, in particular, alarmed her.

"Professor," she said. "Take us in closer to that large Deathlord ship."

Green blinked his eyes. "Clo… closer?" he said in concern.

"I want a full sensor scan," Anna said. "I need to know everything there is about that ship and what it's doing here."

"Princess," said Boone. "Between that ship's escorts and those Shards on our tail, we're going to be pressing our luck by sticking around here any longer than we have to."

"Luck is made to be pressed, Agent Boone. Particularly our kind," replied Anna. "Now take us in close, Professor. If there's one thing I've learned the hard way, it's never to leave anything to chance when it comes to the Deathlords."

*****

While those on the bridge of the Earthship prepared to carry out Anna's orders, Sawbones was busy tending to Mourdock Skyborn in the ship's medical bay. Mourdock gasped, his eyes slamming open. He looked around, disoriented, before his vision focused in on the Stonehooligan.

"Take it easy, man," said Sawbones. "You're safe, now."

Mourdock blinked, looking down at his gut where he remembered being impaled by GorJiro's moonfyre sword. "Where… where am I?"

"You're on the Earthship, in the med bay," Sawbones replied. "We just rescued you lot from the Conclave. Good thing the Princess teleported you all in when she did. You were hanging onto life by a thread."

"Anna?" Mourdock murmured, still trying to get his bearings. Though the wound in his gut had been healed, it still ached terribly. He went to push himself up on the bed, but discovered to his horror that his arm was missing, the phantom limb in its place flailing about.

"My arm!" he cried.

Sawbones grabbed onto him, using her healing powers to keep Mourdock from going into shock. "It's gonna be okay, man!" Sawbones insisted. "Your arm's been severed, but we can grow a new one for ya. You'll be good as new as soon as this is all over, I promise!"

Sawbones' assurance helped to calm Mourdock, until he glanced over and saw Jack and Ravencrow both lying on medical beds. The Harvshodd was coughing and wheezing. Jack appeared to be unconscious, his skin pale with faintly colored corrupted veins visible beneath it.

"Jack!" said Mourdock. "Great Observer! How did he become corrupted?"

"Calm yourself, daggit!" snapped Sawbones. "I don't know what's happened to the Earthman, yet, but his vitals are stable and whatever has infected him seems to be slowly fading."

"Will he be okay?" Mourdock asked, concerned.

Just then, the ship shook as it was struck with plasma fire. Sawbones grimaced. "Assuming the Deathlords don't blow us all up, he's gonna be fine," she said. "Now if you'll excuse me, I gotta tend to that Harvshodd before he chokes on his own blood."

Sawbones left Mourdock and rushed over to Ravencrow. Mourdock turned and looked at Jack, who lay on the medical bed beside him, unresponsive.

"Hang in there, Jack…" Mourdock muttered to his friend. "Just hang in there!"

*****

"EVERYONE HANG IN THERE!" cried Green back on the bridge as he desperately banked the ship away from the Shards that had been harassing them.

Anna glared at the Earthship's viewscreen as they came closer to the large Deathlord vessel which was covered in long spikes. *What the blazes are you?* she wondered. *We've never seen anything like you before.*

"Try and stay on the edge of those capital ships' point defense arrays, Professor," instructed Boone.

"But we shall need to get closer to get a complete scan of the vessel," replied Green.

"If we get in range of those ships' point defenses, we won't be alive long enough to get any sensor readings."

"Fair point," agreed Green. "Scrappy, my boy! See if you can boost our sensor strength at all. We need to keep some distance between us and those ships."

"Redirecting the use of some of the Earthship's sub-arrays now, Professor," Scrappy replied.

As the Earthship flew at the edge of the Deathlord ship's point defense array, pursued by a squadron of Deathlord Shards, Anna saw some movement from the spikes of the vessel. She magnified the image on the viewscreen to show that the tips of the spikes were retracting. Seqis came up by her side, squinting at the image in concern.

"Those things on the ship…" Anna said. "They're not just spikes."

"No, they are not," replied Seqis, grimly. "They would appear to be… cannons."

Just then, something fired from the spikes.

"Your Highness!" exclaimed Krupp. "The Deathlord ship just fired ten unidentified projectiles. They're all heading for different tethers!"

"On the screen!" ordered Anna.

The image of one of the projectiles was magnified as it sped toward its destination. The second the image became clear, there was a collective gasp from those on the bridge. Every face went grim as the chilling realization of what was on the viewscreen settled in upon all who looked at it.

"It's a monolith," growled Rionknidis. "That ship is firing monoliths toward the tethers!"

"That is why the Deathlords needed all these tethers!" said Seqis. "So that ship can seed those rocks to every planet in the Empire all at once!"

Fear gripped Anna's chest. Now that the Deathlord Seed Ship had reached the center of the pocket universe, it could launch any number of those monoliths to any planet it pleased. While the Empire's attention was focused on the battle raging in Maxima, the true threat would be attacking countless worlds without warning. It had to be stopped.

And in that moment, the Earthship was the only thing with any hope of doing so.

"Target those monoliths!" Anna commanded. "Destroy them before they can make it through the tethers!"

"Focusing on those monoliths is going to leave us vulnerable to the Deathlord Shards," cautioned Boone.

"The monoliths are our priority right now," Anna stated. "We cannot allow them to infect other worlds!"

"Oh, dear," murmured Green. "It's times like this when I wish I were a better pilot!"

"Better pilot or no, you're the only one we have at the moment, Professor," Anna said. "Now intercept those monoliths before they can do any more harm!"

Green brought the Earthship toward the volley of monoliths as they sped toward their respective tethers. Boone and the others targeted them and began to fire, the Earthship's plasma batteries spraying out and finding some of their marks.

"Blast it," grumbled Boone. "Even with the Earthship's advanced targeting computers it's like trying to hit a needle with a needle!"

"Keep trying," Anna ordered. "We must not let any get past us!"

"Um… I'm afraid it's too late for that…" said Scrappy. "We missed three of them. They've exited the pocket universe already and are headed toward their targets."

Anna scowled as she looked at the viewscreen. *Blast it!* she thought. *If those monoliths have a chance to spawn Deathstalkers, those planets will be overrun in no time!*

"We have incoming!" reported Krupp. "Twelve Shards are on their way to intercept!"

The Deathlord fightercraft bore down on the Earthship, unleashing their plasma bolts as they zoomed by, the Earthship banking far too late not to take the brunt of the volley. The vessel rumbled as alarms blared.

"Oh, dear!" squeaked Green. "That was not good!"

"Yeah, you might want to try dodging those," grumbled Boone.

"Sage advice, my good man," replied the Professor. "And as much as I appreciate it, I'll have you know piloting a spacecraft is not exactly as easy as it looks!"

"They're coming back around," said Krupp.

"Prepare to engage them," Anna said.

From their stations, Boone and others locked onto the incoming fightercraft, firing the Earthship's weapons as they came within range. The Deathlord Shards scrambled, but not before getting their shots in.

"Shields down to 67%," Scrappy said. "I don't think we can afford to take many more hits like that!"

"We need to get out of here," Boone advised. "We should join up with the fleet over Maxima. At least there we'd have some cover."

"Oh, no," said Krupp. "Sensors show another deployment from that Seed Ship. They've just launched another volley of monoliths!"

On the viewscreen, Anna saw more monoliths fire from the spikes of the large Deathlord vessel. "Move to intercept them!" she ordered, just as the Earthship absorbed more plasma blasts from the Shards swarming around them.

"Look out!" cried Scrappy. "The Deathlord cruisers are now firing at us!"

Green banked the ship away just as a stream of plasma blasts emanated from two large ships not far from them. "Blast it!" cried Boone. "They've moved to put us in range of their point defense arrays! They're trying to cover the deployment of those monoliths!"

"Stay on target!" commanded Anna. "Shoot those monoliths down!"

Green did his best to maneuver through the assault the Deathlords were dishing out, and though the Earthship was able to take out some of the monoliths, others still found their way through the tethers. As she watched the evil rocks make their escape, a sharp pain struck Anna's heart each time a monolith got through to another unsuspecting planet.

"No..." she said in dismay.

The Earthship jostled as it was struck again, causing more alarms to sound. "Shields down to 30%," Scrappy reported. "We can't keep this up, Your Highness!"

"We don't have the firepower to defend all these tethers," said Boone. "We're only one ship, Princess. We can't take on all these Deathlords by ourselves."

Anna frowned. "Then we shall have to enlist some help," she replied. "Open an emergency subspace broadcast to the ships in the Maxima system."

"Emergency broadcast engaged," Krupp said.

"Attention all Imperials in Maxima," Anna said. "This is Princess Glorianna of Legacy Prime. I am on the Earthship inside the Conclave's pocket universe. I know you are fighting hard to protect the planet of Maxima, but there is a far graver threat revealing itself here. A Deathlord Seed Ship is launching monoliths through other tethers leading to star systems throughout the Empire in the hope of infecting all our planets with black rock and the Deathstalkers that come with it. We are trying to intercept these monoliths before they make it through, but we are being overwhelmed. Please, if you can, we need your assistance! Make your way to the pocket universe and help us destroy these ships and these monoliths before they spread their corruption to all corners of our galaxy! The entire Regalus Empire is in peril! I beg of you... heed my call!"

★★★★★

For the first time since the whole ordeal over Maxima had started, Fredreek had been feeling hopeful. Things had started to turn around with the arrival of the Imperial and Redwater fleets. Then, he had learned Wilvelm had survived when they'd received his message about the successful assault on the dark temple on Maxima's surface. Things had been looking as though they had shifted their way, at least until he'd heard Princess Glorianna's broadcast.

Fredreek had known that Seed Ship had been bad news since the moment it had appeared. And now that he knew what its purpose was, he felt guilty for allowing it to enter the tether over Maxima without a fight. Fred had seen first-hand the evil those monoliths brought with them. The thought of them infecting other worlds – possibly even his homeworld of Omnicron – sickened him.

"Call up the entrance to the pocket universe on the viewscreen," he ordered.

Copperhyde did as commanded. Fredreek looked at the image before him. The Deathlords had clustered their biggest ships in front of the portal. Their plasma fire radiated out all around them in a point defense array, making it almost impossible for the starfighters to get close and inflicting extremely heavy damage to any capital ship that got near.

Fredreek scowled at the image as a wild notion crossed his mind. *It's crazy enough that it might work*, he thought. Fredreek accessed his control console and checked the distance from his ship to the portal, doing some quick math in his head while having the bridge's computer run some simulations based on his idea. Sure enough, his plan had some merit to it. Pulling it off, on the other hand, would take a bit of help, and an awful lot of luck.

Fredreek turned to his crew. "Everyone," he said, loudly, "listen up."

All eyes on the bridge turned to him. Fredreek's stomach churned nervously. For some reason, what he was about to say to his crew made him more afraid than what he was actually proposing they do.

"You all heard the Princess tell us what's at stake here," Fredreek said. "You've all seen, first hand, what the Deathlords are capable of. You've seen their raids on your homes and the carnage they've inflicted on the outposts and colonies of this system. You're seeing them turn Maxima into a warzone before your very eyes. Not one of us has gone untouched by their malice. And if something isn't done right now to stop them, many other systems are going to experience their terror first-hand."

Fredreek swallowed hard, before taking a deep breath.

"I have a plan," he said. "It's crazy. And dangerous. And… maybe a little stupid. But I believe it will work. And when it does, this ship, and all on it, will be responsible for holding the line against the Deathlords and stopping them in their tracks. This ship is named *The Shieldbearer* because Lord Skyborn had it designed to defend Maxima. Now, I find it fitting that such a ship will be the shield that guards the whole galaxy… if we all have the strength to wield it."

An eerie silence hung in the air as those on the bridge all absorbed Fredreek's words and what they implied.

"You know what yer askin' of us," said Copperhyde with a scowel.

Fredreek nodded, sadly. "Yeah," he said. "I know."

Copperhyde looked around at the other crewmembers on the bridge, their expressions a mixture of dread and steely resolve. One by one, each met Fredreek's gaze and gave him a nod of consent. Copperhyde fished out his pocket RNGsus[21] device and for the briefest of moments appeared as though he were going to consult it, before grimacing and tossing the tiny contraption away.

"So much fer fortune and glory," muttered Copperhyde. "Guess I'll have ta settle fer being a blasted hero."

A hint of a smile grew on Fredreek's face. "I guess we all will," he said, softly. "Open a channel to *The Colossus*."

"Channel open," replied Copperhyde.

On the viewscreen of the bridge, the images of Amadeus and Starkeeper Drucker appeared. "Yes, Lord Goldstone?" Drucker replied.

"Starkeeper, we need to breach that portal," Fredreek said. "We can't allow the Deathlords to send those monoliths through the tethers."

"Agreed," Drucker said. "But their ships have it blockaded pretty well. It's going to be a fight to push through. We'll take a great number of casualties."

---

21 RNGsus is the god of random number generation. Followers of the Church of RNGsus of Pre-Determined Destiny believe that through random numbers they can be guided toward doing what they need to do to in order to follow the path fate has laid out for them.

"We only need one ship to make it," Fredreek said. "And with your help, I think my ship can be the one to do so."

"What are you proposing, Lord Goldstone?"

"I am moving the *Shieldbearer* into position to make a blind lightspeed jump directly through the portal."

Amadeus's eyes widened. "Fred…" he said, "that's insane."

"It's the only way to make it past that blockade without getting torn to shreds," Fredreek replied. "If we don't make this maneuver now, it's going to be too late. The Princess and the Earthman's ship can't hold out for much longer."

"But a blind jump to lightspeed," said Amadeus. "Fred, if there is anything in your path – even the slightest amount of debris - when you make that acceleration… it could rip right through your ship and tear it apart."

"I'm aware of the risks," Fredreek replied. "But *The Shieldbearer* has an ultanium reinforced hull. If there's any ship here that could survive such a maneuver, it's this one."

Amadeus and Starkeeper Drucker exchanged knowing glances. Amadeus nodded. "What do you need from us?" asked Drucker.

"Clear me a path," Fredreek said. "Get those Deathlord ships out of the way long enough for me to make the jump."

"Leave it to us," Drucker said in response. "Good luck, Lord Goldstone."

"Same to you, Starkeeper. Oh, and Amadeus…"

Amadeus met Fredreek's gaze. Fredreek smiled at him.

"I want you to know, since I doubt we'll get a chance to talk later… I take back every bad thing I ever said about you."

Amadeus smiled, sadly. "And I, you… compatriot."

With that, Amadeus placed his fist over the crest of his Legacy emblazoned upon his chest in a final salute of respect and admiration. Fredreek did the same, before ending the transmission. Then Fredreek, standing straight and tall, turned to the members of the crew on the bridge. "Okay, everybody," he said, loudly. "Time to take the fight to the Deathlords!"

"Aye, aye, Captain!" the entire crew responded.

Fredreek looked over at the empty Captain's chair. When this battle had started, he did not feel worthy of sitting there. But Wil's words before he left echoed in Fred's memory. He'd just asked his entire crew to put their lives on the line, and they'd need a leader to look to if they were going to succeed.

With that, Fredreek Goldstone finally sat down in the Captain's chair of *The Shieldbearer*, officially claiming command of his ship and all upon it. Despite the dire circumstances in which he found himself, Fredreek couldn't help but feel a little happy. After all, he'd finally found his purpose.

He was going to save the galaxy.

# CHAPTER 37

On the bridge of *The Colossus*, Starkeeper Drucker stood at his command station with Amadeus at his side. "Have all starfighters move their engagements away from *The Shieldbearer's* intended trajectory," he ordered. "I want all Redwater vessels luring the Deathlord Dreadnaughts away from there, as well. We need to shift the battle from that area. X.O.!"

"Yes, Starkeeper?" Cobbwell replied.

"Bring us about and angle us toward the Deathlord blockade," Drucker said. "Bring us in at maximum speed. I want engineering at the ready to redirect all power from non-essential systems to the shields. Have repair crews standing by."

"Aye, aye, sir!" Cobbwell said, before going to carry out Drucker's orders.

"Starkeeper," said Amadeus, "may I ask what it is you have planned?"

"A little tactic I once had the unfortunate ordeal of having experienced myself back during the Great Border War[22]," he replied. "It was a strategy Harkon the Black used to interrupt the point defense arrays of coordinated Imperial vessels in order to allow his fleets to approach so they could get within range without being damaged."

"And what is this strategy?"

"We're going to run right into the middle of the Deathlord blockade and overload our shields so that they'll knock back every last one of those blasted ships."

Amadeus blinked at Drucker, as though not understanding what the man had just said.

"We're... what?"

"*The Colossus* has four Mark 7 grade repulsor shield generators," Drucker explained. "If we can push each one to its maximum energy level and then set them to extend the shields out at a fast enough speed, the shields will break down

---

[22] The Great Border War was the most recent war between the Regalus and Visini empires, where the Visini spaceforce, led by Harkon the Black, attempted to conquer Regalus occupied planetary systems.

into a shockwave powerful enough to knock every single one of those Deathlord ships out of the way long enough for Lord Goldstone to complete his maneuver."

"That's incredible!" said Amadeus. "Why isn't this tactic used more often?"

"Aside from the fact that it requires shield generators strong enough to create the shockwave?" Drucker said as he tapped away furiously at his command console in preparation for the maneuver. "The ship that performs it usually never survives."

Amadeus raised an eyebrow. "That… is most certainly a concern."

"Indeed," Drucker said. "Once we overload our shields they won't be back online for some time. It won't take the Deathlord vessels long to correct themselves and begin firing upon us. We're going to be taking quite a few hits."

"Is there anything I can do to assist?" Amadeus asked.

Drucker looked at Amadeus and smiled. "Pray," he replied.

That didn't exactly instill Amadeus with an overwhelming sense of confidence. But before Amadeus had time to think about it any further, Officer Cobbwell approached. "We are in position, Starkeeper," the X.O. said.

"On screen," Drucker ordered.

On the viewscreen of the command station, the Deathlord blockade loomed menacingly before them, guarding the portal as their plasma fire streaked across the blackness of space.

"Time before we reach the edge of their point defenses is two minutes, sir," Cobbwell informed Drucker.

"Bring all but one of the shield generators down and begin redirecting power to them," Drucker commanded. "Focus full power from the remaining generator on forward shields. Maximum thrust. Take us right to the center of that blockade and prep thrusters for emergency burn. We're only going to get one shot at this."

"Aye, aye, sir!" responded Cobbwell.

Amadeus gazed at the Deathlord blockade as it ominously grew larger on the viewscreen. Drucker noted his worried expression. "Regretting your decision to come fight instead of carving out your own Empire?" Drucker asked.

Amadeus shook his head. "Not even a little," he replied.

Drucker smiled at that. "I'll admit, I was as surprised as everyone else when you announced to your system that you would be joining your fleet with mine and taking us to aid Maxima," he said. "Putting the safety of the Empire ahead of your own Legacy, particularly after how you'd been treated, took a great deal of courage. When this is all over, I don't know what the state of affairs will be, but I can tell you this, Lord Evenstar… today, you've accomplished a great honor for your Legacy."

"I would much rather accomplish a great victory for everybody, Starkeeper Drucker," Amadeus replied. "Please see that such a thing is done. It would be so unbecoming to lose my first space battle."

"Fear not, Lord Evenstar," Drucker said. "After dealing with your sister… I have a feeling the Deathlords will be a piece of cake."

At that, both Amadeus and Drucker shared a chuckle before Cobbwell joined them. "We are about to enter the outer range of the Deathlord point defense array," he reported.

"Very well," replied Drucker before patting Amadeus on the shoulder. "Buckle up, Lord Evenstar. It's going to be a bumpy ride."

Amadeus could feel the ship vibrate the moment it crossed the threshold of the Deathlord's defenses. He watched the forward shields of *The Colossus* light up as it absorbed the brunt of the plasma fire, each red bolt blooming into a floral-looking pattern as it met the invisible barrier.

Officer Cobbwell called out the range to their target as they sped closer and closer to the cluster of Deathlord vessels, the intensity of the plasma fire increasing as the distance closed. Suddenly, some of the plasma blasts began to make it through, hitting the hull and causing the ship to rumble from the impacts.

"Forward shields down to 30% and falling," Cobbwell said.

"Steady," said Drucker, as calmly as though he were taking a stroll through the park.

If the Deathlords were concerned about *The Colossus* approaching them, they didn't show it. They held their formation, continuing to focus their fire on the large capital ship as it continued its advance. Soon, more and more plasma blasts were finding their way through the shields. The ship rocked with each impact, alarms starting to blare as it took damage.

"Forward shields at 10%!" said Cobbwell. "Damage being reported on decks nine through twenty."

"Steady," repeated Drucker, his eyes intensely surveying the various readouts at the monitors of his command console. He reached out and tapped a button, opening a voice channel to *The Shieldbearer*. "Lord Goldstone. Are you in position?"

"We are," Fredreek replied.

"Be prepared to execute your maneuver the moment we're clear," Drucker said. "X.O., fire forward plasma batteries."

"Firing, sir!"

*The Colossus* loosed a barrage of plasma fire, focusing on the Deathlord vessels. It caused the Deathlords to break their formation, creating an opening between their cluster.

"They're forming a gap!" Amadeus said.

"They're forming a kill zone," Drucker said. "They think we're on a suicide mission to try and breach the portal. They want us right in the center of them so they can rip us apart."

"And that's exactly where we're headed, isn't it?"

"It is indeed," Drucker said.

Just then, the ship rocked violently as the plasma bolts from the Deathlords began hitting the ship directly.

"Forward shields have failed," Cobbwell reported.

"Stay on course," Drucker ordered. "Bring us right to their center. Have engineering standing by to overload the remaining generators. Status of our armor?"

"Holding for now, sir," Cobbwell replied. "No hull breaches reported, yet. But we can't take this pounding for too much longer."

"Have *The Onslaught* and *The Cobald* ready to cover us," Drucker said. "Prep the maneuvering thrusters for maximum burn."

"Sir, yes, sir!"

Amadeus could feel his hand shaking from the nervous energy raging through his body. How Drucker, let alone all the personnel on the bridge, could remain so calm and collected was beyond him. The ship shook and rocked as its hull absorbed the impacts of the relentless plasma fire, and the closer they got to their destination, the worse it became.

The large Deathlord ships surrounded the lumbering *Colossus* as it raced through their ranks, every plasma battery of the Imperial flagship firing back at the enemy vessels. Streaks of red peppered the void of space, like a deadly blooming rose that raged in every direction. It wasn't long before *The Colossus* was completely enveloped by the enemy ships, all targeting it with focused fury.

Alarms were raging on the bridge as the entire ship jostled from the constant pummeling. Amadeus was glancing at the damage reports that scrolled across the command console faster than anyone could read them. He gripped the rails of the station in white knuckled fear, gaining what little resolve he could from Drucker's cool and collected demeanor as the Starkeeper kept his measured gaze on his readouts.

Then, finally, it was time.

"Shield overload!" Drucker barked. "NOW!"

An electrified bubble formed around *The Colossus* for the briefest of instants before appearing to explode out in all directions, forming a powerful shockwave. The charged explosion of repulsor particles rocketed forth, impacting all the surrounding Deathlord vessels with a powerful collision.

The shields of the Deathlord ships sparkled as they met with the shockwave and the ships were knocked back from their positions, rolling on their axes as they were all thrown for a loop.

Suddenly, the onslaught of plasma fire ceased.

"Emergency burn!" barked Drucker.

"Emergency burn, aye, sir!" responded Cobbwell.

Amadeus felt *The Colossus* rumble, even through its inertial dampeners, as its maneuvering thrusters burned at maximum, moving them out of the trajectory of the portal. As soon as the massive Imperial flagship had cleared the way, Drucker hit a button on his console.

"*Shieldbearer*, this is *Colossus*," Drucker said. "The path is clear."

On the bridge of the *Shieldbearer*, Fredreek and his crew all looked at the main viewscreen in awe.

"Blimey," muttered Copperhyde. "They actually did it. I wouldn't have believed it if I hadn't seen it with me own eyes."

"You ain't seen nothing yet," Fredreek said. "Navigation, are we clear for lightspeed jump?"

"Sensors read the path is clear of debris," said a crewman from the Navigation station. "Lightspeed engines are ready."

Fredreek nodded his head and looked at the looming portal before him.

"Engage," he ordered.

Upon that command, *The Shieldbearer* engaged its lightspeed engines, rocketing across the distance of the battlefield and through the open tether at 99% the speed of light. It returned to normal almost immediately, having exited lightspeed directly beside the Deathlord Seed Ship.

"All plasma batteries – FIRE!!!" cried Fredreek.

*The Shieldbearer* opened fire upon the Deathlord Seed Ship, hitting it with the full force of its port-side plasma batteries while using the rest of its plasma cannons to target the various monoliths the ship was sending out. Starfighters launched from the ship's hangars and immediately began to engage the Deathlord Shards, coming to the aid of the Earthship as it frantically maneuvered through the fray of enemies.

"Deathscream missiles!" ordered Fredreek. "Take out those escorts!"

The last remaining complements of missiles were fired, arcing toward the Deathlord cruisers that were protecting the Seed Ship. The volley caught the ships unaware, busting down their shields and blowing them apart.

★★★★★

Everyone on the bridge of the Earthship cheered at the arrival of the Maxima flagship. Professor Green was especially relieved. "Oh, thank goodness," he muttered. "Dogfighting is most certainly not my expertise…"

"*The Shieldbearer* is hailing us," said Boone from his station.

"Put them through," replied Anna.

Fredreek's face appeared on the Earthship's viewscreen. "Princess," Fredreek said. "Good to see you safe and sound. Well… sound anyway. There are far too many Deathlords around for anyone to be safe at the moment."

"There are, indeed, Lord Goldstone," Anna replied. "But with you now here, I'm hoping to change that."

"What do you need me to do?"

"I must go join the main battle," Anna said. "I'm going to need you to stay here and ensure as few of those monoliths make it out of the pocket universe as possible. The Great Seal of the Conclave has been broken, which means these tethers will close soon. But until they do, every one of those monoliths that makes it out of here represents a planet the Deathlords gain a foothold on."

"I understand," Fredreek said. "We'll hold the line, Princess. If the Deathlords want those planets, they'll have to make it through me, first."

"Thank you, Lord Goldstone," Anna said. "May the Great Observer watch over you."

"And you, as well," Fredreek replied.

Once the transmission ended, Anna turned toward Green. "Professor, pilot us through the Maxima tether," she ordered. "Take us to the heart of the battle."

Professor Green bit his lip, nervously. "As you wish, Your Highness," he replied.

The Earthship maneuvered through the chaos of the Deathlord Seed Ship and *The Shieldbearer's* heated exchange of munitions, emerging through the tether where the Regalus fleets were engaged with the Deathlords. The backdrop of space was peppered with the bright lights of plasma fire as the massive battle raged around the planet.

The faces of all those on the bridge of the Earthship stared at the scene on the viewscreen before them, grimly. "Great Observer," Krupp muttered. "There are so many ships!"

"This is even bigger than any of the battles of the Great Border War," muttered Seqis. "And the Deathlords have far greater numbers than we do."

"Report," said Anna. "What is the fleet's status?"

Boone looked up from his console. "Enemy engagement on all fronts," he replied. "Every ship from Maxima, Redwater, and the 3rd Fleet is engaged with at least two Deathlord Dreadnaughts. Half our drone force has been destroyed. Regalus fightercraft are outnumbered three to one… I'm afraid we're losing this fight, Your Highness."

Anna gazed at the turmoil before her. Hundreds of fightercraft were scattered throughout space, twisting and turning as they engaged in heated dogfights with the Deathlord Shards that sought to overwhelm them. The capital ships were scattered, the Deathlord fleet having effectively isolated them from one another in an effort to cut them off from any support. The Regalus vessels were holding for the time being, but it was obvious to everyone that it was only a matter of time before the Deathlords eradicated all resistance.

"Open a channel for an unsecured ultrawave broadcast," Anna ordered.

"Channel open, Your Highness," Scrappy said from the communications console.

"This is Princess Glorianna of Legacy Prime," Anna said. "I wish to speak to the Deathlord Supreme. Respond."

There was a brief delay before a reply came, which Scrappy put on the Earthship's viewscreen. A collective gasp escaped all who'd come from the Conclave as they saw the image of GorJiro sitting in a command chair, surrounded by Deathlords. The Paragon looked tired and haggard, with an eye missing and half his face scarred.

"Cormac!" Seqis exclaimed in disbelief.

"That is no longer my name," GorJiro replied with a snarl. "My name is Mellegogg, Deathlord Supreme."

"But you died..." said Krupp.

"Death is no obstacle for a Deathlord," GorJiro said.

The members of the Vanguard scowled. "So... you were the traitor in the Conclave this whole time," Seqis said.

GorJiro smirked. "I am a large part of a grand plan, Lord Commander. A plan for which I have toiled a very long time. And now, you see it playing out before you. Nothing can stop it."

"Are you certain of that?" asked Anna.

GorJiro chuckled. "Look before you, Princess," he said. "My fleet is stronger than yours. Your ships have been isolated and will be destroyed as my monoliths infect every planet in your pathetic Empire. Each planet the monoliths land on will spawn a dark temple, and with it, legions of Deathstalkers. You have already lost. My corruption is *unstoppable*."

Anna looked upon GorJiro, the image of Emperor Tarrok gazing upon the smug Nohron Brightshade flashing to her mind. "I will give you this one chance, Deathlord," Anna said. "Pull back your ships and return to whatever dark hole you crawled out of... or you will be destroyed."

GorJiro's one good eye widened at Anna's words before a hearty laugh escaped from him, one which ended in coughing as he grasped at his chest. He gazed at Anna with a wicked smile. "Foolish girl," he said. "I am the greatest living warrior in the galaxy. I have fought in countless conflicts and have always emerged victorious. There is nothing you can say that will intimidate me, nor anything you can do to defeat me."

"You do not believe me to be a threat?" Anna asked.

"No, child. I do not."

Anna gazed at the Deathlord Supreme, her eyes hard and resolute.

"Well, then," she said. "Allow me to make a believer of you."

Anna signaled to Scrappy to end the transmission.

"Your Highness," Seqis asked. "What do you plan to do?"

Anna approached the Earthship's access orb, hesitating only long enough to reply to the Paragon's question. "To show the Deathlords the power of Legacy Prime," she said before closing her eyes and touching the access orb.

Anna could feel the jolt of energy surge through her body as she connected with the Earthship. She could feel the ship's walls, its inner-workings, and most of all, that friendly, familiar presence that existed within it. She became acutely aware of all those the ship carried, as though her consciousness were one with the vessel.

*Please*, she thought. *I ask you now for your help…*

The Earthship responded, asking what it was she needed.

*Jack*, Anna thought. *I need Jack!*

In the Earthship's med bay, Sawbones stood next to Jack as she attempted to heal the corruption which had taken root in him. But as the Paragon Healer used her spiritual energy to attempt to remove the vile affliction, Jack's consciousness drifted to a mental construct where Anna was awaiting him.

"Anna?" said Jack.

Anna smiled. "Jack," she replied. "It's good to see you again."

"Is… is it really you?" Jack asked, his face hopeful.

Anna smiled and nodded. "It is. I freed myself from the slythru's control. But right now, I need your help if we're going to defeat the Deathlords."

"The Deathlords?"

Anna waved her hand and transformed the mental construct into an image of the battle raging around Maxima. Jack looked at the chaotic scene before him with concern. "They're attacking Maxima," Anna informed him. "They're overwhelming our fleets. While we struggle to keep them at bay, they are infecting other planets with their dark monoliths."

"How do we stop them?" Jack asked.

"I have a plan. But I need your help to do it. Will you help me?"

"You know I will," Jack replied, with a cocky smile.

Anna blushed at his response. She knew she could always count on Jack when she needed him most. She held her hands out toward him. "Then let us defeat these Deathlords… together."

Jack took Anna's hands and nodded to her. "Together," he said.

As Anna's and Jack's consciousness connected, on the bridge of the Earthship, all the machinery began to shimmer, as though it were emitting an intense heat. All those on the bridge looked around in alarm.

"What's happening?" asked Krupp, nervously.

"Do not fear," Anna said, a golden aura beginning to appear around her. She opened her eyes, which glowed brightly with golden energy. "It is just the magic of the Ancients at work…"

In the med bay, Jack's eyes opened, as well, glowing with the same golden energy. Sawbones looked at Jack in surprise as the medical table he was on began to transform into a pilot's chair, Jack's hands moving to the two control domes on its arms as the Paragon stumbled back, her healing interrupted by Jack's sudden bout of consciousness.

Mourdock looked over at his friend with concern. "What's… what's going on?" he asked.

"I don't know," grumbled Sawbones, looking around as the walls of the med bay also began to shimmer. "But if I had to guess… something big is about to happen!"

The hull of the Earthship began to glow brightly as it flew through the fray of the battle that raged around it. One by one, the Imperial pilots who were engaged in dogfights looked at their instruments in alarm as their ships stopped responding to them.

Back on the bridge of *The Colossus*, those at their stations began to cry out in confusion. Amadeus and Drucker looked around in concern. "What's going on?" Drucker asked. "Report!"

"Ships systems have stopped responding, Starkeeper!" the ship's pilot replied. "We've lost control!"

"Have the Deathlords somehow hacked our systems?" asked Amadeus.

"Impossible," Drucker replied. "There's no way they could have technology that would allow them to do such a thing!"

Then, all the machinery on *The Colossus's* bridge began to shimmer, as well. Those at their stations backed away, unsure what was going on as the shimmer spread throughout the entire ship.

"Sir!" cried the Weapons Officer. "The ship… all plasma batteries are firing on their own!"

"Engines are engaged," said the Engineering Officer. "*The Colossus* is flying itself!"

"Starkeeper," said the Sensor Technician. "It would appear all Imperial vessels have been taken over and are operating independently of their crews!"

"What could be causing this???" asked Drucker, alarmed.

Amadeus looked at the bridge's viewscreen and smiled, tapping on Drucker's shoulder before pointing at the image of the Earthship as it flew through the battle, glowing brightly, as a golden aura emanated from it.

"Whatever it is," Amadeus said. "I don't think the Deathlords are behind it."

As the Earthship flew, other Imperial fighters began to fall into formation to its rear, breaking off from their engagements with the Deathlord Shards and grouping up behind the Earthship's lead, the other fightercraft giving each vessel cover as they all began to converge.

"It… it looks like all fightercraft are coordinating their attacks, Starkeeper!" reported Cobbwell. "They appear to be breaking away from their individual fights to offer each other cover!"

"How is that possible?" asked Drucker. "Even the most sophisticated A.I. couldn't handle synchronizing that many ships!"

"Sir!" said the Sensor Technician again. "All capital ships are moving to regroup! We're being moved into formation with the other remaining vessels!"

Drucker and Amadeus turned toward the holo-display of the command table, looking at the positions of the various Deathlord and Imperial ships. Drucker's eyes widened as he watched the growing trail of fightercraft weave through the battle like one large monolithic force, attacking both Deathlord Shards and capital ships to give the Imperial vessels cover to regroup.

"Great Observer…" said Drucker as he looked at Amadeus in astonishment. "What could be capable of doing this?"

"There's only one thing I can think of," Amadeus said with a smile. "Legacy Prime."

Anna gazed down at the battle before her from her mental construct as she focused her energy on moving the capital ships to positions where they were needed. Jack flew at the head of all the fightercraft, golden threads from each vessel attached to him as he coordinated all the fighters, attacking the Deathlord ships as needed to give Anna the cover she required.

On the bridge of the lead Deathlord Dreadnaught, GorJiro gazed at the scene before him with growing concern. "What is happening???" he demanded.

"Supreme," the Deathlord Vaxshir, his Lieutenant, replied. "All Imperial ships are converging. They have broken away from our attempts to isolate them."

"How!?" barked GorJiro.

"The Imperial fightercraft," Vaxshir said, pointing out the coordinated force of starfighters that moved as though they were controlled by one mind. "They have successfully engaged our vessels, allowing the Imperial capital ships time to maneuver into formation."

"This is unacceptable!" GorJiro cried. "Destroy the lead vessel! The one all the other fightercraft are following!"

"We are trying, Supreme," Vaxshir said. "But our Shards cannot get close enough…"

GorJiro snarled. "Then call our ships back to us!" he ordered. "Get us in formation, as well! If they want a head-to-head fight… we shall give it to them!"

The terrain of the battlefield began to shift as the Deathlord and Imperial vessels started to draw into their own formations. As Jack piloted all the fightercraft, Anna gazed at the movements of the Deathlord Dreadnaughts.

"The Deathlords are grouping together," Anna said.

"Good," replied Jack. "That'll make this easier. You ready?"

"Whenever you are," Anna said with a smile.

Jack grinned. "Time to show GorJiro what it's like to lose a fight!" he said.

With that, Jack led all the fightercraft in a coordinated assault on the Deathlord capital ships, maneuvering through their point defense arrays and swarming around the vessels like a horde of angry insects, peppering them with plasma fire as all the ships weaved through their ranks. The Deathlord Shards attempted to engage, and though some fightercraft fell to the Deathlord defenses, the monolithic nature of the starfighters all working in unison was too overwhelming for the Deathlord cruisers to handle.

Anna pushed the capital ships forward, focusing all their fire on individual targets as Jack's fightercraft continued to distract and attack the Deathlord fleet. One Deathlord Dreadnaught fell, ripped apart by the Imperial fleet's coordinated efforts, erupting in a bouquet of destruction. Then another Deathlord Dreadnaught fell. Then another.

The Imperial capital ships advanced, working in tandem with one another in their attacks, swiftly cutting down the large Deathlord ships while a few focused on eliminating the Deathlord Shards that attempted to attack them. All the while, the starfighters, led by the Earthship, continued their assault as the long line of fightercraft twisted and maneuvered through the ranks of the capital ships like a mechanical serpent that left nothing but destruction in its wake.

Starkeeper Drucker and Amadeus looked at the battle as it played out over the tactical holographic display table of *The Colossus*. "The Deathlords are out of position," Drucker noted. "They tried to form up, but the starfighters led by the Earthship are hampering their movements…"

"And now that our fleet has returned to formation, the capital ships are able to focus fire on the Deathlord Dreadnaughts while the smaller Imperial frigates focus on point defense to keep the Deathlord Shards from getting close enough to damage us," Amadeus said. "It's brilliant!"

"It is, but the level of coordination required to pull this off would be impossible if it weren't for whatever the Earthship is doing," Drucker said.

"However, now that the fleet has been consolidated… the Deathlord's superior numbers have been marginalized."

"Not that their numbers are going to matter much longer," said Amadeus with a smile. "Starkeeper… we're winning this!"

Drucker smiled at that, as well. "Indeed, Lord Evenstar. It appears as though we are."

More Deathlord vessels erupted, with Shards exploding left and right as the coordinated assault continued. The cruiser GorJiro helmed shook as it was peppered with plasma fire, and a nearby Deathlord ship exploded. GorJiro stared at the carnage on his viewscreen before him in shock and disbelief as his once mighty fleet began to dwindle.

"How is she doing this?" he muttered to himself. "How is this possible???"

"Supreme," Vaxshir said. "Our efforts to resist the Imperial counterattack are failing. If we continue at this rate, our entire fleet will be wiped out."

GorJiro gazed at the fleet positions, his mind racing for any type of solution. But his experience in battle told him that what his Lieutenant said was true. And as the unnerving feeling of failure settled in GorJiro's gut, he grimaced and gave the order he never thought he'd have to give.

"Signal all ships to retreat," he grumbled. "Fall back into hyperspace. We must leave before the Imperials destroy us."

"Right away, Supreme," Vaxshir responded.

GorJiro pulled himself out of his command chair and gazed up at the viewscreen of the bridge as it focused in on the Earthship, which flew with expert maneuvering through the fray of battle, glowing brightly with its golden aura. The Deathlord Supreme hung his head, a dour grimace on his scarred face.

"I am now a believer, Princess," he muttered. "I underestimated you. But I shall not make that same mistake again…"

With that, the Deathlord fleet began to retreat. And Cormac Braen GorJiro finally knew the bitter taste of defeat.

# CHAPTER 38

As the space battle raged outside the Conclave pocket universe, an equally frenzied battle was still being fought between *The Shieldbearer* and the Deathlord Seed Ship as the Imperial vessel continued to target its nemesis and all the monoliths its was launching, flying around the Deathlord vessel as the tethers within the universe began collapsing.

*The Shieldbearer* rocked as its hull continued to take the abuse from the large Deathlord starship, its shields long ago depleted from the relentless assault of the Seed Ship. More and more of the ship's plasma batteries were being destroyed or depleted, and damage reports were coming in faster than Fredreek could keep track of them. But by this point, none of that mattered to him. Fredreek had one mission, and one mission only…

He was going to destroy that Seed Ship, no matter what.

"The Deathlords have adjusted their course!" called out Copperhyde as the Seed Ship turned away from them. "They're headed for the tether back to Maxima!"

"They're making a run for it," growled Fredreek, looking at the Deathlord ship on the bridge's viewscreen. "We can't let them escape."

"Why not?" asked Copperhyde. "We did what we came to do. We stopped them from seeding those monoliths through the tethers! Let's use the last of our engines to get the squick out o' here before this entire space bubble collapses in on us!"

"If that Seed Ship escapes, who knows how many more planets it might be able to infect before it can be stopped!" said Fredreek. "I swear, as long as we still breathe and this ship still stands, we must hold the line against them! And that means stopping them right here! Right now!"

"How do you propose we do that?" asked Copperhyde. "Our plasma batteries are exhausted! Our shields are gone! Our engines are failing! What do we have left to throw at them?"

"The ship," replied Fredreek, his gaze hard and steely. "Set course to intercept. Give me full burn, everything we have left. I mean to ram right through those sons of troggs."

Copperhyde's eyes went wide. "That's madness!" he said.

"The ship's armor will hold against theirs, I'm sure of it."

"The ship may hold, but we won't!" Copperhyde cried. "Inertial dampeners have failed. If we make a burn like that, the lucky ones of us will pass out and the others will be crushed by the gravity it generates. Not to mention, without engines, we won't have a chance of getting out of this!"

Fredreek frowned. "My friend," he said. "You knew from the start there was no chance of getting out of this. Now, take heart. Have courage. And let our final moments count for something."

"So… when ya said you'd make sure I never had to work again, ya were being kinda literal," grumbled Copperhyde.

"What can I say? I'm a man of my word."

Copperhyde frowned. "Ya better be right about this. Be a shame ta die for nothing."

"That it would," agreed Fredreek. "Now everyone buckle up and set course to intercept!"

Fredreek grabbed the safety harness of his seat and buckled himself in, as did those on the bridge who hadn't already done so. Copperhyde scowled as he punched in the coordinates to bring the ship about.

"Initiating bloody suicide plan in three… two… one…" he muttered, before engaging the engines.

*The Shieldbearer* made a sickening lurch forward, pressing those on the bridge flat against their seats as its engines burned, propelling them forward toward their target. The engines disengaged as soon as the ship had its momentum, barreling forward directly at the Deathlord Seed Ship.

Fredreek felt nauseated from the maneuver. He hadn't been prepared for just how unpleasant the sensation of acceleration without the inertial dampeners would be. Some members of the crew had passed out. Luckily, Copperhyde was not one of them.

"Bloody squick, that was awful!" the mercenary muttered.

"How much burn do we have left?" asked Fredreek.

"Enough ta do what ya have planned… I think," Copperhyde replied.

Fredreek nodded as he looked at the viewscreen. *The Shieldbearer* quickly closed in on the Seed Ship. "On my mark, be prepared to engage," Fredreek said.

The Seed Ship began to fire at them, its blasts impacting the ship and causing it to jostle.

"Stay the course!" Fredreek cried.

*The Shieldbearer* continued on its path, the blasts from the Deathlord vessel ravaging its hull. The damage started to permeate the ship as electrical overloads began to occur and personnel stations blew out.

Fredreek gritted his teeth and held on to the arms of his command chair with a white-knuckled grip. *You won't escape me*, he thought as the ship came into range. *You will not pass! I won't allow it!*

"All engines, full thrust!" barked Fredreek. "Ramming speed!"

*The Shieldbearer* lurched forward as its thrusters raged to life one final time. The failing of the inertial dampeners put heavy g-force on all who remained on the bridge. Fredreek could feel the acceleration as if it were a weight on his chest, and his vision blurred. He could hear his crewmates cry out as they, too, bore the brunt of the acceleration.

The Deathlord Seed Ship quickly grew large on the viewscreen and Fredreek was flung forward against his seat harness as the ship violently rocked from the impact. The high-pitched shriek of metal scraping and mangling sounded out, mixed in among the cries of men not lucky enough to have their harnesses hold.

Fredreek could see the Deathlord ship break apart as *The Shieldbearer* crashed through it, pieces of debris fluttering in every direction like dust in the wind as the Seed Ship broke in two, its large halves slowly spiraling away end-over-end. Explosions erupted from the Deathlord ship, powerful enough to rattle *The Shieldbearer* from their shockwaves.

Explosions erupted on the bridge of *The Shieldbearer* as control panels overloaded. Some of the crew were right at their stations when the explosions occurred, hitting them as hard as if they were lying on a grenade. Fires broke out and began filling the cabin with smoke and the artificial gravity finally failed, causing the bodies of Fredreek's fallen comrades to float around the room, as ominous as if they were ghosts cursed to haunt the ship for the rest of eternity.

Fredreek's chest burned. He knew he'd broken his ribs when they'd made impact, having lurched against his chair's harness as hard as he had. He was flirting on the edge of consciousness, but the pain from his chest kept him awake.

The console at his chair, miraculously, was still working. It beeped, displaying sensor data on its flickering screen. Fredreek glanced down at it, then back up at the bridge's viewscreen. Through the haze of the smoke that was quickly filling the room, the large monitor flickered through static as it struggled to live, showing a collection of black monoliths drifting out into space as they fell from the corpse of the Deathlord Seed Ship.

*There were so many…* thought Fredreek. *They could have infested every planet, colony, and outpost in the Empire.*

Fredreek looked over at Copperhyde's station. The mercenary was slumped in his seat, his eyes closed, a large wound on his head from the explosion of his control console. Fredreek frowned.

"It wasn't for nothing," Fredreek said to his fallen companion, sadly. "What we did… it mattered…"

Fredreek looked at the viewscreen as *The Shieldbearer* continued to drift. The readouts at his chair told him the engines were dead, life support was failing, and the power generators were about to go out. Sensor readings reported the tethers were all starting to fail, most of them having already closed. Fredreek looked at the one facing Maxima, the planet framed in the portal, all blue ocean and green continents.

*It's so beautiful…* Fredreek thought.

A strange calm came over him then. A type of resigned feeling that put him at peace with his fate. He glanced down at his control panel, curious. Despite all the odds, the communications array of the ship was still functioning.

*You're a good ship*, he thought. *You've always done what was needed of you. Even now.*

Fredreek tapped the console before him, activating the ultrawave radio and setting it to the correct frequency. Using it would drain the generators faster, but at that point, Fredreek didn't think it mattered much. He opened a channel, hoping against hope he'd be able to reach the person he wanted.

And as luck would have it… he did.

"Wil?" he said. "Wil? You there?"

On the planet of Maxima, Wilvelm Blackfyre was looking out over the wastes surrounding the dark temple he and Grohm had assaulted when he heard his suit's radio crackle. When Fredreek's voice rang out, Wilvelm hit his comm link with surprise.

"Fred? Is that you?" he asked.

He heard Fredreek laugh. "Glad to hear you're still alive, buddy," Fredreek said.

The sound of his best friend's voice made Wilvelm smile. "Yeah, it was touch and go there for a bit but… I made it!"

"Good," replied Fredreek. "Females totally dig war heroes, you know. Would be a shame for you to miss out on all the ladies by being dead."

"Not to mention all the free drinks we'll have coming our way," Wilvelm replied. "There's not a bar in this system that'll charge us! We'll have to come up with some type of impressive title to let everyone know what big shots we are. Something like 'Heroes of Maxima' or the like."

Fredreek chuckled at his friend's suggestion, right before the sadness of the situation exerted his grip upon him. "Yeah… I'm afraid you're going to have to fly solo from now on, buddy," Fredreek said, softly. "I'm… I'm not going to be around to get you into trouble constantly."

As Fredreek's words settled in on him, Wil struggled to come to grips with what his friend was saying. "What are you talking about?" asked Wilvelm.

"I booked a trip right out of the universe," Fredreek said. "And I'm afraid it was one-way."

"That's… no…" replied Wilvelm, struggling to think of what to say. "You can't… you gotta come back!"

Fredreek sighed as he gazed at the viewscreen of *The Shieldbearer*, watching the tether to Maxima slowly shrink, his view of the planet growing ever smaller.

"I wish I could, believe me," he said. "But I'm okay with it. I stopped them, Wil. The Deathlords. I kept them from spreading those blasted monoliths to all corners of the galaxy. I took command of my own ship, stood toe to toe with the bad guys, and I beat them. Me. Can you believe it?"

A cold, helpless feeling gripped Wilvelm's chest as he looked upward, as though he'd be able to see his friend somewhere in the sky. "I… I believe it, buddy," Wilvelm replied. "I always knew you had greatness in you."

"Thanks for believing in me. It always meant a lot," said Fredreek. "Do me a favor, would you? Tell my mom, I love her. And just because I'm going to be gone doesn't mean you're allowed to date my sister. She'll always be off limits, understand?"

"Fred…" said Wilvelm, his voice cracking.

"And when you see my father, tell him…" Fredreek's voice faltered as emotion began to overtake him. "Tell him… I hope I finally made him proud."

"Fred!"

"And thanks for being my friend," Fredreek continued as the tether he gazed at shrank smaller and smaller. "You were better than a brother to me, Wil. Better than I deserved. I hope you have a good life. I truly do. Next time you're at Club Cristo… have a drink for me, would ya?"

Wilvelm looked up at the sky, his vision blurry from the tears streaking down his face.

"FRED!" he cried to the heavens.

"I love you, man," Fredreek Goldstone said.

And then, there was only static.

One by one, the Deathlord Dreadnaughts began to escape through hyperspace windows, withdrawing from the battle. When this happened, the crews on all the surviving starships began to cheer.

Anna looked at the enemy vessels retreat from her mental construct as Jack tried his best to get in parting shots with his fightercraft, taking out one more Dreadnaught before it had the chance to run away. "They're retreating!" Jack said. "Should we follow them?"

Anna frowned. "The fleet is in no condition to do so," she said. "Neither are we…"

Indeed, the level of concentration it had required to salvage the battle had drained Anna, and she could tell Jack was beginning to waiver, as well. As the final Deathlord vessel escaped into hyperspace, Anna finally released Jack, along with control of all the ships.

Her consciousness snapped back into her body as her aura disappeared and the bridge of the Earthship returned to normal. She briefly waivered on her feet before collapsing to the floor.

"PRINCESS!" exclaimed Seqis as he and the other Vanguard rushed to her side.

Anna felt weak and drained. She tasted something coppery on her lips and reached up to find her nose was bleeding. Krupp and everyone else on the bridge of the Earthship looked at the viewscreen in awe. "We… we won the battle!" Krupp said in disbelief.

"That was… amazing…" Boone said, at a loss for words.

"Princess, are you okay?" Seqis asked as he tended to Anna.

Anna wiped the blood from her nose. "I'm fine, Lord Commander," she replied. "Just… please, help me to my feet."

Seqis and Lugard assisted in lifting Anna up. She was dizzy for a spell before she was able to regain her composure. She turned to find all those on the bridge looking at her in wide-eyed wonder. Commander Gunner was the first to step forward, looking down at her with a measure of genuine respect she'd never seen anyone give her before.

Gunner placed his fist over his heart and then knelt before her.

"Hail, Legacy Prime," he said.

All the other Royal Guard followed suit, followed by the Initiates from the Conclave. Even Agent Boone and Professor Green knelt, each one saying the same thing:

"Hail, Legacy Prime."

Anna gazed upon those who knelt before her, a sense of pride and accomplishment welling within her heart. She'd never felt worthy before. She'd never felt as though she were deserving of her position. However, in that moment, she realized she'd earned this acclaim. Despite the recognition from those around her, though, Anna's mind was focused on one thing and one thing only…

Jack.

In the med bay, Jack's eyes returned to normal. He also suffered from a nosebleed as he fell unconscious again, his body going limp as the command chair transformed back into a medical bed. Mourdock looked at his friend in concern. "Jack!" he cried as he tried to get off the medical table he was on to move to Jack's side. "JACK!"

Sawbones stepped up to Mourdock and prevented him from moving further. "Daggit, man!" Sawbones grumbled. "You're in no condition to be moving!"

Mourdock was too weak to resist. He didn't know what had happened, just that his friend needed help. "Please," Mourdock said. "Help him…"

"I'll get to him as soon as ya stop trying to kill yourself," Sawbones replied.

Just then, the door to the medical bay slid open. Mourdock looked over to see Anna standing in the doorway, surrounded by the Royal Vanguard. One look at her and all the pain he was feeling seemed to drain away. His heart leapt. The woman in that doorway was not the same Anna he'd been trying so desperately to heal at the Conclave for what seemed like a lifetime. The Anna he saw, right then, was the real one. His true love had finally returned!

"Anna…" Mourdock said.

For the briefest of moments, Anna did not move. Within the span of a few heartbeats, Mourdock witnessed her look from Jack, to him, and back. When her gaze settled on the Earthman, Mourdock saw the worried look on her face. All her focus was on Jack. Though Mourdock was just as badly injured, he may as well not even have existed.

Anna rushed to Jack's side, cupping his face in her hands.

"Jack!" she said. "Jack? Speak to me!"

Sawbones moved to Jack's side and placed her hands on Jack's chest.

"Will he be okay?" Anna asked.

"He's been through a lot," Sawbones replied. "But he's a fighter."

"Please, help him," Anna pleaded.

"Aye, Princess," Sawbones said. "I'll do my best."

As Anna gazed at Jack in concern, she did not notice the stare she was receiving from Mourdock. It was a look filled with sorrow, confusion, and pain. He'd suffered grievous injury, but none of his wounds hurt as much as what he was feeling right then. Though he was alive, in that moment, when he witnessed the love of his life chose another over him…

The best part of Mourdock Skyborn died.

# Chapter 39

Scallywag stood on the bridge of *The Megavolt*, his men all standing by as its crew brought the ship back out of Eionmeer's atmosphere.

"The portal above the planet has collapsed, Commander," a sensor technician reported. "All our soldiers have returned from the surface of Eionmeer, no casualties reported. The Deathlord threat has been neutralized."

"Good work, everyone," Rintin replied from his command console. "Excellent job."

"Job ain't over yet," Scallywag said. "You lot got any missiles left?"

"Yes, plenty," Rintin responded.

"Good. Target that bloody temple. Blow that blasted thing ta pieces."

Rintin nodded to his ordinance officers. "Temple has been targeted," responded a technician. "Missile strike to launch in three, two, one…"

Scallywag watched the bridge's viewscreen as missiles arced from *The Megavolt* and raced down to the surface, impacting the dark temple there. Mighty explosions bloomed from the multiple impacts, and the once imposing structure collapsed in on itself and crumbled into the remains of the destroyed colony.

Scallywag smiled and looked to Rintin, giving the man an approving nod. "There," he said. "*Now* tha job be over."

"And seeing as we have done our duty and assisted the Regals in fending off this attack, what is to happen now?" asked Rintin.

"I'll tell you what happens now, you blasted fool," said Eisenwolf, glaring at his Executive Officer. "He kills us all, confiscates the ship, and turns it over to the Regals in exchange for a pardon and a reward. Thus is his nature."

Rintin and the rest of the crew looked around nervously at Scallywag's men, who still had their weapons at the ready. Scallywag chuckled and shook his head in consternation before he let out a loud whistle, signaling to his men. "Danny-boy, unseal tha doors," Scallywag ordered. "One-Eye, Kapplan, ReeRee, enact them exit protocols we discussed earlier. Betran, take yer men back to tha ship. Glimmer and her people will stay with me."

As everyone followed their orders, Scallywag approached Eisenwolf, looking the man up and down as though he were a stain of filth on his boot.

"Ya remember last time we spoke, we said next time we met, this thing between you and me was gonna end?" asked Scallywag.

Eisenwolf stood upright. "I take it you mean to kill me now?" he said, stiffly.

"No, I mean ta end this thing," Scallywag said. "I'm sorry, Eisenwolf."

Eisenwolf raised a curious eyebrow. "Sorry?" he said.

"Yeah," Scallywag replied. "I'm sorry about what happened to yer father. He was a good man. A fine commander, too."

Eisenwolf glared at Scallywag with a mixture of confusion and disbelief. "What… what are you saying?" he asked.

"I'm apologizin' to ya," Scallywag replied. "What I did… well, I imagine it can't ever be forgiven. But you weren't tha only one who lost people they loved ta Harkon's rebellion. Me? I lost everything. So I know that kind o' pain doesn't just go away. I ain't askin' ya to forgive me. I ain't askin' ya to like me. But what I am askin' is that ya let go of that pain you've been carryin' with ya all these years and accept my apology."

Scallywag held out his hand. Eisenwolf looked down at it and sneered before spitting in Scallywag's face.

"That is what I think of your *apology*, Red," he growled.

"Well, can't say I didn't try," Scallywag muttered as he wiped the saliva from his face. "Take care, Wolfie. If'n I ever see ya again, trust me when I say you're gonna be the one who's sorry."

Scallywag turned and signaled for Glimmer and her crew to leave with him. He nodded toward Rintin as he made his way for the exit.

"Ship's all yours again, mate," he said.

Eisenwolf and Rintin exchanged curious glances. "You mean… you're just returning my ship back to me?" Eisenwolf asked, suspiciously.

"Oy, what am I gonna do with a ship this big?" Scallywag replied. "Besides, we did what we set out ta do. We helped save tha day. Congrats, Wolfie. If ya play yer cards right, ya might even be able ta get a medal fer this."

"And you're not going to kill us all?" asked Eisenwolf. "You're not going to live up to your reputation?"

Scallywag stopped and sighed. "I know it may be difficult fer ya ta believe, Wolfie… but I ain't tha scoundrel ya think I am. I *want* ta be a better man, and I'm tryin' really hard ta make that a reality. So no, I ain't gonna take yer ship. I ain't gonna murder the lot o' ya. I'm just gonna gather me people and be on me merry way. Scallywag the Red is turnin' over a new leaf. So until next time – cheers!"

Scallywag and Glimmer's crew all turned to leave. Eisenwolf stepped forward, snarling like a mad dog. "So that's it?" he cried. "You just think you get to walk away after all you've done?"

"Yep," Scallywag said.

"This isn't over, traitor!" Eisenwolf called after him. "No matter how far you run or how well you hide, I'll be coming for you! I'll find you! And I won't rest until you, and everyone you care about is dead! Your crew, your friends, and that little Blue harlot will all pay for your crimes! Do you hear me? I'LL NEVER STOP HUNTING YOU UNTIL MY DYING BREATH!!!"

Scallywag stopped and frowned. He looked over his shoulder at Eisenwolf. "Ya sure you don't wanna change yer mind about that?" he asked.

"Never," said Eisenwolf resolutely, his eyes hard and cold.

At that, Scallywag shrugged. "Alright, then…"

Scallywag quickly drew his blaster pistol from his holster and fired it at Eisenwolf, hitting the Visini square between the eyes. Eisenwolf's hateful gaze turned to one of abject surprise, right before his body fell limply to the floor of the bridge. All the other Visini crewmen looked at their dead Captain in shock before their attention turned back to Scallywag, who still had the smoking plasma pistol in his hand.

"Well, back to tha old leaf," Scallywag muttered, bitterly. "Anyone else wanna swear undying vengeance? You?"

Scallywag turned his pistol on Rintin.

"No," Rintin replied, quickly.

"You?" Scallywag asked as he aimed his pistol at Chief Engineer Grunseer.

"Nope, I'm good," Grunseer replied.

"Right," said Scallywag as he holstered his gun. "Carry on, then."

Scallywag proceeded to lead Glimmer and her men off the bridge, with Gage and Smash taking up the rear to ensure none of the Visinis followed them. "Did you really have to kill him?" Glimmer asked as they walked.

"Prolly not," Scallywag admitted. "But I find that when someone swears ta devote his life ta yer ultimate destruction, it tends ta be a good idea ta get rid o' them before they can do any real damage."

"I'm not saying he didn't deserve it," Glimmer said. "But all that talk about you being a better man… I believe it's possible, Scally."

"It obviously ain't."

"I don't believe that," Glimmer insisted. "You've changed. I've seen it. The old Scallywag, the one I knew from all those years ago… he'd have never done what you did here. I may not have believed it if I hadn't seen it with my own eyes, but… you're a good man. Dare I say it… you're a hero."

As Scallywag approached the airlock leading to *The Reaver*, he smiled at Glimmer sadly. "I appreciate the kind words, lass, but ya should know by now…" he said, just as Tarkrane, Kapplan, and ReeRee appeared with weapons drawn. "Never trust a Red."

Glimmer and her crew looked at the pirates in surprise as they proceeded to disarm them.

"Scally, what the blazes are you doing?" Glimmer asked.

"Cuttin' ya loose," Scallywag said as he and his men backed away into the airlock. "Soon as we're clear, the robot is gonna teleport ya onto a confiscated freighter in one o' *The Megavolt's* hangar bays. It ain't tha prize *The Reaver* is, but it'll get ya back home. Figure tha Maxima corvette and the shipping contracts will make up fer any inconvenience. And in case yer worried about any charges from the Visini Empire, I had Dan scrub tha ship's systems of any record o' ya. So ya won't have ta worry about any official reprisals, as long as ya blame everythin' on me, which shouldn't be too hard."

"And what about you?" Glimmer asked. "You're just going to go back to pirating after all this?"

"I aim ta retire from the hero business," said Scallywag. "Never suited me much anyway. It be time ta get back ta bein' up ta no good. That means if ya come with me, you'll eventually either betray me or join me. And frankly, I'd rather yer skin stay blue and beautiful, lass. So I'm afraid this here be good-bye."

Glimmer's jaw set as she glared at Scallywag, her sapphire eyes hard but glassy. "Blast you... you right red scoundrel."

Scallywag looked at Glimmer as though that were the nicest thing anyone had ever said to him. His lips curled into a sly, loving smirk. "I love you, too, by the way," he said softly, right before hitting the door panel.

The airlock door hissed shut between them. But through the round porthole window, their gazes still locked. Scallywag could see a single, glistening tear running down Glimmer's cheek, her eyes begging him not to go.

In response, Scallywag simply winked at her. He then turned and walked away, finally allowing himself to shed his own tear as he did so.

Scallywag marched onto the bridge of *The Reaver*. Betran and the other Yellows from Eionmeer were there. Scallywag looked at them. "Well, lads, a deal's a deal," he said. "You lot did your part. Now I owe ya a ride out o' tha system. Where might I drop ya?"

Betran frowned. "We have no House," he said. "No family. No home. We got nowhere to go."

Scallywag nodded. "We all been there before," he said, before turning to the rest of his crew. "Whaddya think, lads? This sorry bunch o' Yellows pirate material?"

"Their aim be as bad as their attitudes," Kapplan muttered.

"They're ugly and smell like Bova Spunk," chimed in ReeRee.

"Not a single one o' them is of any use," Tarkrane declared.

Betran and the other Visinis shifted uncomfortably while Scallywag smiled. "Relax, ya bunch o' browners," he said. "That means 'yes'. Welcome ta tha crew."

"Yo-HO!" the pirates all cheered, before patting the Visinis on the back and welcoming them.

"Does… does this mean we'll go red, too?" Betran asked Scallywag.

"Maybe," Scallywag replied. "But if'n ya wanna keep yer skin the way it is, I'm givin' ya permission ta refuse any order that might make it otherwise."

"Why would you do something like that?"

"I may not be able ta be a better man," Scallywag replied. "But that don't mean you lot gotta be tha same way. Part of not owing an allegiance ta any House means ya can be whatever ya want ta be. And I'll be browned if I'm gonna stand in the way o' that."

Betran smiled and nodded. "How is it you're nobler than that Blue Eisenwolf ever was?" he asked.

"I ain't noble, mate," Scallywag said, patting Betran on the shoulder. "I'm just the captain o' this crew. And that means I gotta take care o' ya. *All* o' ya. Best I can."

"*Here-here!*" the crew all cheered as Tarkrane approached Scallywag.

"And it be good ta have ya back, Cap'n!" Tarkrane said. "What are yer orders?"

"Right," replied Scallywag. "First off, I want everyone ta greet our new First Mate… Dan."

Dan gave Scallywag a curious look as the rest of the crew gave him a round of applause, complete with a good deal of hooting and hollering.

"Dan! Dan! Dan!" the crew cheered.

"Oh, my," Dan replied. "Master Scallywag, sir… though I am honored by the appointment, I am not sure I am worthy of such a position."

"Oy, rustbucket, ya saved our collective bums more than a few times," Scallywag said. "Not only did ya stage a massive prison break, ya helped us storm a Visini capital ship. If'n that ain't First Mate material, I dunno what is."

Dan looked around at the motley crew that surrounded him on the bridge and all of them nodded in agreement. "Well, then, I shall be honored to be your First Mate and a member of your crew," Dan finally replied.

The crew all cheered. Scallywag smiled. "Great," Scallywag said. "Now get to tha navigation console and set us a course fer deep Visini space. Somewhere near a hyperspace trade lane, if'n ya please."

"Right away, sir," Dan acknowledged.

"Does this mean what I think it means, Cap'n?" Tarkrane asked.

"Aye," Scallywag said as he sat in the commander's chair of *The Reaver*. Scallywag ran his hands over the familiar leather armrests and basked in the energy of the bridge and its crew. He'd been away so long, he'd nearly forgotten the feeling. The feeling of being in command. The feeling of being home. He'd spent too much time fighting his own nature, trying to change his skin. If he'd learned anything in his time away, it was that there was a reason his skin was crimson. He was a Red, through and through. And he'd finally accepted that was who he was, and all he'd ever be.

He glanced up at the viewscreen of his ship, looking at the vast emptiness of space before him and all the possibilities it held. He leaned back in his chair and smiled to himself.

"Time ta remind tha universe… why they should fear *The Reaver*," he said.

# CHAPTER 40

Images of the destruction on Omnicron, Maxima, and Eionmeer all faded into each other – showing the full extent of the destruction and loss of life from the Deathlord attack while somber and heart-wrenching music played.

"Once more, tragedy has stru-stru-struck," came Less Flatfoot's voice as the images played out on the screen. "In the decade since the first arrival of the Deathlords, never have we seen such a brazen and large-scale assault on the Empire. Millions of lives were lost in the attack from Deathlord Supreme Verrutus, and the Battle of Maxima was barely won. Even though we de-de-defeated the vile Deathlords, it is difficult to say this was a victory…"

The images shifted to those of planets with dark temples and Deathstalkers roaming the land. "Enough Deathlord monoliths made land-land-landfall to infect eight other worlds, where even now, efforts are underway to contain the corruption from the dark temples which have sprung up there, putting entire planets at ri-ri-risk…"

The images then faded to those of the Deathlord Dreadnaught fleet from the Battle of Maxima. "The Deathlord ar-ar-armada which attacked Maxima is still at large and could strike again at any time…"

Images of people running from corrupted figures then appeared. "And worst of all, the Paragons we once relied upon to protect us have now fal-fal-fallen in league with our enemy, with reports coming in from around the galaxy of those known as *The Corrupted* using their extraordinary powers to attack innocents and ad-ad-advance the Deathlords' cause."

The scenes of chaos and destruction eventually faded to the serious visage of Less Flatfoot, the holonet's premier digital talk show host.

"The fall of the Conclave, the Battle of Maxima, and the attack of Deathlord Supreme Verrutus and his Secret Army have impacted all cor-cor-corners of the Empire. Not a single one of us has gone untouched by what some are calling the worst-worst-worst attack since the destruction of Regalus Prime. But despite all this tragedy, hope still shines…"

The image faded to one of a busy starship construction platform in orbit around a planet, and photographs of people signing up at military recruitment centers.

"Rebuilding efforts are already underway, with the en-en-entire galaxy coming together in the call to fight back against the Deathlords!"

The images then transitioned to pictures of people being treated in medical centers.

"Those who had been in-in-infected by the slythru creatures are being freed from Deathlord control and getting the help they need to return to normal, thanks to the power of Legacy Prime!"

Then, a picture of Anna came upon the screen.

"But most of all, Princess Glorianna has returned to us! Free from Deathlord control! Already she has-has-has reinstituted the Evenstar Legacy and enacted the defensive measure to take the fight to the Deathlords! And rumor has it the Prin-Prin-Princess is so committed to protecting the galaxy, she has called an emergency summit with galactic leaders to discuss the best course for her Empire and her people going forward."

The image faded back to Less Flatfoot as he gazed into the camera.

"What the future holds for us all is uncertain. But one-one-one thing remains absolutely clear. Now, more than ever, we all must stand united against those who seek to destroy us. Remember what Earthman Jack Finnegan, Hero of the Empire, once said: 'If we are going to survive, we need to stand together and stay strong'. In times-times-times like these, truer words have never been spoken."

Less Flatfoot's serious visage suddenly changed back to his bright, light-hearted, usual self.

"And that's it for our show tonight! Apologies to Tam Lameon, we ran out of time. Tune in tomorrow night when we answer the ev-ev-ever-important question: 'boxers, briefs, or creative use of dental floss?' with Oikazoid fashion expert Gaga Ganoosh! Be here for that, bad Voresh poetry, and more! See you then."

Amadeus turned off the visual display he'd been watching and checked the time on his datapad. He was running a bit late, but he wasn't too concerned. He had enough experience in these matters to know that such important meetings rarely started exactly when they were scheduled to.

Amadeus left his quarters and began making his way through the corridors of Port Longshore, which he'd offered to the Princess as a rallying point for the Imperial Government in the wake of Omnicron's destruction. The conference room, which had been designated for the meeting of the Empire's leadership, was large, its walls appropriately decorated with flags of the Regalus Empire, Legacy Prime, and the Evenstar Legacy. A long elderwood table, big enough to seat all those in attendance, sat at its center.

And those in attendance were numerous. All four surviving members of the Directory were present. Their paranoia over Uleeg Casgor's control had prompted them each to leave Omnicron well before the attack, which had probably saved their lives. Other heads of important Legacies were in attendance, as were the remaining Starkeepers.

Starkeepers Killian, Bennett, and Benedict were all in attendance, as was Starkeeper Drucker who nodded to Amadeus when he entered. General Rustwave was present, along with other high-level military advisors. The only major figure not there was Starkeeper Cohaagen, who had unfortunately perished during Verrutus's attack.

Those assembled did not have long to wait before Princess Glorianna arrived, escorted by all four members of the Royal Vanguard – including the Tygarian Rionknidis, with freshly regrown hands thanks to the Paragon healer Sawbones MacCrusty. The Princess was clad in a resplendent crimson and gold gown, her hair done up with a holographic crown on her forehead.

This was not the same Anna that Amadeus was accustomed to seeing. She did not appear meek, demure, or insecure in the slightest. This Princess appeared harder and more confident in herself. Something about her brilliant blue eyes struck Amadeus as powerful as she gazed at all those who had assembled around the table.

"Gentlemen," Anna said. "Please, be seated."

All in the room followed suit as Anna took her high-backed chair at the head of the long conference table.

"Thank you all for coming today," Anna started. "Obviously, there is a great deal that needs to be discussed, so I will not drag this out with too much ceremony. I would just like to begin by thanking Lord Evenstar for making his planet and his space station available to us so that we can sort out the important matters we need to."

Amadeus acknowledged the Princess. "Legacy Evenstar is here to serve, Your Highness," he said.

"And we are grateful for your service," Anna replied. "Without you and your fleet, it is very likely none of us would be here right now."

Those gathered at the table then offered Amadeus applause in acknowledgement of his actions.

"And without you, Your Highness, it is very likely my fleet would have made little difference," Amadeus stated.

"You are too kind, Lord Evenstar. Now that our pleasantries are out of the way, let us get on to business, shall we?"

"The first order of business should be to establish a new capital," said Director Zirsee. "The sooner we can get back the continuity of government, the better."

"Agreed," seconded Director Jamerones. "We must get the Empire working once more. Re-establishing centralized control is of paramount importance."

"No," Anna said.

All eyes in the room turned to her. "Your Highness?" questioned Zirsee.

"There will be no new capital," Anna stated.

The looks on the faces of the men in the room communicated that they were both troubled and suspicious of Anna and her statement.

"Your Highness," Jamerones began. "Are we to assume that you do not wish to reestablish the governing body of the Empire?"

"I do not wish to continue doing that which isn't working," Anna replied. "Since the destruction of Regalus Prime, the Imperial government has been mired in bureaucracy, which has merely slowed the decay of our Empire rather than protect it. We've been clinging to a peacetime form of government, one which has proven ineffective in our current circumstances."

"Then what are you proposing, Your Highness?" Director Ridsco asked.

Anna took a deep breath. "My protector Paragon Shepherd's last words to me were 'Be Strong'. I believe that mantra extends not only to me, but to the Empire, as well. In order to be strong, we must shed that which makes us weak. Having a capital for a centralized government is too big of a target. Twice now the Deathlords have destroyed the seat of power within our Empire, and twice it has crippled us. I will no longer have it."

"But without a capital, how are we to manage our territories?" asked Director Phenberg.

"We won't," Anna replied. "We will decentralize control of the Empire and grant full power to the Legacies to manage their planetary systems as they see fit."

This sent a murmur of concern through many at the table.

"This will include both the building of Legacy starfleets and the recruitment of Legacy-controlled militia," Anna continued. "We will grant all systems access to the Ancient technology we use for the creation of our military and will allow the Legacies to provide for the safety of their own systems from this point forward, with the greater Imperial fleets dispatched to support them as needed."

"Your Highness," piped up Starkeeper Killian. "Allowing the Legacies to build standing militaries will only give those systems who wish to break off from the Empire the ability to do so without fear of reprisal."

"If we cannot protect them, then they are right to secede from us, Starkeeper Killian," Anna replied. "The damage from the Deathlord invasion is far reaching, and we have no right to exert control over our people at the expense of their safety. There is a reason why so many systems are flirting with independence, and it is because they do not feel the Empire can protect them. If we are to quell this unrest, it must be done by proving to our member worlds that we are deserving of their fealty, as opposed to being entitled to it."

"I can see the wisdom of this strategy," Amadeus spoke up. "Granting more power to the Legacies will allow them to better respond to the unique situations that could crop up in their systems. Giving them the power not only to protect themselves but also to fight the enemy as they see fit, without the micromanagement of the Empire, will ensure the Deathlords will not advance their invasion so easily. And allowing the planetary systems to act as independent cells will make it harder for any Deathlord gain to affect the other systems so adversely. By removing high value targets, we will make it harder for the Deathlords to hurt us."

"At the expense of possibly hurting ourselves beyond repair," grumbled Jamerones. "I am not saying the Princess's proposal doesn't make sense from a certain viewpoint. But if it were to be enacted, what would be the role of the Empire at large? What is to stop our member worlds from breaking off by the droves and fracturing our grand society beyond recovery?"

"The role of the Empire will be a simple one, Director," Anna said. "Our role will be victory. Our role will be to defeat the Deathlord scourge at all costs and to protect not just our people, but *all* people from their evil. The Empire will be the beacon of light in the darkness that it was always meant to be. We will be strong for those who are weak. We will be brave for those who are scared. And we will fight for those who are unable to fight for themselves. We will no longer simply play defense. We must take the fight to our enemies. It is time we went on the offensive, and I propose we redesign our Empire to do exactly that."

The room was quiet as Anna's words settled in on the men who were there. Although many appeared to agree with her, there were just as many who appeared skeptical.

"I agree with this new direction the Princess proposes," stated Starkeeper Drucker. "Without the burden of having to protect so much territory, our fleets will be better able to engage the enemy. I, for one, do believe it is high time we took the fight to them for a change."

Many of the military experts at the table nodded in agreement.

"If this is indeed to be the new mission of the Empire, Your Highness, might I ask what shape you see the Imperial government taking?" Phenberg asked.

"We must be able to react to circumstances as they arise, without being bogged down in bureaucracy," Anna replied. "Let the Legacies deal with the day-to-day management of their people. This means we would no longer need either the Junior or the Elder councils of government. In their stead, I propose we form a High Council, staffed with representatives from each quadrant of Imperial Space, along with military experts whose sole purpose will be to formulate strategies to defeat our enemy. The representatives would coordinate resource allocation while the military experts would coordinate with the Starkeepers to enact our missions."

"I would also propose we allow the Legacies of each quadrant direct access to their appropriate Starkeeper fleets," suggested Amadeus. "By granting open lines of communication to the Empire's military, we ensure that Legacies can receive help as quickly as possible."

"Agreed," said Anna. "In addition to this, I propose the Imperial Government base itself within its own starfleet. By staying mobile, we make it harder for the Deathlords to target us, while ensuring that we can provide support to any of the four Starkeeper fleets as needed."

"We can repurpose the Omnicron Fleet for such a task," offered Starkeeper Bennett. "It will take time to rebuild it, but having a fifth, roving fleet that can be dispatched to reinforce our armadas as needed will certainly strengthen our position."

"I am coming to appreciate this new direction the Princess is offering," said Zersee. "A streamlined council would certainly cut through much of the bothersome red tape our Empire has previously been mired in. But I must ask… will the Directory be in charge of this council?"

"Indeed, I was wondering that myself," Ridsco chimed in. "What role do you see the Directory playing in this new style of government you are proposing, Your Highness?"

"None, whatsoever," Anna said, flatly.

The frowns on the faces of the four Directors in response to the Princess's reply were apparent to everyone in the room. "Need I remind the Princess that Emperor Nameer himself developed the Directory to ensure—" Director Phenberg began.

"I do not need reminding of what Emperor Nameer developed, Director," interrupted Anna. "Need I remind you that Nameer did not develop his system of government until he had won the war with his brother and was transitioning into peacetime rule?"

"So you would simply toss away democratic rule because we are at war?" Jamerones protested. "What of the Imperial Charter? Are we to rip that up, as well?"

"I know this is difficult for the four of you, especially after what transpired with Director Casgor," Anna replied. "The disbanding of the Directory is not a reflection on you men or your abilities. In fact, I shall welcome you all to sit on the High Council as advisors. But in these trying times, we must have decisive leadership – something which cannot be accomplished through our old form of government."

Anna's offer of membership on the High Council seemed to assuage the objections of the Directors, but essentially being 'demoted' didn't appear to please them all that much, either.

"Am I to take it that Your Highness plans to be the one who rules over this High Council?" asked Ridsco.

"No," Anna replied. "I will continue my role as a Constitutional Monarch, under the laws of our Empire, until such time as I am old enough to claim my title of Empress. Thus, I will simply oversee, rather than run, the High Council I am proposing."

"I believe that to be a wise choice, Your Highness," said Jamerones.

"I will, however, exert my right as a member of Legacy Prime to appoint the person I believe to be best suited to run the High Council, as well as to dismiss any members of the council who I believe are not doing their jobs."

The men in the room all nodded in agreement, though some of them obviously did so grudgingly. "If I may be so bold, Your Highness," ventured Ridsco. "Do you have someone in mind for this leadership position?"

"I do," Anna replied, before turning her head and looking directly at Amadeus. "I propose Lord Amadeus Evenstar for the position of Grand Premier of the Empire and chief executive of the High Council."

Amadeus's eyes went wide at the words of the Princess. He no doubt looked as shocked as the rest of those at the meeting.

"*Him?*" cried Zersee, in disbelief.

"Do you have a problem with a direct descendent of Emperor Nameer and the ruler of one of the most important Legacies in our Empire accepting such a position, Director?" Anna asked, calmly.

"Your Highness," interjected Ridsco. "Not to disparage Lord Evenstar, but he doesn't have the kind of experience necessary to take on such an important role. He's barely even had any time as the head of his Legacy."

"Allow me to put bluntly what my esteemed colleagues are trying to be polite about," grumbled Jamerones. "I have suits older than your choice for Grand Premier, Your Highness. Lord Evenstar is nothing more than a boy!"

"A boy who outmaneuvered a Starkeeper, confiscated an Imperial fleet, and mounted a defense against our enemy that protected the Empire from a full-scale invasion," replied Anna. "Frankly, I wish we had more 'boys' like him. Let alone men."

Amadeus couldn't help but smile. He was glad Anna had said it, so he didn't have to.

"Lord Eudox Evenstar was a great man and a great leader," Anna continued. "He was a man who zealously advocated for the kind of strategy we are now going to pursue. I see his best qualities on display in his son, and I have no doubt that despite his age, Lord Amadeus Evenstar is more than up to the task of leading our Empire in this trying time. He not only has my respect but my full faith and trust in his abilities not only to bring the fight to our enemies but also to win those fights."

"I agree with the Princess's assessment," chimed in Starkeeper Drucker. "Lord Evenstar could have opted to use the fleet he'd captured for his own personal gain. Instead, he made the decision to use it to protect the Empire, even as the Empire was persecuting him. He displayed bravery and level-headedness during the battle of Maxima. He has earned my respect as a leader, despite his age. I would encourage my fellow Starkeepers to support the Princess in her nomination of Lord Evenstar as the Grand Premier of this new Imperial Government."

Nods of approval signaled agreement from Drucker's peers. Anna turned and looked at Amadeus once again. "Lord Evenstar," Anna said, "do you accept my offer?"

Amadeus nodded. "It would be my honor to serve you and the Empire, Princess."

"The honor is ours," Anna replied. "Congratulations, Grand Premier Evenstar. I look forward to seeing you lead us to a decisive victory against the Deathlords."

"I promise not to disappoint, Your Highness."

"Then I will now leave the Empire in your hands," Anna said while getting to her feet, the rest of the room following suit. "I trust you'll figure out how to proceed with the restructuring of the government and our new strategy?"

Amadeus bowed in acknowledgement. "It will be my top priority, Your Highness."

Anna nodded in approval before looking at the others in the room. "Gentlemen," she said, "thank you for your time, council, and service."

With that, Anna turned and left the room, followed closely by the Royal Vanguard. Once she had left, all eyes turned toward Amadeus. They were harsh eyes. Eyes filled with judgement, expectation, and doubt. Amadeus knew he'd have to prove himself. He reminded himself to keep in mind that everyone in the room was on the same side. The challenge would be reminding everyone else of that fact.

"Compatriots," Amadeus said, "it's already been a long day and there is much to process after this meeting. I suggest we adjourn for now and start fresh tomorrow. I would like to meet with each of you, one on one, to hear your thoughts and ideas on how to proceed and then to work together to figure out the details of our strategy going forward."

Those in the room all nodded in agreement, even if it were begrudgingly. It might not have been the start Amadeus wanted for his new role in the Empire, but he decided that for now, it would do.

Amadeus's mind was already racing with the different details of how he was going to tackle this new challenge of running the government as he made his way back to his quarters. He was so lost in thought that he barely noticed Kimlee sitting in the living area. She was drinking a glass of expensive nectarplum wine, a dour look on her face. She'd been in a foul mood ever since he'd had Surior escort her off *The Colossus* after declaring he was taking the fleet they'd captured to aid Maxima.

"Kimlee!" Amadeus said when he saw her.

"Amadeus," she muttered, swishing the wine in her glass around. "How was your meeting with the Princess?"

"You won't believe it," Amadeus said, excitedly, as he told his sister the news. Kimlee listened quietly as Amadeus shared with her the details of the meeting and the new position that had been bestowed upon him. When he was done, Kimlee was silent, staring absently into her glass of wine. "Well?" Amadeus finally asked. "Don't you think this is great news?"

"What's great about it?" muttered Kimlee.

Amadeus looked at his sister, confused by her reaction. "What do you mean?" he said. "The Princess is actually instituting some real change! We're finally doing what father always wanted, and best yet, she's entrusting me to carry it out!"

"And this excites you?" Kimlee said with a scowl. "Being Glorianna's puppet?"

Kimlee's response genuinely took Amadeus aback. "What are you talking about?"

Without warning, Kimlee threw her glass of wine at Amadeus. Amadeus recoiled as the glass sped by him before hitting the ground and shattering, the dark liquid it held spilling all over. Before he knew it, Kimlee was on her feet and approaching him, a look of contempt on her face.

"I'm talking about being cowed by an Empire that nearly *destroyed* us!" Kimlee sneered. "I'm talking about living life on your knees instead of being the masters of our own fate! You dear, sweet fool. Don't you see what you've done? For once, we had the upper hand! This could have been the start of something! We could have finally broken free and forged our own Empire! Instead, you gave away the keys to the kingdom. You threw it all away to save our enemies, and now you're submitting to them once more."

Amadeus looked at his sister, sternly. "A kingdom built on sand is doomed to crumble," he responded. "Father believed in the Regalus Empire. He'd want us to defend it."

"Don't presume to know what our father wanted!" Kimlee said, bitterly. "This Empire you think he believed in so much is what *killed* him! It's the very same Empire that is rotting from the inside out, bloated with ineffective bureaucrats, sycophants, and fools – all led by a child who was never meant to sit the throne! *We* should be ruling this galaxy, Amadeus! The Evenstars! Just like how Nameer saved it from the incompetence of his brother, it is up to *us* to save it from the incompetence of Legacy Prime."

"Nameer never wanted power, Kimlee," Amadeus replied as calmly as he could. "He believed in the Empire, as well. He did not break away. Instead he took steps to fix it. He gave up most of his power so that the tyranny his brother forced upon the galaxy would never happen again."

"And look where that's gotten us," Kimlee snapped back. "Ruled by an army of politicians that bicker among themselves instead of doing what it takes to defeat our enemy. Do you honestly think anything is going to change? The bottom-feeders will do all they can to cling to their power, especially in this new government of yours. In times of war, what is needed is a strong hand and decisive action. We had an opportunity to seize the power that is rightfully ours. To do what father truly wanted and finally take the fight to our enemy!"

"And that's exactly what we did."

"You're making the mistake of thinking the Deathlords are our only enemies," Kimlee replied. "Can you truly put our fate in the hands of the Princess once more, knowing she tried to destroy us?"

"She was under the influence of the Deathlords—"

"And who's to say she won't be influenced by them again?" shot back Kimlee. "And if not her, someone else, perhaps? I for one will not stand for that. I will never again allow Legacy Evenstar to be at the mercy of another."

"You have no choice," Amadeus said, sternly. "I am the Lord of this Legacy and I determine the direction of it. Legacy Evenstar will be the pillar that stands strong and holds this Empire together. We will lead through example, as we always have. I will not be responsible for tearing this Empire apart because of my own ambition. Jack was right when he said we need to stay united. Without the support of the entire Empire, we will never be able to defeat the Deathlords."

"Jack is as blind and foolish as you are," Kimlee replied. "You were never meant to rule, Amadeus. *I* was. And I can now see what needs to be done."

"Just so we're clear," Amadeus said as Kimlee moved to leave. "This isn't about the Empire, is it? This is about you and your ambitions."

Kimlee stopped at the door, turning her head ever so slightly to address her brother for the last time.

"Not my ambitions. My destiny. My destiny is to rule, little brother. And that is exactly what I intend to do. With or without you."

And with that, Kimlee Evenstar left.

Kimlee gazed at Port Longshore as *The Handsome Wreckage* moved away from it. The planet of Redwater loomed largely behind the space station. She gazed at it, as though it were for the last time.

Devorian regarded Kimlee for a long moment as he sat at the ship's piloting controls. Though many in Verrutus's secret army had been freed, his slythru remained in control. But without the voice of its master to guide it, Devorian's slythru no longer knew what its purpose was. In absence of that, it chose to continue to follow the one being its old master felt was in alignment with his grand plan. Namely, Kimlee Evenstar.

"Are you sure about this, my Lady?" Devorian asked. "With your brother's new position, you could make a legitimate claim to the leadership of your Legacy—"

"No," Kimlee said, flatly. "I do not want it. I do not want anything handed to me any longer. I wish to forge my own path. I wish to conquer, as I was meant to, and create my own Legacy. One that no one will have the power to take away. Not my brother, not the Princess, and certainly not the Empire."

Devorian frowned. "It will be hard, my Lady," he said. "Without the wealth or influence of your Legacy behind you, convincing others to follow you will be a most difficult task."

"No more difficult than overtaking a Starkeeper fleet, I imagine. We did the impossible once, Mr. Westlake. We can do it again."

Devorian smiled. "Far be it from me to ever underestimate you, my Lady," he said. "So, tell me… how shall we start building your new empire?"

Kimlee was quiet for a long moment as she stared out into the void of space, contemplating her next move. "You once spoke to me of friends of yours. The ones you called 'The Liberators'. Do you believe they would still assist me?"

"Possibly," Devorian replied. "I know all the right people to introduce you to, and I have no doubt that you would be able to charm them into backing your plans."

Kimlee smiled. "Good," she said. "If I plan to lead a revolution… I am going to need a great deal of revolutionaries."

# CHAPTER 41

The persistent beep of the medical monitors woke Banjax, the Endolan's eyes fluttering open. His vision was hazy at first, eventually coming into focus on Heckubus Moriarty who loomed over him. The robot's ocular orbs regarded him with interest, dilating as Banjax regained consciousness.

"Ah!" said Heckubus. "You've finally awoken! Excellent. How do you feel?"

Truth be told, Banjax felt horrible. His entire body – what was left of it, anyway – ached, and the medication he was on made everything seem hazy. But despite his sorry state, he was cognizant enough to know Heckubus Moriarty was the last thing he wanted to see.

"You…" grumbled Banjax, his throat dry and his voice hoarse.

"Yes, 'tis I! Heckubus Moriarty! Evil genius extraordinaire and now *undisputed* supervillain of the galaxy!"

"Get… out…"

"I see you are still upset that I outsmarted you. Don't be. I outsmart everybody."

"You… blew me up…" grunted Banjax.

Heckubus chuckled. "I did, didn't I?" he said, gleefully. "In my defense, you were trying to kill me at the time. But that is neither here nor there. The doctors expect you to make a full recovery, albeit with the help of a few more cybernetic upgrades. But, hey, who *needs* full use of their lungs, kidneys, or liver to function, anyway, eh?"

Banjax moaned.

"You may be wondering what it is I'm doing here, since I obviously have no vested interest in your well-being or current prospect of vitality," Heckubus continued, completely oblivious to Banjax's misery. "Tell me, do you remember Princess Glorianna coming by to visit you earlier?"

Banjax's memory was hazy. It felt like he'd been living in a dream for weeks. But he did have some recollection of a blonde-haired girl visiting him, her voice reaching into the darkness and showing him a way out of his mental prison.

"I… yes…" he replied.

"It would seem the Princess has acquired a unique skill due to her ordeal with Verrutus," Heckubus said. "Apparently, she is able to make psychic connections to those who are infected with slythru and assist them in freeing themselves from the creature's influence. I asked her specifically to help you do just such a thing. Now I must ask… can you feel the influence of your slythru, still?"

Banjax blinked his eyes for a moment. "It's… it's still there…"

"Yes, it would appear that once the slythru successfully melds with a host it can never be removed," Heckubus explained. "However, the Princess's recent actions should have broken the control it had over you. So next I'll inquire… are you, Banjax, now back in control of yourself?"

Banjax hesitated briefly before answering. "Yeah… I think so…"

"Excellent!" exclaimed Heckubus, twiddling his fingers. "I'm going to require those with slythru connections such as yourself as we continue to hunt down those of the Secret Army who are still under Deathlord control."

"Hunt down?" growled Banjax. "You're asking me… to work for you… again?"

"Well, I'm not so much *asking* as I am *telling* you you're going to be working for me, again," Heckubus said. "Once a Henchman, always a Henchman, I like to say! And to be frank, you're far too competent to allow you to go off on your own when I can utilize your skills for my own selfish and brilliant ends."

"Slag… off…" sneered Banjax.

"Yes, yes, yes, you have every right to be reticent considering how thoroughly I spanked you while you were under the slythru's influence," Heckubus said, brushing off Banjax's animosity. "But look at it this way – as my Henchman, you will be upgraded to the most high-tech cybernetics available. Not only will I optimize your internal replacements to make you faster, stronger, and better – I will have the most state-of-the art bionic arm installed on you, as well as make available the latest weaponry, gadgets, and starcraft at my disposal. You shall want for nothing, Henchman! How's that sound?"

"Slag… off…"

"Excellent! It's a deal then," Heckubus stated. "Your bounty hunting skills shall be most useful for my future plans. I am glad we could come to this mutually beneficial agreement, which mostly benefits me!"

Banjax scowled. "I didn't agree—"

"Shhhhhh!" said Heckubus, placing his metallic finger over Banjax's lips, mushing them together into silence. "No need to thank me. You'll find I can be a benevolent overlord for those who succeed in the tasks I give them. And I have no doubt you will accomplish everything I require of you once you are back on your feet. But until such time, rest, Henchman. Regain your strength. You shall need it."

Heckubus then increased Banjax's pain medication on the monitoring equipment, sending the injured bounty hunter back off to slumber before he could object any further. When Heckubus exited the room into *The Collosus's* medical bay, Agent Boone and Hunchy were both waiting for him.

"So, what did he say?" asked Boone.

"Nothing of consequence," Heckubus said, dismissively. "Nevertheless, he's onboard."

"Oh, happy day!" Hunchy said as he hopped up and down. "New friend for Hunchy to make! Hunchy excited to be part of old Master's team! Does old Master know how Ruthless Cyborg Bounty Hunter like his coffee?"

"No, I do not!" snapped Heckubus. "I do not concern myself with such trivial details, you twit! That is what I have you for. Ask him when he wakes up again. And be sure to have the doctors make arrangements for all his necessary upgrades! I wish to have Banjax up and operational as soon as possible."

"Oh, yes, old Master! Hunchy will do so right away!"

As Hunchy scurried off to carry out his orders, Boone looked at Heckubus. "So… robot…" he started to say.

Heckubus held up a metallic finger to signal Boone to stop talking. "Uh, uh, uh!" he said. "I would prefer you now refer to me by my official title: Heckubus Moriarty – *Destroyer of Worlds!* Mwuahahahahaha!"

Boone frowned. "You didn't destroy any worlds," he muttered.

"I did so."

"You destroyed a massive glob of slime."

"It was the size of a planet!" Heckubus argued.

"It didn't have any land mass, atmosphere, moons, or any other thing that would classify it as a planet."

"Bah!" cried Heckubus, with a wave of his hand. "It had a population in the millions stretching out across the galaxy!"

"Technically, it was one guy," said Boone. "You are the destroyer of *one* guy."

Heckubus narrowed his ocular orbs at Boone. "Can't you just let me have this one?"

"No."

"Ugh! Fine!" lamented Heckubus. "Keep your sycophantic flattery to yourself! It makes no matter. All that matters is Verrutus is no more, and soon what remains of his Secret Army will be exposed and dealt with."

Heckubus began walking out of the medical bay with Boone at his side. Hunchy quickly caught up with them, hobbling along a short distance away from his two masters. "Verrutus may be gone, but the Deathlord threat is greater than ever," said Boone. "This Mellegogg guy is still at large with his Deathlord fleet and according to the case files Chief Alabaster was personally overseeing, there are supposedly two more Supremes out there that we know nothing about."

"Indeed. Moredread and Ashtoroth," said Heckubus. "No doubt they think they are more evil than I as well! Which, of course, means I shall have to mercilessly destroy them, too."

"Hard to destroy someone we have zero intel on," said Boone. "At least with Mellegogg, we can research all we have about his true identity. These other two are completely unknown to us."

"Fear not, Henchman! I excel at dealing with things that I know nothing about!"

"Obviously," said Boone with just a hint of sarcasm. "But it's the I.I.A.'s job to uncover these types of mysteries. Without Chief Alabaster around anymore to guide the ship, we're now at a disadvantage, at least until a new Chief is appointed. And even then we can only hope whomever the bureaucrats appoint is half as good as Alabaster was."

"I would not concern myself with such matters just yet, Henchman," Heckubus said. "The priority for the I.I.A. now is to build up its intelligence network so that these mysteries are quickly solved. And as it just so happens, I already have put into place things which shall help your pathetic agency to do precisely that."

"Have you now?" asked Boone, suspiciously. "And what exactly have you put into place?"

"Intelligence offices on every capital ship in the fleet, for starters," said Heckubus as he approached a door down the corridor. "It is important that the I.I.A. remains decentralized, mobile, and networked to ensure intelligence is quickly disseminated as it is gathered. As you are about to see, the office I've set up here on *The Colossus* is part of this brilliant new infrastructure I have developed."

"Uh, huh," said Boone, cautiously. "And what else have you put in place?"

"Various other things you needn't concern your puny little mind with," replied Heckubus, dismissively. "But one very important factor in the intelligence equation is going to be that of personal intelligence."

"Personal intelligence?"

"Yes, intelligence from individuals scattered throughout the galaxy."

"And how are we supposed to gather intelligence on that kind of scale?"

"You are about to see, Henchman. You are about to see…"

Boone and Hunchy then followed Heckubus into a room off the corridor, its door opening to reveal a comfortable anteroom with couches, tables, and even a quaint little bar. The Wild Ones were all in attendance there, lounging comfortably while playing a game of *Loquir*[23]. They quickly stood up when the others entered and nodded in acknowledgement toward the robot as he approached.

"Boss," said Buchignani.

"Ah! Minions! I see you are all here. Excellent!" stated Huckubus. "At least, I see there are four of you here. Where is your invisible companion? I should like to finally meet him."

"Sorry, boss," drawled Buchignani. "Aneel already took his share and left."

"Left?" said Heckubus, confused. "Where did he go?"

"Ee-yo. He went back home to Teeneque," said Buff.

"Teeneque?"

"The invisible world where all the invisible people live," said Kamm.

---

[23] Loquir is a popular card game within the Regalus Empire, which somewhat resembles poker.

Heckubus gave the group a confused look.

"Yeah, we don't really understand it either," muttered Siv. "But, you know, that's Aneel."

"Don't worry. He'll be back," said Buchignani. "Once he's run out of money, he always comes back."

"Ee-yo! Aneel is *terrible* with money!"

Though Heckubus was tempted to ask what an invisible deaf mute could possibly spend all his money on, he thought better of it when he realized he honestly didn't care. "Agent #00B2EE$^n$ has filled me in on your heroics during the siege of Megabase Cygnus," Heckubus said. "And as impressive as your skills were in avoiding an assassination, escaping from a prison, and assaulting a fortified control room all to save an entire planet – it is even more impressive that you were so selfish as to demand a ridiculously high reward before agreeing to do so. Bravo, minions! You have earned what little respect I have for inferior beings such as yourselves."

"Thank y'kindly," said Buchignani.

"And in addition to my respect, you have also earned an obscene amount of digicredits, not only for your actions on Megabase Cygnus, but also for your service to me while I misled Verrutus and his Secret Army." Heckubus nodded toward Hunchy, who approached each Wild One and distributed digicredit cards to them. "As promised, here is the rest of your payment, in full. I'd say try not to spend it all in one place, but I'm not one to engage in such futile endeavors."

When Hunchy was finished handing out the digicredit cards, the Wild Ones each slid them through their datapads to check their balances. Buchignani let out a low whistle. "Dancin' Dixie," Buchignani muttered. "If I'd known savin' the Empire paid so well, I'd have become a patriot long ago."

"Indeed, you middling lot of jackanapes[24] have proven to be far more reliable than I ever could have anticipated," Heckubus said as he paced among the ranks of the outlaws. "As far as minions go, you all served as a passable group with slightly more intelligence than I am used to dealing with. You should feel proud of yourselves! Well… maybe not proud… let's say you should not feel disappointed in yourselves! Yes, that's better."

The Wild Ones all eyed each other. "Uh… thanks?" replied Kamm.

---

[24] Jackanapes are extremely large, ape-like animals, known for being one of the dumbest species in existence.

"And if you are impressed by your current account balances, I can assure you, there is plenty more where that came from, if you are interested. Which I assume you all are."

"Ain't gonna turn down a meal ticket when I see one," Buchignani replied. "What ya got in mind, boss?"

"Though you all are indeed filthy outlaw scum, you are my kind of filthy outlaw scum," Heckubus said. "Which means you can easily network with other, filthier, kinds of scum. I want you to go back out into the galaxy and keep me appraised of what is going on out there in the underworld. I want to know of every scheme, scam, and heist that is being planned. I want to know who the big and little players are. In short, I want to know everything you can possibly tell me. For this service, you shall be well compensated. How does that sound?"

"Ee-yo. You're asking us to be… spies?" Buff asked.

"I'm sorry, do you have a moral objection to ratting out your fellow lowlifes in exchange for boatloads of easy digicredits?" asked Heckubus.

The group all looked at their account balances again.

"Nope," each one said in turn.

"Didn't think so," Heckubus said. "Now, off with you! Earn your pay, you imbeciles! And if you run into any other imbeciles who may be useful, send them my way so that I may recruit them, as well. You'll, of course, receive a finder's fee when you do. Now out of my sight!"

Before he left, Buchignani tipped his hat toward Heckubus. "Pleasure doin' business with ya, tin man," he drawled before turning and heading out of the room.

When the group was all gone, Boone looked at Heckubus and crossed his arms judgmentally. "Was it my imagination, or did I just see you set the stage for an underworld criminal conspiracy using Imperial funds?" he asked.

"That's one way to look at it," replied Heckubus as he left the anteroom and entered an office that had been set up with a dazzling array of visual displays, each monitor showcasing images from many different planets. "Another way is that you just saw the start of a new intelligence network designed to replace that which the Empire lost with the destruction of Bob. The underworld criminal element is exposed to a great number of dealings meant to be kept hidden from the universe at large, and through them, we may very well be able to get insight into future Deathlord schemes."

Boone raised an eyebrow. "You expect me to believe that you're suddenly interested in fighting the Deathlords and defending the Empire?" he asked, skeptically.

"I can assure you, I do so out of completely selfish and evil reasons, and not with a shred of compassion, loyalty, or sense of duty."

Boone frowned. "Well, better the devil you know, I guess…" he muttered. "If Alabaster were here, he'd demand you keep him in the loop with what you find."

"But, alas, Alabaster is not here any longer," Heckubus said. "So I suppose you will have to do."

"Me?" asked Boone.

"Oh, yes, I neglected to mention – you're the new public head of Imperial Intelligence."

Boone's eyes went wide. "What?"

"I've already cleared it with the Princess, who has agreed to put your name forth for confirmation to this new High Council she's set up," Heckubus said. "You have proven yourself a trustworthy and resourceful henchman. I'm now only *slightly* disappointed that I didn't get to kill you on our first meeting, which is quite a step up as far as you're concerned, if I do say so myself. I'm going to need someone like you close by to carry out my orders in the conflicts that are to come."

"Someone like… what a minute…" said Boone, trying to comprehend what the robot was telling him. "If I'm the new head of Imperial Intelligence, I'm the one in charge."

"You're the new *public* head of the organization," said Heckubus. "But the actual inner workings of the I.I.A. will be handled by someone far more suited for them."

Boone frowned as Heckubus's words began to settle in on him. "Oh, no," he muttered. "You're not saying…"

"That's right, Henchman!" exclaimed Heckubus as he sat behind the large intelligence desk in the new command center and steepled his fingers, diabolically. "Meet the *real* Chief of Imperial Intelligence. Mwuahahahaha!"

# CHAPTER 42

Wilvelm looked out to the horizon where Capitol City used to stand. It had been completely destroyed, along with half of the planet of Omnicron, during Verrutus's attack. Countless lives had been lost on the surface, and what had once been considered one of the centers of modern civilization had all but been reduced to rubble.

The Goldstone Legacy had just started the rebuilding efforts, as evidenced by the many construction devices hard at work in the hazy distance as the skeletons of buildings were once more being erected. But Omnicron would never be the same, and everyone left on the planet knew it.

*It's such a nice day*, Wilvelm thought as he looked up at the sunny blue sky and felt a cool breeze waft over him. *At least we can be thankful for that much.*

Wilvelm turned to look at the collection of people at the reception. It was filled with the elite of the Omnicron system and the few surviving planetary leaders who had been spared from Verrutus's carnage. There was food and drink aplenty, with everyone hob-knobbing and talking about the various issues that faced the planet now that the Imperial capital would no longer be occupying it. But it was still a somber occasion. There was hardly anyone in the system who hadn't experienced tragedy on a scale never thought possible.

The Shrine of Hydrion stood tall and proud at the head of the gardens where the reception was being held. It was a tower built of sandstone in the tradition of the Ancients, meant to commemorate Emperor Hydrion's victory over Edvard the Undying and his Twilight Empire. It was the closest thing Omnicron had to an Ancient Temple, and Wilvelm felt it was a fitting location for the memorial.

As he made his way through the din of the event toward the shrine, he saw Lady Casemere and her daughter Farrah – Fredreek's mother and sister – exit the structure walking arm in arm. Lady Casemere's eyes were noticeably red and puffy from crying. She had seemed the picture of poise before the unveiling ceremony had started but had since broken down many times. Farrah looked beautiful as ever, with her lightly freckled face and her mother's flowing red hair. Her beauty was a thing to behold even when it was marred by sadness.

"My Lady," Wilvelm said to Lady Casemere as he approached her. "I'm sorry I did not get a chance to express my condolences before the ceremony. It has been hard getting planetside without the Capitol City spaceport and the lack of portgate access. I fear I almost didn't make it in time."

"It's okay, my dear Wilvelm," Lady Casemere said as she embraced him tightly. "Your presence is always welcome."

"I wish… I wish I could have saved him…" Wilvelm said, starting to get choked up himself at the memory of his friend.

"There was nothing you could have done," Lady Casemere replied, herself tearing up once more. "You were both in such a... terrible situation."

Lady Casemere gave Wilvelm a kiss on the cheek, then wiped her eyes with a handkerchief and continued toward the reception. Farrah stayed behind and gave Wilvelm a hug, as well. "Thank you for coming," she said.

"Of course," Wilvelm replied. "I wouldn't have missed it for anything."

Farrah pulled away and looked toward her mother. "It's been so hard on her," she said. "She loved Fredreek so much. Your message that he spoke of us before the end… it's been a great comfort to her to know his family was in his thoughts."

Wilvelm nodded, sadly. "And how are you holding up?" he asked.

"Not very well," Farrah replied, "but better than my father. He has been putting on a brave show for the public, but he's hurting worse than any of us. He blames himself for putting Fredreek in that position in the first place."

"He shouldn't," Wilvelm said. "There was no way of knowing what the Deathlords had planned. And to be honest, if Fredreek hadn't been there… we may not have been able to stop them."

Farrah nodded. "I think father knows that. But it doesn't make it any easier."

"No, I suppose it doesn't."

Farrah smiled sadly and gave Wilvelm a kiss on the cheek. "Fred loved you like a brother, you know," she said.

"And I, him," Wilvelm replied. "Since he died… I feel like there's a part of me that's missing."

Farrah gave him an understanding pat on the hand. "That's a feeling my family knows all too well," she said. "But the best any of us can do is to carry on and honor his memory."

Wilvelm nodded. "If you'll excuse me, Farrah, I wish to go pay my respects," he said.

"Of course," she replied, sending him off with another embrace.

Wilvelm entered the shrine, the tall, domed rotunda housing a statue of Emperor Hydrion, the walls inscribed with his most famous quotes. Wilvelm made his way past that to the addition which had been constructed for the new monument. The branching chamber was still filled with candles and the smell of incense from the ceremony, which had served as both a funeral and a dedication.

The rounded chamber seemed tall and cavernous. Etched into the walls were the names of all who gave their lives in the battle of Maxima. A holographic collage of the star system rotated high above, giving the chamber an otherworldly feel.

Against the wall was the large golden statue of Fredreek, standing tall and proud with the animetal[25] representations of *The Shieldbearer* and other Maxima ships slowly rotating around the base of his likeness. On the statue's foundation was a bronze plaque which read: *Lord Fredreek Goldstone, The Shieldbearer That Defended The Universe.*

Urion Goldstone stood, alone and silent, gazing up at the likeness of his only son. He had been very composed as he had given the eulogy earlier. Though Wil wanted to pay his respects to his fallen friend, he hesitated to interrupt Urion's time with the monument. As he turned to go, he heard Urion's voice speak out.

"Is that you, Wil?" he asked.

Wilvelm turned back toward him. "It is, my Lord," he replied.

"Come," Urion said. "Pay your respects."

Wilvelm made his way to Urion's side. The man's face looked serene as he gazed upon the statue. But Wilvelm could see the pain in his eyes.

"The Paragon Engineers did a good job with his likeness, don't you think?" he said.

"They did, indeed, my Lord," Wilvelm agreed.

Urion nodded. "Do you think… do you think Fredreek would have liked it?" he asked.

---

[25] Animetal is a metallic compound that can be made to move and change shape when electricity is run through it.

"Of course," Wilvelm replied. "He'd have liked it more if it had been a statue of him drinking with many beautiful women attending to him, but I'm sure he'd have been proud of it."

Urion had to laugh at that. "Yes, indeed," he muttered. "I used to get so upset hearing about his partying and antics. The one thing I wanted, more than anything, was for him to distinguish himself and bring honor to our Legacy..."

Wilvelm nodded. "That's exactly what he did," Wil replied.

"Turns out, I didn't want that at all..." Urion said, his chin quivering. "What I really want is... *I want my son back!*"

Tears formed in Urion's eyes, staining his cheeks as they ran down his face, his carefully maintained façade cracking as emotion overtook him. Wilvelm lowered his head, giving Urion a chance to compose himself. Urion wiped the tears away with the back of his hand and took a deep breath before speaking once more.

"The Deathlords have made a terrible error," he stated. "I don't care if it bankrupts my Legacy. The Goldstones will devote every resource at our disposal to defeating these monsters. Ships, troops, technology… I don't care what it takes. The time for politics is over. If my son's sacrifice is to mean anything, then I must take it to heart and commit to doing what he did. Fight. And by the Great Observer, that's exactly what I'll do."

Urion turned and looked Wilvelm in his eyes.

"I understand you've petitioned Legacy Prime for a Blackfyre-led Alpha Force contingent that will be specifically trained to assault these dark temples of the Deathlords," he said.

Wilvelm nodded. "The surviving members of Alpha Force MX017 and I are the only soldiers with actual experience assaulting the temples," Wil replied. "I feel that if we're going to fight this invasion, we're going to need teams dedicated to destroying these monstrosities."

Urion nodded. "I have no doubt Mourdock Skyborn will support you in this, seeing as how you are a member of the Rim Legacies," he said. "But I'll ensure you have my full support, as well. Anything you need, Wil – anything at all – you come to me, and I'll make sure you get it."

"Anything, sir?" Wilvelm asked.

"If it's within my power to grant you, you'll have it."

"Does that include a Rognok?" Wil asked.

★★★★★

Wilvelm emerged from the shuttlecraft onto the hangar deck of *The Colossus* where he was greeted by an administrative android and a Stonehooligan Paragon by the name of Sawbones MacCrusty. Though Urion Goldstone's support had cleared away many of the legal issues surrounding Wilvelm's request, there was still one big hurdle to overcome – and that was getting the Rognok to agree to join him.

"Paragon MacCrusty?" Wilvelm said as he approached.

"Aye," the Stonehooligan responded. "You must be Lord Blackfyre?"

"You can call me Wil," he said. "How fares your patient?"

"As well as can be expected, I suppose," Sawbones replied as she began to lead Wilvelm deeper into the ship. "I consider myself a good doctor, but even I'm flummoxed by Rognok physiology. Since there is no documentation on such things, I've been having to wing it when it comes to the blasted thing's treatment."

"Is he healing?"

"Best I can tell," Sawbones replied. "Frankly, I'm amazed he's still alive. Our medical scans showed so much trauma, it was a wonder the Rognok could even move at all."

"Considering what I've seen Grohm is capable of, I guess I shouldn't be surprised," Wilvelm said. "If I didn't know any better, I'd say he can't be killed."

"Oh, the Rognok can be killed, believe that," Sawbones said. "From what I can gather, each time the Rognok suffers a trauma, his body heals and adapts to lessen the impact of that trauma should it be repeated. It makes him tougher and stronger, for sure, but it also serves to weaken his central nervous system."

"What does that mean?" Wil asked.

"It means, the stronger a Rognok gets, the shorter his lifespan becomes," Sawbones explained. "Eventually, the stress put on the Rognok's body becomes too great, and it begins to shut down. I'll have to do more testing and analysis, but so far, that's what I've been able to gather."

That bit of information troubled Wilvelm. "But... can he still fight?" he asked. "How long until it becomes too much for him?"

"Daggit, man, I'm a doctor, not a fortune teller," Sawbones grumbled. "As I said before, there's a lot we don't know about Rognoks. But one thing we do know is that they love to fight, so I'm guessin' Grohm will do so whether it's bad for him or not. From what I've seen, he's already one of the toughest Rognok's we know about, which means he's been through some bouts of massive trauma already. Hard to say what's going to be the thing that pushes him to his breakin' point. But my guess is that if he can survive a fall from orbit and go on to fight his way through an army of Deathstalkers, then he might still have quite a bit of time left in him. But don't quote me on that."

Sawbones led Wilvelm to the ship's medical bay and then to the recovery room, which housed Grohm.

"He's in there," Sawbones said with a nod of her head toward the door. "Not sure what you plan to say to him. He ain't exactly chatty."

"He doesn't need to talk to me. He just needs to listen," Wilvelm replied.

Wilvelm entered the room. Its sterile white walls and floor made the room feel brighter than it was. Two medical beds had been pushed together to accommodate Grohm, but they didn't look used. The massive alien instead was sitting cross-legged in the corner with his eyes closed. His skin looked almost back to normal, appearing coarse and grey once more – though it was still marred with blackened and discolored patches.

"Hello, Grohm," Wilvelm said.

Grohm opened his red and black eyes and peered at Wilvelm.

"You remember me?" Wilvelm asked. "We, uh… fought a bunch of Deathlords together."

Grohm snorted. Wilvelm wasn't sure if that meant Grohm did remember or not, but he chose to assume he did. Wil grabbed a nearby stool and pulled it up toward Grohm, sitting on it and looking the Rognok in the eyes.

"I don't know if anyone has updated you on what's been happening since our assault of the dark temple down on Maxima, but it's not very good. Though we were able to route the Deathlord strike fleet and prevent them from seeding all their monoliths, numerous planets within the Empire were still infected by the ones that got past us. It seems the monoliths have formed new temples on these infected planets and they're being used as beachheads from which the Deathlords can invade."

Grohm growled at that news.

"My sentiments, exactly," Wil responded. "The planetary militias and the Imperial forces are busy mounting resistances to the Deathlord incursions, but until we take out those temples, they're just going to keep coming. I'm forming a special attack force with the sole focus of assaulting the temples and the monoliths they house. And to be frank, we could really use your help."

Grohm just stared at Wilvelm, so long that it became uncomfortable.

"Um… so what do you say?" Wilvelm asked. "Would you be willing to be a part of the squad? We could use someone fearless like you on our side."

Grohm frowned and looked away. "Grohm not fearless…" he finally said.

Wilvelm raised his eyebrows in surprise at Grohm's response. "What are you talking about?" he asked. "You went toe-to-toe with the Terrormancers on Essox and Maxima! They didn't even make you flinch!"

Grohm's lips turned into the hint of a snarl as he gazed off toward a corner of the room. "Grohm felt it," he said. "Grohm was terrified. Just like Regals were. Just like you."

Wilvelm blinked at Grohm, not knowing how to respond to him. "But… you didn't seem like it. The way you fought…"

"Grohm chose to fight instead of fear," Grohm continued. "But was difficult. The fear was so strong, it made Grohm weak. Made Grohm want to run. Want to hide. Want to… not fight."

Grohm hung his head, looking ashamed.

"Grohm not join Regals," he said. "Grohm's emotions… getting stronger. Harder to control. Is why Grohm was banished from Rognok. Regals think Grohm strong? Grohm fearless? Is not true. Grohm is weak. All Rognoks knew this. Is why they called Grohm – Grohm the Weak."

Wilvelm nodded, finally understanding what Grohm was telling him. "You know, I experienced the same fear you did while fighting those Terrormancers. I know what you were going through. I don't think I'd ever experienced that type of fear in my life. It was crippling. I could barely function when I felt it. So I understand why you think feeling things like that makes you weak. But you inspired me to overcome that fear and fight back. Seeing you stand against those Deathlords… it made me believe it was possible. And without you and your inspiration, Grohm, I'd have never been able to help you take down that temple. You seem to think emotions are a liability, and to be truthful, some are. But they can also be advantageous. Did you know there's a word for feeling afraid but not allowing it to control you?"

Grohm looked at Wil with a curious glance.

"It's called 'bravery', and it's not easy to do." Wilvelm continued. "You may think feeling fear makes you weak, Grohm. But being brave… that takes a certain kind of strength not everyone has. And you? You have more bravery than anyone I've ever met. Which means you're also the strongest being I've ever met."

Wilvelm placed his hand on the Rognok's shoulder.

"You're not Grohm the Weak. Not to me," he said. "To me, you're Grohm the *Brave*."

Grohm grunted and looked away. Wilvelm couldn't tell if that were a positive or a negative reaction from the massive alien.

"We need more like you," Wilvelm continued. "We need men who are brave. Brave enough to fight the worst the Deathlords can throw at us. Brave enough to stand against the Terrormancers and not to run. You can teach us, Grohm. You can teach us how to be brave. And if you're willing to share your strength with us, we'll share ours with you. You don't have to be alone. You can be a part of something greater. And when you are, you'll know a strength you never before believed existed. Because we're stronger *together*."

Grohm was quiet for a moment before turning his gaze back at Wilvelm. "Grohm… the Brave?" he said, as though trying the title on for size.

"Grohm the Brave," Wilvelm said with a nod. "The Deathlords are trying to use fear to defeat us. But fear has no effect on the brave. That should terrify the Deathlords. And if you ask me, I think it's high time we gave our enemy something to fear."

Wilvelm extended his hand toward Grohm.

"Are you with me?" he asked.

Grohm looked down at Wilvelm's hand. For a moment, the Rognok didn't move. But then, he stood, rising to his full height. The alien's red and black eyes met those of Wilvelm, and Grohm took the man's hand in his, sealing their pact.

"Grohm with you…" he said.

# Chapter 43

Jack had felt like he'd been in his medical bay for years. Anna had ensured he received the best medical care the Empire had to offer, which ended up amounting to doctors who were so nervous about treating a Hero of the Empire under direct orders from the Princess, that they erred on the side of an over-abundance of caution and had restricted Jack to a long period of medical observation.

Apparently, Jack had been in a coma for about a week after helping Anna to mount a defense against the Deathlords in Maxima. He woke up feeling like death warmed over – not just from the wounds he received while fighting GorJiro, but also from the rigors of breaking the Great Seal and absorbing whatever it was that the Ancient vault shot at him.

The good news was that whatever corruption had taken root in Jack while breaking the seal seemed to have gone away. Though the doctors who were tending to him were flummoxed by the strange malady, they were relieved that Jack seemed to heal himself of it. For all intents and purposes, Jack was back to normal – even if he did feel as though he'd been run over a couple of times by a steamroller.

When the doctors cleared Jack to leave his medical bay, Jack jumped at the chance to get out of bed and go for a walk around *The Colossus*. Jack had never been on a capital ship before, and he wanted to check it out. But more than that, he wanted to see his friends again.

So many people Jack had come to care about had died, but of all of them, he felt Shanks' loss most acutely, followed by that of Flitter. The Orean had been like a sister to him, and the sacrifice she'd made to save Jack during his fight with Blackmane, Krixus, and Desmodus still haunted him. Though Jack had come to accept the loss of Pennywise and Shanks, thinking of Flitter still brought tears to his eyes.

Scallywag was no longer around, either, having flown away with his ship and with Dan. Heckubus didn't seem all that interested in visiting. Professor Green was occupied trying to decipher some weird disk he'd gotten from the Eionmeer temple. Grohm had suffered some major injuries, but he seemed to be on the mend. Krupp and the other Unlikelies were still mourning Flitter and the loss of the Conclave. And Anna seemed incredibly busy trying to help the Empire recover from the Deathlord invasion. That was okay with Jack. He knew all of them were safe and well and that there would be time for them later. But there were a few of his friends Jack wanted to check in on immediately to see how they were doing.

One such friend was Moon Ravencrow, who was also under observation in a private medical bay. When Jack entered, Ravencrow was seated on his medical bed, his eyes once more covered by the dirty blindfold Jack had become accustomed to seeing him wear. The covers of his bed were tangled and messy, wrapped around the Harvshodd's stunted legs. When last Jack remembered seeing him, Ravencrow had been close to dying from his wounds. Now, he seemed close to dying from boredom.

"Humph," Ravencrow muttered grumpily as Jack entered. "You again."

Jack smiled. He figured if the old Harvshodd was in a bad mood, then he must be feeling better. "S'up, R.C.?" he asked. "How you feeling?"

"Old," Ravencrow replied. "Too many war wounds, not enough wars. You seem to be doing better."

"Well, I still feel like I've been run over by a truck a couple of times," Jack said as he pulled up a chair to Ravencrow's bedside. "But the doc says I'm going to make a full recovery."

Ravencrow nodded. "So it would seem. You are indeed a hard one to kill, Earthman. I'll give you that."

"I would have been dead many times over if it weren't for you," Jack stated as he sat down. "Not just because of your training, but because you risked your life to come to my aid."

"Is that why you're here? To thank me?" asked Ravencrow, dismissively.

"No," answered Jack. "I wanted to know why you would help me so much, seeing as how you're also the bounty hunter that's been working so dang hard to capture me all this time."

Ravencrow frowned. "That's a good question," the alien muttered. "One I often found I would ask myself over the course of our interactions."

"Ever come up with an answer?"

"Humph!" snarled Ravencrow. "None I like."

Jack nodded. "So, why didn't you just grab me?" Jack asked. "You had plenty of opportunity while we were at the Conclave. You could have knocked me out, heck, even killed me if you'd wanted. Why didn't you?"

"Other than the fact that you chose the one place in the entire universe to hide where it would have been impossible to successfully abduct you? I would never have disrespected the Conclave by doing so. I may be a lot of things, but above all, I'm a member of the Order of Peers. I swore to do a duty when I joined their ranks, and I always take my duties very seriously. As long as you were in the Conclave, I would never have allowed myself to act as Stalker Crux in any capacity. I was merely trying to keep an eye on you until such time as you left and I could resume my task of bringing you in."

Jack looked down and picked at his nails. "So what's a guy who takes his duties as a Paragon so seriously doing moonlighting as a bounty hunter?"

Ravencrow shrugged. "The money is good," he replied. "But the challenge it presents is what I really enjoy. When you hit a certain level of skill as a Paragon, it becomes difficult to find things that will occupy you. Things that will allow you to push your boundaries. To learn new things. Bounty hunting helps me to do that."

"So you became a bounty hunter because you were bored?"

"Basically," Ravencrow replied. "It was either that or become a duelist like GorJiro, travelling from place to place across the blasted galaxy looking for idiots to kill so I could brag about how good of a fighter I am. But that didn't appeal to me. I could get the same rush hunting down bounties, and at my level, the ones I was hired to bring in were always a nice challenge. I used to think that would be the only thing that could occupy me anymore. At least… until I got to know you."

Jack raised an eyebrow. "What do you mean by that?" he asked.

Ravencrow sighed. "I've never been much interested in teaching," he said. "Never was a good fit for me. Learning about The Void… it's a personal journey. It's something one must discover for himself. And the more I learned to embrace it, the harder it was for me to share what I had learned. Most people can't bring themselves to understand The Void, because it is unknowable. Therefore, I never felt as though I had much to offer at the Conclave. But then… but then *you* came along."

Ravencrow tilted his head toward Jack, the hint of a smile growing on his face.

"You have a natural affinity for The Void, boy," Ravencrow continued. "It's raw and unrefined, but it's there. I've seen it. Training you… teaching you…

sharing my knowledge with someone who can actually use it… it was more fulfilling than I'd have liked to admit."

Jack smiled. "You saying you liked teaching me?"

Ravencrow chuckled. "Maybe a little. Guess you taught me a thing or two, as well. Go figure."

"So where does this leave us?" Jack asked. "You going to try and collect on your bounty now that I'm out of the Conclave?"

"The bounty has been rescinded by the Princess. There's nothing to collect any longer."

"I heard you take soulbound oaths on all your bounties," Jack replied. "Doesn't that mean you have to complete them no matter what?"

"Pah!" spat Ravencrow. "That's just some nonsense I tell idiot customers so I can charge them ridiculous fees for my services. Like I'd be stupid enough to bind a bounty to my very soul."

Jack nodded. "We're cool then?" he asked.

"Yes, I suppose we are," Ravencrow replied.

"Well, that's a relief," Jack said as he leaned back in his chair. "You were a real pain in the butt."

"Yeah, that's why I get paid the big bucks."

Both Jack and Ravencrow had a chuckle at that.

"So what are you going to do now?" Jack asked. "Going back to bounty hunting?"

"Possibly. I haven't decided yet."

"You know what you *could* do?" Jack ventured. "You could help re-establish the Conclave."

"Humph. Heard about that, did ya?" Ravencrow asked.

"A few people were talking about it," Jack said. "With the Conclave pocket universe gone, they need to start training Paragons again. You're a member of the Order of Peers. You could really help with that."

Ravencrow shook his head. "There's nothing I can do to help, boy," he muttered. "Paragons were an endangered species to begin with. Out of every million living beings, maybe *one* of them had the potential to become a Paragon. And that was with the accelerated learning environment the Conclave offered.

Without it, it's an even less likely scenario. I don't need to have to watch the news to know that the Paragons corrupted by the Deathlords are wreaking havoc on the galaxy, and the ones that aren't are being looked upon with suspicion and mistrust. We're a dying breed. At this point, any attempt to rebuild will just be prolonging the inevitable."

"That's kinda a crappy way of looking at things."

"Doesn't make it any less true."

Jack sighed and got to his feet. "Well, I hope you change your mind, dude. Despite what you think, you really are a great teacher. And one of the best living Paragons we have left. You could do a lot of good if you wanted to."

"And I suppose, from the tone of your voice, you're going to have a role to play in establishing this new Conclave?" asked Ravencrow.

"I've learned a lot already. But my training isn't complete. I need to finish what I started."

"Are you sure about that?" Ravencrow asked. "You may not be a Master Paragon, but you're better trained than anyone you could most likely cross paths with."

"Even Mellegogg?"

Ravencrow frowned at sound of the name. "No," Ravencrow said, sadly. "Not him."

"And that's why I have to continue my training," Jack said. "I have a quest I need to complete. And in order to do that, I have to be able to face any obstacle in my path. Even ones as big and scary as Mellegogg." Ravencrow was quiet for a long moment. Finally, Jack decided their conversation had come to an end. "Take care of yourself, Master Ravencrow," Jack said. "I hope you reconsider. It would be nice to train under you again."

As Jack turned to leave, Ravencrow spoke. "What if there were another option?" the alien asked.

Jack stopped and gave the Harvshodd an inquisitive look. "What other option?"

"What if I were to take you on as my apprentice?" Ravencrow offered. "Would that be something that would interest you?"

Jack's eyes went wide with surprise. "Apprentice?" Jack said, dumbfounded. "Me… and you?"

Ravencrow shrugged. "You'd mentioned before about how Paragon Shepherd offered to take you on," he said. "Why not me?"

"How… how would that even work?"

"Not sure, really. I've never taken on an apprentice before. But I imagine it would be similar to how we operated at the Conclave."

"You mean, I annoy you until you teach me something useful?"

"Sounds exhausting, doesn't it?" Ravencrow replied with a chuckle.

Jack was quiet for a moment as he weighed the Paragon's offer. "You're actually serious? You'd really take me on? Teach me to be a Master Paragon, just like you?"

"Yes. But make no mistake about it, boy. What I am offering you is not something to be taken lightly. If you accept it, the path you'll walk will be a difficult one. Any adversity you think you had to endure at the Conclave will be a drop in the bucket compared to what lies in wait for you along this road I'll be leading you down. It will be hard. Brutal. Unforgiving. I will show you the depths of The Void, and there is a very real possibility you will not survive it. But if you do… then I believe you could very well become the greatest Paragon this universe has ever seen."

Ravencrow's words stunned Jack. "Really?" was all he could manage to say.

"As much as it pains me to admit it, yes," Ravencrow replied. "You have what it takes to be great, Earthman. You have courage. You have heart. And you have an iron will. I have never met one such as yourself. A fighter with the will to win and the constitution to do what's right… even when it's the hardest thing in the world to do. That's a rare combination indeed. But more than that, I've seen how you inspire those around you. How you push them to be better than they are. Show them what they are capable of. You did it with your companions on your adventures, you did it with the students you were grouped with at the Conclave, and… and you did it with me, as well."

"I did?"

Ravencrow suddenly looked uncomfortable, as though it pained him to speak about the subject. "You became my student, yes. But you also became something more than that. Something I never expected. You became my friend. And you've earned my respect."

For some reason, the Harvshodd's words resonated with Jack. He couldn't help it. He felt a little choked up that Ravencrow would acknowledge such a thing. "Thanks, dude..." Jack was finally able to say. "That means a lot, coming from you."

"Let's not make a big thing of it," grumbled Ravencrow. "But it's because of this respect that I'm making you this offer. And if we are to do this, then you'll need to devote yourself to it completely. That means cutting off all ties you currently have and giving yourself over to your training."

"What do you mean 'cutting ties'?" Jack asked, suddenly wary.

"You'll have to let go of those closest to you," Ravencrow warned. "All your friends, all those you care about... you will not be able to see them. And you must give up all your possessions – anything that could possibly distract from your training must be let go of. This includes that ship of yours."

"I'd... I'd have to give up my ship?"

"You must give up *everything*," stressed Ravencrow. "You must come to your training unencumbered and free from all obligation and responsibility. This is the only way I know how to teach you. If you are not able to cut your bonds and shed your burdens, then I will not be able to help you. So you must choose. Your training? Or your ties?"

Jack was quiet for a long moment. "Can I think about it?" he asked. "You don't need an answer right now, do you?"

"Take your time, but don't take too long," Ravencrow said. "If I haven't heard back from you by the time I'm ready to leave this blasted hospital, I'll just assume your answer is 'no'."

Jack's mind wrestled with the offer that Ravencrow had presented to him as he left the Harvshodd's medical bay. Part of him wanted to jump at the chance to train under Ravencrow exclusively. The idea of becoming a master of The Void and learning to harness its power greatly appealed to Jack. But the other part of him wasn't willing to pay the price Ravencrow was asking.

How could he leave his friends? How could he leave his ship? How could he leave Anna? Why wasn't it possible to maintain his life and his connections while continuing his training? But that was the nature of Ravencrow and his teachings, wasn't it? They were never what one was expecting.

As Jack struggled with his decision, he decided to seek out an opinion he trusted. Someone he knew would be honest with him and also knew the value of what Ravencrow was offering. Though he hadn't seen Mourdock since the battle with GorJiro, Jack felt he could still count on him to offer good advice. And for once, maybe Jack had something to offer Mourdock, as well.

After regaining consciousness, Jack had learned all about what had been happening while he was in the Conclave, particularly in Maxima. Though Mourdock had risked his life fighting Mellegogg, he'd lost so much more than he could have possibly known about. His father was dead. His mother was dead. One of his best friends died. His home planet was attacked. Couple that with the serious injuries he'd sustained, and Jack couldn't help but worry about him. After all, Jack knew what it was like to lose everything one cared about. Now, more than ever, Jack knew Mourdock needed a friend to rely on.

Jack finally arrived at Mourdock's private medical bay. The doors hissed open to reveal that Mourdock was not in his bed. He was standing in front of the room's window, looking out into space. His body seemed uneven with his arm missing, a medical brace strapped to the stump of his shoulder. Mourdock was strong, but apparently the effects of the Corruption were still lingering with him, despite having overcome its influence. His once perfect skin was now pale, with the shadows of the corrupted veins still visible underneath. His once luxurious blonde hair was now brittle. And his once perfect features had grown gaunt and angular.

Jack entered the room, waiting for Mourdock to acknowledge his arrival, but he never did. Instead, Mourdock opted to quietly stare out into the dark void of space. After a long, awkward silence, Jack decided to speak.

"Hey," Jack finally said. "I came to check in. See how you are doing."

Mourdock didn't respond. He barely even moved.

"I'm sorry I didn't come by sooner, but the doctors didn't want me out of bed until they could tell whether or not I was fully recovered," Jack continued. "Apparently, being shot by a highly concentrated beam of Ancient knowledge isn't exactly good for you... and I've done it twice now."

Again, Mourdock remained silent.

"Look, I heard about what happened to your parents... your planet..." Jack said. "I just want to let you know how sorry I am. I know what you're going through..."

"Do you?" asked Mourdock, still not bothering to face him.

"I lost my entire planet, remember?" Jack said. "I lost my mom. My friends. Everything I ever knew. So, yeah, I do."

"You know nothing of what I have lost," Mourdock replied, quietly.

Jack sighed. "Okay," he said, trying to be sensitive to what Mourdock was going through. "Maybe I don't. But I want you to know I'm here for you. As a friend."

A bitter chuckle escaped from Mourdock upon hearing that. "As a friend…" Mourdock said slowly, as though he were repeating the punchline to a bad joke. "Some friend you turned out to be."

Jack frowned. "What's that supposed to mean?" he asked.

Mourdock was quiet for a moment as he continued to stare out the window. "What type of a man falls in love with his friend's fiancée?" Mourdock asked. "At what point does that friendship become nothing but a mask for betrayal?"

"Dude, what are you talking about?" Jack asked, approaching Mourdock as his concern over the direction of this conversation grew.

"I am talking about your lies," Mourdock replied. "I'm talking about your love for the woman that is to be my wife."

Jack looked at Mourdock, confused. "But… you said you didn't care about my feelings for Anna," he said. "That I was free to love her no matter what…"

Mourdock abruptly turned, his face twisted in an anger the likes of which Jack had never seen.

"That was before I knew she felt the same way about *you!!!*" Mourdock screamed.

Mourdock's words hit Jack harder than any blow could have. He was frozen in shock, unsure of how to respond. All he could do was look into Mourdock's eyes, which gazed at him with pure, unadulterated hatred. Mourdock's face was so tight with barely restrained anger, he was hardly able to breathe, his pale face growing red and flustered.

"M—Mourdock…" Jack finally said. "I… I…"

"You are not my friend," Mourdock said. "You never were. You took the one thing I held most dear in my life away from me. And now… I have nothing left."

"That's not true!" Jack objected.

Mourdock stepped toward Jack, his face inches away. Despite his weakened state, Jack had never seen Mourdock look more threatening than he did that very moment. "There is no use denying it," Mourdock said through gritted teeth. "I know what I saw. Now take this warning to heart, Earthman, because I will only give it to you once. Go. Go far, far away. Do not come near me or Anna ever again. You are no longer welcome in my presence. You are no longer welcome in the Empire. You are dead to me. And should you ever dare to show your face again, I swear on the souls of my parents… I *will* kill you!"

Mourdock had made the threat with such steely passion, Jack knew he truly meant it. So powerful was the anger Mourdock was directing toward him, Jack was forced to take a step back, feelings of hurt and sadness raging within him.

Without another word, Mourdock turned his back to Jack, gazing out the room's window into the vast empty void of space once more. Jack looked upon his former friend, a tear welling in the corner of his eye.

"I'm… I'm sorry…" was all Jack could manage to say.

Jack had come to Mourdock seeking advice, and in a way, Mourdock had made his decision easy for him. Jack and Mourdock had been through so much together. Their friendship had survived the corruption that had plagued the Conclave. It had survived the betrayal of GorJiro.

But in the end, the one thing it could not survive was their love for the same woman.

# CHAPTER 44

Anna looked down at the stone disk on the table as Professor Green finished his debriefing of what he'd learned before Eionmeer's Caretaker had fallen to the corruption of the dark temple. She reached out and touched the disk, tracing her finger around it, trying to get a sense of whether or not she could connect to it and unlock the secrets it held. Anna frowned when she realized she could not.

"So you believe this disk contains historical records of the Ancients and their wars with the Eternal Enemy?" Anna asked.

"That is what we were told, Your Highness," Green replied. "But in all honesty, it could be much, much more than historical records. There could be any number of things on this disk – from blueprints of Ancient technology to instructions on how to achieve enlightenment – why, the possibilities are limitless!"

"But we won't know unless we find some way to access what is stored on it," Anna muttered. "Is there any way of doing so?"

Professor Green frowned. "I'm afraid the normal avenues of researching the disk are not available to us any longer," he said. "Normally we would attempt to use a temple to interface with it, but with both the temples of Regalus Prime and the Conclave destroyed, there are no more Ancient temples with functioning access orbs known to us at the moment. Our second option would be to try to use an Ancient relic to decipher it, but again, all collections of Ancient relics have been destroyed, as well. This means we shall be forced to use more conventional methods to try to interface with the disk… but doing so will be very complicated and could take years."

"Years will be a small price to pay if we can learn more about our enemy from this piece of stone," Anna said. "Anything you need to unlock this disk, I shall make sure you have it."

Green's face lit up. "Oh!" he exclaimed. "Does this mean I'll be the one leading the research team?"

"You'll be doing more than that, Professor," Anna replied. "You'll be running all of the Maguffyn Corporation from here on out."

It was not often that Anna had known the Professor to be at a loss for words, but this was certainly one of those times. Green simply blinked at her, as though unsure of what he'd just heard her say. "The… the Maguffyn Corporation?" he stammered.

"No other entity in the Empire has the resources to deal with Ancient technology like the Maguffyn Corporation does," Anna said. "And with Armonto Virtuoso missing, it is without a CEO. It will need someone with extensive knowledge of the Ancients to lead it forward. Frankly, I cannot think of anyone better qualified in that regard than you. So? What do you say, Professor?"

Professor Green nervously fidgeted. His large eyes were still wide with surprise as he struggled to find the words to respond. "Oh… oh, dear… oh, dear…" he muttered.

Anna tried not to smile, but she found the Professor's nervousness endearing. "Professor, I would not be making you this offer if I didn't have complete faith that you would be able to do the job."

"Yes, I understand, but… well… I've never run a company before! Let alone the largest company in the known universe!"

"I believe you're smart enough to figure it out," Anna said, reassuringly. "And you won't be alone. You'll have all the support you could possibly need. Trust me."

Green glanced upwards, wistfully. "CEO of the Maguffyn Corporation?" he mumbled, thoughtfully, as though trying the title on for size. "Surely there are others far more qualified for such a position than I?"

"Do not sell yourself short, Professor. Under Armonto Virtuoso, the Maguffyn Corporation was corrupted. We not only need someone with a top-notch intellect to guide the company, but we need someone with a good heart to help heal the damage Virtuoso left in his wake. I can think of no better person for such a task than you."

Green nodded. "I'm not going to lie… having access to the entirety of the Maguffyn Corporation's research on Ancient technology is tempting. And having those kinds of resources at my disposal would greatly speed up our research into the disk…"

"Does this mean you'll take the job?"

Green finally smiled and nodded. "It would be my honor, Your Highness."

"I had hoped you'd say that," replied Anna with a smile of her own. She extended her hand, which Green shook excitedly. "Congratulations, Thaddius Rebbibald Green, new Chief Executive Officer of the Maguffyn Corporation. I expect great things from you."

"And I shall do my best to fulfill those expectations, Princess!" Green replied before scooping up the disk. "Now, if you will please excuse me, there is much work to be done! And I am eager to get started!"

"Of course," said Anna. "I will have Premier Evenstar see to it you have everything you need to transition control of the company and its resources to you."

Anna and the Professor left the briefing room together, parting ways once they entered the hallway of *The Colossus*. While Green walked away, excitedly muttering to himself all the things he should be doing now that he was one of the most important people in the galaxy, the Princess began walking to her next appointment with Seqis, Dahuud, and her new chief of staff Tebbara Fetch in tow.

Fetch had previously been governor of the settlement on Eionmeer, so he had a great deal of executive experience which Anna was coming to rely on as she assumed a greater role in the running of her Empire. But more than that, Fetch and the Princess shared a link through their slythrus, just as Anna did with the rest of her new security detail, run by Commander Gunner.

Aside from the fact that the men who'd been at her side on Eionmeer gave their loyalty to her because of her role in freeing them from the slythru influence, there was a strange sensation of trust between them. It was as though the shared trauma of having been slaves to the slythru united them, and the links the dark creatures had to one another gave them all a sense of one another's true intentions. It was for this reason Anna had quickly entrusted her affairs to Fetch, despite not yet knowing him all that well.

"Your next appointment is already waiting for you in your office, Your Highness," Fetch informed her.

"Thank you, Tebbara," Anna replied. "After this meeting I should like some personal time to meditate, if you do not mind."

"I shall clear your schedule for an hour afterward. Will that suffice?"

"It should. Thank you."

Anna entered the office that Starkeeper Drucker had given to her when she'd boarded the ship after the summit at Port Longshore. He'd offered to give her his own offices for her use, but Anna refused, not wanting to displace him. Though not befitting of royalty, the office she'd been granted had everything she needed to conduct her business – and that was all Anna really cared about.

The Royal Vanguard and Fetch stayed in the anteroom as Anna went to her private office where Krupp was sitting. The Paragon was both patiently waiting and nervously sweating in anticipation of her arrival, shooting to his feet the moment she entered the room.

"You-your Highness!" he said, his voice cracking with nervousness.

Anna smiled at him. "Tell me, Paragon Krupp… how is it you can charge into battle to face an army of Deathstalkers, yet I am the thing that intimidates you?"

Krupp smiled at that, wiping the sweat from his brow and awkwardly drying his hand on his white robes. "In all fairness, Your Highness, the Deathstalkers were not nearly as pretty as you are."

Anna had to laugh at that, which seemed to put Krupp more at ease. "Please, sit," she said, gesturing to the chair in front of her desk. Krupp did as she asked while Anna took her seat, smiling warmly at the awkward young man who was across from her.

"The Empire owes you and all the other Paragons who fought on Eionmeer a great debt," she said. "I want you to know that though I may be your Princess, in my eyes, you and I are equals."

Krupp nodded at that. "That is most kind of you to say, Your Highness," he replied. "Frankly, I'm not sure it's deserved. Though I have the title of Paragon now, I still feel like an Initiate. I have not progressed in my training as far as most who have such a title and I feel as though I still have much to learn."

"You have proven you've learned the important things," Anna replied. "Being a Paragon isn't simply about the skills you possess. It's about being the best you can be. And judging from your actions, Paragon Krupp, you are indeed one of the best this universe has to offer."

Krupp blushed at the compliment. "Thank you, Your Highness."

"And it is for this reason I will be entrusting you to re-establish the Conclave."

Krupp's eyes went wide at that. "Come again?"

"In my conversations with your friends, they all told me that you are not only a good leader, but also a good teacher. They said they can always rely on you to help guide them to do what they must to succeed. The Conclave was a place of learning, and if we are to train new Paragons, I cannot think of anyone better to oversee such an endeavor than a teacher. Wouldn't you agree?"

"With all due respect, Your Highness, surely there are Paragons far better qualified to do such a thing than me," Krupp said. "There are other members of the Order of Peers who still survive, and other highly skilled Paragons throughout the galaxy…"

"You are a highly skilled Paragon," Anna stated. "And as of today, I am appointing you to be a member of the Order of Peers, as well."

"M… me?" said Krupp with astonishment. "But… compared to Masters Highclaw, Savage, and Hodapp, I'm not at all deserving of such a thing!"

"Compared to Master GorJiro, you deserve that and far more," countered Anna. "I realize this offer comes as a surprise, however, of all those who survived the destruction of the Conclave, every last one of them has expressed nothing but faith and support of you, Paragon Krupp. But above all that, I'm told you and Jack are close friends. Is this correct?"

"Yes," Krupp replied. "He's one of my best friends."

"Then that is all the proof I need to know you are the right man for this job."

"Even if that is the case, Your Highness, re-establishing the Conclave will be… almost impossible, I'm sorry to say. Without the time constriction the pocket universe provided, training new Paragons will be a long and difficult endeavor. Initiates could spend lifetimes unlocking only the most basic of skills."

Anna leaned back in her chair. "Tell me, Paragon Krupp. What do you know of the Order of Luminadric Monks?"

"Um… not much," Krupp admitted. "Just that they were created by Emperor Nameer to advise Legacy Prime on moral and spiritual issues."

"The Luminadric Monks are far more than advisors," Anna said. "They are Paragons in their own right. And I have already reached out to them concerning the possibility of using their temple to train new Paragons."

"Does their temple also have time constriction capabilities?" Krupp asked.

"No. They have something… quite different. But the monks are able to use it in their training, just as I am confident you and your new Initiates will, as well. But with so many Paragons having fallen to the corruption of the Deathlords, it is vital that we get a new Conclave up and running, so that we can create a way to counter those the Deathlords have claimed. So what do you say, Paragon Krupp? Will you answer your Empire's call?"

Krupp hesitated for only a moment before a resolute look settled on his face. "After Regalus Prime was destroyed, I swore to myself that I would find a way to fight back against the Deathlords," he said. "I came to realize afterward that I am a poor warrior, but there is more than one way to fight. If this is how I can make a difference, then this shall be how I fight against the evil that is plaguing this galaxy – by being as good a teacher as I can be. Yes, Your Highness. I will answer your call. It will be my honor to serve you and my fellow Paragons by rebuilding the Conclave."

Anna smiled. "I am glad to hear it, Paragon Krupp," she said, getting to her feet and shaking Krupp's hand. "Please, let me know if there is anything I can do to assist you in your endeavor."

"I will, Your Highness," Krupp said before taking his leave.

Once Krupp had gone, Anna sealed the door to her office and sighed. So many things required her attention now that she was taking a more active role in the ruling of her Empire. There once was a time when she would have welcomed the increased responsibility, but that was before she'd finally tapped into her abilities. Now that she had an idea what she was capable of, she felt all her duties as a ruler were nothing more than a distraction from the development of her powers.

Anna sat upon the floor of her office, entering her meditation position as the Luminadric monks had taught her, and attempted to make contact with her Source as she had done when trapped in her mental construct. But once more, she found the process of doing so to be increasingly difficult.

Though Anna had unlocked powerful abilities when she'd been forced to face Verrutus, she could already feel the knowledge she'd gathered from her ordeal begin to slip away. When the experience had been fresh and she could utilize the power of an access orb to help free her mind, she was able to do amazing things. But now, remembering how to do such things was like trying to remember the details of a dream, and the more time that passed, the more those details faded.

She wanted to access more of her genetic memories and to tap into the wisdom which lay with her ancestors. She wanted to reach out and make connections with the machines based in Ancient technology, as she had in the Battle of Maxima. But more than anything, she wanted to return to the spider web of slythru connections Verrutus had woven and free the rest who remained enslaved.

Indeed, when the Imperial government was running smoothly once more, that is what Anna intended to devote herself to. She felt it was her duty and responsibility to free any and all who remained under the influence of the slythru. The acceptance of the slythru as a part of her gave her a certain measure of control over it. She could sense those who had been infected. She could see the slythrus sticking from their necks. She could even reach out and communicate with them and show the host how to break free. And yet, whenever she did so, there was a part of her which knew that using her dark side in such a way gave it power.

Even then, as she meditated, trying to free her mind and tap into the power that she knew she had, she sensed the presence of her dark companion. Though it was no longer in control, it still lived, and would always live, waiting to try to take her over once more.

*Not free…* Anna could hear her dark companion hiss. *Never free!*

*You do not frighten me,* Anna responded. *You may whisper in my ear. You may influence my decisions. You may even tempt me into dancing into the dark where you'll exert your control. But so long as I have those who anchor me to the light, you will never have true power over me. Never again!*

It was then Anna saw an image of Jack in her mind's eye. He appeared to her as he had when she realized what it would take to defeat both Verrutus and her dark companion. Just like Atashah was the anchor for Nameer, Anna accepted that Jack was her anchor. He was always the one who inspired her. Who guided her. Who loved her unconditionally, even when she probably didn't deserve it.

Since their shared experience in uniting to fight the Battle of Maxima, Jack had been on Anna's mind. She'd been to visit him numerous times in the medical bay as he recovered, each time feeling more and more certain about her feelings for him.

All her life, Anna had been subject to a set of rules she felt she did not have the power to break. The biggest of which was her engagement to a man she did not love. Though Mourdock Skyborn was a good man, he did not make Anna feel like Jack did. He did not make her happy. And after all she'd been through, Anna realized how important it was to be happy.

Though she'd been struggling long and hard with her decision, that vision of Jack finally cinched it for her. She made her choice. Though she knew there would be a great deal of political fallout in the wake of it, she simply could not go on living a life she did not feel was right for her. She decided she would break off her engagement to Mourdock Skyborn and instead pursue the relationship she truly longed for.

She wanted to be with Jack. And it was as simple as that.

When Anna exited her meditation and opened her eyes, she felt as though a huge weight had been lifted from her shoulders. She could finally admit it to herself – she was in love with the Earthman! And now that she could be honest with herself, she could finally be honest with others, as well. She was ready to make a proclamation to the entire universe: Princess Glorianna of Legacy Prime and Jack Finnegan were finally going to be together!

As Anna got to her feet, Fetch opened the door to her office, bowing to her apologetically. "Pardon the interruption, Your Highness," he said. "But Earthman Jack Finnegan is here to see you."

"Jack?" said Anna, her heart leaping with excitement. "He's been released from the med bay?"

"Apparently so, Your Highness," replied Fetch. "He's requested an audience. I thought you'd like to know right away."

"You thought correctly, Tebbara. Please send him in."

Anna straightened her gown as Fetch retreated into the anteroom. She felt uncharacteristically nervous with the anticipation of Jack's arrival. But she supposed that was only natural, considering she planned to confess her feelings to him.

When Jack entered he was looking as healthy and vibrant as ever. Anna smiled at the sight of him. "Jack!" she said as she embraced him. "It is good to see you up and about again!"

"It's good to be up and about," Jack replied.

Anna thought it odd that Jack did not seem to return her embrace with any particular enthusiasm. Nor did he appear to have any excitement in his voice. This caused Anna to break off her hug, feeling as though she may have overstepped a boundary of which she was unaware. "I… I came to visit you many times in the medical bay," Anna said. "You, um… you weren't conscious, though."

"Yeah, I know how that goes," replied Jack. "I feel like that's what I did with you for, like, years at the Conclave."

Anna nodded. "Believe it or not, those visits were more important than you know. I was able to glimpse snippets of them. Every time I did, it gave me hope and allowed me to fight against the slythru. You helped me to hold on."

"That's great!" replied Jack, looking awkward. "Um… I'm glad I could help."

Anna frowned. "Jack… is there something wrong?"

Jack sighed. "Yeah… maybe… I'm not really sure," he said. "I don't know exactly how to tell you this, but I'm going to be going away for a while, and I'm not exactly sure when I'll be coming back."

Jack's words felt like a knife had just pierced Anna's heart. "You… you're leaving?" she asked, confused.

"Master Ravencrow offered me an apprenticeship under him and it kinda requires me to leave all my friends and possessions behind," Jack explained. "I've given it a lot of thought, and… uh… I think it's best for everyone if I take it."

Anna turned away in an attempt to hide the emotion she was experiencing. *It's not best for me!* she wanted to cry. *I only just got you back – and now you wish to leave?*

"I see…" was what Anna said instead.

"I need to complete my training, and with the Conclave gone, this is the best way I know how to do it," Jack explained. "Now that you're safe, I figured it would give you and Mourdock more time to reconnect."

"Me and Mourdock?" Anna asked. *What about me and you?*

"He… he really does love you, Anna," Jack said. "He's a good guy. The two of you… you deserve one another. I, uh… I don't want to get in the way of that anymore."

Anna turned to look at Jack, but Jack was unable to meet her gaze. Sadness gripped her as she realized that though she'd fallen in love with Jack, he must have lost his feelings for her completely. "I understand," Anna said, quietly. "Did… did you come to say good-bye, then?"

"Actually, I'd hoped you'd do me a favor?"

"Of course. Name it."

"Would you look after my ship while I'm away?" Jack asked. "I can't bring it with me, and you're the only one in the universe I trust to keep it safe while I'm gone."

"Your ship? Yes, of course," Anna replied. "I'll make sure nothing happens to it."

"Thanks," Jack said. "That means a lot to me."

"It means a lot to me knowing that one day, you will return to claim it," Anna said.

Jack finally met Anna's gaze. Her eyes told him everything she felt about him and the only response he could give was a look of sadness and regret. "I... uh... I should get going," he said. "Ravencrow wants to leave as soon as possible."

"Must you go so soon?" Anna asked, desperate to keep him around.

"I think I need to," Jack replied. "It's... it's just better this way."

A feeling of powerlessness washed over Anna. All of a sudden, all the confidence she'd gained during her ordeal with Verrutus left her and she felt like that helpless, insecure, unworthy little girl she used to be. In the back of her mind, she could hear her dark companion laughing.

"Jack, I—" Anna said, wanting to confess her true feelings to him.

Jack gave Anna a look, as though saying he knew what she was going to tell him and pleading with her not to. Anna stopped herself, swallowing her emotions.

"I... wish you good luck," she forced herself to say. "I want you to know you are welcome back anytime you desire, and your ship will be here waiting for you. As will I."

"Thanks, Anna," Jack replied. "I knew I could always count on you."

There was an awkward moment between the two as neither knew how to say good-bye to the other. They could have kissed. They could have embraced. They could have even nodded to one another. But instead, Jack simply turned and walked away.

The moment the doors closed, Anna could not hold herself together any longer. A sob escaped from her and tears began to flow. She clutched at her chest and dropped to her knees, her heart breaking.

After all her trials and tribulations, she'd finally achieved some much needed victories. She'd beaten Verrutus. She'd beaten Mellegogg. She'd even defeated the slythru which had taken control of her. But despite all those wins, she'd just lost the one thing she'd needed most of all.

She had lost the one person she trusted to keep her anchored to her light.

# CHAPTER 45

The professional image of reporter Danton DeGoosey was being displayed on a holoscreen in a darkened room as the intrepid newscaster began his segment.

"This is Danton DeGoosey, coming to you live from the planet of Maxima as the fallout from the Deathlord invasion continues to play out. Though the scourge of the dark temple and its Deathstalker army affected the entire planet, nowhere did it have as much of an impact as the planet's capital city of Highpoint, right here on the Hilavan Plateau."

The image cut to B-roll footage of desolate streets littered with destroyed vehicles and property, before fading to teary eyed residents who were returning to their ransacked homes.

"The Deathlords left nothing in the city untouched. From residences, to businesses, all were laid to ruin," said Danton's voice-over.

"I still can't believe something like this could happen here," said one older Endolan[26] as he gazed at the wreckage that used to be his storefront. "I spent forty years building this business, and the Deathlords came and wiped it away in a day. You think you're safe living in a big city… but ain't nothing safe from Deathlords no more."

"But far worse than this terrible destruction is, undoubtedly, the loss of life," the voice-over continued as it cut to various memorials filled with teary-eyed mourners.

"My wife was ripped apart by those creatures," said one distraught man. "So many people were killed by those blasted things! How could this be allowed to happen? How???"

Danton continued. "And as tragic as the deaths that occurred during the invasion are, perhaps even more troubling are those whose fates remain uncertain…"

The image cut to a memorial wall in the Equinox temple, with the holoimages showcased before candle-lit vigils of those who went missing during the invasion.

---

[26] Endolans are dark skinned humanoid aliens with a vestigial third eye.

"My daughter is still missing!" said a sobbing woman as she spoke to Danton. "We got separated when those creatures flooded into the city. I don't know if she's alive or dead! I'm still looking for her, but I don't know where she could be!"

The image then cut back to Danton DeGoosey, his somber face gazing into the camera.

"Despite all the tragedy that's been inflicted upon Maxima, a ray of hope has arisen. There are reports coming in that hundreds, if not thousands, of civilians were saved from the Deathlord attack, kept safe in the famous Equinox temple, here behind me. According to those who lived through this harrowing experience, they survived because of the actions of one very brave man."

Hand-held footage of Zarrod disguised as Hasatan appeared on the screen. The doors to the Equinox temple opened to reveal him looking battered and wounded, but still standing, his moonfyre sword in hand. As the Peacekeepers who had been guarding the inside of the temple rushed up to him, he collapsed in their arms.

"As this amateur footage taken just minutes after the attack ended shows, a man by the name of Paragon Marvus Hasatan survived the overwhelming onslaught of Deathstalkers," reported Danton. "Eye-witnesses say he single-handedly guarded the entrance to the Equinox temple, keeping all those inside it safe from the Deathlords."

The image then cut to an interview with the Peacekeeper Lieutenant who'd lead the evacuation.

"It was the bravest thing I've ever seen," the Peacekeeper Lieutenant said. "One man, against an army of those creatures! He held them off. Probably saved the lives of everyone in the temple by doing so. As far as I'm concerned, Paragon Hasatan is a true hero."

The image then cut to the High Pontifex, surrounded by grateful looking practitioners. "Praise be to the Great Observer!" the High Pontifex said. "For he looked down upon us in our time of greatest need, and sent a savior to answer our prayers! And that savior's name is Hasatan!"

"Bless him!" the congregation all proclaimed. "Bless Paragon Hasatan!"

The image then cut back to Danton DeGoosey. "The 'Hero of Highpoint' as Paragon Hasatan is being called, has been embraced by members of the Church of the Great Observer all throughout the Rim as those here on Maxima continue to spread word of the Paragon's bravery in defending the lives of civilians during the Deathlord attack. Already, social media and the ultraweb are raising this previously obscure Paragon into galactic prominence for his selfless deeds. But all one needs to do is walk the streets of Highpoint to see the impact this humble warrior has had on the people of this planet."

Street art of Hasatan's face adorned the sides of buildings, with the word 'Savior' written beneath it. Processions of people, all projecting holoimages of Hasatan, marched through the roadways of the city.

"There are many heroes that came out of the invasion," one woman said as she spoke to the camera, holding up a holoimage of Hasatan as she did so. "But they were all busy fighting the Deathlords. Paragon Hasatan was the only one who was fighting to protect the people! My family and I are alive today because he chose to put his own life on the line to guard our temple! If you ask me, that makes him the greatest hero of them all!"

The interview cut away to Danton once more.

"Already, there is talk of Paragon Hasatan being nominated by the Rim worlds to represent the fourth quadrant in Princess Glorianna's new Imperial governing council – talk of which is further boosted by the fact that Paragon Hasatan is the personal mentor of Emperor Ascendant, and now Legacy head, Mourdock Skyborn. As his support here in the Rim grows, news of his actions continue to spread virally throughout the ultraweb, as trend-tags such as #HighpointHeroForAll and #ImWithHasatan surge on social media platforms. And as word spreads, it seems as though this particular Paragon is destined to be more than a just a hero. He's to be a leader. This is Danton DeGoosey, Galactic Imperial News Service, Maxima System."

As the program cut away to commercial, it was muted. Armonto Virtuoso smiled with satisfaction as he turned his attention away from the newscast and back to a clear glass box filled with tiny insects, which he proceeded to scan with a datapad.

His new workshop was dark, but was slowly starting to come together as his worker-bots went about setting it up to his specifications. Since arriving at the location, Armonto mused to himself how peaceful his life now was, away from the bustle of a city and the responsibilities of running a company. Had he previously known that striking out on his own would feel so rewarding and fulfilling, he'd have figured out a way to kill Casgor and Verrutus long ago.

But he wasn't truly working on his own. He had a new partner now – one who was shaping up to be far more reliable than the last two. Armonto looked over at his workstation console as an alert popped up, telling him a visitor was incoming.

Armonto set aside his datapad and broke himself away from his study of the insects to approach a large metallic platform which began to glow brightly as it was energized. Armonto stood patiently, hands behind his back, as the platform engaged. In a flash of light, Zarrod in his Hasatan hologuise was revealed to now be standing upon it.

Zarrod squinted and peered into the darkened room, the only light emanating from the various computers and electronics that had been set up within it. The joints of worker-bots whirred as they went about assembling the various workstations and machines Armonto had repurposed from the Maguffyn Corporation before fleeing Omnicron.

"Supreme," Armonto said. "Welcome."

Zarrod stepped down from the platform, appraising the progress of Armonto's lair with approval. "Things are coming along nicely, I see," he said. "Travel here is much more convenient now that you've gotten your man-made portgate operational."

"It is indeed," Armonto replied, looking at the platform. "Now that we are able to develop our own portgate network, we can go anywhere we desire, undetected. I could not have achieved such a breakthrough without your assistance. Your instructions on Servuchur were quite invaluable. It finally allowed me to stabilize the digimatrix needed to create such a thing."

Armonto turned toward a large nearby cube, which contained a swirling and moaning soul within. Next to the digimatrix cube was a chair with the lifeless body of Hylda Whaller strapped to it. Armonto sighed.

"Pity," he mused. "She was a good assistant."

"Now that you've perfected the soul transfer to your digimatrix device, how long will it take you to enact the rest of our plan?"

"Hard to say," Armonto replied. "If I had a team working beneath me, probably a couple of months. However, working solo, it will undoubtedly take longer. Possibly years."

"If years are what it will take, years are what you shall have," Zarrod replied.

"And you're confident you can deliver such an amount of time?"

"Do you still doubt me?"

"Admittedly, any doubts I may have harbored about your abilities have been eliminated, seeing as how everything that's occurred has played out precisely as you'd said it would," Armonto replied. "Not even Verrutus had that ability. It gives me a certain level of confidence in you that I did not have with my previous partners."

"Good," said Zarrod. "You and I have achieved exactly what we need to enact our plan. Both the Empire and the Deathlords are in turmoil. Neither side lost in their latest conflict, but neither did either side win. Mellegogg's plan worked just enough to weaken the Empire, but not enough to destroy it, and thanks to the Princess and the Earthman, the Deathlords did not achieve the decisive victory they'd hoped for. From this chaos springs opportunity, which I intend to take full advantage of."

"And now that you are set to be a part of the new High Council as a hero of the Rim, that should not be too difficult."

"Indeed," Zarrod said. "My ploy to position myself as a hero during the invasion of Maxima could not have worked better. When I control all the resources of the fourth quadrant, I'll ensure you have everything you need, Mr. Virtuoso. You can count on that."

"A refreshing change from dealing with that insufferable Uleeg Casgor, that's for certain," Armonto replied. "And your choice of location for our secret base of operations is a most impressive one. Not only is it spacious and well-hidden, it meets any energy requirements I could possibly ever need."

"You may thank the Conclave archives for that," Zarrod said. "Now that your portgate is up and running, no one will ever be able to find us."

"At least not until it is too late to stop us," Armonto added.

"It is already too late to stop us," Zarrod stated. "Everything is playing out exactly as I have foreseen, and it will continue to do so until our ultimate victory."

"And you are confident there will be no surprises that may adversely affect our chances for success?"

"I am," Zarrod replied. "Nothing can surprise me any longer."

With that, Zarrod deactivated his hologuise, removing it from his wrist so that it could be recharged. When he turned back toward Armonto Virtuoso, he noticed the man was giving him a curious look.

"What is it?" Zarrod asked.

"Forgive me," Armonto said. "Your true appearance is just… not what I was expecting."

"Have you never seen a Deathlord up close before?"

Armonto raised an eyebrow. "With all due respect, my colleague… you look nothing like any Deathlord I have ever seen."

Zarrod did not know how to take that comment. It was true that without his armor, he was a shadow of his former self. But he still looked enough like any other Deathlord not to warrant such an observation. Zarrod then walked to a nearby computer station and called up the console's facecam, displaying his image on the viewscreen.

What he saw staring back at him was a face he did not recognize. He was no longer a skeletal visage. His face was now fleshed out, with scaly jet-black skin. He'd grown something resembling a nose, and his mouth had begun to form lips. But the most noticeable difference were his eyes. They no longer glowed fiery red. Now, they were proper eyes – white, with green colored irises. Zarrod gazed at his image in shock and confusion.

*Human…* he thought. *I… I look… like a human…*

Zarrod reached up and gingerly touched his new features. He noticed even his hands looked different. His fingers no longer had claws. They were now covered in a rough flesh. It suddenly occurred to him that the strange sensation he'd experienced when the Earthman had been breaking the Great Seal of the Conclave may have been him transforming.

Zarrod scowled. His farsight ability had allowed him to manipulate events to play out exactly as he'd wanted. And yet, the Earthman had yet again done the one thing Zarrod had not accounted for.

He'd surprised him.

# EPILOGUE

The boarding ramp of *The Phantom Menace* lowered, revealing the planet upon which it had just landed. Jack gazed around at the thick jungle foliage, a light fog hanging in the air like a hot, wet blanket. It was so humid, it was hard to breathe. Jack frowned, looking at his surroundings with a certain amount of disappointment.

"What's this planet called again?" he asked.

"It doesn't have an official name," Stalker Crux said, his robotically modulated voice piercing the ambient jungle sounds ringing out around them. "I call it Primaevus."

Jack squinted at his companion. "Um… isn't that Old Solar for 'large pile of excrement'?" he asked.

"Is it?" replied Stalker Crux. "Thought it meant 'young world'. My Old Solar has always been terrible. Either way, the name is appropriate."

"You're as bad at naming stuff as I am."

"One of the few skills we're equal in, I suppose," the bounty hunter replied. "Make sure you have everything you need. We will not be returning to the ship."

Jack hefted his backpack onto his shoulders and nodded. He had packed everything he thought he'd require – some clothes, some hygiene products, a little bit of food, and Shepherd's journal. He figured he could simply learn to manifest anything else he needed during his training, and it kept the pack from being too burdensome.

He followed as Stalker Crux descended the boarding ramp and began making his way through the jungle. Jack was still getting used to his mentor's alternate form. It appeared that Ravencrow rarely ever walked around in his true form, at least outside of the Conclave. Mostly, he travelled in the guise of Stalker Crux. Jack had preferred it when he'd been able to hang out with Ravencrow as an ugly little Harvshodd. The imposing cyborg bounty hunter get-up could be a bit too intimidating for Jack's liking.

It didn't take long for Jack's clothing to cling to him like a second skin and his hair to plaster onto his head as though he'd just been swimming. The humidity of the planet was stifling. Jack wondered if Ravencrow was even aware of how uncomfortable the climate was while in his Stalker Crux form.

"So, like, is there a reason you picked this place to continue my training?" Jack asked. "Is there something special about it?"

"There is," Stalker Crux replied. "I came across this place long ago in my travels. No one else has yet to discover it. Not the Empire, not the Visinis, and certainly not the Deathlords. There are no indigenous peoples other than animals on the planet. We'll be well hidden here and free from distractions. Oh, and then there's this…"

The two came to a cliff that looked out over a valley, revealing a pyramid-shaped Ancient Temple below them. Its façade was crumbling and overgrown with foliage and vines, and as with other temples, its top was flat, as though unfinished. Jack raised his eyebrows in surprise.

"Whoa," he said. "Is that what I think it is?"

"Only if you're thinking it's a long lost Ancient Temple," Stalker Crux replied. "Otherwise you'd be wrong."

"Dude!" Jack exclaimed. "That's where we're going to be living? Does it have a Great Seal inside? Or any kind of weird powers? Or relics? Or technology?"

"Come find out," Stalker Crux said before continuing down a path toward the valley.

Jack followed his Master as they made their way toward the temple. It took a while for Jack to adjust to his surroundings but he was starting to acclimate to the heavy jungle atmosphere by the time they reached their destination. Jack looked up at the towering temple in excitement and wonder, trying to guess what awaited him inside.

It turns out what awaited him was a large, dirty, derelict temple. The sandstone bricks were beginning to crumble, the markings and etchings on the walls and pillars within were so weathered as to be barely visible anymore. Vines and plant-life had broken through the floor and walls, slowly overtaking the structure and bringing various annoying insects along with them. Sparse rays of sunlight shined through where parts of the ceiling had collapsed, giving off what little light there was within.

"Quaint," muttered Jack as he followed Stalker Crux over the broken, uneven floor, deeper into the temple. "How is it the Ancients can build temples that can float in space and exist at the center of planets, but they can't build something that can withstand weeds?"

"The Ancients were wise enough to know that one shouldn't fight nature, boy," Stalker Crux replied. "When you look around and see an Ancient wonder being defiled by weeds, I see a structure that welcomes all forms of life and nurtures it. For all we know, the plants on this world could have been made by this very temple and it is responsible for all life on it."

Jack promptly swatted an insect that had landed on the side of his neck. "Hope it's not too attached to all the life here," he muttered.

"I wouldn't worry too much about that," Stalker Crux replied. "As far as nature is concerned, death is just another part of life."

Jack and Stalker Crux continued to trek through the temple until they emerged into a large chamber shrouded in darkness. Stalker Crux took out a few illumination orbs and activated them, tossing them into the air where they hovered and revealed their surroundings with their soft light.

The chamber was partially collapsed, with one of its walls in rubble and one of its large pillars lying on the floor where it had fallen long ago. But the ruins of the chamber did nothing to obscure the large, circular stone seal that was embedded in the ground at the room's center.

"Here we are," Stalker Crux said as he approached the seal.

Jack looked around, confused. "What is this place?" he asked.

"This is what makes this temple so special," Stalker Crux replied. With a wave of his hand, there was a low rumble as a stone kiosk rose up from the floor and an access orb sprang to life over it. Stalker Crux placed his hand on the orb, and the stone seal before him receded, twisting out of the way to reveal a swirling pink and purple vortex beneath.

Jack's eyes grew wide as the light from the vortex lit up the chamber, causing shadows to dance among its pink and purple hues as its light bounced off the walls like sunlight bouncing off water.

"Whoa," Jack said, under his breath.

"Beautiful, isn't it?" mused Stalker Crux. "Take a closer look. It's safe."

Jack walked past his mentor and approached the edge where the floor dropped off into the vortex. The energy below him swirled chaotically, with flashes of lightning snaking through the twisting tempest. There was a low rumble coming from the whirlpool of energy, like the muted sound of a storm raging. In a strange way, the sight reminded Jack of the old tether in the Conclave, only far more visible and violent.

Jack gazed into the dark center of the vortex with curiosity. "What… what is this?" he asked.

"It's a Nexus node," Stalker Crux replied.

"A Nexus node?" Jack said as he began to turn back toward his companion. "Isn't the Nexus some prison the galaxy dumps their worst criminals into—"

Just then Jack was hit with a green stasis bolt. The energy engulfed him, completely paralyzing his muscles and holding him in place like a skin-tight cage. Jack didn't even know what had happened until his gaze settled on Stalker Crux and the bounty hunter's smoking shoulder cannon, which slowly retracted.

"I wouldn't exactly call it a prison," Stalker Crux replied. "But whatever it is, it's a place no one ever comes back from."

A rising sense of panic was growing within Jack as he realized he was currently helpless and unable to move, let alone speak. His mind raced as he desperately tried to think of something he could do to escape his current predicament.

"Don't bother trying anything. The stasis field is designed to make it hard for you to concentrate. You won't be able to manifest anything while under its influence," Stalker Crux said as he pulled a small disk from his thigh and set it on a nearby rock.

*Why?* Jack wanted to ask, wondering if this were some kind of strange test his mentor was putting him through. Stalker Crux hesitated for a brief moment before speaking once more.

"Know that I take no pleasure in what's about to happen," he said. "But this is all I could think of to do, for both our sakes."

Jack wanted to cry out. To yell and scream at the one he'd put his trust in – the alien he'd thought was his friend. But instead, he was helpless to do anything but watch as Stalker Crux activated the subspace communicator disk and the holographic image of Armonto Virtuoso appeared above it.

"Stalker Crux," Armonto said. "It is about time I heard from you."

"I have the bounty you hired me to get," Stalker Crux replied, gesturing toward Jack. "My soulbound oath to you has been fulfilled."

"So it would seem," Armonto said, his holographic image looking over toward Jack. "However, I believe the terms of our contract were that the Earthman be killed."

"The language of the contract stated the Earthman was to be 'eliminated'," Stalker Crux said, "which I plan to do by feeding him to the Nexus."

Armonto raised an eyebrow. "I don't know how I feel about that. I'd much prefer to witness his death myself."

"You can witness him suffer a fate worse than death," Stalker Crux said. "No one ever returns from the Nexus. It's as good as killing him. The Earthman will be gone forever, sentenced to whatever nightmare lies beyond that portal. You'll never have to worry about him again."

Armonto sighed. "Very well, if you insist," he said, sounding bored. "Get on with it, then. I have things to do."

Stalker Crux turned and approached Jack, the boy's heart pounding furiously in his chest as the menacing bounty hunter got closer.

"I lied to you when I said I don't soulbind my contracts to myself," Stalker Crux said. "It's something I always do. When failure means death, there is an added challenge to the task of bounty hunting, which I needed in order to do it. Despite all that has transpired, my employer kept your bounty active. I'm afraid you and I were always destined to end up here."

Stalker Crux stopped in front of Jack, Jack's eyes looking up at him, not understanding.

"I know you're feeling confused and betrayed right now," Stalker Crux continued. "And I'm sorry for that. I did come to develop a certain fondness for you, boy. I told you from the start that I was no teacher, but during our time together, I did teach you. I helped you to grow. I was the one who carried you through your training. But that ends here. I'm through carrying you. From now on, you will have to carry yourself."

As the being Jack had thought of as a teacher, a mentor, and a friend loomed over him, he was helpless to do anything but gaze upon the cold, masked visage of Stalker Crux as the red hued visor gazed back at him with a soulless stare. Stalker Crux leaned forward, his robotically modulated voice soft and cold.

"Let this be my final lesson to you, boy," he said. "Trust only in The Void. Because in the end, nothing else deserves it."

Upon hearing those words, a single tear escaped from Jack's eye and ran down his cheek. And with one shove of Stalker Crux's hand…

Jack fell backward, into oblivion.

*Earthman Jack Will Return In…*

# EARTHMAN JACK

## VS.

# THE DEADLY NEXUS

# An Important Note From The Author

Dear Reader,

I hope you enjoyed this latest adventure in the Earthman Jack Space Saga. Please know I am working hard to produce the next book in the series. Being an independent author (i.e. a writer with no money) can be quite a fulfilling profession, but it can also be a lot of work.

Since I do not have a big publisher behind me to help get my books into stores and do publicity for my work, I rely on the fans of my book to help spread the word. If you enjoyed this book and would like to support it and the series it belongs to, then you can do the following things to help me out:

1. Write a positive review on Amazon.com. Readers rely on reviews from other readers when deciding whether or not to give a new book a try. This is one of the best things you can do to help promote this book to others. Please take a few moments to do so.
2. Recommend the book to people you know. Word of mouth is a powerful way to help new readers discover books they may like. Be sure to tell your friends and family about the book!
3. Request your local bookstore and library to carry a copy. It can be difficult to get independent books into brick and mortar stores. If enough people request a book, then stores will start carrying them. This can be a great way for new readers to stumble upon these works.
4. Recommend this book on social media. If you're an active user of services like Facebook, Twitter, and the like, be sure to let your friends know about this series by linking to the books in it within your posts.
5. Sign up for my mailing list. This way you can be notified about updates on the series and when new books are released. You can sign up at: www.EarthmanJack.com.

Doing any of these will go a long way in helping to support this series. With the support of fans like you, I hope to expose a whole new generation of readers to Earthman Jack and his exploits.

Thank you very much for your support!

Matthew J. Kadish

Author: Earthman Jack vs. The Conclave Of Corruption

## Special Thanks To:

Dayna Burnell

Hazel Godwin

Dan Grover

Andrew Taylor

Scott Tulleners

Your Feedback & Support Made This Book Possible.

If you enjoyed this book and would like to support the series, please sign up for the author's newsletter at:

www.EarthmanJack.com

Made in the USA
Columbia, SC
28 October 2017